SARAH'S
JOURNEY

To Marcia
Best wishes
David Beasley
Nov '04

DAVID BEASLEY

Beasley, David, 1931-
    Sarah's Journey / David Beasley.

ISBN 0-915317-14-1

I. Title.

PS8553.E14S27 2004   C813'.54   C2003-907004-2
cover: Eric Rustan

I dedicate this book with much love to Michelle.

2nd printing

DAVUS PUBLISHING
www.kwic.com/~davus
519-426-2077

150 Norfolk St. S.,   P O Box 1101
Simcoe, ON N3Y 2W2   Buffalo, N.Y. 14213-7101
Canada   U.S.A.

ORDERS: WWW.KWIC.COM/~DAVUS

ESCAPE

Those who have seen quadroons and octoroons will remember their peculiar style of beauty, the rich olive tint of the complexion, the large bright eyes, the perfect features, and the long wavy black hair. A hundred romantic associations and mysterious fancies clustered around that class in the South, owned, as they often were, by their own fathers and sold by them.—*The Story of Jane*

1

In 1806, there was no longer the fear of sudden attack by Indian raiding parties, the smashing of babies' heads and the loss of women-folk to the savage hinterlands. The Delawares and the Mingos, not with-out apprehension that certain whites might massacre them on a whim, lived along the river in peace with the whites. Thus, despite an oppres-sive shadow cast over Brown's Island by the steep hills on both sides of the river, Sarah felt safe from the brutality in those hills—the drunken rampages of the foul-mouthed, unpredictable youths and their indul-gent fathers. Sometimes, though, she would imagine rapacious eyes watching her on the island as if waiting for an unguarded moment to attack.

Sarah Kinney was sixteen years old. As she watched the sun break through the dawn, lighting the spring air as if with invisible tinsel, this day seemed the most important in her life. She had fed the farm slaves their morning meal when she saw the sun from the kitchen window and sensed a power that spoke through nature: the surrounding forests and hills and in the great sugar trees covering the northern part of her island, where she wandered in the hour or two that she had free of her chores every week. From the window, she watched the Ohio River sweeping by to those far-off places like New Orleans that she imagined she would never see.

She thought of her mother Molly Kinney, a mulatto slave of Colonel Richard Brown, who died giving birth to her in 1790, and tried to picture her from her sisters' descriptions. Her sister Fanny, who was born on the journey from Maryland to Virginia six years earlier, was eventually sold to Dick Dawson, a free coloured man living in Wellsburg, the seat of Hancock County, Virginia, a few miles down-stream. Sarah's oldest sister, Nell, became personal attendant to Mrs.

3

Honor Brown. The Colonel gave Sarah to his house slaves to raise.

At six, Sarah understood that she was a slave. The abject obedience of the blacks transferred a fear into her at the same time that the superior attitude of the whites raised a wall of rejection against her. She also learned the difference between a house slave and a field slave but did not fully understand her position until Nell told her that the master was their father. She knew a kind of affection from the Colonel, who would pat her on the head at times and call her a pretty girl.

Once she overheard the Colonel defending the need for slaves with his brother Hugh, who believed that owning slaves was not Christian. The Colonel enlisted slaves for the rebel army in the Revolutionary War on the promise of freedom after the War, which, he admitted, caused him the occasional prick of conscience when he knew that such freedom was illusory in a slave state like Virginia.

Sarah remembered her childhood on this little Island, about three miles long in the Ohio River between Virginia and Ohio, the games played with the children of the slaves who lived in huts near the house, and the wild boy George Brown, Hugh's son and the Colonel's nephew, who swam across to the island with Indian boys from Ohio to mix in their games. Sarah liked George, who was two years younger, because he acted so free in everything he did, and, unlike Colonel Brown's white children, he treated her as a friend.

Most of Colonel Brown's slaves worked for his white family in Hollidays Cove on the Virginia side of the river, but they were few relative to the numbers owned by his neighbours such as the Campbells, who had vast acres on the hillsides. Slaves were up before dawn working till after sunset, clearing timber and growing the crops that the flatboats would carry to points south in trade for manufactured goods and fine things like cloth and wine. Strikes of the whip and imprisonment in stockades were everyday reminders that they had no will other than that of their overseer. Sarah grew up hearing cries and screams for mercy every morning along the banks of the Ohio River. Fear of punishment and of the auction block in Wellsburg, where families were separated and sold to different parts of the country, kept slaves cowed. The trade on flatboats down the river gave the women hope that when boats stopped to pick up goods from Colonel Brown's farm on the mainland, there was a stranger meant for them.

Henry Lewis was just such a stranger, but he did not come by boat. He walked out of the bush one day and asked Colonel Brown for work. He was a free Negro, he said. The Colonel, glad to get a strong, intelligent man in his twenties, who was willing to work for little more than his keep, sent him to supervise the slaves who were pulling boulders out of the shallow parts of the river and planting wheat and corn on the southern part of the island. He was even more pleased when Henry Lewis asked to marry his slave Sal, which was Sarah's slave name.

Sarah liked Henry Lewis because, although his skin was dark, he was free and could look men in the eye. He was bold and wooed her like no other black man could. She found a new status with him—a hope for the future, a step towards freedom. Sarah was almost white because her mother Molly had been mulatto. Molly's father had been white but because her mother was black, according to the law, she was a slave. White men on the frontier, who recognized practically no law, recognized that one. Their identity depended on it.

"Penny for your thoughts," Fanny said from behind her and giggled.

Sarah turned to embrace her sister. "Oh Fanny, I want to thank God for this day!"

"You're a lucky one," Fanny whispered. "You got a real man and he's free. You got a chance with him as I always told you. Ma would have been proud."

The sisters tightened their embrace and then quickly let go afraid that someone would see them.

Sarah had two dresses: one for everyday wear, which was ragged, and one for occasion, which she mended to look good. As she put on her good dress and tidied her hair, she thought of the hut she would move to that night. Recently built, it smelt of pine. Henry put in a wooden floor, which distinguished it from the others of hard earth. Fanny helped her decorate it with coloured cloth that the Colonel gave her and some chairs and a table where she could prepare and set out meals. Henry could afford to buy food in addition to what field hands received. Most of his money, he said, he was saving to buy Sarah's freedom.

In mid-morning, she and Fanny stepped into a rowboat sent by the Colonel to bring them to the main farmhouse. The Colonel's oldest slave took this duty seriously and tried not to smile at the excited whispering of the girls. He helped them out of the rowboat with ceremonial precision and escorted them as if they were his daughters to the farmhouse. Nell came running to them and embraced Sarah.

"I saw Henry all spiffed up, looking real nice," Nell said, "He's gone ahead with Dick."

Sarah looked up at the house to see Mrs. Honor Brown and her two daughters watching from an upper window. The Colonel, dressed in full military regalia and with the steel blue eyes of a commanding officer, walked from the house to a carriage with two horses waiting. The Colonel was in a good mood and joked with his son Richard, a tall man with a mild philosophical expression and twinkling green eyes. The son climbed into the wagon to take the reins and the Colonel sat beside him, adjusted his sword and nodded to his son, who drove to where the three sisters stood. The girls climbed into the back of the wagon where they sat on clumps of straw.

"Alright Colonel, sir," the old slave cried. "They's all comfortable."

The wagon moved ahead and Sarah felt she was beginning a journey into a new life. As they passed through the Cove, Sarah waved at some of the coloureds whom she knew, and they waved excitedly back at her. Word had got round that she was being married this Saturday morning and some of her friends had made an effort to be on the streets to greet her. Hugh Laird was walking toward them along the river road and hailed the Colonel to stop. Hugh was the teacher in the Cove. Whoever was educated in these parts had gone to Laird's school for a couple of years. The Colonel had invited Laird to teach his white children, and Hugh had enjoyed talking to the house servants whom he encountered, particularly Sarah, who, as he told the Colonel, would make a good student should he allow her to learn. The Colonel was reluctant to set a precedent and feared the criticism from his fellow settlers should he send Sarah to school.

"You got one of my girls, there, have ya, Colonel?" Hugh said with a slight slur as he often began drinking in the morning, particularly on a Saturday morning. His hair was tossed by the wind off the water and his cheeks were ruddy.

"Marriage day, Mr. Laird," the Colonel said. "We're late starting. Don't want to delay Mr. Doddridge."

"What a beautiful day for it!" Hugh almost sang and reached into the wagon to clasp Sarah's hand. "It's a good omen, my dear. I wish you happiness."

Sarah gushed her thanks, and, as the wagon moved away, she looked at Laird standing in the road and watching them go, and she wondered why he had not married.

When opposite Steubenville whose fort and houses they saw across the river, they turned inland through the thick forest over small rolling hills and into fertile valleys for three miles. St. John's Episcopal Church stood in the centre of a long stretch of level ground. A simple log cabin, it served the Episcopalian community for miles around. It had been built by its very dedicated minister, Joseph Doddridge, who now approached the wagon when it stopped under one of the trees at the front of the Church.

Doddridge was a tall, well-built man with fair complexion and black hair. The Colonel felt humbled in his presence because the man's earnestness and devotion to the Christian message and his great learning set him apart from other men. The fact that he became a medical doctor to support himself as a minister gave him added prestige in a community where most people were illiterate and blasphemous.

While the Colonel's son helped the women down from the wagon, the Colonel chatted with the Reverend. Doddridge's sharp blue eyes seemed to pierce him as if searching for signs of failure, shortcomings, sins. But when the Reverend turned to greet Sarah and her sisters, his eyes glowed with compassion, and he held out his hands to Sarah. The Colonel recalled then how the Reverend hated slavery, and he felt uncomfortable. But the moment passed quickly as Doddridge told them that Henry and his best man were waiting in the church and strode away to prepare for the ceremony.

Richard Brown Jr. accompanied Sarah's sisters into the church where they waited by the open door. Sarah was alone with the Colonel

7

now. She felt a sudden shyness and looked at the ground. The Colonel, resplendent in his uniform, had supreme power in her world. Only God was more powerful because God worked through nature whereas the Colonel worked directly through human beings.

"You will make Henry a good wife, Sal, won't you?"

"Yes, sir."

"You can cook as good as your mother."

"Yes, sir."

"I loved your mother's cooking," he said in a rare outburst of affection.

Sarah nodded and sensed that the Colonel was trying to express his connection to her, despite the law, the custom, the barrier between master and slave that stood between them.

"You and your sisters are good girls," the Colonel said reflectively. "I'm glad you got a good man who will care for you."

"Yes, sir, so am I," Sarah smiled and looked up into the Colonel's bearded face. His beard was flecked with white hair.

Colonel Brown smiled at her and tightened his lips signifying he would say no more. Sarah listened to the birds singing in chorus all about them. It was God's way of celebrating her marriage day, she thought. Hugh Laird was right about this being a glorious spring day.

Richard Brown Jr. stepped from the Church and beckoned to them. The Colonel gave his arm to Sarah, and she, with mixed feelings of eagerness and trepidation, put her hand gently on his sleeve and walked with him into the little church. Her two sisters fell in behind her as the Colonel led her up the aisle to the altar where Henry in a suit and tie stood with Dick Dawson, a man of medium height slightly shorter than Henry and with light brown skin. Henry turned and his face lit up into a broad smile. Sarah thought she saw love in his deep brown eyes and took courage from his strength and assurance.

The Reverend Doddridge glided in long strides to stand before them and began reading earnestly from a prayer book. Sarah let the words pass over her. She was too excited to concentrate on their meaning. She sensed only that they were meant for her. But she responded when she had to, and she felt the ring slip onto her finger, and she embraced Henry with a fervour that surprised even herself. Everyone smiled and the Reverend gave his blessing upon them. When the couple came to the register, Henry signed for them both, and Sarah made a small "x". Then, they were back in the sunlight and riding alone over the hilly road in the one-horse shay that Henry borrowed from Dawson. The others followed at a distance.

Henry happily joked with her over the responsibilities of marriage that the Reverend had impressed upon them, and she clapped at every point and repeated them and emphasized them and admonished him with impish humour to live up to them.

When they got back to the Colonel's homestead, they found a knot of people waiting for them at the servants' quarters. To Sarah's surprise, there was a feast laid out on a long table, which had been dragged from the kitchen onto the lawn. The Colonel's neighbour, Mrs. Butler, stood beaming as she waited to receive them. Sarah fell into her arms in gratitude and Henry expressed his wonderment. When the Colonel's party arrived, they sat in chairs near the table or stood eating in small groups near-by. The Reverend Doddridge arrived on horseback and joined in the festivities in a jovial mood. Fanny was talking animatedly with Dick Dawson and her sister Nell. Mrs. Honor Brown came to congratulate Sarah and stood beside the Colonel chatting with the guests before leaving. There was no sign of her two daughters, not even at the windows of the house. Sarah had sensed their indifference and did not expect them to congratulate her. Richard Brown Jr. remained for a while and said good-bye to Sarah when he left.

Sarah's friend Mrs. Butler remarked how happy she looked; Mrs. Butler had encouraged her to marry Henry, a free Negro, because he could buy her freedom. Slavery happened to you whether you were white or black, whether you arrived as an indentured servant from Ireland to be bought from your ship's captain and herded into the interior or you came from Africa to be sold on the auction block. As the settlements increased and the Indian threat disappeared, colour would become more important as a mark of slavery. Sarah should be thankful, Mrs. Butler said, because she could pass for white in a world which was becoming more conscious of race. But she had to get her freedom.

When Henry signalled with his eyes that they should depart, she and Mrs. Butler embraced. Sarah valued their friendship and at times marvelled at it. Mrs. Butler was unique among "whites" because she accepted Sarah without reservation.

Henry rowed Sarah back to the island. They entered their little hut, closed the door, and fell hungrily at one another. Sarah was no longer a simple slave girl. She was Mrs. Henry Lewis.

2

Sarah and Henry, happy in the first years of their marriage, worked hard, Sarah cooking for the Colonel's family when they came to live on the island for the summer months and for the field hands the year round while Henry worked in the fields and crated goods to be shipped south and sometimes to the north as more and more foundries developed in Hollidays Cove. Henry felt more at home on the island than he had anywhere in his life. Being free, he could travel at will to neighboring towns and, sometimes, took Sarah. She noticed that he was uneasy on their trips to Wellsburg or over the river to Steubenville and Mingo town. For a long time he remained silent about his past and made only references to his work as a skilled artisan in Maryland. But after their son Henry Jr. was born a year into their marriage, he confessed that the welts on his back were not from fights but from the lash, the result of his first attempt to escape from a plantation in Kentucky. After three months he was forced by hunger to come out of the bush. He refused to let his spirit be broken by the whippings, the solitary confinement and the starvation diet. Eventually his owners saw that he was more valuable to them when working rather than smouldering with resentment in the stockades. His eyes fired with hatred as he recounted the brutal treatment meted out to the slaves for no known reason or offence. As he worked as a blacksmith and fashioner of farm equipment, he escaped most of the beatings, but he had to feign abject submission to avoid sudden and unpredictable savagery by the white overseers. By comparison, life on the Brown farm was paradisiacal. Henry swore that he would never again be a slave and asked Sarah to be vigilant.

Sarah was devastated at first. All her high-flying expectations that some day Henry would set them up free and independent shriveled like a balloon. Worse, her newborn son was doomed to be a slave. For a week she went about in a gloomy state and avoided worried queries from her friends. Resentful at Henry for lying to her, she, nevertheless, became sympathetic and forgiving. She understood that he could not reveal his secret until he was certain of her. She loved him more now. Yet try as she would, she could not extinguish that slight pain of disappointment underlying her life from that moment. Their fate lay in the good graces of Colonel Brown more than ever.

Henry reasoned that by hiding in a slave state he tricked his pursuers who would look for him in a free state like Ohio and Pennsylvania. As the years went by and Sarah gave birth to a girl, whom she called Molly after her mother, she persuaded herself that Henry was right. She let herself hope that Henry was free in fact if not in name, that he could establish himself as an independent settler like Dick Dawson and free her and their children.

Henry proved to be good with horses and took care of the Colonel's stables eventually, which meant that he worked less in the fields. He was reluctant to strike out on his own, however, and kept putting off the decision to leave Colonel Brown's employ. Sarah also felt secure under the protection of the Colonel and did not want to challenge the ambivalence of her position lest her assumption that she might one day be really free was proven wrong. Contented with their life on the island, they raised their children with confidence that their basic needs would always be met. Life as an independent settler on a small piece of land was too precarious. Would the Colonel let her go in any case? Even if he were inclined to free her, his white family might persuade him against it.

During the years that Sarah was raising her young children, George Brown stayed at the home of his cousin Richard Brown Jr., who lived a short way upriver from Brown's Island while George attended Hugh Laird's school in the Cove. Sarah was delighted to see George when he came to the island on occasion and reminisced with him about his wild young days. George was still fairly wild and spurned the religious practices of his father and uncle. He wanted a business career.

The old Colonel spent more time in his island home in these years. His grandson, who lived with him, adopted the general attitude that slaves were not humans but things who were set on earth for the pleasure of their masters. When the vicious treatment of a thirteen-year-old girl slave by her owners became known, causing widespread disgust throughout western Virginia, the grandson showed no pity for the brutalized dead girl. It was this attitude that offended Richard Jr. and resulted in his son being raised by the Colonel, who, it was hoped, would inculcate humane values in him. Sarah, however, divined that the Colonel could have no effect on his grandson's warped personality. She kept her children out of his sight.

Nature was a strong component of people's lives. The wilderness, although hacked at and burnt back, still dominated the scenery: the howling wolves, the sharp cries of hunted animals at night, and the song birds in full-throated calls throughout the day. The tall ancient trees were majestic witnesses to the spirit of the world and held a special meaning for Sarah and the other slaves, rooted, like them, to one place communicating silently, like them, to one another, and tied by their very essence, like them, to the great wilderness of absolute freedom which lay beyond the hills and far back from the river. It was all they had, and they looked to the trees for comfort and reassurance almost as much as they looked to God.

Henry Lewis loved to hunt the deer, bears, turkeys and the elk which roamed the forest. Some of the game he brought back he gave to Sarah for the family. Most of it he sold or bartered to tradesmen in the Cove. Sarah was as diligent as the other women spinning yarn, weaving cloth and linen. All clothing for the families was made on the farm. The increasing trade with ports down river and the manufactories appearing in the Virginia Panhandle and southern Pennsylvania brought little relief from these household duties.

As more and more settlers passed through the area or stayed to buy land from the Campbells and other early settlers, Hollidays Cove flourished. More of the island was cleared to grow wheat and became the main source of bread for the area. Among the people who came on business to see the Colonel was Beseleel Wells, the son of a friend who had fought alongside the Colonel in the Revolution and in Indian skirmishes on the Ohio River, where he was killed and scalped. Beseleel was a trader and ran flatboats down to New Orleans. The Colonel admired him and his brother Richard Wells, who were partners, for their resourcefulness. He made the brothers executors of his will.

Sarah, as a very good-looking woman, attracted the attention of male visitors to the island but none more than Richard Wells, who, out of sight of the Colonel, made lascivious remarks to her. She told Henry about his attentions, but he could do nothing other than reassure her that the man knew the Colonel would not allow such behaviour toward his female slaves, that is, if he knew of it.

Sarah's life of hard work and strict obedience continued until one fatal night in mid-February 1811. A cold wind from the north and swirling snow caused everyone to build large fires in their hearths to keep warm. Sarah gathered enough wood to last the night and kept her small fireplace alight. Henry Jr. was four years old and Molly was over one year. The children were sleeping and Sarah was sewing by candle-light awaiting the return of Henry from Wellsburg, when she heard shouts from the main house. She went to the door of her hut and saw flames and huge clouds of smoke coming from the bottom level of the house. The grandson was running about excitedly calling for help. Slaves rushed from their huts with buckets to the river side and returned to throw water on the flames but to little avail. The fire, whipped up by the wind, consumed the homestead in a short time.

The Colonel's personal attendant was comforting his wife as they gazed fearfully at the flames. Sarah rushed to them to ask about the Colonel. The old man had not got out. He had gone to his study to keep his accounts as he often did at night, but this time the candelabra he worked by must have fired a curtain. The slaves were being urged on by the grandson to keep dousing the flames, but, in the end, the fire, having reduced the house to ashes, died out in the wind.

Henry arrived breathless from the Virginia shore and gasped that the residents of the Cove were sending a boat load of men headed by James Campbell to help. He hurried Sarah back to their hut and went out to meet the boat, from which they heard the men's voices approaching despite the noise of the wind in the trees.

Henry feared the unpredictable James Campbell, the toughest and roughest of his family, whose father brought goods over the mountains to trade with pioneer settlers and made a handsome profit within a few years. At his death, James inherited the best land on the hills overlooking the Cove and married the same year that Henry Lewis married Sarah with the difference that he had been 59 and his bride, Margaret MacDonald from Canada, had been 14.

"Where's Colonel Brown?" Campbell shouted to the grandson as his boat ran against the shore.

The boy, in tears, pointed to the smouldering house. Campbell led the men with him as close as they could get to the heat and peered about for signs of the Colonel's body. The slaves stood back and watched them. A sense of bewilderment and dismay held them in shock. What would happen to them now? they wondered. Brown had been a stern taskmaster, but they knew that most owners were worse.

Henry first spotted the body. It was stretched out over what remained of the floor. Although scorched, it was still recognizable as the master of these domains. About him were strewn burnt account books, large leather bound volumes.

"See the old man, do you, Lewis?" Campbell snorted. "Well, he'll have to stay there for the night till we fetch him tomorrow morning."

The men took the grandson across the river to the Colonel's home in the Cove to inform Honor Brown of her husband's accidental death. That night the river froze over. Henry told some of the slaves that it offered them a rare chance to walk over the ice to Ohio and escape into the wilderness, but they were too afraid of being caught and whipped. Moreover they did not know where to go. Their chance of survival seemed better with the Brown family for the moment at least. Henry tried to console Sarah, who regretted the Colonel's death, not only because she was fond of him but because he offered her family security as long as he lived. Now that he was dead, the menace she had often felt from the hills looking down on their island suddenly seemed more intense.

3

In the morning, Richard Brown Jr. and James Campbell came to retrieve the Colonel's body from the ruined house. Campbell looked red-eyed from drinking and his temper was short with his slaves, who moved quickly at his command. Sarah and her small son watched as Campbell's slaves put the remains of the Colonel on a horse-drawn sleigh and walked behind the frosted body atop the sleigh moving against the snow-capped hills. Sarah, sad and apprehensive, hugged her son to reassure him that she would always remain with him.

Brown's slaves gathered their meagre belongings into sacks which they hoisted on their shoulders and when all were ready to depart they followed Henry onto the ice. Sarah carried Molly and led young Henry by the hand while her husband carried their belongings. The cold sliced through their light coats and their feet went numb. When the slaves reached the Brown homestead shivering with the cold, they were doubled into huts already occupied by slaves. Sarah and Henry were given a hut for themselves out of deference to Henry being a free man.

That night a thaw descended out of the hills and by the next morning the ice melted in the river. The Colonel's body lay in a coffin in the front parlor, and, later in the day, after all the relatives and settlers had viewed it, the slaves were instructed to file by and pay their last respects. All of his body was covered by a blanket, but his face, which had escaped the flames, was viewable. He had a look of slight surprise despite the fact that his eyes were closed and his white hair and beard were combed with care to make him appear to be in peace.

The Reverend Joseph Doddridge officiated at the Colonel's burial service in the log cabin church in the woods. The settlers took up most of the seats, but there were some left near the door for the house slaves such as Sarah and her sisters. Doddridge reminded them that the Colonel led them in defending against Indian attacks and building a series of forts to which they could flee when wars broke out. After the service, Sarah looked up to see George Brown give her a broad smile when he passed.

The Colonel's lands and the rents from them went to his widow, son and two daughters. He freed the couple who were his personal slaves and bequeathed their son to his grandson. He declared Sarah's sister Nell free whenever Honor Brown died. The remaining slaves were to be sold after the Colonel's debts were settled. Sarah thought that Colonel Brown looked upon her as special to him and would free her or give her some hope of freedom in the future. But now she realized with a taste of bitterness that money meant too much to the man. She tried to hide her disappointment from her children, and they, being too young to understand, were lulled into thinking that their life would continue as it had been. Henry heard that James Campbell planned to buy Sarah, or Sal as the settlers called her. She had a good reputation as a cook, but it was her good looks which was an attraction, according to the gossip among the young toughs whom he overheard on the street and who mocked him as he walked by. Would Campbell employ him? He had several weeks to decide on a course of action before the executors settled the Colonel's debts and put the slaves up for auction in Wellsburg.

Campbell had a reputation for ruthlessness, drunkenness, and piti-less ferocity. Willful and obstinate with immense influence along the Panhandle, he was in the gang of whites who massacred a village of Christian Indians. Henry and Sarah whispered in the bed they shared with their children and turned over their thoughts until they admitted that their only choice was to ride out their fate where they were. At least, as a free man, Henry could give some protection to his family, and if Campbell did not employ him, someone in the Cove would. Sarah fell asleep in Henry's arms for the last time. Before dawn as Henry rose sleepily from bed to take up his duties in the Browns' stables, the door of the hut flew open and Richard Wells, his lean face leering, confront-ed him with the words, "Henry, these folks claim they own you."

Two burly white men stepped round Wells, pushed Henry back against the wall, and bound his wrists in an iron clamp. Henry looked in terror at Sarah.

"You're our shitty little black slave," one of the men cried. "And you're goin' back to good old Kentucky where you fuckin' belong."

The other man laughed with glee and gave Henry a shove out the door.

"Say good-bye, Sal," Wells smirked. "You won't see him again."

"You'll never keep me!" Henry shouted in fury.

"After the tanning you're gettin'," one of the men said, "escape won't even go through your mind."

"Henry!" Sarah shouted and tried to get to her husband, but Wells pushed her back warning her she would get a whipping if she did not let the law proceed. His clipped nasal voice with its hard-edged menace frightened her.

Sarah sank down on the bed and listened to Henry's voice shouting that he would be back until he could no longer be heard. Wells stepped outside and shut the door with a knowing look. Sarah buried her head on the bed and groaned softly. She feared her children would be taken from her as was usual in slave auctions. Her only hope was that James Campbell really would buy her family.

Within days of her husband's removal back to Kentucky, Richard Wells began to hover about her. Dispirited as she was, she formed a hatred for this man, whom, she suspected, had discovered the truth about Henry and informed on him to collect the reward. Fortunately his brother Beseleel, in settling the Colonel's affairs, frequented the Brown homestead, which made him cautious. Fortunately as well, George Brown, now a handsome lad of nineteen and nearing the completion of his studies with Hugh Laird, noticed Wells's attentions to Sarah. Partly for Sarah's sake and partly for his own, for he recognized with surprise the strong attraction that he had for her, he informed his cousin Richard Brown Jr. He suggested that, with spring upon them, Sarah be returned to the island to cook for the field hands tending the crops.

Until the slaves were sold, Richard Brown Jr., had the authority to use them as he wished. He dispatched Sarah and her children to the island along with a body of slaves, who erected a new central house. Richard asked George to oversee that work.

Sarah fixed on the idea that George could be her protector and prevent her sale to the South. As she expected never to see Henry again, she encouraged George's obvious interest in her when he visited the island—cautiously at first and more boldly as he responded to her charms. George was a virgin but anxious to experience love. All of his desire fastened on Sarah. He loved the proud carriage of her body, the light-brown tinted white skin, the handsome face alive with intelligence, and the full figure which at times caused him to grab her hands and gaze into her eyes with meaning. Sarah's black background, almost hidden in her physiognomy, intrigued him as a mystery, an unknown element of her personality. As soon as the house was built and Sarah and her young children moved into one of the rooms, George contrived to stay the night with the excuse that it was too risky to cross the river in the evening.

Sarah helped him to arrange his bed, and, while she tucked the linen sheets under the mattress, he put his arms around her. They fell together on the bed, and the heat of their passion drove them tightly together. With cries of yearning and professions of love they made love until exhausted. Sarah excused herself to check on her children asleep in the other room; her mind was in turmoil because she felt that she had betrayed her husband and yet she loved George Brown and her need for love had never been greater at this troubling time in her life. Watching over her sleeping children and reflecting that Henry had lied to her that he was free and destroyed her dreams and brought her and the children to a life of misery, she remembered the wild bravery of the young George when they were children. She returned to George's bed. They made love again during the night.

George met the morning with unimaginable joy and Sarah gave thanks to God that He had brought George to her. She had wondered what it was like to make love with a white man. George, who had a good figure, was of average stature with a kind, strong face and an innate sense of rebellion against authority, which she liked. If only their relationship could last, she thought, but she sensed it was doomed on that first morning they lay together. George had his life to follow. He would not be tied to a slave girl whatever he decided to do. She clung to him for that spring and into the summer months until he had to return to his father's farm to harvest the crops. Their good-bye was tearful and cheerful by turns. He swore never to forget her, and, since she was his first love, she knew he never would.

By this time, the Wells brothers had paid off most of the Colonel's debts and divided his estate among his white children. Ignoring a suggestion that the slaves be sold to local settlers, they decided that more money could be got for them by auctioning them off in Wellsburg to dealers, who would take them for resale to southern plantation owners. Disgusted, Richard Brown Jr. talked to Philip Doddridge, lawyer for the estate. Doddridge, who could cut to the core of any issue and come up with an unassailable argument, persuaded the Wells that the Colonel's house slaves were too talented to send out of the county and, as for the field hands, their experience of working this particular area of land was invaluable. If local buyers could be found, the slaves would be reprieved from the horror of plantation living. No action would be taken until after the fall harvest.

Fanny tried to keep Sarah's spirits up with predictions that the Brown family would keep her because she had served the family well. Nell, as Honor Brown's personal slave, heard the discussions within the family and reported the latest decisions. There was a complication. Sarah was two months pregnant and would be unable to disguise the fact much longer. She was happy that she was having George Brown's child but apprehensive about the reaction among the Brown family members. Births among the slaves were usually greeted with mild interest by the settlers; they were considered offspring of their owners or overseers if they were not readily seen to be the result of love-making between two slaves. In Sarah's case, George's father Hugh, a very religious man, might take out his anger on Sarah and cause her to be banished to some distant land. She was concerned for George as well because the family could well turn against him. She asked Nell to tell George the next time he was visiting his aunt that she wanted to see him. But the fall season had come upon them with the trees and bushes ablaze in reds, yellows, mauves and russet, and George had not returned. Nell, whose close relationship with Honor Brown was valued by both mistress and slave, confided in Honor about Sarah's condition.

As a widow Honor Brown had more authority than when she was the wife of the powerful Colonel because now she had property and seemed to represent her late husband's wishes. Chagrined but under-standing, she gave the matter some thought, and, when she developed a slight fever, she told Nell that she would feign serious illness, which would bring George to her bedside. Her doctor, who had seen numbers of his patients die from swamp fever, alerted the family, already shak-en by the Colonel's sudden death. The Browns and the Wells came to the homestead in the Cove and worriedly talked among themselves about the disposition of her property and slaves. Hugh Brown, riding his favorite horse, and George Brown, jogging alongside his father, trav-eled the fifteen miles south along the Ohio shore of the river. Hugh Brown talked to his wayward son about the Methodist religion and the importance of believing in the Christian message in order to live a ful-filling life. George listened and responded with mild objections and dif-ferent opinions. His friends rebelled against the strict and rather quaint views of their elders and valued force and cunning rather than piety.

When they reached the passing place formed by a sandbar which stretched under the surface of the river to the north end of Brown's Island, George mounted the horse behind his father. The horse waded across, the current running up to the level of its neck and wetting the trousers of the men. On the island, they walked beside the horse along a trail through the heavy timber glowing with colour. George felt a closeness to his father and the joy of being alive. He thought then of Sarah and hoped that he would catch a glimpse of her as they passed by the huts on the south end of the island. He saw her as he was preparing to mount behind his father to cross over the shallower fork of the river to the Virginia shore. She ran out from one of the huts and was looking anxiously at him. He smiled broadly until he noticed the swelling of her stomach and gave her a questioning look. She nodded as if in agreement, and, he, stunned, stood undecided whether to go to her or obey the summons of his father, who was impatient to continue. He mounted the horse and crossed the river without a backward glance. His head swirled with impressions, memories of their love-mak-ing, and fears. At first, George decided to hide his indiscretion from his father; should Sarah charge him with being the father he would deny it. By the time they arrived at the Brown homestead, Honor had recov-ered and their relatives were leaving for their homes.

Nell managed to intercept George in the hallway and whisper that Sarah had to see him. The urgency of the message and the sense of reliance upon him that it carried made denying his fatherhood seem small and cheap. He stepped into his Aunt Honor's room suddenly aware that the womenfolk knew everything. She was sitting in an armchair by the window and watching her daughters and their husbands depart.

"Is it true," she asked without turning to look at him, "that you are the father of Sal's child?"

George mumbled "Yes" and stood with a look of despair.

She turned to him and smiled sympathetically. "You know, don't you, that Sal is a child of your Uncle Richard's."

George nodded.

"Your child will be a slave too," she said. "We will do what we can to keep Sal and her children together. James Campbell wants her, but we won't sell her until her child is born. In that way he will be responsible for the new baby as well. I think that is best, don't you, George?"

George cleared his throat. "Who knows about this?"

"None of the family, but we shall have to discuss it with the executors."

"Richard Wells?" George asked in alarm. "He wanted to harm Sal."

"Nell told me as much," she said. "We can manage it without Richard."

"I'm truly sorry, Aunt. I shall live a cleaner life hereafter."

'You tell your father now, and then send him to me. I think I can soften his attitude."

"I'm glad you recovered from your illness," George said, relieved, and kissed her forehead.

Honor Brown acknowledged his concern with a nod. "You could make a good man, George. Put this behind you and use the experience to guide you in future. Good-bye, nephew."

George, choking back his emotion, left her with gratitude. He met his father walking along the hallway to Honor's room and, taking him gently by the arm, pulled him into a vacant bedroom across the hall. George confessed to fathering a child and briefly explained what his aunt intended to do. Hugh Brown's shocked expression made a lasting impression on George, but his father's recognition of his son's contrition followed swiftly after the shock. Hugh patted his shoulder and said a few words of encouragement that, after all, the child was to be born into slavery and would be taken care of. Since the importation of slaves from other countries had been forbidden for decades in Virginia, slaves had to be bred in the state, thus encouraging owners to have children by their slaves. Although Hugh opposed slavery in principle, he conformed to the common opinion that slaves were necessary for the economy, which put George's indiscretion outside any moral censure. Although troubled on a deeper level, Hugh resolved to pursue this argument in his discussion with Honor Brown. It was what Honor would welcome.

George waited outside the house for his father, who in less than half an hour joined him and, saddling his horse for the return journey, counseled his son again about the difficulties he would face in life and the necessity of seeking God's help. George accompanied him to the river and watched him wade to the island and disappear into the woods. He admired his father more than ever now. The old man had covered over his displeasure and given George encouragement. Only the next day did word come to the home of Richard Brown Jr., where George was staying, that Hugh had missed the sandbar when crossing to the Ohio side, and he and his horse were swept away in deep water. Their bodies were not found for another three days. George was heartbroken and blamed himself for causing his father's distraction. Richard Brown coaxed him out of such thoughts gradually and managed to persuade him to remember the goodness of his father and his Christian attitude to his fellow man. George, who had intended to speak to Sarah, now decided against seeing her and returned to his father's farm by crossing upriver. As he set to work with his brothers to bring in his mother's wheat, he could not shake off despondency and a feeling of worthlessness.

Sarah heard from Nell what the family intended to do with her. She was glad that she would not be sold until after her child's birth in the winter of 1812. But she yearned to see George again and was bitterly disappointed, although not surprised, that he made no attempt to meet with her. She thought that the sudden death of his father had much to do with it. Certainly that tragedy had overshadowed whatever small problem she had caused. Early in the winter, the slaves were sold, some locally, some to be auctioned in Wellsburg.

Sarah and her two children were moved to Honor Brown's farmstead in the Cove for the winter, and she was let off some of the more difficult household duties as she approached her time for giving birth.

4

When Sarah gave birth to her daughter in April, she heard that George Brown took his brother's place in an Ohio Regiment, which was to fight against Canada. She laughed when she pictured him trying to conform to military discipline. Their daughter was going to be beautiful and might have a promising future because she was white. Sarah called her Fanny. When the Reverend Doddridge baptized her, her sister Fanny was present as godparent.

When Fanny was a month old, Sarah and her three children moved to the Campbell homestead on the Heights overlooking the Cove. Campbell knew that he had swung a very good deal, especially as two of Sarah's children would soon be old enough to work.

The Campbell household reflected the willful and pragmatic nature of its autocratic head. Margaret MacDonald Campbell was 22, the same age as Sarah. In six years of marriage she had borne Campbell three children and was pregnant with a fourth. Margaret asked her husband to acquire Sarah because she could no longer cope with all the household duties and look after the children. Sarah's reputation as a good cook and her thoroughness in sewing and mending made her indispensable.

Margaret's dealings with Sarah were direct and unassuming, unlike anything Sarah had experienced with white women. She was from Canada, from somewhere north of Lake Erie, a strange country because, as Margaret told her right away, the people there had banned slavery. Margaret's father, a wily Scot, who had moved from Nova Scotia to farm in Upper Canada, as a condition for relinquishing his young daughter to the vigorous but old James Campbell, required Campbell to take her two brothers into his household. Since Campbell found the brothers, John and Candor, good drinking companions and agreeably deferential to him in all things, he assented. The brothers, seeing no future in their father's impoverished existence, readily accompanied Campbell back to his slave-supported empire in the Virginian hills. They offered him their expertise in building grist and saw mills and they constructed a distillery which brought Campbell a lot of money and popularity locally. By their father's instructions, they were to protect their sister from domestic abuse at the hands of the oft-drunken Campbell.

Campbell treated Margaret fairly well. He vented his spleen on his slaves, who lived in a large cabin some distance from the main house. Two or three times a week the brothers heard the groans and cries as Campbell made his will known to them with a bull whip and other devices. Several of the slaves, now grown men, were children he had spawned throughout the years. Only when nearing sixty did he feel that he needed a wife for his sexual and spiritual needs. The young Margaret in her purity made him think that he had at last created a spiritual union. He was a Presbyterian and began attending the church, for which his father had given a small piece of land. His Godliness, however, lasted only for Sunday morning. The rest of the time he was "a thin-skinned, ornery cuss," according to the brothers MacDonald.

Like his itinerant trading father, James Campbell carried goods to settlers through Kentucky, Tennessee, Ohio, Michigan and into Canada. He knew all the Indian paths and where the new settlements were springing up. Sarah, while waiting on table, heard him talk of these far-off places and describe the people he met. She dared not show on her face any interest in his stories and the power that they had on her imagination, but when she was alone she allowed herself to dream of these lands that seemed wonderfully free and accepting. By contrast, the Campbell farm was oppressive and threatening. The black slaves cringed at Campbell's appearance and worked like machines all day and into the night. The men stuttered and shuffled and refused to look at anyone from the main house directly in the eye. The women were sullen. All were in rags and very thin for Campbell gave them little to eat. When he left on a trading venture, he put one of his brothers-in-law in charge. Only then could the slaves breathe easier and work at a normal speed.

Sarah and her children slept in a small cabin big enough to hold a bed and table that was near the main house. Campbell, when drunk in the evenings, would open the door and stare with amusement for minutes at a time before he would sing out a "good-night, my pets" and retire to his house. Sarah was fearful of what he would do. She had heard the stories of his predations, and she feared for her children's safety. But she knew that there was something in her that intimidated Campbell as if he feared violating a certain quality that she had. Her closeness with his wife may have given him pause, but that was not restraint enough when he was truly drunk. Sarah became Margaret's personal attendant and Margaret eventually became confident enough in Sarah's character to confide in her about her marriage and personal matters. White women, Sarah concluded, were almost like slaves, except that they had a better position or rank in the family. She realized that Margaret had little influence over her husband on any matter, yet, although married when young, she had refused to let her spirit be broken by the tyranny of the home. Sarah was a help to her in that way because Sarah's spirit was not broken and both women took sustenance from one another. But Sarah, of course, had had a master more benevolent than the scarifying James Campbell. How long she could keep up her courage under this man in this atmosphere became a worrisome question. She clung strongly to her faith for support.

Campbell let her attend Doddridge's log cabin church only once a month when she had to walk the four miles. Doddridge went out of his way to speak with those slaves who were permitted to attend his church, and, as a medical doctor, one of the few in this part of the country, he often gave his services free to sick slaves whose masters would not pay for their care.

Sarah managed to keep herself in Margaret Campbell's good graces by diligent attention to her needs and to make herself valuable in

James Campbell's eyes by cooking good meals. When James went on his alcoholic binges, he visited the slave quarters and never made it to Sarah's door.

A year passed. Spring was in the air when one evening as Sarah lay in bed with her children, she heard a sound outside her cabin window. Fearing that Campbell would make his appearance and assault her, she clutched her children to her and trembled in fear and with determination to resist. She watched the door move gently and knew that it was some other presence.

"Who is it?" she said calmly.

Quickly, as if in a blur of movement, Henry Lewis stepped into the room and closed the door behind him. "Sarah!" he whispered in almost a cry of relief. "I've come back!"

Sarah stared in amazement at this sturdy man with grizzled whiskers and ragged clothes. "Henry!" She saw the happiness in his face that, nevertheless, had aged greatly since she last saw it. "You escaped?"

Henry threw his head back in pride and laughingly said, "Third time. They can't make me a slave." He rushed to her and threw his arms about her as Sarah clutched him to her.

She smelt the stench of the swamp on his clothes, and her happiness for him turned to wonder as she imagined the hardships he had endured. "I love you, my husband," she choked. "I missed you so much."

"I got through all the pain they give me," he said, tears running from his eyes, "by thinkin' of you and the young'uns."

"Daddy!" young Henry cried and threw his arms about his neck.

Henry put an arm about his boy and held him tightly, then reached for Molly, who stared in doubt at this man, and kissed her cheeks. Henry saw the white baby in bed with them and frowned. "Is that your child, Sarah?" he asked angrily.

"I didn't think you was comin' back," she explained. "I couldn't help it."

Henry reared back, his black face contorted with disbelief and fury. "A white man! You did it with a white man? Who?"

"He's long gone," she said, regaining her composure. "He means nothin' to me."

There was the sound of a plank falling outside. They fell silent, listening. They heard the wind blowing stronger and relaxed. Baby Fanny began to cry and Sarah tried to quieten her.

"I'll fix her," Henry said bitterly.

"No!" Sarah held Fanny close to her. "Don't you hurt her."

"I only got a few minutes," Henry whispered urgently. "They knows I'll be comin' to see you. I chanced it tonight only 'cause there's no moon." He stripped off his thin garments, dirt-laden and torn, and dropped them on the floor. His strong physique, his piercing black eyes and his strong broad hands came as if in a primal urge toward her.

"No, husband!" Sarah cried in alarm. "I'll scream!"

Henry stood back in disbelief and looked blackly at the white baby.

"You want to kill her, don't you?" she cried angrily. "Fanny's mine. You can't come near me."

Henry's passion drained out of him as he stood naked before her. Cursing her, he seized his clothes and quickly dressed. "You just killed us," he said. "You look after my young'uns," he warned.

Sarah spoke softly to him. "You're a brave man, Henry, and I love you, but my children, white or black, are mine. You're an escaped slave and we can never be together again in this life. I've got to fend for myself and my children. You can't help no more."

"I'll look after my children," he said reprovingly. "Don't you doubt that." He stepped over to touch the heads of Henry and Molly while Sarah moved the baby behind her as if fearful he would seize her and strangle her. Henry's temper could flare up instantly although he was a mild-tempered man by nature. "Good-bye, Sarah." Henry turned to the door and stood listening for any sound beyond it in the night. "I hope no one heard that white bastard crying," he whispered bitterly back at her.

"Where you goin'?" Sarah asked.

"Indian country. Ohio most likely," he said. "They's goin' to be lots of bounty hunters tracking me down. They loves me in Kentucky," he added with a smile. "You are my only woman, Sarah. I'll always remember you." He turned his head away with sudden emotion. "God help us poor creatures." He swung open the door and disappeared into the blackness of the night. The flame from Sarah's lone candle shuddered in the sudden breeze as the door slowly swung shut.

Sarah stared at the door for a long time. She worried that he would be caught, although she knew that from his years in the region he had traced all of the smaller paths and Indian trails. She clasped her hands and said a prayer for his safety. His unexpected reappearance in her life provoked conflicting emotions. She wanted to love him, but she saw the hatred in his soul for the white man and for Fanny, her innocent and lovely child. By risking capture in her presence, he put her and their family in danger because it would imply to the whites that she was harboring an escaped slave. The thought of the whipping, maiming and separation from her children for such an offense acted as a brake on any desire to accept him back as her husband. As a fugitive, he had to be gone from her life, and she sensed that, as he swam across the Ohio river at that moment, he was thinking the very same thing. At least, she knew he was free, and, at least, he had shown her that he would not remain a slave. That fact was important to both of them, but fundamental to him as a man.

For the next weeks Sarah was closely watched. James Campbell ordered a couple of his slaves to patrol the grounds at night. Sarah heard them often outside her door. She was forbidden to leave the Campbell property. During the day she had to keep her children with her while she did her household duties. Usually they played with the Campbell children but James Campbell thought that Henry Lewis would risk anything to see them and could be caught more easily if they were with her. Sarah marveled at the speed with which Henry had crossed the country. His pursuers believed such a feat impossible and that, if he tried to see his wife and children at all, he would appear about a week after he actually saw her.

As time passed, the sharp-eyed men whom she encountered on the Campbell farm became fewer and finally disappeared altogether. James Campbell began to resent the fact that Henry had not turned up and suspected that he had eluded his surveillance somehow. Campbell, a bulky farmer with a husky, beefy face and an all-knowing smile of cunning, allowed Sarah's children to play with his own again and sometimes watched them. Occasionally he called young Henry to him. The bright-eyed mulatto boy of five years approached his master with a frightened look. His mother had told him to say nothing about his father, and he chose to say little to Campbell when the old man began to quiz him. "Yes, massa" and "No, massa" were the only words that Campbell could coax out of him. Henry feigned ignorance that he even had a father. Campbell seemed satisfied that he was a slow-witted boy and that he had not remembered his father, but he resented being unable to ferret out the fact that Henry Lewis had seen his family. He should have visited long ago. Campbell was willing to bet that he had. But it would have served no purpose to torture Sarah into confessing that her husband had come to see her. The slave had come and gone; any chance of catching him had been lost. The reward money for his capture was lost too.

Glumly, Campbell began to look upon Henry's eluding of his surveillance as an affront to his authority, and, as time wore on, he began to concentrate his displeasure on the weakest partner of this "crime"— Sarah. When he mentioned his belief that Henry Lewis had made a fool of them to his wife, Margaret tried to convince him that it was not the case. Sarah would have given some indication of it to her, she said, but in no way, through her emotions, body language, or slip of the tongue had she acknowledged that she had seen her beloved husband. Campbell, however, had followed his hunches throughout his life and inevitably discovered that they were more reliable than the opinions of other people. He pretended that the matter was of no importance to him, but it rankled in him nevertheless.

The sixty-six year old farmer had had to put up with several annoyances recently. He worked hard to build up trade for his staples, but competition from other farmers eroded his business, forcing him to sell off parcels of his land to new settlers, who, bringing skills in mining the ore in the hills and in manufacturing implements for both house and farm, cut further into his share of the trade. The furnaces, erected in the vicinity of the Cove, produced cannons and cannon balls, which were shipped via rivers to the American forces on Lake Erie for the war against Canada. Cloth manufactories in the area flourished provisioning the army and navy. Thus young entrepreneurs were getting rich and showing less respect to the old-time farmers. These new industrialists did not use slaves. The professional class that catered to their wishes dared to state their views against continuing slavery in western Virginia. The boldest was the lawyer Philip Doddridge, who had been winning cases against slave holders under a technicality. Virginia required an immigrant settler bringing slaves into the state to register them within one year, which, by diligent searching of the court files, Doddridge's law clerks discovered that many settlers had not done. Doddridge helped slaves to sue for their freedom under *formo pauperis*—legal aid. As farming became more labour intensive, the value of slaves rose, and Campbell warned his farming friends that they would be ruined by these court invasions of their property.

Campbell terrorized his slaves to prevent them from thinking that they could find some legal way to win their freedom. He sent them to be whipped by the sheriff or to be dunked by the ducking stool, held under water until almost drowned. The public, gathering in the mornings to watch this sport, jeered and cheered as slaves groaned, cried and shrieked with pain. Slaves in all skin colours from coal black to lily white endured such treatment for days on end, and often stayed locked in stocks in the town square until they were needed to work on the farms. Sarah, on shopping errands, recognized slaves that she knew and learned that they suffered for no offence other than to be the object of their master's displeasure. She wondered how long it would take for Campbell to come bursting into her little cabin. She prayed that she might be spared. It seemed, however, that God was not listening because the slaves who were tortured were good Christians and called to God as their only protector.

5

Henry Lewis, after leaving the Campbell farm, escaped into the Ohio wilderness. His mind spun with anger and pain. Sarah was lost to him now. He spat with fury as he thought of the pressures put upon him to never run away again. He would rather live on the fringes of society than as a slave at its centre. The system in its arrogant assumption that it was right ground down the human element in man. Henry preferred death to recapture. He had traveled a long distance through Kentucky and Ohio to reach his family in the Virginia Panhandle by living off fish and berries, skirting settlements and sticking to the woods. He should be relieved, he told himself, that his family was still all right, but Sarah's white baby seemed like a reproach to him as if taunting him with his failure to protect her from the depredations of her masters.

He was very, very tired and the night was very dark; he stumbled on along an Indian trail that he knew led westward until he came to a small clearing and found a bed of branches near some bushes a distance from the trail. He fell on them and with the sounds of beasts on the hunt in his ears, he sank into a deep sleep.

He awoke in early daylight to a rustling sound near him and sitting up with alarm he saw that a wild boar was rooting in the branches at his feet. Startled by his sudden movement, it reared its head, stared at him, and, turning its heavy body, it ran away into the trees. Henry stood up and listened. He detected the sound of a stream, and, pursuing the direction from whence it came, he soon located it and drank his fill. He seized some plants growing in a little backwash and breaking off their roots, he chewed them, sucking in the juices and chomping on the fibres. For a man who had been fed little in his slave days, Henry had a strong physique. He was resourceful in finding food—stealing it when necessary and cultivating it secretly. When he lived in the Panhandle, he became friendly with some Indians who lived in Mingo town, a few miles down the Ohio River. They were Senecas and taught him how to distinguish the edible from the inedible vegetation in the forest. When the influx of whites became unbearable, these Indians moved to the western end of Ohio, where they settled in a community of Shawnees and Senecas in Logan county, the only Indian settlement left in that part of the world. It was to this distant country that Henry Lewis headed in hopes that it would give him refuge. A few Delawares wandered about the state in small groups, but they could offer him no help as they were preoccupied with their own survival. As for the white settlements, none was safe for an escaped slave. All these things Henry turned over and over in his mind when he toiled in the stables on his Kentucky plantation. Now that he knew that Sarah could take care of the children without him, he gave up on the idea that he could live near-by in Ohio and make visits periodically to see them. Better for him to make a totally new life, to become as one with the wilderness, and as one with those other victims of the new white empire. It was better for Sarah, too, because he was useless to her now.

Henry took a few days and nights to penetrate through the forests westward to Logan County. Occasionally he came upon a small settlement of Quakers, where he found food and shelter. On these occasions he stayed as much as half a day longer to help with the work to thank them for their kindness. On his way he met many kinds of travelers: migrants in a train of wagons heading westward, isolated wanderers such as bearded and ragged frontiersmen, solitary Indians, and the dangerous outcasts from society. He no longer feared pursuit by his Kentucky masters as they would have had no idea where to begin looking for him. The sense of freedom he felt re-invigorated him every dawn when he awoke to face the adventure of a new day whether raining or shining. Often he wished that he had a gun when he encountered elk and deer gliding through the trees in the semi-darkness and pausing in the shafts of sunlight that broke through the canopy of leaves above. He had kept hunger under control until the last day when he stumbled weakly into an Indian encampment and fainted face down on the hard earth in the central clearing. Squaws came to his aid, pulled him into a cabin and revived him with sweet-smelling herbs. When he sat up and looked around him, one of the women gave him a bowl of mashed corn meal and, with a nod of gratitude, he dipped in his hand and scooped the food into his mouth, trembling with anticipation.

When the men returned from the hunt, he was brought to the leaders and answered their questions. Satisfied that he would bring no retribution upon them, they gave him the right to stay with them. Henry would learn their ways and work with their strong young men to keep the community safe from invaders and supplied with game. It was then that Henry recognized one of the Senecas he had known in Mingo Town and realized that he must have vouched for him, but the Indian, expressionless among the leaders of the council, gave no sign that he knew him.

Henry was assigned to live with an old Shawnee couple who had lost their sons in land skirmishes with whites. The old man took a liking to him immediately and made it known that Henry was his son from now on. He was tall and muscular and his face showed the signs of a wounded man who had overcome his setbacks and made his peace with life. His name was Kokataw and he was the best horseman among them. As soon as he had assessed Henry's abilities in the hunt and became satisfied of his potential as a leader, he began teaching Henry about horses in a way that Henry, the enslaved stable hand, had never known. Horses were not dumb animals but spirits, wild and wonderful, and related by sensitivities of the mind and sensualness of the skin to mankind. That was why the two relied on one another for survival. Man took care of the horse in a firm and gentle way and the horse took care of man as a duty, and, sometimes, as a friend. Kokataw sold his horses to settler and Indian alike, but not before he observed the buyer with animals and taught him to respect them.

These Indians had managed to resist being pushed westward by uniting against all attempts to acquire their lands and by learning trades that could make them useful in the white man's economy. For instance, Kokataw's wife, a tall woman with traces of her former beauty, knew the secrets of herbal medicines and was often sought out by settlers to come to the aid of their families, who had been stricken by disease that their medicines could not cure. She taught Henry the power of certain herbs and how to use them correctly.

Bounty hunters tended to stay away from Indian settlements because they were known to disappear without a trace when they moseyed through them. Henry, owing to his knowledge of English and his Negroid looks which spared him from random attacks that Indians might expect to encounter among whites, often did official business for the Indians in the white towns and earned the trust and respect of his adopted people. He learned to ferret out the news in these towns from people who knew what was happening in distant places such as local rebellions of Negroes, skirmishes with Indians, and the business of strangers who were traveling in the vicinity. Eventually he took a wife, a lovely Shawnee girl, but this was only after he had heard that his pursuers from Kentucky had given up looking for him.

He wondered about Sarah and his children, but he dared not visit them again in his first years in Logan County. Not only would he just bring them trouble, but his inability to help them hurt him to his soul. His struggles to live by hunting in a diminishing wilderness and his assimilation into the Indian community took all his time and effort. Some day, he hoped, he would find a way to communicate with them.

6

On a hot evening in the summer of 1813, James Campbell's tall, bear-like form appeared at Sarah's door. She was dozing and her children were fast asleep. Campbell said that her mistress wanted to see her and to come with him. Margaret, pregnant again, had been complaining to Sarah that this growing child made her sicker than any of her other pregnancies so that Sarah followed Campbell without the least suspicion. On entering the house, Campbell turned to the back rather than to the front where Margaret's bedroom was located. Sarah, surprised, wondered if Margaret had moved to the back of the house because of the cooler breeze that could be caught there. Campbell opened the door to a room with a large bed that was used by guests on occasion. He motioned to her to sit on the bed beside him.

"Don't be afraid of me," he smiled. "I want to explain something to you."

Sarah sat timorously beside him and looked at him with consternation as she feared that Margaret was sicker than she had thought.

"You know I like you," James said seriously, "and now I need you. You will sleep with me here for a while every night beginning now."

Sarah gasped, "But the missus?"

"She's asleep and she ain't ill," he chortled. "Or leastways, she's too ill to entertain me."

Sarah stood up, "Please massa, my children need me."

"They're just fine," he said with an edge to his voice. "You stay with me a coupla hours and then go back to them."

Sarah with a sinking feeling tried to think of a way to escape; she thought of protesting that she could not do anything to hurt her mistress but knew the uselessness of such a defence. If Campbell had been in a drunken rage, she could have resisted him more easily than she could now. She looked distraught, which made Campbell chuckle.

"Come, Sal, take your dress off," he whispered as he threw back the sheet covering the bed. He stood up and began taking off his clothes and throwing them on the back of a chair.

Campbell owned her body and soul, not only by law but psychologically. He was the provider of shelter and food for her children, who would suffer if she refused him.

Dropping her clothes on the floor and lying on the bed, Sarah suppressed the feelings of disgust and hatred that thickened her throat. Campbell was beside her immediately, sucking her breasts and fondling her body. She tried to forget that he was old, tried to think of George Brown and stared at the ceiling as he entered her. He reached a climax and rolled to one side while she suffered the pain of feeling useless. After a few moments, when she rose to leave, he pulled her back and held her by his side and caressed her. She lay as if wooden and prayed that he would let her go. Within half an hour he made love to her again. About two hours after he first took her into his arms, she left

35

him sleeping and returned to her children. Depressed but rejoicing in their presence, she crawled into bed with them and fell asleep.

The slave bell awakened her before dawn. Drowsily she prepared for her household duties of making breakfast for the master's household and attending to the wants of Margaret. At the breakfast table, Campbell ignored her as usual and Margaret suspected nothing. Sarah could not help feeling guilt when she looked at Margaret, whose stomach had begun to swell and whose pleasure in her expectant motherhood seemed to radiate from her. But she suppressed all feeling and prepared her mind to accept the commands of her master for as long as he wanted her. In this way the summer months passed, she visiting the back room of the main house for an hour or two once a week. Inevitably the household learned of it but pretended not to notice. To have remarked upon it would have been dangerous. If Margaret knew, she gave no indication that she did. Her preoccupation was with her new child, another boy.

When she lay with Campbell, Sarah experienced none of the love she had felt for her husband and George Brown. Campbell treated her as if she were a sexual instrument. He probably treated his wife the same way, she thought. He was too arrogant to understand anyone's viewpoint other than his own. His belligerence was noticeably less of late, and Sarah thought that she may have been responsible for taming him. He loved her body and some of his day must have been passed thinking of it rather than inflicting punishments on his slaves, she thought. Occasionally he descended into his angry, destructive stage of drunkenness and did not show up in the back room. Sarah waited patiently for him for two hours and returned to her cabin at such times. He did not take his anger out on his slaves either. He stayed in the Cove drinking and carousing with friends until he passed out. Word would be sent to his house, and one of Margaret's brothers, John or Candor MacDonald, would leave his bed, hitch a horse to a wagon and go down in the darkness to bring the old boy home.

Sarah had only sporadic contact with her sisters at this time. When Fanny gave birth to Dick Dawson's son, she hoped Dawson, as a free coloured man, would free her, but Dawson wanted to persuade his slave-holding community that he could be trusted to be one of them.

Fanny, who was lighter in skin colour than he was, resented him, and Dawson, reacting to her attitude, began to treat her harshly. For this reason Fanny was unable to move as freely as she had in the past and could communicate with Sarah only by the slave grapevine. Her sister Nell, on the other hand, kept an eye on all that was happening in the community through her central position as Honor Brown's personal maid. Honor was awake to all the gossip and Nell, being close at hand when visitors called, took in everything she could. Sometimes she would arrange by a slave messenger to meet Sarah in the Cove at the times Sarah went shopping, and they could have a few moments together to exchange information. It was the sharp-eyed Nell who was the first to notice that Sarah was pregnant. Sarah did not need to tell her that James Campbell was the father. Nell simply put her hand on Sarah's arm in sympathy.

Campbell returned to his wife then. The fall arrived in blazing colours. The slaves worked hard to harvest the crops. Everyone was too busy to think of Sarah's pregnancy, which was taken as a matter of fact without comment. Sarah hoped and expected that her child would be white. She knew that Campbell would care nothing for it and would give her no special treatment, but the child would have a better chance of survival in the world at large. She tried hard to make her children feel that as human beings they were a part of God's love as much as any other human being, including the master. Her own problems and disappointments she locked away in a compartment of her mind and gave her smiles and affection to her children without stint. She rarely mentioned Henry Lewis, and, when young Henry asked for him, she said that he would return to see them when he could.

Sarah named her new son Israel. He was white like Fanny. She took the name from the Bible because it meant the promised land. Perhaps this child would lead the slaves to freedom; at any rate, he was white and symbolized freedom. She nursed him through the summer of 1814, and, with the help of her other children, she kept him healthy when influenza and other infectious diseases were taking away children down in the Cove. James Campbell paid no attention to the child and became rather hostile to Sarah. He seemed to have lost that little respect that he had for her, as if her giving birth was some serious misdemeanour and break-down in morality that he found hard to forgive. Knowing that his wife suspected him, he thought it necessary to accuse John MacDonald of fathering the child. John, thin and wiry, smiled bemusedly at the suggestion and refused to reply to Campbell's taunts and accusations, which he made at unexpected moments, as if he were trying to catch John off-guard.

Israel's whiteness became an affront to him. As the boy crawled about with the other children, he refused to watch them as he did formerly. Despite his overbearing ego, his bluster, his ruthlessness, and his lack of pity for man or dog, Campbell had a streak of fairness running through his body. When one of his brothers deserted the family and changed his name to live in Tennessee, he carried his inheritance by mule pack to him, when he could easily have pocketed it himself. This element in his character made him uncomfortable when he looked at Israel. He could not rationalize his discomfort; he knew it had something to do with being white and being a slave and belonging to him, but he could not admit that he had made a mistake or that he had to correct a wrong. Such reasoning was not a part of his nature, but the unfairness bothered him. It began to work in him causing him to drink more and be trundled home more often by the MacDonald brothers. He became meaner to everyone around him as if a waspish devil had entered his mind and glared out through his eyes at all things moving.

Strangely he became somewhat more friendly with Sarah's two mulatto children: Henry and Mary. He took Henry into town with him when he had business collecting rents, banking, buying provisions, and let him handle the horses that drew the wagon. This was challenging for a nine-year old. He instructed the cooking staff, including Sarah, to teach Molly to cook and wait on table. Sarah was fearful that Molly would burn herself or drop plates because she was just six, but she had no choice and watched over her as carefully as she could.

Campbell's solicitous attentions to her oldest children and his marked dislike for her youngest two confused Sarah. But she understood his dislike for her. She was distinguished in her carriage and her looks, which was enough to shame a man as boorish as Campbell had he known the meaning of shame, but it was her protectiveness and love for her children that made him inexplicably angry. Her love for Israel contrasted with his disdain for the child in such a way as to make him question himself, for which he blamed her. But his antipathy did not express itself with force; it remained concealed like an evil spirit behind his eyes or like a snake waiting to strike out. Whoever its target might be could not be discerned. One reason it remained contained was Sarah's superior nature that intimidated him. The woman Campbell had lusted after and had silently raped now became inviolable because she loved a child whose whiteness was attributable to him.

From Campbell's farmhouse on the high curve of the rolling hills above Hollidays Cove, Sarah looked down at Brown's Island as if it represented a secure time of her life that had been lost to her forever. How menacing these hills had looked to her then! And now she was a part of this menace, living in it and fearful that it would strike her at any moment. Her strong spirit was all she had. God in the person of the Reverend Doddridge was sympathetic but unable to help her. Margaret MacDonald Campbell showed some independent spirit, but she was not strong enough to stand up to her husband. Her two brothers would rather go along with Campbell's wishes than risk his wrath by opposing them. Richard Brown Jr. had taken up his lands in Pennsylvania and the Brown family had forgotten about her; she was just a piece of property that the family had sold; all her thoughts of blood-relatedness and years of toil for the family had in the end meant nothing.

Campbell's resentment took almost three years to find its violent expression. It was a small incident that like a match touched off an inferno. Three year old Israel had taken it into his head to explore his surroundings and wandered into the private quarters of the Campbell home. Usually Campbell would have been out supervising work in the fields or in town visiting with his business associates, but that day he was suffering from a migraine. He heard a crash in his room and looked up to see his glass candle lamp lying broken on the floor and the small table on which it had stood toppled onto its side. Looking curiously at the debris was Israel. With a shout Campbell leaped to his feet and seized the small boy. Carrying Israel screaming through the house to the front porch, he sat on a straight-backed chair, put Israel over his knees and began to slap his rear very hard. The wails of the boy brought all the houseworkers running, including Sarah, who aghast stood waiting for Campbell to finish his punishment. When he gave no indication that he would stop, Sarah shrieked and ran to take back her son, but Campbell pushed her away with one arm and continued the punishment. Sarah screamed for Margaret Campbell to stop it, but Margaret, who had just arrived at the scene was pregnant and fearful of intervening less she receive a beating that might damage her child. Sarah got to her feet and tried again to wrestle Israel away from Campbell, but this time he punched her in the face, stunning her, and shouted to two white overseers to take her to her cabin. As the men pulled Sarah away and gestured to her frightened children to get to their cabin, Campbell began beating the child again as if he intended to kill him. At that moment, an old house slave, who had served Campbell's father and helped raise the Campbell children, ran up to him and seized Israel from his arms. She took the screaming child away before Campbell could react, so surprised he was at her boldness. Glowering, he ordered Candor MacDonald to bring the child back, but Candor, glaring darkly in disapproval, simply stood looking at Campbell. With stares of alarm and hatred from all sides ranged against him, Campbell cried after the old lady rapidly retreating to the servants' quarters that he would not forget her disobedience. All knew that stark retribution would follow and expected Campbell to begin meting it out. His migraine worsening, Campbell went back inside the house, and, seizing his head in both hands, walked unsteadily back to his bed. "Bring me water, Margaret!" he cried back at his wife. "And keep everyone quiet. I want quiet!"

After about half an hour, the old slave, named Alice, had rocked the frightened little boy to sleep and returned him to Sarah, who in tears thanked her. "What will happen to you?" Sarah asked fearfully.

"Don't worry 'bout me," Alice smiled. "You look after your young'uns. He's a mean man, the meanest of the Campbells. Watch out for him, now." She left to return to her duties in the house.

The white overseers told Sarah that she was to remain in her cabin until she was sent for. They returned to the fields and sensed the restlessness in the slaves as they whispered their fears among themselves. The overseers too felt uneasy at the prospect of Campbell losing his temper with a small child. It was a display of weakness, they thought, and tended to undermine their authority. Knowing Campbell only too well, for they had vicious disputes with him, they were apprehensive about the punishment that he would certainly inflict on all and every-one who had dared to question his right to do his will.

It took three days for Campbell to wreak his vengeance on Sarah for giving birth to a white child, which, it was said around town, was his. Sarah had no warning that it was coming. She had been told to resume her duties and assumed that the affair had been forgotten. But on a Friday night, Campbell in a drunken rage walked up the hill from the whisky tavern, took a bull whip from the barn, strode to Sarah's lit-tle cabin, pushed open the door with his shoulder, and stood facing a frightened Sarah and her four children. He lashed the whip to demon-strate its strength, and, without a word, began lashing at all of them in the one bed. Sarah put her body between the leather and her children but was unable to take all the lashings. Her skin was flayed and bleed-ing, the children were howling and clinging to her, and Campbell was smiling gleefully. Fortunately for Sarah, Campbell knocked over the table and extinguished the candle casting the room in darkness. He kept slashing at the bed but many of his blows missed their targets as Sarah had pushed her children onto the floor and told them to get under the bed. She kept to one end of the bed and curled up in a ball, yet even then she felt the breath knocked out of her with each blow and the sharp sting of the leather cut through her. Crying for mercy, she was on the point of despairing for her life when the old lady Alice appeared in the moonlight in the doorway and shouted at Campbell to stop. Turning awkwardly to stare at her, Campbell became more enraged and crying "Out!" he brought his whip upon her, knocking her to the ground. She tried to crawl away as he pursued her, whipping her on the ground and shouting abuse at her. Then as she lay motionless, he threw down his whip, seized her by the back collar of her dress and dragged her to the barn. He stepped into the barn, and Alice, thinking he was gone, dared to groan, but he was back with a rope in his hands. He quickly fixed a noose and slipped it over the old slave's head and threw the other end over a beam near the door. Sarah had crept to the door of her cabin in time to see Campbell haul Alice into the air. She

41

screamed in horror. At that moment, the MacDonald brothers came rushing from the house and shouted at Campbell to let the rope go. But he fastened it to a hook on the side of the barn and left the old lady dangling and strangling. The MacDonalds rushed to undo the rope, but Campbell lashed at them with his bull whip, knocking them down. With Margaret shouting helplessly from an upstairs window of the farmhouse to distract Campbell's attention, Candor MacDonald ran at Campbell, avoided the lash of the whip and tackled him to the ground while John undid the rope from the hook and gently lowered Alice to the ground. John ran to her and took the rope from her neck, but he was too late. Alice was dead. John, furious, ran to help his brother who was rolling on the ground with Campbell. Together they managed to subdue him. Escorting the dazed Campbell into the house with a firm grip on his arms, the brothers took him to his room and tied him to his bed. It was only then that the slaves appeared from their quarters, and in a low lamenting moan they took up Alice's body and carried it to their quarters. Margaret instructed two of the slaves to help Sarah and her children into the back of the farmhouse where she ran to administer whatever aid she could. Sudden silence seemed to claim the night. The shouting, crying, whipping, and lamenting ceased as if the horror had disappeared into the darkness.

Sarah was too badly hurt to walk, but her children, although cut and bleeding, ran to the back of the farmhouse where they sensed protection. Shocked and frightened they sat in silence while Margaret, white-faced and stern, attended to their wounds. The two house slaves put salve on Sarah's wounds. One remarked that she was lucky that the whip had not cut her face severely. She had not lost her beauty.

Sarah was just thankful that her children had escaped without being badly hurt. Poor Alice, she moaned, and she felt guilty that the old, defenseless woman had to save her once again, but this time with her life. The pain, the searing hot cuts on her body, and the sickening turmoil in her mind as she sensed that she would have to endure such punishment again and again, sank her into depression and despair. The deafening cries of Campbell as he struggled against the restraints swept through the house and made the house slaves tremble. Margaret too looked deeply worried. She wrung her hands as she confessed to

42

Sarah that she did not know what they could do to save her.

The fear in those around her, even in the faces of the MacDonald brothers who had taken liberties with Campbell that they had never dreamed they would, somehow gave Sarah strength. She suddenly felt capable of standing up to this man. She called her children to her and told them as they clung to her legs that they were going to their home and going to sleep. "If you want to help me," she said to Margaret, "please tell lawyer Doddridge about us. He's our only hope now."

Campbell's bellowing suddenly ceased. A silence fell over the house. John MacDonald smiled. "He's sleeping at last." He looked at Sarah thoughtfully and hitched his wiry body up as if he were screwing up his courage. "I'll see Philip Doddridge tomorrow. We'll see what we can do. But old James," he sighed and looked at Margaret, "he's an ornery fella."

Nodding her thanks, Sarah led her brood back to the little cabin and closed the door. There was no lock, but she felt secure now that Campbell was tied for the night and sleeping off his drunken rage. It was tomorrow that she feared, but, in the meantime, she fell into a deep sleep, exhausted as were her children, sleeping beside her. Disturbing dreams of Alice woke her twice in the night but she fell asleep again immediately.

Alice's funeral was held the following afternoon. The Reverend Joseph Doddridge conducted a short service on the Campbell property where Alice had lived her life and where she was to be buried. Campbell allowed only the house slaves to attend; the others could not miss their day in the fields. Campbell went into town to be with his drinking companions and to avoid the embarrassment of facing Doddridge. Alice had been about his own age and had grown up on his father's farm with him. He could not understand what had possessed her to interfere between him and his slaves. She knew her place and she certainly knew his temper. Her rash action was going to have repercussions. News of her hanging would circulate and turn some people in the community against him. Even his own brothers on either side of his farm were going to Alice's funeral, an act that he perceived as defiant of him, especially as they had not set foot on his land for ten

43

years at least. The MacDonald brothers had embarrassed him in front of his slaves, which concerned him, but they prevented him from doing more damage, for which he was grudgingly thankful. He saw them as a burden and a helpmeet, a balancing influence in his running of the farm. As for the cause of this mess, he ordered that Sarah and her children remain in their cabin and be fed only bread and water as punishment. He needed time to think of a proper and practical punishment for them. He would like to sell the lot of them, but traders did not want to take small children because it was hard to find owners who would pay for their upkeep until they could do real work. And in Sarah's case, two of her children were white, which meant that they would find it easier to escape someday. He needed to talk the matter over with his friends in the Cove, all of whom owned slaves.

Joseph Doddridge looked very grim as he consigned Alice's body to the grave. He had officiated at many such burials of slaves who had been killed by accident or in a rage by their masters. The law favoured the masters, and, consequently, no witnesses would testify against a master. Most people regarded it as a material loss: the slave lost his worth to the farm and the master lost the monetary worth of the slave. God, whom they all worshipped on Sundays, had nothing to do with it. Doddridge called by at Sarah's cabin as he was leaving the farm. He was shocked by how badly she had been cut by the whip and disturbed by the look of fear on the faces of the children, who seemed to have been stunned into a permanent silence. He patted the eldest gently on their heads and spoke kindly to them, telling them that God loved them and that everything would be all right.

Sarah broke down at his words. The tears which she had held back now flowed at the sound of his gentle voice. The confidence that this large man engendered in those he comforted overwhelmed her. Patience, he cautioned, patience would see everything come right in the end. "John MacDonald will see my brother today in Wellsburg and I will talk to him tonight," he smiled cheerfully. "Don't worry now, my dear girl. We will do what we can." He hugged Sarah to his large frame, and, overcome by her distress, he turned his face away to control his emotions. He strode from the cabin to his horse, which was tethered to a hook on the barn near to where Alice was hanged.

Doddridge, despite his apparent confidence, worried over Sarah's chances of success. His brother would take the case in *forma pauperis* that guaranteed a person without means to sue in court represented by counsel, but in recent years his successes were fewer. As the communities in the Virginia Panhandle became more prosperous, the juries were peopled by the more prosperous merchants and landholders who had less sympathy for the poor and their rights before the law than previously. Even the best lawyer in the nation, which his brother had been called, was unable to sway the prejudiced minds of these richer folk, to whom the hardscrabble lives and frontier attitudes of earlier settlers meant nothing. It all depended, of course, on what sort of case that Philip Doddridge could bring against Campbell; indeed, if he could find any grounds to go to court at all. Moreover, Campbell was one of the most powerful men in Brooke County. How could a poor slave girl hope to win her freedom against a man with influential connections to every industry in the area? He sighed with exasperation. The Church had to do more to aid these people. He had come to the conclusion that the Church should be involved in helping them to escape such an evil system as a last resort. He had established churches in Ohio and Pennsylvania to help settlers form Episcopal centers of worship and his contacts with ministers in the Methodist and Presbyterian faiths gave him a wide web of communication. Many ministers felt the way he did about slavery, but others still supported the system, and, of course, the Church could not be seen as officially endorsing efforts to free slaves. Sarah would have to take a stand in court against Campbell before thoughts of freeing her from this ogre in illegal ways could even be contemplated.

Doddridge looked at Brown's Island as he descended the hill into the Cove. The whole southern half of the island now was cultivated. The great trees remained on the northern half but soon they would be felled for the prices that their hardwood was bringing in the flourishing economy. He reminded himself that after he saw the sick in his clinic in the town, he had to ride out to the Brown farmhouse to visit Mrs. Honor Brown. She was dying of an ailment for which he could find no source. All he could do was comfort her and reassure her of God's love.

When Campbell returned for his evening dinner he was sober. He said very little to his wife and stayed away from his six little children, whom he usually liked to sit and talk with before they went to bed. He told Margaret that he did not care how useful Sal was around the house, he had to make an example of her. He was sending her and the children to the town prison for a while. He did not want them on his property. The experience in prison would be good for them, he said sarcastically. When Margaret tried to protest, he silenced her with a gesture and an angry look. He told John and Candor MacDonald, who sat silently at the table, to take Sal and her children down to the Cove in one of the farm wagons in the morning. They finished the meal in silence. Campbell sensed their disapproval, but he relished doing whatever he wanted over their objections. He did not know that John had seen Philip Doddridge that day and that Doddridge had agreed to take Sarah's case. As far as he was concerned, the imprisonment of Sarah for a spell was the end of this particular matter. He would bring Sarah back only after the loss of her cooking could no longer be endured. By sending Sarah to jail, however, he unwittingly was assuring Doddridge access to her and making it possible for the clever lawyer to build a case against him.

7

At this time Philip Doddridge was 34 years old and widely respected for his forensic talents. His law practice spread through western Virginia into Ohio and Pennsylvania from his office in Wellsburg. His ability to lead a jury along his line of reasoning and his sense of humour made him a formidable opponent in a courtroom. When his reputation as a member of Congress spread nationwide, Daniel Webster, the famous orator from New England, said that Doddridge was the only man he feared to debate. His familiarity with the Brown family and its slaves throughout the years as their family lawyer brought her predicament close to his heart. The happy young girl he had seen on Brown's Island was now a beaten woman languishing in prison with her terrorized children. Although there seemed no grounds for legal action, Doddridge knew that in every case a reason could be found to challenge what was taken for granted. Since he was too busy to attend to Sarah himself, he assigned her case to his assistant Alexander Caldwell, who was just a few years younger than Doddridge and destined for a brilliant career as a judge. Caldwell was also from the family of an early settler who like the Browns and the Doddridges hailed originally from Baltimore. Caldwell was friendly with James Campbell and just the year before had lent Campbell money to tide him over in a year of bad harvests. Campbell would get no leniency from him, however, as he was as committed to ameliorating slavery as was Doddridge, though he was considerate of an owner's right to his property so long as that property was not abused. As he listened to Sarah's story in the hot, poorly-ventilated prison cell in Hollidays Cove, he came to see a side of Campbell that he had not imagined. The man had disgraced the reputation of the old settler class by his irrational actions. Caldwell remarked too that Sarah looked white and that two of her children were white, which, as he gleaned from her description of Campbell's anger, may have caused Campbell's deep resentment. He left her with assurances that he would find some way to free her from Campbell's tyranny and asked her to have hope in the legal process. When he had gone, Sarah felt a sense of relief for the first time. The fact that such clever men were working on her behalf made her think that Campbell could be beaten. She told her children to pray for their lawyers that they might find a way to deliver them from slavery.

At this time Honor Brown died and left a modest sum to Sarah's sister, Nell. Since Nell was freed according to the Colonel's will, she could live with her husband Grady who ran a hardware store in the Cove. She was in a position to help Sarah if she won her freedom. She visited Sarah in the slave prison and tried as best she could to prevent punishments from being meted out to the mother and her children such as placing them in stocks in public to humiliate them. The jailer, a mulatto, would soften the punishment because he had to live in the community and shopped at the Grady store. The whippings and near-drownings administered to the other slaves constantly unnerved Sarah. Screams and cries, uncontrollable sobbing and furious shouting—all the noises of the oppressive prison house—compounded the feeling of condemnation which the walls of the building seemed to hurl against her.

Nell understood Campbell's resentment of Sarah. Campbell's long life was spent defending his property and his right to do whatever he wished. Now in his seventies, youthful in body and still rigidly opinionated in mind, he could not forgive a living contradiction to his belief that slaves were inferior. Sal was not broken by his seduction of her, by bearing his child; she was as proud as ever and maintained her pleasant and even disposition despite the indignities he showered upon her. If he could have seen her despair in her private moments, he would have been gratified, but Sarah, out of her devotion to her children, kept up a bold front in public.

Caldwell found court records for the county revealing that when Colonel Brown moved his family and slaves into Hollidays Cove from Maryland in 1784, he neglected to take the oath required by law that he register his slaves within ten days of arrival. Not until 1791 did he register his slaves. Moreover, he did not mention Molly, Sarah's mother, because she was dead by then. Consequently, according to Caldwell, Sarah was free and her children were born free. The Justice of the Peace in Wellsburg listened to Caldwell's argument and gave his opinion that Sarah was justified in suing Campbell for her freedom. Sarah was jubilant. When Fanny came to see her in prison, Sarah told her that they had actually been free all the time they were enslaved. Fanny, astounded and just as excited, asked Sarah to help her get free of Dick Dawson. She confessed that he had been assaulting her for a long time as she refused to sleep with him until he freed her. Her life had become miserable. He was jealous of her and afraid that if she was free that she would leave him. He was right about that, she said angrily. She could no longer abide him. That he would keep his own son a slave showed what kind of a man he was. He was no better than a white slaver. Sarah calmed her down and swore that Caldwell would help her too.

Caldwell was concerned over this new development because Philip

48

Doddridge bought the seven-year old Fanny in 1791, at which time he advised Colonel Brown to register his slaves otherwise he could not sell Fanny to him. By buying Fanny, Doddridge recognized her as a slave, and by selling her when a young woman to Dick Dawson, regardless of his hopes that Dawson would free and marry her, he had reaffirmed her status as a slave. True, her mother Molly was not registered. That was the main point in the argument for freeing all her descendants. Fanny should have been registered seven years earlier. But Doddridge could not appear in court to argue that she was not a slave when he had owned her at one time, and if Fanny was a slave so was her sister Sal. It was bad luck, made worse by Caldwell having to argue the case himself.

When Campbell received a writ from Caldwell accusing him of trespass, assault and battery and false imprisonment because Sal and her children were not slaves, he reacted with fury. He was on the point of instructing that severe punishment be meted out to Sarah when the MacDonald brothers intervened and persuaded him that he would injure his defence irreparably. He did not consent to allow Sarah to return to the farm immediately and left her to endure the torments of prison until the end of summer. In September, John MacDonald collected a thin and worried Sarah and her children from the prison and returned them to their cabin near the Campbell farmhouse. The next day Sarah was back to cooking and working in the household. Margaret MacDonald welcomed her with sympathy and smiles of encouragement. Sarah was relieved, especially for her children, whose good spirits returned as they joined in play with the Campbell children. She sensed that Campbell dare not abuse her with such violence again because the case was being watched by the leading men in the county and the public was talking about his killing of Alice. When she met him, she kept her eyes averted and he pretended not to notice her. Such was the hostile state of domesticity while Sarah waited expectantly for the case to come to trial.

He was unnerved by the attention the case was getting and angered by criticism from the religious community. Having, with his father, the packhorse merchant, established a Presbyterian Church on their lands, and watched with dismay the intense young minister Ma

Curdy preach there to intense excitement in 1802 when the parishioners jerked and shivered, fell down and bolted up in proclaiming God rather than the only other choice he gave them, the Devil, Campbell rued the consequences. "The Great Falling Down," led to the "Great Revival" religious movement in the Western Country. Of the several social causes which came out of it, Campbell was most disturbed by the advocacy of the abolition of slavery and, rarely attending church since the revivalists, whom he called fanatics, took over, now forsook it altogether. He intended to rely on his business connections and his influence as a leading landowner as weapons accrued over a long life to defeat the young lawyers challenging his authority.

Since the registrar who had taken Colonel Brown's statement on his slaves in 1791 was dead, Caldwell brought his son and his widow, who had witnessed the Colonel making the statement, to testify on Sarah's behalf. He had the court officer and the jailer testify to both Sarah's and Fanny's incarceration with their children in the slave prison, the one in the Cove and the other at earlier periods in Wellsburg. These witnesses came to the County Court in mid-October to record their statements and ten days later Campbell's witnesses made their statements.

The trial at the County Court in November was short. The foreman of the jury, James Brown, a shoemaker in Wellsburg, owned slaves. Sarah and Fanny sat side by side on a bench with William Caldwell while James Campbell and Dick Dawson sat with their lawyer a few yards from them. Sarah watched the white slave owners of the jury smiling and laughing at a comment made by one of them and wondered how Caldwell was going to convince them to free Fanny and her.

Caldwell presented his argument in a matter-of-fact tone and concluded that Sal and Fanny should be set free and awarded damages for the injuries done to them and their children. He brought forward his witnesses to Colonel Brown's slave registration and introduced the document, which he said was central to the issue of freedom for Sarah and Fanny. Caldwell called the jailer to describe the condition of Sarah and her children when they were sent to prison. The jailer was reluctant to go into detail, but through persistent questioning, he told of the bruised and battered bodies that he received and of the instructions from the owners to punish them even more. Caldwell, in his stiff formal style, made it clear that their owners wanted dumb obedience from their slaves. They wanted to beat out of them any thoughts that they may actually have been free.

Sarah and Fanny held hands during the testimony and tried to keep tears from coming to their eyes. To the spectators in the courtroom, the sisters had proven by law that they were actually free. Some seemed sympathetic and others looked on in pity. Dick Dawson, the free coloured man, squirmed uneasily and looked guiltily at Caldwell when he was referred to as a slave owner without a sense of responsibility and without a conscience. In his case Caldwell wanted $1000 in damages. Damages from Campbell he left unspecified until the issue of Sarah's freedom was decided.

Campbell's lawyer Charles Hammond looked at the jurymen with a broad smile. He was a drinking buddy of Campbell's and was well-known to the men on the jury because he had practiced in the county for years and went out of his way to make friends and be ready to give advice in a homespun manner to anyone he encountered. His argument was simple: Sal was a slave of Campbell—he bought her as a slave and kept her as a slave. His witnesses testified to the truth of Campbell's statement. They had been at Campbell's farm many times over the years and saw Sal working there as a household slave.

Sarah stared in disbelief at these men. She had served them at table on occasion and seen them in the Cove when she did the shopping, but what did it matter what they said? The issue was that Campbell treated her as a slave when by law she should have been free. She grew alarmed at the last witness for Campbell. He was Richard Wells, the trustee for Colonel Brown's will. He gave Sarah a hard look when he stepped up to testify and smiled thinly like a stage villain. Sarah whispered to Fanny that he was an evil man who made Henry Lewis's capture possible. Colonel Brown, Wells said, always treated Sal as a slave and her mother Molly had been a slave in the Brown family for all her life. In no way could anyone assume that Sal was free. He produced a Bill of Sale for Sal from the Brown family to James Campbell. As for Fanny, he responded to Hammond's whimsical reference to a kettle calling the pot black by producing a Bill of Sale for Fanny from the Brown family to Philip Doddridge. Hammond, a large stout man with a warm, ingratiating smile, told the jury that technicalities could not affect the bare facts that Sarah and Fanny had been slaves for their entire lives. If a mere technicality were sufficient to separate a man from his property, then the law of property was in grave danger. No, it was too basic to the security of the citizenry and could not be tampered with by a flimsy technicality such as delaying the act of registration of a handful of slaves. His message seemed to alarm members of the jury whose inclination was to support Campbell in any case. Caldwell, in his turn, argued that the so-called technicality was an important barrier against the importation of slaves and that Colonel Brown's neglect was a serious breach of the law that merited the jury's strong disapproval. Regardless of the sale of Fanny and Sal, the fact is that they should not have been sold. Sal and Fanny were legally free and to deny that would be a miscarriage of justice.

The jury took a brief quarter hour to reach a verdict: it decided that Sal and Fanny were slaves, as Campbell claimed that they were. Both women were crestfallen, but Caldwell quickly told them not to despair, that he would appeal the verdict, which, he said, was in contradiction of the evidence. Campbell beamed a smile at the jurors and thanked his lawyer, whom he arranged to meet later in the day in the Cove to celebrate his victory. Dick Dawson was shunned by Campbell and barely acknowledged by his lawyer. He took Fanny solemnly away with him. Sarah waited until Campbell called her and told her to get in the back of his wagon. The way back to the Cove along the shore road was beautiful with all the trees in bright reds and yellows. Nature looked so free and happy to her who felt so imprisoned and hopeless. Candor MacDonald drove the wagon and after dropping Campbell off at his favorite tavern in the Cove, he took Sal back to her cabin and her expectant children. Candor made just one remark to Sarah: "It's hard to get justice in Virginia." The same thought occurred to the clerk who copied out the case for the court files and, as, he thought, for posterity; he wrote, "No Justius in Virginia."

Sarah cried when she was alone. There was still some hope that a new jury in the Superior Court could save her and she clung to that

belief to prevent her falling into depression. Her poor children depended on her. If the courts failed her, Campbell's meanness would show in
all its force. He could sell them all off individually to different areas of
the country. Sarah would rather die than let that happen. For the
moment she had to put her trust in Alexander Caldwell and hope that
with God's help he would win their freedom, but, with the establishment against her, she had to prepare herself for failure. The slaves on
the farm looked with admiration at her, and her case had been spoken
of in the Cove with sympathy and support among both whites and free
coloureds. But Campbell was stubborn and unlikely to change his position. He relished beating her in the courts. Juries of slave-holding
white men were never going to support her claim, but there was a
chance of a miracle happening. Sarah readied herself to cook the
evening meal and tried to put thoughts of the trial out of her mind. Her
last thought as she walked to the farmhouse was of her sister Fanny
and her son Richard. They would not be joining her appeal. Dick
Dawson had been spoken to very severely by Philip Doddridge and
would be mistreating Fanny no more, it seemed. It was better for Sarah
too if she pursued her suit alone.

Campbell tried to get her to drop the appeal by making difficulties
for her. He deprived her family of food at certain times; her movements were restricted; Henry Jr. and Molly, now 10 and 7, were put to
work in the fields. Sarah, however, proved that she could be just as
stubborn as Campbell and met his provocations with firmness. As winter came and Campbell spent more of his time in the Cove, Sarah and
her family had less fear of punishment and took what joy they could in
visits from Nell Grady and her husband and from Mrs. Butler, who
always brought food and sweets for the children. Mrs. Butler encouraged Sarah to continue fighting for her freedom and comforted her
when her worries became too much for her and she would break down
to unburden herself of the pain and humiliations she had to endure.
Mrs. Butler was helpful too when the children were sick by bringing
medicines and by calling the Reverend Doddridge when the illnesses
were serious.

The Reverend followed Sarah's case and kept up her spirits whenever he saw her. He complained to Campbell when Campbell refused to

let her attend church service and made the old man back down. Secretly Doddridge was involved in helping slaves to escape but only in a secondary position and only when the chances for escape were excellent. His work as a minister riding from Wellsburg into Ohio and Pennsylvania and his work as a doctor, which included turning part of his home into a hospital, gave him wide influence and a certain authority among free-thinking people. Escapes were almost always upon the initiative of the slave, who, beaten, threatened with ill-treatment and lack of food, had no recourse but to try to live in the wilds until caught and dragged back for more inhuman treatment. Sarah commiserated with the poor creatures who had tried to get away and suffered the terrible consequences of being caught, like her own husband. Henry told her of the tortures his captors had put him through in order to persuade him not to run away again. The expense of hunting him down seemed to motivate the owners to be as vicious as they could, but the more punishment Henry received, the more determined he was to escape again. She wondered if Henry was still alive. If Henry had been caught, Sarah thought, how could she expect to escape with all her children. She admired his spirit above all else. His determination to be free influenced her thinking and imbued her with a courage that she doubted that she could have sustained on her own. She was given hope by a minister like Doddridge and a lawyer like his brother; but these people were intent on overthrowing slavery by legal means, which was a slow and uncertain process; they were whites facing white slave owners *en masse* who resorted to violence and intimidation to keep control and reassure themselves that slave revolts would not occur; and they had to argue against the propaganda that slavery was natural which decades of legalized slavery imprinted upon the minds of the white population. Moreover, Sarah sensed that her children's whiteness presented a subtle threat to the slavers, creating uncertainty and causing them to react more severely. The jurors declared them slaves to uphold the virtue of slavery against the growing clamour of abolitionists and not from any judgment on their particular case. Alexander Caldwell understood this and consulted with Philip Doddridge when he returned from the state legislature during a recess.

"We'll never get sympathy from a jury in these parts," Caldwell snorted. "Not so long as the issue comes down to property and the rights of owners."

Doddridge, tall like his brother and built just as broadly, smiled at his partner's exasperation. He reached up to smooth back his pony tail, a habit of his when he was thinking of strategy in a case. "The judge to whom we will be appealing will have even less sympathy. He accepts appeals only on points of law. You can argue that Sal is a good woman who loves her children deeply and is prosecuting this case mainly to free them, but unless you can get conclusive proof that Colonel Brown intended her to be free, he is likely not to hear the appeal."

"I've talked to Richard Wells," Caldwell said. "Behind that cynical facade, he seems to have a soft spot for Sal. If we could persuade him to change his tune and testify that the family regarded Sal more as a family member than as a slave and that the family allowed Campbell to take her because no one else was able to support her and her children, then we could make a stronger argument that Brown did not register her mother Molly as a slave because he did not regard her as a slave."

Doddridge shook his head. "The judge won't listen because he will know that Brown freed Sal's sister Nell in his will and that I bought her sister Fanny. In one way I made a mistake by including Fanny in the case, but if we had not included her, Campbell would have done so, and we would have been hurt worse than we are. I bought Fanny to save her from being sold to the plantations and thought that I found a good home for her with Dawson. But that man disappointed me." Doddridge said again what he had repeated to himself many times as if he were continually blaming himself for the predicament they were in. "I fear, Alex, that we cannot save Sal and her poor children through the courts."

"But we have Sal on appeal," Caldwell said encouragingly. "We will keep the argument as narrow as we can and focus on Brown's fail-ure to register his slaves. A judge as meticulous as Daniel Smith would have to agree."

"I wish I could be with you in court," Doddridge sighed. "If you do win an appeal and the case can be heard at the Superior Court in Wheeling, perhaps then I can help you. But that's wishful thinking." He brushed his pony tail. "I think your attempt to change Wells's testimony will be valuable. But Campbell has influence with his friends and I won't bet on winning him over."

"Campbell's losing friends," Caldwell frowned. "He's borrowed too much too often."

"He owes you a lot of money, doesn't he?" Doddridge smiled. "After this case, you'll have to drag him through the courts to see any of it."

"I have to admit that just contemplating taking him to court gives me pleasure," Caldwell laughed. "After what he did to Sal and her young children," he suddenly grimaced, "I wish I could charge him with something worse than being in debt."

Doddridge punched his shoulder lightly. "If you deprived him of Sal and her children, you would hurt him to the very core. I wish you well. But I fear we are running against the tide. By the way, I hear that one of Sal's children, the girl Fanny, was fathered by young George Brown."

"The minister?" Caldwell's voice jumped with surprise. "That's hard to believe."

"He was a wild fellow till he got salvation," Doddridge smiled. "The story goes that after he came back from the War he went to a religious meeting with his brother and was quite taken by the shaking and trembling of the congregation. The experience convinced him to be a missionary amongst us sinners. He's somewhere riding the Methodist circuit in the eastern part of the state."

"Should we tell him about Sal?" Caldwell asked, wondering if Brown could help in some way.

"Nothing he can do," Doddridge said. "It will just add to his guilt and drive him deeper into religion. We have enough fanatics without adding to the number," he smiled.

"Too bad," Caldwell said sadly. "She needs a friend now."

Doddridge nodded and said good-bye with a wave of his hand and went on to other business. Caldwell returned to numerous files lying on his desk, all requiring a clear and emotionless mind. Richard Wells, as he suspected, had a soft spot for Sarah hidden behind his resentment of her for rebuffing his advances. Caldwell working upon his regret that Sarah was sold to Campbell, finally persuaded him to join other witnesses against Campbell in the preliminary hearing in Wellsburg.

Caldwell related the news to Sarah, who was surprised and ecstatically grateful to God for giving her hope. That evening she prayed to Jesus, pouring out her heart to him, reiterating her pain and loneliness, and asking him to save her children. Margaret Campbell encouraged her with kind words but she could show no overt sympathy because Campbell demanded her absolute support in all he did. Her brothers were circumspect and dedicated themselves to running the farm. Sarah for the first time had some confidence that she would be victorious. She went about her duties with a happier step and a confidence that she had not known since she and Henry lived together on Brown's Island.

Campbell, however, was able to put off his trial till the fall with the excuse that he was too ill to travel. As a respected man in his community he was taken at his word. He reasoned that with Caldwell and Doddridge behind her, Sal could very well win her appeal; he could not afford to lose her now that he was in debt to several people. Sarah swallowed her disappointment and treated the delay as just one more barrier to overcome while Campbell used the time to work out a stratagem to sell Sarah quickly and effectively close the case against him.

8

One evening as Sarah was tucking her small children into bed in her rude wooden cabin, Campbell threw open the door and pointed to her disinterestedly, as if he considered her an object of no further use to him. A scrawny young man with a hard lean face and long black hair took her fiercely by the arm and told her to come with him.

She pulled her arm away and looked angrily at Campbell.

"I sold you, Sal. You and your two whities. You belong to Samuel now."

Shocked, Sarah looked round at her children and running to them, embraced all four as if to shield them from the harm that had come upon them swiftly like a wide-winged hawk. "Give me time, massa, please."

The young man drew back at the sound of the pain in her voice, but Campbell shook his head. "Get her out!" he barked and turned on his heels to leave.

"Mr. Caldwell will get after you," Sarah shouted tearfully.

Campbell paused as he thought of whipping her for her insolence, but she was no longer his, and he smirked at the slave dealer waiting by his wagon in the dark as if to say that this troublesome woman now belonged to him.

Samuel, the dealer, bought the white skinned children, who were four and two and still needed a mother, but not the ten-year old Henry and the eight-year old Molly who were old enough to live without their mother and being brown were easily identifiable as slaves. Samuel, struck by Sarah's good looks, got her for a good price. After he was finished with her, he intended to sell her and her two whities to a plantation in the deep south. Samuel smiled to himself at the pleasure and profit that was to come his way. He was approaching middle age, but he was still athletic and strong, and he thought himself good-looking. He was a bachelor because, he explained, the slave business kept him on the move buying and selling in different parts of the country. He was a hard bargainer and had made a good sum of money. Every living thing was a potential opponent. That was why he was satisfied with the price that he forced Campbell to take since he knew that Campbell feared he would lose in the courts. He strode to the cabin and told his helper to get the children into the wagon while he took care of Sarah. The children were crying now and Sarah was clasping Henry and Molly to her as Samuel coolly pried her arms away from them and with his strength forced Sarah out the door and into the wagon where he locked leg irons about her ankles. The chains were attached to the wagon allowing Sarah very little movement. As she sat disconsolate in the back, the young man placed Fanny and Israel in her arms and she looked up to see another house slave run to her cabin to comfort her crying children. The wagon lurched forward and headed down the hill to the river road leading to Wellsburg. Sarah's last glimpse of the

Campbell house was of an upstairs window lit by candlelight and the worried face of Margaret Campbell peering into the night.

The slavers' pens in Wellsburg were unclean and smelling of urine. There was a heavy gate fronting on the street which opened onto a mud lane alongside of which the pens were ranged. Each pen was gated and locked. Samuel had twenty pens and would pack several people into one if he had a large number of slaves to control. Sarah heard the low moaning of men and women, sorrowing over their separation from their loved ones or giving voice to physical pain from the whippings and tortures they had endured. Some slaves were partially insane from the treatment they had received but sufficiently viable for work on the plantations picking cotton or tobacco under the supervision of an over-seer. Sarah panicked when she heard them and mumbled a short prayer to God to get news to Caldwell of her plight. She and her two children were put in a pen by themselves.

There was a small aperture which allowed air and faint light to invade the blackness. A dirty straw mattress on the dirt floor served as a bed. Sarah sat on it and rocked her children to sleep. Her mind raced from one possibility to another. Could Caldwell rescue her? Would the court help her? Had Campbell negated the possibility of an appeal? Was she to be abandoned and her children taken from her? What could she do to save them? To all her questions she had the foreboding of evil and helplessness. Finally, her mind hurting and swirling, she fell asleep and at some time in the night dreamt that her husband Henry broke down the door of the pen and rescued her and the children. Henry's broad smile and confidence calmed her and his afterglow remained with her as she awoke to the clatter of the opening of the door to her pen.

Samuel, leering, stood in the early morning light holding out a brown dress made from the cheap material used for slave clothes and told her to take herself to the well where she would find a pail marked by her name. Sarah sensed that he had a special interest in her, but he said nothing as he hurried way to deal with his other slaves. The man could suddenly turn on her and make things worse for her, she thought, but he could also be the means of her salvation. She gathered up her children, found the well and bathed behind some blankets thrown up on lines to shield the bathers from prying eyes. The cold water and bits of soap slid over her skin refreshingly, and, as she washed her hair in the pail, she began to hope again. Her children were splattering water at one another and laughing, and she too laughed with them. She washed Fanny and then little Israel and dried them on a ragged towel that was lying on the line. A male voice called her harshly, and, hurriedly pulling on her new dress, she cried that she was coming.

The thin young man who had been with Samuel the night before stood waiting impatiently for her. He led her and her children to a long log cabin in which there were several long tables at which black slaves were eating. She took a seat at one of the tables and lifting her children onto her lap she fed them the bits of fish and bread that made up their breakfast. There was silence in the room, save for the sighs and coughs of the slaves and the sounds of their eating. Intimidated by the solemnity of the place, the children made no noise and looked about the tables with apprehension. Suddenly numbers of slaves stood up and filed out the door. Sarah heard the rumble of carriages come up, stop, and load up with slaves. She wondered what her destination would be and looked round at the young man who was walking towards her.

"Sal, bring your kids. You'll be sewing today. Come on, hurry up."

She followed him to a small carriage driven by a black slave dressed in a green suit and wearing a black top hat. He told her to get on the back seats. When she and the children were seated, the young man told her, "My name is Derek. I'll be here when they bring you back."

The wagon took her away from the river into one of the streets running on the side of the escarpment to a frame house painted in white. The front door opened when the carriage stopped and a large woman stood waiting impatiently for Sarah and her children to walk up the lane to the house. When Sarah was directly in front of her, the woman looked surprised at the whiteness of her skin and she gazed in dismay at her white children. "You workin' here for the day?" she queried, frowning at Sarah as if she had come to the wrong house.

"Yes, m'am," Sarah said and smiled.

The woman frowned disapprovingly. "I hope you can do the work," she said. "I got lots of sewing to be done. Here, I'll take the chillun," she took Israel from Sarah's arms and held out her hand for Fanny. "They can play in the back room. Come in." She closed the door after Sarah and strode to the back of the house with the children, followed closely by Sarah. "They can play with the toys that belonged to my chillun."

Israel squealed with delight when he saw some toy wagons and horses and as soon as he was put on the floor he scrambled to them. The woman took a doll from a wooden box and gave it to Fanny who held it with amazement. She led Sarah into a larger room where there were a number of dresses laid across a bed. "This is where you work. I got materials you need on the dresser over there. Just ask me if you need somethin'." She looked at Sarah questioningly, her long face as unreadable as a weather-worn tablet.

"Do you want me to make dresses after a pattern?" Sarah asked.

"That's the idea," the woman said. "The pattern is there. Just follow it." She strode away to another part of the house.

Sarah applied herself to the work, which, after she studied the patterns, was like sewing she had done for the Brown family. She could hear her children playing in the next room, and, when they called out to her, she was quick to respond and take them to the outhouse or reassure them if they fell and hurt themselves. The children had learned to be quiet and well-behaved and to obey their mother's every wish as if they knew that great danger could come to them if they did not. The woman looked in on Sarah occasionally and brought her a lunch to share with her children for a little while. It was dark when the wagon came to take Sarah and her children back to their slave pen. The woman told Derek that she was pleased with the work and wanted Sarah to continue with her.

When Sarah and her children got off the back of the wagon, she saw Alexander Caldwell standing at the doorway to the slave pens. She smiled at him with gratitude, but he looked at her glumly. "We didn't expect this to happen." he said. He patted the children's heads and watched as they ran into the small yard on which the pens fronted.

"Can you do anythin'?" Sarah asked hopefully.

Caldwell screwed up his face in doubt. "We'll do what we can," he said and reached out to take Sarah by the elbow in a sympathetic gesture. "I spoke to the slave dealer, Samuel. He didn't seem to know that your case was progressing on appeal. Campbell told him only that he won the case against you."

"Is Samuel going to make Campbell take us back?" Sarah asked suggestively.

"Too late for that," Caldwell shook his head.

Sarah felt her heart drop. She put her hand on her brow as if to squeeze away the pain in her mind. "What am I going to do?" she cried plaintively.

"We're not going to let you be sold south," Caldwell said firmly. "Samuel knows that he will be held liable for any thing that happens to you so long as your case is not decided. In the meantime Samuel has agreed to put you into a bigger and better pen because you're going to be here for a longer time."

Sarah nodded her thanks and smiled slightly as if Caldwell's efforts had given her a ray of hope.

"Be careful," Caldwell counseled her. "Give Samuel no reason for selling you. We'll find some way out of this mess."

Sarah felt relieved that someone was looking out for her. She had been on her own for so long and withstood the ugliness that had come to her and her children with all the inner resources she could call upon. Alone, she would have crumbled long ago, but it was fear for her children that kept her resisting, yearning for freedom and keeping up her pride.

Derek appeared behind Caldwell and waited respectfully.

"When Mr. Doddridge begins something, he always finishes it," Caldwell said. "Be assured of that, Sal."

"I trust you, Mr. Caldwell," Sarah said gratefully.

Caldwell turned to Derek. "You escort Mrs. Lewis and her children to their new home."

"Yes, sir," Derek said.

"And make sure you look after them well," Caldwell frowned.

"Yes, sir," Derek said, his long thin face blanching with alarm at the responsibility Caldwell was charging him with.

Caldwell smiled at Sarah. "It may be some time before you hear from us. But don't despair."

Sarah gained strength from Caldwell's visit. She called her children who ran to her in the near darkness, a half-moon and stars giving light to the courtyard, as they followed Derek.

They were housed in a shack with a family of slaves who worked in the kitchen preparing meals for Samuel and his slaves. Sarah was given a small room near the door. There was a bed in it and a dresser with a mirror. There also was a chair. Sarah silently thanked Caldwell when she saw it. The urine smell was gone and the room was clean. A couple of candles on the dresser cast a warm light over the wooden floor. Sarah had not experienced such comfort since she worked for Colonel Brown, she thought. At Campbell's she had no chair and no dresser. A shout from the main cabin warned her that the night meal was on the table.

A black girl in her teens, sprightly and smiling mischievously, entered the room. "I'm Siva. Come with me, Sal. We eat in another room." Siva picked up Israel, leaving Sarah to follow leading Fanny by the hand.

They came to a long table in a smaller room just off the kitchen and next to a long dining room where the slaves were fed and where Sarah had eaten breakfast.

"Food's on the table," Siva said, pointing to three bowls with soup and bread. "The rest of us here have eaten already."

Sarah sat her children at the places and fed Israel as she fed herself. Siva, who had dashed away to the kitchen, hurried through the room carrying a large tray of plates. Behind her rushed a young man with a soup tureen. Sarah glimpsed an old woman cooking at a stove before the kitchen door swung shut.

Siva came back and sat at the table. She seemed friendly. Unlike the other slaves, who, sunk in misery, had no time for anyone else, she seemed to take an interest in Sarah's welfare. "Massa' tells me you be here a long time. Thass good. Ma and me do the cookin'. Rupe helps us when he can. What's massa' planning for you?"

Sarah shifted uncomfortably. "His plans are not my plans," she said.

"Well, you is white almost," Siva laughed. "You got big ideas, ain't you?"

Sarah felt a shiver of apprehension. She suspected Siva of spying for Samuel. That's how she lived better, like other slaves she had met who were ready to betray confidences to improve their own condition. "Ideas?" she countered. "What do you have on your mind?"

Siva laughed defensively. "You got a lawyer, so I hears. You tryin' to prove you are free. But even if you gets free, what you gonna do? How you gonna live?"

"We'll cross that bridge when we come to it," Sarah said. "Fanny dear, you're spilling soup. You got a napkin, Siva?"

"We got paper," Siva got up abruptly and went into the kitchen. She came back immediately with some strips of meat and sweet potato in a dish and a sheet of old newspaper, with which she began wiping the front of Fanny where soup had stained her dress.

Sarah helped herself to the meat and waited for her children to finish their soup before serving them the most substantial food that they had seen in a long time. From the large room came Derek's voice shouting to the slaves to return to their pens: it was lock-up time.

"You don't have to go yet," Siva said, getting up. "I've got to see to the women and I'll come back for you. You'll have time to eat," she smiled and dashed away.

Sarah, fearful that her children would not have time to eat the meat, tried to hurry them up. Siva's brother Rupe rushed by on his way to the kitchen. He gave Sarah a big smile. He was several shades darker than Siva. Sarah wondered if she could trust him more than she could Siva. She had learned to recognize the spies among the household slaves through watching the actions of betrayal when she was growing up and hearing of the injustices done to innocent slaves by the lies and misrepresentations of these informers who would do anything to cut down rivals for what little favours and attention they could get from the master. But Sarah needed friends in order to survive. She had to find someone she could trust. Thankfully, the children finished the meat and potato before Siva returned.

"There's a pump outside the cabin," Siva said. "You can wash there now. Then I'll lock you in. You want to make sure that everythin' is taken care of before I locks you in 'cause nobody's gonna unlock your door before early tomorra."

The children had learned to be regular in going to the toilet and washing themselves quickly because, if they did not, it would cause problems for their mother who would be berated and sometimes whipped if they made messes. When Siva bolted the bedroom door behind Sarah, the children fell asleep immediately. Sarah stirred with worry about her oldest children with Campbell and then about her uncertain situation until weariness forced her into sleep.

The next morning she was awakened by the slave bell. Thus began another day like the first. She sewed for the same expressionless woman, was picked up by the lean-faced Derek, was fed by the friendly but untrustworthy Siva, and slept the same restless sleep. She rarely saw Samuel as he was constantly away buying and selling slaves. She could make no friends among the slaves because none was there for long. One day a family arrived and two or three days later would be marched to the auction block in town and disappear. Her lawyers never came to see her. Occasionally she would get messages from them, assuring her that they were keeping her case before the court and that Henry and Molly were being treated reasonably well by Campbell. Thus her life passed uneventfully until about a month or so, she was not certain of the date as she never saw a calendar, when lying in bed and worrying as usual, she heard the bolt of her door being slid back stealthily. She sat up, curious as to whom it might be and fully expecting Siva to step into the room. A man stepped into the room and closed the door behind him. In that second when he was framed in the doorway, Sarah recognized the shape of Samuel. She had no time to react before he was upon her and tearing at her thin nightdress, baring her naked and kissing her body with passion. Too frightened to struggle she spoke calmly. "Massa, don't do this, massa. There's no need, massa." But Samuel stripped off his own clothes, held her in a tight embrace, sucked her breasts, and drove his penis against her. Lying back, she accepted him and made her mind go blank. She felt him explode into her. After a moment, he pulled away, quickly sought out his clothes, put them on, and without a word, stepped quietly out of the room, bolting the door behind him.

Sarah lay dazed, comprehending that she had been raped but unable to focus on the act. Subconsciously she had expected Samuel to assault her and was not surprised when he did, but, gradually, as she felt her helplessness, she began to cry, and she reached out to touch her children who were lying still asleep near her on the bed. Then she grew angry and allowed a deep hatred for the man to overwhelm her, until exhausted from crying, she relegated it in her mind to an incident which she had to forget. Samuel could hurt her worse than raping her, she thought, and, as long as he wanted her, he would keep her from being sold. She clung then to the hope that he still wanted her. After the rape he could want to get rid of her. Some men were like that. Through the next few weeks, she wondered which of the two reactions would dominate him. She had her answer when he visited her again and raped her as he had the first time. She was now prepared to steel herself to accept his behaviour and to find consolation that she and her children were safe from the auction block as long as it continued. Every three or four weeks during this stage of her captivity, Samuel's wiry body would descend on her like a rapacious hawk and in minutes would disappear into the darkness as if carried away on wings. Sarah felt herself in limbo. She had lost hope in her court case. Campbell was powerful enough to avoid an appeal, particularly when he was no longer the owner of the slave who brought the action against him. The courts were too busy with more important appeals than to be clogged up with in *forma pauperis* cases. She tried to keep up her spirits for the sake of the children but when she heard the wailing of the slaves in the pens as mothers were separated from their children and husbands from their wives, she lay petrified.

In the summer of 1819, she became pregnant. She knew the signs well enough. She feared to tell Samuel lest he turn in anger upon her. But, as she grew bigger, she had to tell him and suffer the consequences. Otherwise, Siva would inform on her and that would be worse. On Samuel's next monthly visit, as he lay recovering from his orgasm, Sarah told him that he was the father of her child. Samuel sat up and swung his feet onto the floor. He stayed motionless as he thought, and, for the first time, spoke.

"This will end," he said quietly, his voice husky. "I'll keep you till the baby comes."

"You won't sell me?" Sarah choked. "You won't take me away

66

from my babies? You won't sell your own child?"

Samuel slipped on his clothes and wordless glided out the door, slid the bolt, and never returned to visit Sarah in the night.

9

During her pregnancy Sarah worked just as hard as before and just as silently, interrupting her work only to tend to her children who played together in the next room. The tall, long-boned woman, who paid Samuel for Sarah's services, sometimes showed interest in the children. She brought them toys which had been cast off by her grandchildren, and she seemed to want to communicate with them but held herself back as if afraid to overstep some unseen boundary.

Likewise, Derek, who continued to deliver her and other household slaves to various establishments in Wellsburg, kept their relationship on a cool businesslike level. Sarah guessed that he knew that Samuel was the father of her child; he tended to help her in and out of the wagon with a solicitude that amused her.

Siva's attitude took a subtle change when she knew of Sarah's pregnancy. Having been raped by Samuel and left without a sign of tenderness, Siva escaped being sold by promising to watch his slaves and report to him. She sympathized with Sarah and argued with herself that she could make an exception of her. She and her mother began to give her better food and they helped care for her children. Siva smuggled sweets to Fanny and Israel that none of the slaves had ever seen, let alone eaten. Expecting to be sold to the southern plantations once the baby was born, Sarah anxiously waited for an opportunity to contact Alexander Caldwell, but she could not ask Siva to meet him because slaves were not allowed to communicate with anyone; she was sure that Siva's sympathy for her did not extend to risking severe punishment on her behalf. Fortuitously, she found a more trustworthy messenger in her sister Fanny.

Several weeks into her present imprisonment, when she was being carted to work in the early morning, she saw Fanny walking at the side of the street and carrying a basket of food. Fanny, curious about the occupants, and expecting to see miserable slaves being taken to the auction block, stopped to look in the back of the wagon. Her eyes met Sarah's and she gasped and made as if to run to her, but Sarah put her finger to her lips and signaled for Fanny to follow. Fanny walked behind the carriage discreetly, falling back a distance but always keeping it in sight until she saw Sarah and her children enter a house under the supervision of a tall white woman. Fanny decided to walk along the street running behind the house and since the streets ran on the side of the escarpment, she was able to look down on the house and through the back windows. She saw Sarah sitting and sewing and looking up anxiously at the window. When Sarah saw her, Sarah beckoned her to come toward the window. There were trees and bushes to conceal Fanny's approach, which she made in a leisurely fashion while she watched Sarah carefully raise the window.

As Fanny came under the window, Sarah bent down and whispered hurriedly, "I'm in Samuel's slave pens but here every day. Tell Mr. Caldwell I'm with child and Samuel's going to sell me. Where's my Henry and Molly?"

"Oh Sarah, they're goin' to sell you south?"

Sarah nodded, "Where are my children?"

"At Campbell's. They're just fine. Nell's lookin' out for them." Their hands met and clasped tightly before Sarah pulled away quickly and put down the window. Fanny hurried back to the street and continued on her way to Dick Dawson's home. Thus it was that a means of communication was set up between the sisters, though, fearing detection, they used it rarely. Fanny told Dick Dawson about Sarah's fear of being sold, and he delivered a note to Caldwell.

Sarah's plight alarmed Caldwell, who had been unable to persuade the court to hear an appeal because, for one reason, Caldwell had been unable to produce any truly new evidence that might have persuaded the jury to render a different verdict. Philip Doddridge, realizing that Sarah could not be freed legally, suggested to his brother that the

Methodist Episcopalian Church find a way for Sarah to escape with her children. Some slaves had found refuge with Churches in Ohio and Pennsylvania and been guided through the forests to safe havens in those states and in Upper Canada, but they had been able-bodied and made their initial escape unaided. Sarah, pregnant, with two small children, would be physically unable to put up with the hardship that such an escape demanded. Moreover, the Church could not be seen to be breaking the law regardless of how great the cause. Philip asked Joseph to make George Brown aware of Sal's fate, and, to Joseph's quizzical expression, Philip simply said that it was important that George know.

George Brown had become a very persuasive preacher through the years. The Great Falling Down craze had snared him. The ungovernable emotions of many hundreds of people entered his mind and soul, and, although he did not throw himself upon the ground or rock back and forth for hours as the spirit moved him, he was imbued with the power and the energy of the message. Before he drowned, George's father had spoken to George about doing good in the world, and this last conversation came back to haunt George until he gave himself into the service of God. His studies changed him and his days were spent with other people's troubles and in building the church in frontier areas where the need for spiritual leadership was great.

When he arrived in Wheeling, where his predecessor was stoned out of town for preaching against slavery, he bravely insisted that no man had the right to own another and that the brutality of coercion was a grave sin in the eyes of God. This time, the men did not attack; their leader, remorseful, confessed that he could not go through with his intention to sell two girl slaves to the southern plantations. The following evening George went to the man's home and, in the presence of two light-skinned young women, who had no inkling of their impending sale, the owner signed papers giving them their freedom. The slave owners in Wheeling regarded the owner's action as an isolated incident by someone who could afford to lose property. They branded the Reverend George Brown a dangerous man.

Joseph Doddridge rejoiced in George's success, and, on George's rides north into the Panhandle, he made it a point to include him in

meetings of Methodist Episcopalians in Steubenville. Doddridge minis-
tered in a church there and knew Dr. David Stanton, a profound thinker
and strong anti-slaver, who led a secretive group which organized
escape routes for slaves. Although Stanton criticized Episcopalianism
for its hierarchical structure, which, he said, kept its parishioners
under its boot, his wise counsel in anti-slavery matters brought him
into close association with Episcopalian ministers.

Alarmed at Sarah's condition, Joseph Doddridge went to see Sarah
in the evening as she returned from her day of sewing. Derek and the
other young toughs guarding the slaves gave him hostile looks but dared
not interfere with his visit to his parishioner. The tall, big-framed
Reverend with silvery hair stood like a standard of hope to the slaves in
the muddy, wretched-looking yard into which they were led from the
returning wagons. Some wore chains and others muttered as if half-
mad while their keepers hurried them along to their pens. When Sarah,
her head held high, with her two white children in tow, came to the
yard, she broke into a radiant smile and came to the Reverend to grasp
his hand.

"I must talk to you," Doddridge said. He noticed that she was
quite big with child. "Can we speak in your cabin?"

She nodded, but just then Samuel strode up from out of the dim
light and spoke in a loud, harsh voice, which, despite his bold attitude,
betrayed his uneasiness. "What do you want with her?"

Doddridge gave him a withering look. "We are discussing the baptism of her child," he said.

Samuel, chastened, nodded, and added quietly, "Eatin' time is
soon. She don't want to miss that." He walked away to attend to some
other slaves, who were chafing at being shoved and cursed by the men
herding them into their pen.

Doddridge reached down and gathered Fanny into his arms. As
Sarah carried Israel ahead of him towards the shack, she noticed Siva
and her brother watching them from the door of the main cabin.
Doddridge noticed them too and sensed that such curiosity meant that
their conversation must be kept very quiet. Sarah put Israel on the bed
and sat beside him. The Reverend put Fanny down to run about and sat
on the room's only chair.

"When do you expect your child, Sal?" he asked in a low voice, intimating that she was to speak softly.

"Early March, I think," she whispered. "Then I think Samuel will sell us all."

"We're going to help you. Do you want to escape? go to Canada?" he asked, unsure if she understood the hardships and danger involved.

Although surging with excitement and disbelief, she kept her voice low and controlled. "Oh, if only!," she sighed. "Ever since Margaret Campbell told me about it, I wanted to."

Doddridge looked at the door and whispered, "We could fail. All depends on timing. We'll set a date for baptism two weeks after the baby is born. In that two weeks you must be ready to escape with your children."

"How do I get away from here?" Sarah asked worriedly. "They watch me close."

"We'll find a way. Is there someone you trust?"

"Not here," she cautioned. "My sister's master, Dick Dawson, might be able to help. He knows where I am."

"Good," Doddridge smiled cheerfully. "I'm asking the Reverend George Brown to help us. Do you remember that wild boy about your age who used to play in the woods on Brown's Island? Well, he's a good minister in our Church now." He noticed Sarah blush and wondered if she loved the man.

"Yes," Sarah nodded eagerly, scarcely believing that she would see George's confident face and engaging smile again, "I remember him. I can't believe that you could do this for me, Reverend." Tears welled in her eyes.

Doddridge stood up and patted her shoulder sympathetically. "One of us will be in touch again. I'll inform your slave-trader that baptism will be in mid-March or so. That gives us two-months to prepare. Cheer up, Sal. God shall help us. He is on our side."

Fanny went screaming to the Reverend as he walked to the door and clung to his legs. "I love you, my child," Doddridge said and, raising her, kissed her cheeks. "You be good and do everything your mother tells you. Will you?"

Fanny nodded and smiled, and when Doddridge put her down, she stood happily watching him leave.

Sarah sank onto the bed full-length and put her hands over her face. The worry, the fears, the inevitability that depressed her seemed suddenly lifted. She felt alone no more. The strong presence of the man of God and all he represented were going to free her and her little children. They had taken pity, just like Jesus Christ did in the Bible. It was up to her to be sharp and to stay strong. Her children's future depended on it. Then, as if a shadow had shaped itself in the room to haunt her, she thought of Henry and Molly, her beloved children struggling to live in the evil confines of Campbell's farm. She would have to leave them behind. Pains of regret and remorse would not cease regardless of how she reasoned that she had to sacrifice them so that her other children could live free. The sound of the bell for the evening meal reminded her of the power of slavery against which any scheme could fail regardless of the good intentions of her friends. Now despondent again, she walked with the children to the main cabin and met a curious Siva at the door.

"That your preacher?" Siva asked off-handedly. "He take an interest in your chillun. That doesn't happen round here much."

"He's good," Sarah said. "He could help you if you trusted him."

Siva's grin faded. "Only help we can trust is among ourselves," she said resentfully. "Like I'll trust you if you trust me."

Sarah thought then of seeing Henry and Molly. "We can put that to a test," she replied and looked Siva in the eye.

Siva was taken aback. "I'm ready, anytime." She went into the kitchen to fetch the meal of beans for Sarah and her children.

Sarah thought she might put her to the test, but not directly. When Siva returned with the food in one large plate, Sarah seized her hand and, looking up at her earnestly, whispered, "You don't need to lock the cabin door every night, do you, Siva. I'm too fat to run anywhere, and I'm not ready yet to see myself and my unborn baby ripped to pieces by the dogs," she smiled.

Siva regarded her seriously for a few seconds. "All right. I can leave it unlocked when the massa is away. Who you want to see anyway?" she added impishly.

"None of your business, girl," Sarah laughed and began feeding

Fanny and Israel.

Siva walked away with a giggle. She, herself, had snuck out on occasion to see a man. She was not going to deprive Sarah of that same pleasure. She sensed the intensity in the woman and understood her need. When Siva came through the small eating room again, she stopped by Sarah's side and whispered into her ear. "Massa's goin' away to-night for three days. I can lock up the dogs tomorrow night, for sure."

Sarah looked at her anxiously to see if she really meant it, and, satisfied, nodded in agreement.

Throughout the next day at work, Sarah planned how she would get to Campbell's. It would be too dangerous to travel on the road, although she would have to take the road in some places near Hollidays Cove where houses were close to the river. There was an old Indian trail alongside the river which could be used for most of the way. She would likely not encounter anyone in authority on the trail, but sometimes people were attacked at night by thieves and she would have to be vigilant. It was a Saturday so that most people who left their homes would be drinking in the taverns. And the next day, Sunday, she could rest up because the slaves were not hired out on Sundays.

If only she could trust Siva, she thought; if only God would soften her heart just this once. She knew Siva liked Fanny and Israel; maybe she would understand if Sarah told her that she had to see her other children who were so young and defenseless and without their mother's love. But she decided against telling her. She would compromise Siva if she were caught. She had to trust in God.

When Derek drove her back to the pens, she thought that he looked at her suspiciously, and she wondered if Siva had told him, or did he guess at something? Was there something in her manner which made him doubt her? When she took the children to eat, she looked questioningly at Siva, who smiled and said, "Yes, yes, all's alright, Sal." The consequences of being caught were too horrible to think about. She would be whipped and maybe miscarry. Her worry came out on her face. Siva stopped to put a hand on her shoulder. "You do what you gotta do," Siva said. "All's we can do is look the other way. We'll do that. Don't you worry."

In the early evening, when the children were asleep, Sarah put on her ragged coat and crept into the hall outside her door. She listened for any movement in the darkness outside and quietly opened the outside door and closed it behind her. She peered into the darkness, then back at the main cabin where there was some candlelight from one of the rooms where the white guards lived. Possibly Derek was awake. She ran across a patch of ground and came to a wire fence. She knew where the low part of the fence was located and breathing heavily from the load of her baby she straddled it and eased herself over it to the ground on the other side. There was a light dusting of snow, enough to show footprints if she stepped in it, but there were earth patches beside it which she was careful to step on and avoid the snow whenever she could. When she got to the river, the light was dim because the sky was overcast and the moon's light came through faintly. She set out along the path with determination and swept her eyes constantly over the ground ahead of her for any sign of danger, and she listened over the faint lapping sound of the river for boats in the water. After an hour of walking she heard oars pulling over the water and some men's voices raised in drunken jibes and laughter. When they came near, she hid behind some bushes until they passed by. She felt lucky that the night was darker than usual and the hardness of the frozen ground meant that she could travel faster. Her fear of detection kept her moving swiftly. Finally, after three hours of walking steadily, she came upon the houses by the riverside, and, cutting through fields with the sounds of dogs barking in the distance, she reached the roadside and continued into Hollidays Cove without encountering anyone. As she climbed the hill toward Campbell's farm, her walking became more laboured and her body seemed heavier, but she refused to stop and rest because her time was too short. Campbell's dogs had been taken out of the cold for the night and were probably in the main farmhouse and in the barn. Sarah knew them and felt she could prevent them from attacking her when they identified her, but the problem of keeping them from barking until they knew her worried her. Luckily, only one old hound was roaming the grounds near the slave cabins and Sarah called his name softly before he saw her. He poised, his head raised in question, and then ran toward her to lick her hands. She patted him to calm him, ran quickly across an open area where the moonlight could catch the outline of a figure and entered one of the slave cabins where Fanny had told her that her children slept at nights. Sarah stood adjusting her eyes to the darkness inside the cabin until she discerned the two children sleeping together on a straw mattress on the floor. There were some slave women sleeping near them. Kneeling beside them, Sarah placed her hand on Henry's brow and caressed him until he awoke. She took him in her arms and tears came to her eyes and fell on his cheeks.

"Mummy?" he whispered. "Is it you?"

"I'm here, my darling. Just for a while. Have you been good? Have you been my man?" She tried to sound cheerful.

Henry began to cry silently. He knew the danger that his mother was in but he could not help himself.

"Have you been taking care of Molly? Are you well?"

"Yes," Henry managed to say.

Sarah reached over and gently rolled Molly back and forth with her hand. Sleepily Molly sat up and wiped her eyes with the back of her hand.

"My dearest child," Sarah said and held her firmly to her and kissed her until she was wide awake.

"Mummy!" Molly cried with excitement.

"Ssh!" Henry hissed.

Sarah grappled them both to her and swayed with them back and forth as she felt their young lives enter her body and be at one with it. "My lovely children, Mummy's come to see you just this once. Mummy had to see you. She may be going away, but do not worry, my lovely ones, Mummy will be safe with your brother and sister."

"Where are you going?" Henry asked. "Are they sending you down river?"

"I can't tell you now, child. But remember whatever happens, Mummy loves you." She kissed Henry very long on the forehead and then kissed Molly.

One of the sleeping women stirred, cleared her throat and sat up. She stared at Sarah and her children as if witnessing a ghost.

Sarah knew her. "I've come for only a few minutes to say good-bye. Have my children been treated well?"

"Huh," the woman snorted. "The ole' massa's got no choice but to treat them well. He's been gettin' the treatment from Massa Margaret for sellin' you down river. He daren't do nothing."

"Please look after them for me. See that they grow up good."

The other two women woke up at this point and looked in wonder at Sarah. "We thought you was finished," one woman said.

"I wanted to see my children. You make sure they ain't harmed."

"Nell can do that better than us," said the other woman. "But we'll try. They's good children. God bless you, Sal."

Sarah looked at her children. "Can you light a candle, please. I want to see them clearly. I may be gone a long time."

Molly clung tightly to her at these words.

"But I'll see you again," Sarah said consolingly. "We'll always be in touch through your Aunt Nell, I promise you," she said firmly. "I want to be proud of you. Do what's right."

One of the women lit a candle and handed it to Sarah while another woman went to the doorway and sat watching for anyone coming. Sarah gazed on the faces of her children and wiped at their tears with her hand. "Always remember that Mummy loves you, and someday we'll be together again. Always remember that."

"Will you come see us again?" Henry asked, sudden worry crossing his young face.

"I can't," she admitted, "but be brave and look out for one another. You must depend on one another." She paused to look into their faces as if attempting to engrave on her mind every feature, every expression that looked up at her adoringly and tearfully.

"Someone there!" the woman at the door warned.

Sarah blew out the candle and hugged her children as if it were for the last time. She waited with them in the darkness, silently, and thought of the years that she had spent on Brown's Island, the happy years with her husband, now either recaptured, or hiding in some remote forest, or dead. Her poor enslaved children. What would become of them under an evil, willful master like James Campbell? Would he sell them eventually when they got big enough to fetch a good price? She hoped that God would help her to prevent that.

"He's gone," said the woman by the door. "It was the skinny MacDonald goin' to the shit house."

The slaves laughed quietly and Sarah gave one last tearful hug to her children, kissed them, and stood up. "Have to go," she said. "Got to be back before dawn." She moved to the door, looked out into the darkness, and strode several steps when she felt a tug at her dress. Henry had run after her and was pulling at her dress to keep her. She stooped, hugged him and disengaged her dress carefully from his grasp. "You are Mother's big man. I'm countin' on you, Henry, my child. You take care of your sister. Don't let anything happen to her."

"Good-bye, Mummy," Henry whispered. "I love you."

Sarah stumbled more than ran away from the shacks into the covering of the trees. Tears streamed down her face, but bracing herself for the journey back to Wellsburg, she steeled herself against all sentiment. She had her other children to think of now. Her sisters would have to look after Henry and Molly, who would grow and develop according to the principles she had tried to instill in them. Her younger children needed her guidance now. As if to emphasize this, she felt a sharp kick in her stomach. She paused and patted her belly affectionately, then stooping she sped along by the bushes and trees down to the road back to Wellsburg.

10

Sarah stepped aside in the blackness at the roadside to watch several carriages with singing drunken men pass by on the way to the Cove; she worried at the time lost. She guessed that it was now past two in the morning, and it would take her three hours of fast walking to get back unobserved. She stayed on the road, despite the sharp stones that cut at her feet, for as long as was wise, because she could travel faster. Her body, aching with the load she carried, she fought all temptation to rest. Suddenly, up ahead, she heard horses' hooves cantering over the stones and ducked behind bushes off the road. Two lean young white men with rifles rode by. They had the long-haired, rough look of Samuel's guards. She wondered with a thrill of fear if they were looking for her. Worried now about her children, she almost ran through a field to the riverside to take up the pathway. She tried to console herself with thoughts that those men were looking for someone else. There were always patrols hunting for runaways. Possibly they were bounty hunters up from the South. If they were from Samuel's surely Derek would have been one of them. But she could only be sure when she got to the cabin. Could Siva have betrayed her? she wondered. Could she have set her up just to win the praise and confidence of Samuel? The light was stronger here as it reflected off the water. She found that she was moving faster than before. Her worry made the pains in her back and feet disappear as she sped towards her children. Since it was Sunday morning, people would be rising later than usual. On any other day she would have met someone on the trail by now. She thought God must be with her.

At last, she came to the turn in the trail that she recognized as leading into Wellsburg, and, suspense welling in her heart, she scrambled through bushes and over the low part of the wire fence, and, uncaring whether anyone saw her, she ran to the cabin door, opened it and stepped inside to lean against the wall and catch her breath. She listened to the silence. It was still dark. All seemed to be as she had left it. She tiptoed to her room and found her two little children sound asleep. They were safe, she was safe, and Siva had not betrayed her. She sank onto the bed, and, feeling exhaustion and tiredness sweep over her, she fell into a deep sleep.

Sarah awoke to the sounds of her children playing. They had no toys but they used their imaginations to pretend they had toys like the ones they played with at the tall woman's house. A bright early morning sun burst through the lone window, and Sarah guessed that she had slept for about two hours. She heard a knock at the door. Sitting up, brushing back her hair, she called warily, "Come in."

Siva stood in the doorway. She was smiling cheerfully. "Just came to get the little ones for breakfast. You look tired, Sal. Stay there and I'll bring you somethin'."

Sarah showed her gratitude in her eyes and watched as Siva led the children out of the room before she fell asleep again. Siva kept the children with her for the morning and did not return them to Sarah until noon when Sarah was awake and looking forward to the rolls and cheese that Siva brought her. Siva asked no questions and stayed just long enough to tell her that Samuel had sent word that he would be coming back a day earlier than expected. Sarah nodded and smiled gratefully. She felt satisfied that she had seen Henry and Molly. They knew now that their mother loved them and, regardless wherever she was, thought of them. She had to plan for the future. She had to escape, but the difficulties seemed insurmountable. She wondered when the Reverend Doddridge would help her. Just how could he get her away from Samuel. Surprisingly, as she was thinking of Doddridge, her door was thrown open and Derek stood sternly looking at her.

"You got a visitor," he said rather angrily as if it was her fault that he had been disturbed. He turned away and motioned to someone to enter the room.

Sarah's heart seemed to leap when George Brown in a minister's coat came to her, put his arms about her and kissed her cheek.

He looked apologetic. "My dear Sal. Well, you've had quite a time of it, I hear. But you look as pretty as you always did. Are these your children?" He looked down at the two of them playing on the floor.

"Yes, George," she smiled proudly. "They're mine and Fanny is yours."

George dropped to one knee and pulled Fanny to him. She struggled against his chest, but Sarah told her that the Reverend was a friend, and Fanny began to look at him interestingly.

George Brown had grown handsomer with age. His wildness had been replaced with a gentleness of nature and his warm personality had become a mature geniality. "I didn't know what had become of you, Sal. I'm sorry that I have been so busy working and studying that I just lost track of my early life." He looked at her as if asking her forgiveness.

Sarah looked at Fanny. "You left me somethin' precious, George, somethin' of yourself. There was nothin' you could have done. I tried for my freedom but ole man Campbell beat me."

"The Reverend Doddridge told me everything," George said compassionately. "We're going to get you away from here. You and your children are not going South. You can be sure of that," he added grimly. "We have friends in far off places." He looked at Fanny and caressed her fair hair. "So Campbell decided you and your innocent little children were troublemakers and had to be sent down to toil in the cotton fields." He shook his head as if at the wickedness of man.

Sarah pointed at the door, and George, silently getting to his feet, strode to the door and opened it. Siva stood in the hallway, made wide eyes at Sarah and muttered, "Derek told me to listen." As she walked away, she called back, "I couldn't hear you anyways."

George closed the door and smiled at Sarah. "We'll send you messages through your sister from now on. I just came to give you hope, my dear Sal. We'll get things ready right after your child is born. That's when they'll least expect you to go."

Sarah nodded. "Never thought you'd be a minister of the Lord," she laughed suddenly.

"It is funny, isn't it," George said, his eyes glinting with humour. "But the bug bit me and won't let go. I'm glad in one way, Sal; it brought me to serve you. I felt guilty for a long time. Somehow, now I can make atonement for some of the wrong I did you."

"You did no wrong to me," Sarah smiled. "Other than my husband, you are the only man I loved. You gave me joy when I was down. You and your wildness gave me courage, and I've had to use what you gave me an awful lot lately."

George blushed and bowed his head. "I want to pray with you, my dear. Will you say the Lord's Prayer with me please." He knelt on the floor and gathered the two children to him and, reaching forward, placed his hand on Sarah's head as she leaned from the bed towards him. He and Sarah said the Lord's Prayer together, their voices beginning slowly separately then joining in unison and in strength. When George looked up he kissed Sarah lightly on the lips, patted the heads of the two children, and wiping a tear from his eye, he went to the door. "Can't stay," he mumbled. "I loved you, Sal. If I don't see you again, you remember that. I won't forget you."

Sarah smiled tearfully at him and nodded understandingly as she watched him close the door behind him. His visit had rejuvenated her. She was confident now that she would escape because George would be looking into the details and planning as much as he could, as much as fate would allow him. She took out the small Bible that she kept under her mattress, the Bible that the Reverend Doddridge gave her years ago, which, although she could make out no more than a few words, comforted her.

Rumours that Canada was the promised land spread through the slave population. Veterans returning from the War of 1812 told of fighting black regiments and warned that blacks were free in Canada. When abolitionists surreptitiously spread the word in the south, the slaves knew it was true because when caught the abolitionists were quietly murdered.

In spite of her long walk to Campbell's, Sarah suffered no adverse consequences from her pregnancy. Her worries over Henry and Molly and her guilt at leaving them behind had been assuaged. All her thoughts were concentrated now on the escape. A visit from the Reverend Brown to Samuel, who was himself an Episcopalian although not a church-goer, persuaded him to go easy on Sarah. A few days before the baby was to arrive, Samuel told Sarah that she could stay in the cabin and rest. There was altogether too much attention being paid to her, Samuel thought, when mothers like her were being sold on the block every day. He resolved to sell her as soon as physically possible after the baby was born.

A black midwife was called to attend Sarah when she felt labor pains. Siva took the children into her room and amused them. Her mother joined her when the birth seemed imminent and allowed her to go to Sarah's room and help the midwife. The slaves in the pens had been waiting for the birth and had wished Sarah well with kind words and smiles from a distance so that there was an air of expectation in the camp. All of them, except for Siva's family, had to depart for their daily hiring out, before the birth happened. The child came without complications in the morning. It was a girl. She was white.

Sarah took her baby from Siva with the happiness that she had experienced after bearing her other babies, but, as she gazed down at the helpless little child, she thought with a sinking heart how difficult her escape was really going to be. The girl needed constant attention. Could she survive being carried under trying conditions through forests, in hiding, in the cold nights, for possibly months? Siva brought the other children to gaze at their sister. Sarah smiled at their amazement, but the sudden thought that they might perish in the escape upset her, and she turned her mind to George Brown, who even then was working to save her from being sold to a crueler master in the South.

Brown and Doddridge agreed that if Sarah and her children could make the initial break and get to the river unobserved without help, then there was a good chance they could be spirited to the other side. Since Sarah and her children could pass for whites, their advisor, Dr. Stanton, suggested that a boat take her upstream as far as possible before detection was likely, and she could hide the first day in a safe house on the Ohio side. From there she could go by carriage north-wards. The unpredictability of events, which they had experienced in other escapes, kept them from planning in much detail from that point. Sarah would need a man to escort her; otherwise, she could not get far with three small children. Her escape was fixed for the third Saturday after the birth.

Joseph Doddridge visited Sarah to baptize the new baby ten days after birth. He found that she had been given more freedom than usual. The young guards allowed her to stray with her children from the pen area and play with them on the grass by the riverside. It was March and still too cold to stay out long, but Sarah made a point of going out with her children two or three times a day. She suspected that Samuel was prearranging her sale to catch the ministers and lawyers interested in her welfare by surprise. Siva promised to inform her if she or her brother heard any plans affecting her. Siva and her brother witnessed the baptism. Doddridge asked Sarah what she was calling the baby.

"I finished with family names with my first three, then Israel got a biblical name. Now I want something distinctive, Reverend. Can you suggest one?"

Doddridge smiled and thought for a moment. "Well, she was born in early March about the time of the Roman goddess who was charged with caring for the sacred fire. She was the goddess of the hearth. You want a home, don't you, my dear?"

"I dream of a home of my own," Sarah said with passion.

"Perhaps this child will symbolize that hope," Doddridge suggested.

"Yes," Sarah said excitedly. "What was the goddess's name?"

"Vesta," he said.

Sarah thought for a moment, formed the name with her lips, gazed at the baby in her arms, and nodded. "I like Vesta," she said.

Doddridge proceeded to baptize the girl, dipped her in the water, and returned her crying to Sarah's arms. He thanked the others for attending, and, after they spoke to Sarah and left the room, he whispered to Sarah that she was to be on the riverside with her children just as it became dark on the next Saturday evening. Dick Dawson would be waiting for her in a small boat. He clasped her hand and said, "God be with you."

Sarah's words of thanks got caught in her throat, and she watched him leave the room with a mixture of exultation and fear. She now became very concerned that Samuel would try to sell her before Saturday. Later in the day, she walked out with her children to the river bank and tried to discern where Dawson would try to land his boat. About twenty-five yards upriver from where she stood was a tiny beach between two boulders. She decided that that was where he would come ashore. Her heart began to beat faster as she looked over the river at the free state of Ohio, its strand of flatland alongside the river backed by a high escarpment that she feared she could not climb in her present state. She thought of the kind men who were risking long prison terms to help her, and she gave thanks for Dick Dawson who was risking everything. She had to be as sharp as she could be so as not to fail anyone. She had trained her children to be silent when need be, but Vesta was just over two weeks old. She could cry out at any time. Sarah rocked her and comforted her. If God cared about her, she thought, He would make sure that Vesta stayed quiet.

Late in the afternoon on the following Saturday late in March, Sarah dressed her children as well as she could in their poor clothes and put on the two dresses she had under her only coat. She had been nervous for the past two days and had not slept much in anticipation of this moment. Samuel and his sharp-eyed employees paid her no attention. Siva left the cabin door unlocked at nights. The sun was low in the sky and still carried the essence of winter over the hard ground, although in mid-day its increasing brightness promised warm weather within days. The forest floor was cold; the thick vegetation held the snow and ice in its grasp and only reluctantly surrendered it to the warmer weather. Sarah felt she was leaping into the darkness. She had no idea what route she would take north or how far she was to go before finding a permanent refuge. Margaret Campbell's stories of Canada and its great forests had intrigued her, but she wondered how she could survive there and how the settlers would treat her knowing that she was an escaped slave. As she led her children slowly to the green sward on the river bank that had been their playground for the past week, she looked back at the slave cabins and the ugly pens where so much misery had resided for decades and went on and on without cease as if in tune with some cosmic necessity. She felt strong. She learned from her previous births to exercise and recover to begin working right away. Her baby was light to carry too, and, despite its incontinence, it was easier to handle than if it were months older.

She anxiously scanned the river in the dimming light for a boat. A flatboat drifted by in mid-river on its way south. She led her children to the water's edge and watched the brown water and listened for sounds of an approaching vessel and of footsteps and voices on shore behind her that could be threatening. She held her baby close to her so as to comfort her and prevent her from crying with the sudden coolness coming down the river. The sun sank behind the hills and moments later a graying clarity graced the atmosphere. Seeing more clearly than in the sunlight, she observed a small boat with a man sitting in it close to the Ohio shore. The light grew grayer and just as a veil was drawn over the water she saw the man start to row the boat. A calmness came over her and her anxiety gave way to determination. Calling softly to Fanny and Israel she led them by one hand to the small opening between the two boulders that she had remarked when she made her visit to Campbell's. Just as they reached the little beachhead giving them room to stand where the river water lapped at the sand, she detected men's voices coming along the trail. Gathering her children to her, she huddled by one of the boulders and threw her dark coat over them. Sensing her fear, the children stayed silent. Two men, whom Sarah recognized as Samuel's guards, were deep in argument as they passed by them on their way upriver. She stayed still for a long time before she relaxed and breathed easier. Turning about to look out at the river, she saw the boat approaching the green sward, and distinguishing Dawson's squarely built figure, she gave a soft whistle. Dawson stopped rowing and looked about him. She whistled again, and, detecting her, he brought the boat into the space between the boulders. Without a word she helped the children climb into the bow into Dawson's hands, and then handed him the baby before she, knee deep in the freezing water, climbed aboard. Dawson immediately began rowing into the river and northwards. Sarah, picking up Vesta from the floorboards where Dawson had put her, signaled to her other children to sit facing her on the floor of the boat. The soft scraping of the oars against the gunwales sounded like an announcement of her escape, but no one seemed to be listening.

Sarah looked back at the receding shoreline and was satisfied that they had not been seen, but now the problem was to avoid boat traffic. While other ships showed lantern lights, Dawson kept the rowboat dark. The night fortunately was dark. Dawson worked the oars smoothly and as noiselessly as he could. Sarah sensed his nervousness and fear. She wondered if she should speak to him and try to calm him but thought better of it; he might become alarmed at any noise from her. In public Dick Dawson appeared at ease and in control, but she knew that he was constantly in fear of being mistaken for a slave or reenslaved by some unprincipled slave-dealer. The practice of capturing free coloreds by surprise and shipping them south on vessels dedicated to that service had become greater of late now that slave traffic between the states was being discouraged. Trapped in some large plantation and chained night and day to a work detail, a free man could appeal to no one. But Dawson's fear was greater now. Certain death would come to him if he were caught. Only his indebtedness to Philip Doddridge and his belief that Doddridge could save him if necessary brought him to perform so foolhardy an act. Since the trial, he had come to respect Fanny and resolved never to ill-treat her, although he kept her his slave. He looked at Sarah, faintly shaped in the dim light, and felt pleased that he could help free her, the sister of his Fanny. But only when his part in the rescue was finished would he rejoice in it.

A cold wind began to blow against them after what seemed like a couple of hours. Sarah seeing that her children were shivering, opened her coat and beckoned them to come close to her. They crawled to her and huddled against her as she spread her coat about them. The shore was invisible. Clouds obscured the moon and stars. She could no longer restrain her curiosity.

"Where are you takin' us, Dick?"

"T'other side Steubenville," Dawson said quickly.

"What then?"

"White man, carriage," Dawson said between breaths.

Sarah divined what her route would be—straight to Wellsville, Ohio, at the tip of the Panhandle. The plan was to get her as far away as possible before Samuel and his men missed her, which should not be until Monday morning. Even then they might not think that she had escaped and would not begin searching until later in the day. It was best to avoid Steubenville where someone might see her with Dawson. She was known by some people in Steubenville because she visited there on occasion with the Browns when she lived on Brown Island. She began to cough and tried to suppress it. Up ahead was Steubenville. She could see the lights left burning on the dock for any night traffic on the river. Dawson stayed in mid-stream as he rowed cautiously by the town.

"Not far now," he said.

Fortunately they met no river traffic. Within a half-hour, Dawson pulled closer to the Ohio shore. The moon reappeared in the sky then and shed some light on the shoreline. Trees stretched up skeletal-like and behind them lay the forest black and alive with cries of animals and the lonesome howl of the wolf. Dawson coasted close to shore where a narrow dirt road ran just a few yards back, dipping and rising, twisting and turning with the contour of the shore. There was a slight inlet and into this he guided the boat, stroked the water a few times and brought them into the shore. She peered at the impenetrable darkness, half-afraid that their contact was not there. The boat rode up on the land and its bow stuck on some roots. Rising and extending his hand to Sarah, Dawson took Fanny and then Israel from her and put them on shore. Sarah took his hand and, carrying Vesta, stepped onto the land. She stood wide-eyed, listening and hoping.

Dawson made the grunting sound of a mountain lion. They waited, watching, trying to see into the darkness. Dawson was just about to grunt again when a man with a long beard stepped from some bushes in front of them.

"Sal?" he asked.

"Yes," Sarah whispered.

"I am Thor."

"Thor?" Dawson asked. "Then that's fine. Safe journey, Sarah."

"You leavin' us?" Sarah asked bewildered, unsure of the stranger.

"I'm staying the night in Steubenville. Avoid suspicion," Dawson chuckled, feeling relieved that his role in the escape was finished.

"My thanks with my whole heart," Sarah said, "and my love to dear Fanny."

Dawson cleared his throat and pushed off from shore.

"Come quickly," the bearded man said. He had already picked up the two children, one in each arm and was carrying them to the road.

Sarah followed quickly with Vesta, who had fallen asleep. She sensed this man was from her Methodist church. His black coat and hat and his long black beard added to a sense of rightness in his actions which had come to identify Methodists who firmly believed in their moral authority, although they might be contravening the law.

"We've got a ways to travel tonight," Thor said as he led the way to a carriage standing by the side of the road.

It was a one-horse cabriolet with room enough for the two small children to fit behind the main seats on which she and Thor sat. Thor covered the children with a heavy blanket and threw a rug over Sarah's lap. Sarah drew it up around her shoulders so that it provided shelter for Vesta in her arms. With a crack of the whip, Thor headed north at a canter. Sarah sensed his nervousness, which, when mixed with her apprehension, made her sit up in high alertness. Aside from the animal cries from the forest, however, she encountered nothing to alarm her. One carriage coming towards them passed by with a mere nod from the farmer driving it. The night was dark enough to make their faces indistinguishable to others. No one could have suspected that she was other than the wife of a farmer who lived in the neighbourhood.

With her children safely asleep under the rug despite the jolting of the carriage, Sarah mentally urged the horse pulling them to run. She felt the miles drift by in the dark night to separate her forever from her hated bondage. Life was hard for pioneers and that helped them understand the hardships faced by their slaves, but the vicious southern planters made their slaves do all the work and they had no understanding of the hardships. Even her skills at sewing and cooking would find no use in the south because those jobs would have been filled. There was only field work. Better to die running away than under a whip in a cotton field, she thought. The cold air whipped her face and kept her wide awake, ever watchful for danger. Thor said not a word. She felt the strength of his presence, a protectiveness, a firm support, and her mind raced back to the people who planned her escape. But now she had to depend upon peoples of different beliefs. Wellsburg, she had heard, was Quaker country, which had recently adopted its name to honour one of its founding families. She would be safe there probably, but afterwards how could she get through the forest all the way to Canada? Despite the exhilaration of fleeing unobserved successfully, she began to dread the route ahead of her. She felt back to touch the heads of Fanny and Israel as if to reassure herself that they were all right. Thor glanced at her and said, "Not far to go, Sal. We made good progress."

The road dipped closer to the water just before they reached the town which was drowned in darkness. The sounds from the forest died away. Now that she was almost at their destination, Sarah felt the cold like ice throughout her body. She stifled a cough and wiped at the mucus dripping from her nose. Thor guided the carriage through the main street, its clapboard stores and stone houses looking like lonely sentinels set to watch the centre of town, and he turned into a side street to stop in the lane of a large house.

"This is the place," Thor said. "They'll be waiting for us."

Sarah looked up to see candles being lit by the front door. Thor helped her down and took Vesta from her. Two men came running up to them. Thor signaled to the two children fast asleep behind the seat and they clambered onto the carriage to lift them out and carry them, still in a deep sleep, indoors. Thor followed them with Sarah, walking stiffly, close behind him. One of the men returned to take the horse and carriage to a stable. This was all accomplished silently. Sarah, apprehensive, entered a large room with a great fire to which Thor led her and set Vesta down in a chair facing it. He rubbed his hands and signaled to Sarah to do the same. As she warmed herself, a plump, pleasant woman approached from another room.

"Welcome to our home," she said kindly. "Your children are in bed." She picked up Vesta. "I'll take care of her. You must rest."

Sarah reached out in alarm and then, understanding that she must trust these people, she smiled, and feeling a tiredness flowing over her from the effects of the warmth, she muttered a thank you. She followed down a hallway to a small room where a trap door stood open. The woman pointed to it and said that if she climbed down, she would be safe for the night.

Wondering where Vesta would stay the night but too tired to even question the suggestion, she slowly descended a ladder to a small room lit with candles in a single holder. A thin woman waited there for her. She wore a white Quaker hat and came to her with her hands outstretched.

"I have filled the tub there," she pointed to a bathing tub in one corner, "with warm water. Please bathe and you will fall asleep right away," she smiled. She pointed to a bed made up with sheets and covers. "I'll take your clothes and put new ones in the room before you waken."

Sarah let her help take off her worn, coarse slave clothes, and naked she walked to the bath and stepped into it. The woman was climbing the ladder when she looked up. "Thank you," Sarah called after her. She felt her fears evaporate as she gave herself trustingly to the care of these people.

"I'll look back to see that you don't fall asleep in the water," the woman said.

Sarah sank into the warmth and felt the cold ease out of her limbs. She seized the soap at the side of the tub and scrubbed herself quickly all over. This was a pleasure she had rarely experienced. The water turned brown with the dirt that Sarah scraped from her body. Then, quickly, before the warmth overcame her, she stood up, dried herself, walked to the bed and crawled beneath the covers into oblivion.

11

When Sarah awoke, she sat up with a start. The room was lit by a solitary candle but it gave sufficient light for her to make out the clean dress and bonnet that awaited her in a chair. She first thought of her children and her escape. She remembered that she had to trust these Quakers but she was anxious to see her children. She stepped quickly to the chair and clothed herself in the soft garments. She had not worn such fine clothes in years, and, despite her worries, she took a sensual pleasure in feeling them on her body. She looked in a mirror set beside the candle, brushed back her hair, put on the bonnet, and, smiling at her disguise, climbed the ladder to the floor above. The daylight in the windows had a sunny mid-day sense, and Sarah realized that she must have slept at least six or seven hours. All was quiet. Sarah, deeming it unwise to call, went from room to room until she came to a kitchen where the thin woman she met last night was cooking over a stove. The woman turned to her with a slight surprise.

"You're up! Your children are awake and eating in the room over there." She pointed to a small room off the kitchen. "I'm frying eggs for us."

Sarah went into the small room and rushed to hug Fanny and Israel who were spooning porridge into their mouths.

"Mommy," Fanny cried. "We got away, didn't we, Mommy?"

"Yes, we've done well," Sarah said. "But where's Vesta?"

"Sleepin'" Israel said.

"In the room where we slept," Fanny added. "She's bin looked after by the kind lady."

As Sarah went back to the kitchen to ask if she could see Vesta, the plump Quakeress carried the baby down the hall towards her. "Your little one is hungry too," she smiled.

Sarah took Vesta, kissed her, and, sitting on a chair in the corner, gave her a breast to suck. Both the women set the table in the kitchen with plates and cups and then added eggs and bacon and potatoes. The plump woman, who said that her name was Patience, brewed coffee. The smells of the food and the kindness of these women gave Sarah a momentary relief from fear. Putting Vesta in a crib in the corner, she sat down at the mid-day meal with them and listened to them discuss the possible steps that they should take next to effect her escape. Finally, after they saw that Sarah had eaten, Patience asked Sarah if she could travel again that day.

"We can keep you here, but the men think that you should get away to Salem while no one is yet lookin' for you."

Sarah nodded in agreement. "I'm all right and my children are the same."

"You see," said the thin woman, "you can pass for white folks, you and your children. That's why we dressed you that way. You pull your bonnet close over your head as if keeping out the cold and no one will think you're escaping."

"I'm afraid my voice will give me away," Sarah said.

"Don't matter," the thin woman said. "Lots of us come from south of here and speak like you. A man will travel with you. Just leave everything to him and pretend to be preoccupied with your children. There's so much movement of strangers round here that no one's goin' to suspect."

"We'll pack a lunch for you," Patience smiled. "It's just a day's journey."

Sarah looked worriedly between the two of them. Many slaves had been caught or turned in by people for reward money. Was it going to be as simple as riding in a carriage in the company of a white man?

91

"After Salem is the difficult part," said the thin woman, as if divining Sarah's thoughts. "But we'll cross that bridge when we come to it."

"Will Thor be takin' us?" Sarah asked quietly.

"Thor's back in Steubenville," Patience said. "He's Methodist. One of the brethren will take you for the next lap. We don't know who it'll be."

"He'll be here for you in about an hour. It'll take about five or six hours to get to Salem with a good horse and buggy," said the thin woman. "We must be thankful that the roads are still hard. If it were warmer, they'd turn to mud and it could take twice as long."

"Luck is with us so far," Patience smiled. She stood up and looked in on the children in the small room. "They're ready for more," she smiled at the thin woman and went to the stove to fill two plates with eggs and bacon. "This will give them strength for the long trip." She took the plates to the children.

"Do you know where I go after Salem?" Sarah asked the thin lady. "You said that it'd be the hardest part."

"Cleveland."

"Cleveland!" Sarah gasped. "It's far away, isn't it?"

"It's back country, mostly forest. The road's dangerous at times. It's because you and your children can pass," she explained. "That's why we're taking you directly. And because you got young children who can't be exposed too much. You understand?"

"How is it dangerous?" Sarah asked alarmed.

The thin woman shook her head. "They'll inform you at Salem."

Vesta began to cry and Sarah smelt the defecation that seeped through the cloth binding her. Patience, returning to the table, led Sarah to a room down the hall and brought out a basin and water for Sarah to bathe her baby.

Sarah felt humbled by the kindness of these people. Without their help she could not have gone far before she was recaptured. How long could she have crawled through the underbrush with her children, she wondered. She was desperate enough to do it, but she knew Samuel and his men would have tracked her down with bloodhounds soon enough. Even if she failed to get free, she would remember these people with gratitude, she thought. When she finished bathing Vesta and calming the child, she returned to the kitchen to find a young blond man sitting at the table.

"Hello, Sal," he said with a beaming smile. "I'm your new husband."

"Alvin!" Patience admonished him.

"Well, she's got to start treating me like a husband," he retorted. "We got to sound free with one another, like a husband and wife."

"I can do that," Sarah laughed. For the first time she was able to laugh and it felt wonderful. The young man exuded confidence, and his eyes twinkled. There was not the slightest condescension in his manner.

"Don't draw attention to yourself," Patience warned. "Alvin's new to this, so we've got to make sure he doesn't think it's an adventure."

"I know," Alvin smiled. "My aunt thinks I'm reckless when I'm really just ready to take risks. They are different," he winked at Sarah.

"It's after noon," the thin lady warned. "You'd best be off." She came to Sarah with a black coat lined with fur. "This will keep you warm."

Fanny and Israel wearing new coats came into the kitchen with Patience. "Be good," Patience told them. "Do what your mother tells you."

Fanny and Israel nodded tensely. Those words seemed to cut them off from the past hours and put them back into the region of fear that they had known for most of their young lives. They ran to Sarah and stood by her side. Sarah took up Vesta and followed Alvin out the back door to a carriage pulled by two horses. It was covered and looked as if it belonged to a prosperous person. Sarah guessed that it would be less likely to be challenged than a more modest conveyance. She was being asked to act the role of a white person of means. Her white children would serve as a testament to her own legitimacy. They all climbed in the carriage. Sarah leaned back to kiss Patience on both cheeks and wave to the thin lady who stood in the doorway watching them go. Alvin cracked the whip and the carriage leaped forward. Soon they had traversed the town centre and were moving swiftly into the countryside where some of the land was cleared. The farms cut out of the forest were surrounded by timber fences. Many trees, punctured to let the life out of them, stood like scarecrows, their dead limbs fallen to the ground and some of them ready to be tumbled by the strong winds of spring. Log cabins stood on rises of ground. Orchards sometimes appeared by the roadside, their denuded trees beginning to bud. The road rose as the carriage climbed deeper into the forest. Soon there was no sign of habitation, just the narrow dirt road, the silence of the trees and the occasional gurgle of streams fed by the melting snow. Sarah, watching the land from the carriage window, sensed that Samuel was just discovering that she was gone and was beginning to search for her. He would go to Campbell's farm to see if she had tried to rescue her older children. He would look for her throughout the Panhandle first because he could not have suspected that she was as far away as Salem. But after Salem? The thin lady was right. That would be the difficult part.

Sarah did not have to pretend to be white because she felt white by inheritance. She thought of herself as connected more to the Brown family than to her mother's family; even at that, her mother's mother had been mulatto. Sarah thought that her relative whiteness was a further reason for seeing herself as free. The natural dignity with which she carried herself and a forthrightness in her manner that presumed an equality with white people provoked Campbell's resentment. It also angered some black field slaves, to whom as a house slave she thought herself superior. She learned early in life that everyone was an individual and different. But, it was how she dealt with others that determined how they dealt with her. If blackness was a stigma in society then she would bring up her children as whites. She glanced at the pink and white skin of Alvin and his blond hair, characteristics that gave this young man a right to become whatever he wished in this society. She did not envy him as much as she hated the system that favored him and tried to destroy her. But here he was, privileged, throwing his advantage to the winds in order to help her. He too must have thought like her and regarded human beings by their individuality, not by their skin color.

As if he sensed that Sarah was thinking about him, Alvin spoke up for the first time. "Sorry I'm not more communicative. I've been on my guard for anyone I might know but we're far enough from town now that it's unlikely I'll meet someone."

"What would you say if you did?" Sarah asked.

"I'd say that you were a family friend that I'm helping out."

"Is that all we have to be worried about?" Sarah asked.

"Oh no!" Alvin shook his head. "When we come into Lisbon, we have to avoid the officials who can stop us on the slightest suspicion. I've timed it so that we arrive as its getting dark so few will be in the streets."

Sarah instinctively reached for her children as if to protect them from the prying eyes of an enemy.

The road they were pursuing still rose into the hills of softly rolling contours. Sarah saw few signs of habitation. The ground was rocky and the forests very thick. She pictured slaves, less fortunate than herself, finding their way through the forest at nights and watching the north star for guidance. Her own poor Henry may have settled deep in some forest like that and be hunting and fishing to keep alive.

"You've got good children," Alvin said. "I've never seen two children so quiet and well-behaved. They obey you, don't they."

"Out of necessity," Sarah smiled. "And even dear little Vesta doesn't make a noise. It's as if they've learned through my body, sort of soaked in my fears and thoughts."

Alvin gave her a quizzical look. "How come you're so white-lookin' and white-speakin' and you're still a slave?"

"Haven't you seen white slaves before?" Sarah asked, amused.

"Sure, I've seen 'em," Alvin confessed, "but I didn't know 'em well enough to ask 'em that question."

"It's a matter of law," Sarah sighed. "If your mother's a slave, you're a slave."

"And what do the black slaves think of white slaves?" Alvin asked.

"Some of them envy us because we get to do house work while they mostly work in the fields, but they know that we're all in the same boat and suffer the same things." Sarah soothed Vesta and rocked her gently in her arms. "Can we stop by the next stream," she asked.

"Sure," Alvin said looking askance at Vesta.

Within minutes they crossed over a culvert made of logs jammed together and stopped at the side of the road. The pale light of the afternoon sun filtered through the trees and the rustling sound of the stream below seemed like a whisper in the silence. Sarah stepped out of the carriage and carrying Vesta gingerly stepped through the bushes and down the steep side of a ravine.

"Can we come?" Fanny shouted.

Sarah looked back as if to say 'no' but catching Alvin's delighted smile, she nodded, "You can come but stay close to me now."

"Away you go," Alvin laughed, helping Fanny and Israel out of the carriage. He rejoiced to see them running with shouts of joy to their mother and clambering through the bushes and sliding carefully down the hillside. Raised as a Quaker, Alvin believed in the spontaneity of expression and the integrity of the individual. When slave children could behave like children, instead of the subdued and cowering little animals whom he had often seen, he felt that all the risk he took was worth it many times over.

The ravine was deeper than Sarah had thought at first, but she had no choice because Vesta was stinking and needed a washing. When she reached the stream, she stood on some rocks and lowered the naked Vesta into the cold water. Vesta cried in delight and splashed about her while the other children went upstream and drank the water and played in tall bushes. Sarah wrapped Vesta in a dry cloth which Patience had given her and beat the dirty cloth against the rocks until it was clean. Scooping up Vesta she went the short distance upstream to drink the water and fetch her children to return to the carriage. Just as she finished drinking and was calling Fanny to bring Israel, she heard men's voices from the road above. They sounded angry and belligerent. Dashing to her children she pushed them into the bushes and huddled, listening. The sound of the stream muffled the voices but she sensed that Alvin was being confronted by some men. She feared that it was a posse looking for her. The bushes and trees were too thick for her to see the road and for those on the road to see her. She cuddled Vesta and rocked her slightly to make her contented.

Alvin was seated on the carriage and waiting patiently for Sarah's return when he was startled by two horsemen who appeared in the road before him. They were lean, straggly-looking men with mean faces that belied a hard life scrabbling a living from the soil. One of them with a beard rode his horse directly to Alvin while the other looked about for a sign of any other person near-by.

"Watchya doin' here, Quaker?" asked the bearded man. "You prayin'?" He smiled wickedly.

"Just restin'," Alvin said. "I've come a long way."

"Those horses look pretty good," the man kept smiling. "Don't they look good," he said to the other man who rode up to him.

"Sure as hell do!" The other man had a hoarse voice with a deep tone that seemed threatening to Alvin.

"Our Quaker boy is just restin'. We could borrow his horses while he's restin', don't you think?"

"Sure as hell could," said the other man, smiling broadly now.

"You'd take my horses and leave me stranded?" Alvin asked incredulously. He was thinking of Sarah and hoping that she would not appear with the children. These men would harm them.

Without a word, the two men dismounted and unhitched Alvin's horses from the carriage. They seemed to be in a hurry now that they were stealing. The man with the hoarse voice let out a gleeful laugh as he rode off in the direction of Wellsville holding the tethers of Alvin's two horses, beautiful chestnut mares.

"Now you just sit there, Quaker boy, and don't indulge in any violence and evil thoughts," said the bearded man. "We'll look after your horses just fine." He spurred his horse and cantered after his friend.

Alvin watched them go with relief. They could have been killers, not just thieves. He saw that they had long knives and one of them carried a rifle slung in his saddle. There was no other route for them to travel but to Wellsville where many people knew Alvin's horses. But for the moment Alvin concentrated on getting Sarah to Salem. They were a few miles from Lisbon. About a mile up the road Alvin knew a Quaker farmstead where he could borrow a horse, but he could not leave Sarah and her children alone in the forest while he went to get it. He got down from the carriage and stepped part way down the hillside of the ravine. Seeing no sign of Sarah, he called her name softly. Sarah answered by stepping out of the bushes into a slight clearing where he could see her looking up at him worriedly.

"Come!" he cried. "They've gone."

Sarah called to her children to follow her and together they climbed the hillside, seizing onto bushes and tree branches to pull themselves up. When on the road, which at this point was like a wide trail, Alvin explained that they had to walk for about a mile where they could get help. At the slightest noise of someone coming, they were to take cover in the forest. The children listened attentively. Alvin picked up Israel and lifted him astride his shoulders. Sarah carried Vesta. Fanny ran in front of them happy to be leading them out of difficulty.

"Those men were desperadoes," Alvin said to Sarah. "They could have done anything."

Sarah, too tense to speak, nodded and tried to calm herself.

"They'll get caught, I think," Alvin said hopefully. "They look suspicious with two horses in tow. If they try to sell them in Wellsville, they'll be caught."

They continued in silence as the sun dropped in the sky. Sarah felt Vesta getting heavier in her arms as they walked. Turning a bend in the road, they saw a log cabin on a hill crest far back from the road. There was smoke coming from the chimney.

"I know these people," Alvin said, putting Israel down. "They've helped runaways. But let me go ahead to be sure."

Alvin led them over the field covered with a fine skein of snow and called out as he came near to the cabin. The door swung open. A big man stepped out. He was frowning in a bemused way.

"Lost your way, Alvin?" He looked down the pathway at Sarah and the children. "Come in and get warm. Welcome to you all." He swept his arm back toward the open door and, nodding at their murmurs of thanks, followed them into the one large room of his cabin. A fire in the hearth gave light and warmth to every corner of the room. A small window at the far end with a pane of glass caught the dying rays of the setting sun.

Alvin introduced their host, Big John, to Sarah and the children and explained what had happened to them.

"It'll be dark soon," Big John declared, looking at Vesta. "You'd best stay here for the night."

"Too risky," Alvin said. "We've arranged for refuge in Salem.

We've got to get there tonight."

Big John looked into the fire for a moment. "I understand," he said. "But I've just two horses. Best thing—you take my wagon and one horse to Salem while I go with the other horse to get your carriage down the road. When you return you can pick up your carriage. Sound all right, brother?"

"That's good," Alvin nodded. "We'll be on schedule then."

"Thank you," Sarah smiled, hardly daring to believe in this man's goodness.

Big John leaped to his feet. "Here now, take some of this cheese and bread with you." He took a home-made loaf and several thick cuts of cheese from behind the stove and stuffed them into a cloth bag. "You young'uns will be hungry soon," he said beaming at Fanny and Israel and handing the bag to Sarah. "Let's get started." He led the way outside to his barn behind the cabin.

"Wait a moment," Alvin said worriedly. "People in Lisbon are bound to know your horse and wagon. They'll think we stole it."

"Good thinkin', Alvin," Big John cried. "Now that's what I admire about this young man, Miss," he said to Sarah. "He has prescience." He went to a corner of the barn and tore a piece of paper off a hook. He took a small pencil out of his pocket and wrote, "Loaned to my friend, Alvin," and signed his name. "That ought to do the trick," he said, handing the paper to Alvin. He turned to his horses and led one of them to an open wagon where he hitched it. "Nothing fancy like yours," he said. "But you can pretend to be poor farmers."

"I've come down in the world already," Sarah laughed nervously.

"Freedom's like that," Big John laughed with her. "Up and down, up and down." He took Vesta, while Alvin helped Sarah and her children onto the wagon seat, and chucking the baby under the chin, handed her up to Sarah. "Take care of yourselves, now. We don't see many pretty ladies like you come through here, and it gives the heart a rise to meet someone like you."

"Thank you, Big John," Sarah said leaning forward to offer her hand and feeling the rough hand of the farmer tenderly hold it for an instant.

Alvin flicked the reins and the horse pulled the wagon out of the barn.

"Follow that trail," Big John shouted, pointing to a wheel-rutted lane leading behind the cabin. "You'll catch the road on the other side of the hill. Short cut," he said.

Sarah and Fanny waved good-bye to him as the wagon moved swiftly up and over the crest of the hill.

"I think he really wanted you to stay the night," Alvin said. "He lost his wife over a year ago. He's kind of lonely, I suspect."

"It's too bad we couldn't," Sarah said. "I like him."

"Trouble is, his farm is watched whenever there's reports of runaways in these parts. He's never been caught because he's isolated out here and bounty hunters, sheriffs and the rest of them don't like to camp out for long on the off-chance that they'd catch someone, so he knows how to outwait them."

They came upon the main road and Alvin, to make up for their delay, urged the horse to trot all the way to the village of Lisbon, which they entered as the sun sank behind the horizon and the air grew perceptibly colder.

Just a handful of people stood outside the collection of cabins and watched Alvin drive his horse at a walk through the village. It was almost dark which made it difficult for anyone to distinguish people. Sarah sat straight and confident to show that she was a white woman intent on her business. She smelt cooking of the evening meals emanating from the cabins, and, remembering the bread and cheese that Big John had given them, she broke off pieces of both and gave them to Fanny, Israel and Alvin to eat as they continued into the forest. The trail wound upwards for a few miles and then began to descend. They saw in the moonlight the rolling hills, one behind the other in a descending contour, and the horse, sensing his load becoming easier, began to pull harder as the wagon coasted down slowly toward the valley in which Salem lay.

"You've got a big lead on the slavers," Alvin said encouragingly. "The best thing is to get you straight to Cleveland, but that's over seventy miles and there's no settlements along the way. It's going to be hard on you. You've got to lay up in Salem till we figure out a way to get you and your little ones through the forest. The Brethren can shel-

100

ter you now, but it's goin' to be your Methodist people to guide you after Salem."

"Is there a road?" Sarah asked concernedly.

"Not as good as this," Alvin said, "and this one is barely passable most times of the year. You'll have to travel on foot or by horseback, I guess. I never been much beyond Salem."

A wagon approached from in front of them. Alvin pulled his wagon as close to the side of the trail as he could, leaving just enough room for the other wagon to pass. A heavy-set man and his plump wife sitting in the front seat of their wagon looked closely at Alvin and Sarah. Behind them were three young men, presumably their sons. Pulling up his wagon beside Alvin's, the man greeted them in a loud voice: "Where are you going, stranger?"

Sarah tensed, wondering if he were one of the officials Alvin had mentioned.

"We're meetin' kin folk in Salem," Alvin said.

"Pretty late to be takin' your family on a visit," the man observed.

"Got held up by bandits," Alvin said. "Stole our horses so we had to get another one."

The mention of bandits startled the man and his wife. "How many of 'em?" the man asked.

"Two," Alvin said.

"Tall, thin, sort of scruffy?" the man asked.

"Yes," Alvin nodded. "Looked like they'd as soon kill you as look at you."

"They're the same as we saw in Salem," his wife exclaimed to her husband. "And you thought they could scout for us," she added sarcastically.

The heavy-set man squirmed uncomfortably and turned to look back at his sons. "You hear that?" he demanded. "We got taken in."

"How do you mean that?" Alvin asked innocently. He felt uncomfortable about these people which is why he mentioned the thieves so soon, so as to take their minds off looking for runaways, as he suspected.

"There's escaped slaves come up this way and we got the responsibility to keep a look-out for 'em," the man grimaced, "and those men said they could help us."

"And you were ready to pay them," his wife snorted.

The boys sniggered behind them.

"They'll be caught when they get to Wellsville," Alvin said.

"Well then," the man tried to sound business-like, as if his wife's comments were unworthy of a reply. "We wish you a good journey." He put the whip to his horse and nodded agreeably as he passed.

During this exchange Sarah sat in demure attentiveness and smiled at the man's wife as if amused by her boldness in criticizing her husband. She was tense under the surface but managed to appear at ease. When the wagon disappeared into the darkness behind them, she let out a long sigh of relief.

Alvin smiled. "Our first real test of passing for white. You did great, Mrs. Lewis."

"They were lookin' at us so hard I was afraid of being found out," Sarah confessed. "But the Lord was with us."

"Amen," Alvin added and urged their horse forward.

Other wagon drivers and horsemen they encountered showed little interest in them, so eager were they to get to their homes. They arrived at a stone house on the main street of Salem about three hours after they were expected. Alvin drove up the lane leading to the house, stopped in front of the stoop, helped Sarah and the children out of the wagon, and knocked on the large wooden door. After a few minutes when no one appeared, Alvin began to worry that they were no longer expected, but a stern voice addressed him from the side of the house. "Brother!"

Sarah turned to see a man of middle height and middle-age with a stern face and thin spectacles balanced on a large nose. He held a glass lantern lit by a candle and gestured impatiently for them to come round to the side of the house. Alvin took the children by the hand and Sarah followed him with Vesta, whose weight, although relatively light, was beginning to make her arms ache. Their host waited by a side door and pointed for them to enter. They stood in a hallway while they waited for the man to lock up the door and take the lead. They went through two small rooms, the second of which was a private library with more books than Sarah had ever seen.

"Had an accident?" the man inquired.

Alvin briefly described the theft of his horses.

"Could have been worse," he said. "Bad characters comin' in from the east. Used to kill Indians, now they kill us." He pulled a sash on the side of the wall and a large wall bookcase seemed to split down the middle as the two halves moved apart revealing a wooden door. He unlocked the door with a long key and, opening it, stepped aside to allow Sarah and her children to enter ahead of him. "Usually keep it locked," he said. "But you can come and go, if you remember to pull this sash on your side to close and open the bookcase."

The room was larger than any room Sarah had lived in, and it was furnished with comfortable chairs and two beds. A window looked out at ground level. Noticing Sarah's glance at the window, the host explained that it faced the forest which grew close to the back of the house.

"Look here," he said sharply and walked to a corner of the room, pulled back a rug, and, stooping, picked up a trap door. "A passage leads into the forest. If you're in trouble, use it." He smiled at Alvin. "Was used to escape Indian attacks in the old days when this was a family fort. Made sure it was part of this house." He let the trap door fall shut. "Name's Horace Dour," he said, extending his hand to Sarah and shaking hers warmly. "I know yours and all about you and your types." He looked at Fanny and Israel who were playing on one of the beds and loving its softness.

"I'm thankful to you," Sarah said, trying to conceal her fatigue.

"Tut, tut," Horace shushed her. "You've got a long and difficult road ahead. I'm just a brief stopover and glad to help you to a new life, my dear. Hungry? Food's been waiting for a while." He turned on his heel and gesturing for them to follow, led the way back through the two rooms and down a short hallway to the kitchen, where laid out on the table were plates for all of them. "Cooked you my favorite stew," Horace said enthusiastically, and taking a pot off the stove began spooning the stew onto the plates.

The smell of the food drew them directly to the table. Sarah suddenly sensed how very hungry she was, and she looked at her children with admiration for uttering no complaint. But before they began to eat, she insisted they wait until she thanked the Lord for their deliverance thus far. Horace took Vesta from her arms and placed the baby in a wooden cradle on a table near the sink.

After Alvin ate several spoonfuls and tasted the beer that Horace put before him, he asked how dangerous it had been of late.

"People here are good," Horace said. "If they see bounty hunters, they let me know. But it's bad from here on."

"You got a plan?" Alvin asked uneasily.

Horace nodded. "Don't worry. You sleep well and get back safe to Wellsville. We'll get this young lady safe and sound to Cleveland."

Sarah wondered why Horace was alone and where the women of the house were, but she was too reticent to ask. She gathered from the conversation that Horace had made money in trade and built this large stone house in the village to reflect his leadership in the community. Other stone houses were built beside his and across the street to begin forming a nucleus of wealth in Salem, which was the most enterprising settlement in this part of Ohio. Horace's austere expression and abrupt manner of speaking covered a kind heart and a concern for the less fortunate, but his temperament seemed made for business. Sarah could tell that he enjoyed his wealth. When there was a lull in the conversation she ventured at last to ask about the ladies of the house.

"When expecting visitors," Horace said quickly, "they visit relatives. Safer that way." Noticing that the children had finished their stew, Horace took the pot and spooned more on their plates. He looked gratified that they began eating again with gusto.

"How long can we stay here?" Sarah asked.

"Best to wait a couple of days till we know what lies ahead. Your guide is coming down from Cleveland now and he'll tell us what we need to know."

"You're in good hands," Alvin said. "May God be with you, Mrs. Lewis." He stood up to shake her hand, but Sarah, rising to her feet, hugged him to her and conveyed her everlasting thanks to him in that gesture.

"Need sleep, don't you?" Horace said to Alvin with a smile. "Your bed's ready for you. Come with me."

Left alone with her children, Sarah reflected on her good fortune in distancing herself so far so soon from Wellsburg. If Samuel had published a reward for her return in the newspapers, it would take some days for the news to reach these parts. The people along the way had turned a seeming impossibility into a reality. She was still far from her goal of freedom for her children, but they had withstood the journey with a stoic composure and a fearlessness that made her love them all the more. She had trained them to absolute obedience, which they recognized from the cradle as necessary to their survival. Vesta too had weathered the journey well so far. Sarah carried her all day and breast fed her whenever she cried for milk. She loved this child who seemed contented so long as she was safe in her mother's arms, despite the shaking and bouncing of the wagon over the rough roads, the cold, and her concern that she was transmitting her fear to her. She washed the dishes in the sink when they finished eating and was leading her children back to their hidden room when Horace caught up with her.

"You will find bedclothes in the closet in your room. Sleep well, little ones," Horace said to Fanny and Israel who looked at him in awe. He accompanied them to the door of their room and closed the bookcase behind them.

Sarah went to the back window and stared out at the blackness of the forest, in which she would wander uncertainly until she found light at the other side. She prayed that her children would stay healthy for the journey. She put Israel and Fanny into one of the beds and took Vesta with her in the other. She blew out the candle and thought again of the humane treatment she was receiving from these Quakers. She pictured the benevolent smile of the Reverend Joseph Doddridge reassuring her that she would overcome the dangers ahead.

During the night it rained heavily. By morning the streets of Salem were mounds of mud. Wagons sank up to their axles. Horace Dour was working at his accounts when Sarah came out of her hidden room.

"Good morning!" he cried cheerfully. "You'll not be going today, that's certain."

"I don't want to be an inconvenience to you, sir," Sarah said.

"Nonsense! Breakfast? Bring your children." He sped away to the kitchen while Sarah went into her room to retrieve Vesta and send Fanny and Israel out ahead of her.

The blazing hearth in the kitchen drove away the chill of the early spring air. Sarah laughed to see Fanny and Israel break from an early morning stupor into excited chatter at the smell of coffee and oatmeal with molasses. She saw Horace smiling sympathetically at her as if to say that he knew that they were eating better than they had at any time in their short lives.

In the afternoon Horace Dour brought a tall slim colored man called Alick to meet Sarah. A mixture of white, Indian and black, he wore a serious expression as if he had been through much and would find nothing to smile about ever. He said all was ready to travel on the morrow. Alick had traveled the route several times, in particular during the War of 1812 when he brought supplies to the American forces by pack horse that way. He was to pretend to be Sarah's special servant conducting her and her children to her husband on a farmstead outside Cleveland. Sarah and her children were to go by horseback, and she was to sit side-saddle like a lady. Colonel Brown had allowed Sarah to learn to ride on Brown's Island but not side-saddle. Her children looked pleased, although they had not been on a horse. Campbell allowed only those slaves who cared for the stables to ride and exercise his horses. Sarah wondered whether she had the stamina to ride such a long distance while clutching Vesta to her chest. She told herself that her reward for making the attempt would be greater than any pain she might suffer.

"You will have to leave your Quaker clothes behind," Horace warned. "We have clothes that will mark you and your little ones as born to the purple, or, at least, well-born," he smiled.

"Going up in the world again," Sarah thought to herself.

"If your lady pleases," Alick said and bowed, "we shall leave at dawn. Please dress warmly."

"Leave that to me," Horace said briskly. "And now, good-afternoon, my dear Alick."

"Be sure you are not late," Sarah said breezily to Alick as she had seen the ladies at Colonel Brown's home treat servants.

Horace cried, "brava!" and gave Sarah a tap on the shoulder as he strode from the room.

"Where does Alick go?" Sarah asked.

"He stays with friends in the village. He is a very private person and can be comfortable only with certain people. You will find that he is an excellent guide. And now, for your clothes tomorrow." He dashed down the hall and disappeared into one of the rooms.

The sun rose in a clear blue sky. Sarah, seated on a large gray mare and, holding Vesta, followed the chestnut stallion on which Alick rode with Fanny and Israel seated in front of him. Israel laughed with joy as he sat on the horse. The trail was muddy and washed away in places— impassable by carriage. Alick said the journey would take them two to three days if all went well. Alick carried food in his saddlebags and a pistol in his saddle pocket. Sarah had changes of clothing in her saddlebags.

Vesta, whom Sarah feared would fall ill from constant exposure and the jarring movement, adapted well and fed at her breast several times a day. Fanny and Israel treated the escape as a great adventure and took in all the strange scenes and the people they met with fascination. As Sarah experienced the impenetrability of the forest, fears of the wilderness that she associated with the savagery of the Indian wars of her youth swept over her. She would have been too terrified to travel on her own. Forests were mysteries into which people disappeared. The various Indian trails crossing the one that they were following would have led her in circles, and having to depend on strangers for sustenance, she would have found enemies rather than friends. When they were several miles out of Salem, Sarah asked Alick to stop. She gave him Vesta to hold while she dismounted and remounted astride her horse and took Vesta back.

"Side saddle is too uncomfortable," she explained. "I can't make it that way."

Alick allowed a flicker of a smile to cross his lips. "Not likely to meet one in these wilds who'll give a damn that a well-born lady is riding astride. Sometimes those Reverends plan too much."

"How are my darlings?" Sarah asked, looking at Fanny and Israel clinging to the saddle horn.

"We're all right, mommy," Fanny said.

"It's fun," Israel laughed. "But I want to go faster."

"Trying to get 'em to relax," Alick smiled at them. "They're learnin'. We'll stop in three hours to eat." He lapsed back into silence.

Sarah sensed animals watching them from the gloom of the forest and occasionally she heard a crashing through the underbrush, but she saw only birds, some with colorful coats, and heard their songs. Sarah had not heard songbirds like this since she was small. The industries of the growing settlements had brought silence to the forests. Families of the original settlers were like the birds that fled the harsh conditions of a developing economy, she thought. Hordes of new settlers filled their places and forges grew and as the countryside began looking meaner, conditions for slaves worsened. The new settlers were opportunists who never knew the value of human relationships and treated slaves, not as helpmeets in the battle against nature, but as objects to make them rich. Some from the early settler class, typified the voracious new settler in his viciousness, for example James Campbell. If Campbell, Sarah thought, had met Alick, he would have found some way to kill him for his independent spirit as a colored man. But then Alick, she suspected, had handled many Campbells. She felt confident in his guidance. He exuded an air of mastery of any situation.

Thoughts of freedom and of raising her children to be citizens swept over her as she fed Vesta. The fine clothes she wore gave her a sense of that freedom. They were dark such as ladies wore for riding, but she would be able to wear clothes of any color, anything she wanted. Her children could be educated. They could be gentlemen and ladies. The future was going to obliterate those years of humiliating slavery, turning men into fools and women into obsequious clowns, trying to please their masters to avoid punishment. How glad she was that she started life in Colonel Brown's house, where she developed an independent spirit strong enough to defy Campbell. The taste of freedom she just experienced with the Quakers, the feeling that she could be accepted among people for herself, and all the little things that came along with being treated as human, the courtesy, the consideration—no, she could never return to slavery. She would kill herself first.

They came to a clearing of short grass and large stones on the crest of the hill. Below them she saw the rolling hills of a black-branched forest dropping away to a plain in the distance. The level land ran on into the horizon. Here and there were green clusters of firs and some trees were sprouting green buds.

"Good land for farming some day," Alick said. "There's a stream half-way down where we'll eat." He urged his horse onward.

The snow melting on the forest floor formed a torrent of water, which they heard rushing through the trees as they approached the area where Alick intended to stop. But Alick, reining in his horse, threw out a cautionary hand. Sarah pulled up behind him and stared in the direction he was looking. She heard only the water tumbling down the hillside. They stayed still for a couple of minutes, and then Sarah saw a figure move out of the trees with a horse trailing behind it.

"Stay close to me," Alick said to her. "Ride up almost even, but let me be in front."

Sarah brought her horse almost even with Alick's and together they rode down to meet the stranger, who, she made out as they drew closer, was a rather tall white man who seemed to take no interest in them, at least, he was concentrating on filling a pot with water from the stream. Alick led Sarah to a point upstream from this man, and, handing Fanny and Israel over to her by propping them on the front part of her saddle, he directed his horse to where the man was drinking from the stream. Sarah watched as Alick conversed with the man who now she could assess as about six feet tall and in his forties. The children wanted to get down and drink from the stream, but Sarah restrained them with sharp words that alerted them to danger. Presently Alick returned and dismounting tethered his horse to a near-by tree. He took down Fanny and Israel and watched them run to the water and stare down at it rushing past.

"He's prospecting for land," Alick said to Sarah raising his voice to be heard above the sound of the water. "Says he's going to Cleveland." He took Vesta from Sarah while she dismounted. "Fact is, Europeans got all the land round here cheap years ago. He could be a land agent. He has a German accent. Could be planning to bring in German settlers."

"What do we do?" Sarah asked anxiously.

"I told him you were going to your husband. Said you were Irish."

"Good," Sarah smiled.

"He seems friendly," Alick warned. "We need a name for you. They'll be lookin' for Mrs. Lewis."

"I'm Mrs. Sarah Kinney," she said.

Alick unpacked the food from his saddlebags while Sarah went to her children who were running along the shore of the stream and laughing at the fish they saw. She saw that the stranger had built a small fire back from the stream and was cooking some meat on a spit. She bathed and cleaned Vesta in the water. How beautiful and peaceful the wilderness was, she thought, and how secure she felt with Alick to protect her. She saw that Alick had built a fire and collected water in a pot which he was boiling. She called to her children who came obediently to her and walked with her to Alick who was sitting on his haunches and stirring pemmican in the pot. Alick laid out some boiled eggs on the ground that Horace Dour had given them, and he motioned to Sarah to begin eating. The children cracked them open and ate hungrily. Alick laid the heated strips of pemmican on a rock, and, after they had eaten the eggs, they chewed away at the pemmican. Sarah saw the change in her children. Their sense of freedom brought a bubbling mirth to their faces. She, however, could not relax until she had reached Canada. How easily expectation could become disappointment! How quickly paradise could become hell!

The stranger broke camp first. He destroyed his fire with a stick and poured water on it. Then lifting his hat to them, he mounted his horse and headed north. Alick waved in response, but Sarah pretended not to see him.

"We'll wait a bit and give him a good start. He's moving faster than us," Alick said.

"Where did he come from?" Sarah asked.

"The bush. Could have been lookin' at land."

Sarah let the children play while she washed herself in the stream and Alick broke camp. They set off at a leisurely pace, Alick holding the children tightly as they tended to be drowsy after their exercise and eating. Vesta was sleeping in Sarah's arms. The afternoon sun began to weaken and reflected off the tops of the trees but failed to penetrate deeply onto the pathway, which was in semi-light. They stopped a couple of times to attend to their toilet in the woods. Sarah felt her stiffness when she dismounted so unaccustomed she was to riding. Once they encountered a family on horseback and in a small carriage heading for Salem. Although the men in the family appeared to want to stop and talk, Alick explained that they were behind schedule and they hurried on.

They were on flat ground. Occasionally they would come upon clearings where timber fences had been erected and small log cabins stood back from the road, but these cabins had been abandoned and were broken and desolate-looking. Alick explained that their isolation had driven some settlers mad. Others, finding that land prices were kept high, went further west. The land was fertile but one could not live off peaches and vegetables alone. Human contact became the primary ingredient to the founding of a settlement. And then, making a living off the land seemed easier than it actually was, Alick smiled.

Sarah thought of the hardships of settlement. The cold, the illnesses, the lack of medical skill, the fear of attack by forces unknown, perhaps drunken Indians or drunken white men, or desperadoes looking for a lark. That is why whole families, including cousins and in-laws, migrated together. They faced the harshness of the natural world in support of one another, and they could survive. Would Canada be in that primitive state? she wondered. Margaret Campbell had told her that it was being settled quickly by Europeans and New Englanders and had painted pictures of thriving communities working the land. Sarah refused to think of what she could do to survive there. All her energies were put to getting there.

The sun was setting when they came to a small clearing with a log cabin sitting back from the trail. Smoke was coming from its chimney. Stumps of trees and huge wounds in the soil where trees had been uprooted gave a forlorn look to the place. There was a log shed behind the cabin that seemed big enough to shelter horses. Alick recognized the horse of the German tethered to a rail outside the shed and he mentioned it to Sarah.

"We could bunk in the woods," he said, "but it'll be too cold tonight. Have to take shelter here."

Sarah sensed his reluctance. "What's the matter with it?"

"The man there is ornery.... charges too much, but he knows what I think of him.... Shouldn't give us trouble, but be on guard."

"What's he goin' to do?"

"Steal, and more if I weren't with you."

"I got nothing so he doesn't worry me. Just so long as he's not a slave catcher."

"He'd be one if it paid more," Alick smiled.

Alick led the way to the front door of the cabin which stood open. He dismounted and entered while Sarah rode forward to take the reins of Alick's horse and speak to her children who looked very tired and clung to the horn of the saddle to keep from toppling over. They waited, listening to the sounds of men's voices from inside the cabin. Presently Alick appeared and took Fanny and Israel down and then held Vesta while Sarah dismounted.

"You'll have a corner to yourself and the children," Alick said. "We'll get them fed and put them to bed."

Sarah nodded in gratitude and moved stiffly into the cabin behind the children. Some light came from the one window and there were a number of candles. Some smoke from the fire in the hearth clung to the ceiling and the room had the smell of burnt meat. Sarah saw the German sitting at the lone table near the hearth and eating. Alick took her to a corner of the room sheltered by a bearskin rug and pointed to a bed raised a few inches from the floor. While she helped Fanny and Israel take off their clothes and get ready for bed, Alick put Vesta on a cushion beside the bed and went to the hearth. When the children had crawled under the covers, Alick returned with a plate of food for them— some potatoes, fish, bread—which they ate with their fingers. Sarah washed herself with water from a basin and smoothed back her hair. She took off her coat, laid it over a chair and straightened her dress to try to look presentable. She heard Alick talking with a man with a strange accent, whom she took to be the German. By the time she was ready to eat, her children were asleep. She took the empty plate carefully from the hand of Fanny and decided to return it to the kitchen area. She sensed that Alick wanted her to remain secluded behind the curtain, but she was curious about the inhabitant of the cabin whom Alick appeared to mistrust.

Alick was sitting at the table and talking with the German. A short, wiry man with sharp eyes stood by the stove where he was cooking. He broke into a smile when he saw Sarah approach. Alick looked surprised, and the German quickly got to his feet to bring a chair to the table for her.

"I was bringing a plate to you, Mrs. Kinney," Alick said. "As soon as it was ready."

"Ready!" said the cook, and, slapping fish and potato on a plate, he set it in front of Sarah's chair and took the plate she was carrying.

"Thank you, Mr.—" she paused expectantly.

"Wiler," said the cook. "I own this place and take in travelers, m'am."

"And this is Mr. Braun," Alick said, nodding at the German.

"Pleased," said Mr. Braun, taking Sarah's hand and kissing it. He waited until Sarah sat before re-sitting. He had a powerful-looking frame and a long head with an ingratiating smile.

Sarah smiled at Alick as she began eating. "Please continue your discussion."

"It's about the difficulty of finding settlers," Braun said. "It is a big job to clear land here. Big trees, too big."

"It can be done," said Wiler, settling into a chair at the table. "Little by little."

"Ha, you want business," said Braun, "but people from Germany I bring are poor." He turned to Sarah. "Where does your husband settle?"

Sarah finished swallowing some fish, and Alick replied for her. "Near Cleveland. There's goin' to be a big trading port there one day."

"He's smart," said Wiler, "but it'll put a load on you, Mrs. Kinney. The work's hard."

"I'm not afraid of work," Sarah said.

"Life's all the same," Wiler added. "You gotta love nature the way I do. Do you love nature?"

Alick laughed. "She's not going to be a hermit like you. She's got children to bring up."

"Your little one seems pretty young to be takin' a trip like this,"

113

Wiler observed. "You must a been in a hurry to see your husband again."

Sarah had a momentary fear that she was to be discovered, but she smiled and appeared relaxed. "She's a good baby and travels well."

"I go to Cleveland too," said Braun. "Perhaps we ride together?"

"We leave at dawn tomorrow," Alick said unenthusiastically.

"Better to have company, I think, is that not right?" Braun asked Sarah.

"Yes," Sarah said. "I don't know the dangers, but if we meet any, we would be better to meet them together."

Braun looked satisfied and sat back in his chair. The night had been black for some time and the candles were burning low.

"I go out before dawn," Wiler warned. "Huntin's good then."

"We'll settle now then," Alick said quickly, pulling out a bag of coins.

Sarah said good-night and shook Braun's hand, which he extended to her as if they had come to an agreement. Sarah thought that he missed a woman's company and was looking forward to traveling with her. As she retired behind the bearskin rug, she saw the men go to their cots set against the wall on the other side of the room. In a moment the candles were extinguished, and, hoping that on the morrow they would meet no hardship greater than fatigue, she crawled beside her children .

12

Sarah awoke in the darkness to the sound of feet moving stealthily over the floor boards. She heard the cabin door open and close and remembered that Wiler went hunting early. She lay pondering this fact while listening to the breathing of her children. She heard an occasional snore from one of the men and guessed it was Braun. Then unexpectedly she heard a whisper beside the bearskin that concealed her bed from the rest of the room. She recognized Alick's voice and whispered back.

"We have to get out," Alick said. "Get the children ready. I'll get us breakfast."

Sarah saw a flare of light as he, holding back the bearskin, lit a candle and handed it in to her.

Sarah sensed that his concern had something to do with Wiler, and she awoke Fanny and Israel, who, still sleepy, groggily helped her clothe them. Vesta, disturbed by the activity, began to cry. Sarah picked her up, rocked her, and gave her her breast to suck. When they came to the hearth, which Alick had set alight, Sarah saw Braun sitting on his bed and pulling on his socks and shoes. Alick was stirring porridge and spooning it into bowls for each of them. Sarah put the bowls on the table and found spoons while Alick fetched milk from a box outside the front door.

"Mein Gott!" Braun swore. "There is no light, no dawn yet."

"Ain't had sleep anyways," Alick said. "Put a pan on the floor beside Wiler's bed so when he got up he'd knock against it, in case I dozed off. Sort of a safety alarm."

"Wiler's gone hunting, hasn't he?" Sarah asked.

"He's gone to get his friends who live a couple of miles back in the bush," Alick said.

"You think he wants to rob us?" Braun asked surprised.

"*He* won't do it," Alick said, taking a mouthful of porridge.

"How many men will do it?" asked Braun, still looking surprised, even unbelieving.

"Half a dozen or so," Alick said. "I thought he'd leave us go because of the children. But he sees us as weaker prey, I think."

"That is foolish of him," Braun said. "We have guns."

"You sure?" Alick asked.

Braun stood up and went over to his saddle and equipment which hung on a rack near the door. He began feeling frantically over his equipment and then turning to Alick in shock, he said, "I see what you mean."

"People have disappeared along this trail," Alick warned Braun.

115

"Wiler is one of the loudest complainers, but I suspect him. If he wants to hunt when the animals come out at night, he'd best do it early in the evening. The animals he wants should be back in their beds by now," he smiled at Sarah. "He's not expectin' us to go for another hour or so when it's light. So we'll be ahead of them if we move fast."

Sarah was terrified for her children. Her worried look made Alick try to comfort her.

"I've got a gun," he said. "And they don't like to get hurt. You ride between Mr. Braun and me. Mr. Braun, will you take Israel on your saddle?"

Braun seemed pleased at Alick's trust in him. "Willingly." He smiled at Israel. "We'll keep these bad men away, won't we? I have a long knife in my boot pocket," he said emphatically. "I can use it pretty good."

Sarah felt too nauseous to finish her porridge, but Alick insisted that she eat it as they might not be able to stop for a long time. He went out to saddle the horses.

"Don't be afraid, lady," said Braun. "We can look after you." He stood up and patted her head.

Sarah felt tears spring to her eyes at this man's kindness and blinked them back. "Thank you, Mr. Braun. You are a chivalrous man." She hurried her children to finish eating. Fanny wanted to go to the toilet. Sarah grasped her hand swiftly and took her to the outhouse that stood behind the cabin. They stumbled over stones in the dark.

"Mommy, are we in trouble?" Fanny asked as she sat on the seat. A faint light in the sky was enough for them to make out the shapes of things.

"We'll be in trouble till we get out of this country," Sarah said.

She heard Alick leading the horses from the shed to the cabin, their hooves knocking on shale that broke through the grass beside the cabin, and then a loud cry of exultation. Sarah looked out of the outhouse at Braun brandishing his rifle.

"I have my gun!" he announced to Sarah. "Leaning against the shed." He held it out at arm's length.

"To make you think you left it there," Alick said. "When it gets light, look at it closely. Are we ready, Mrs. Kinney?"

"Fanny!" Sarah said.

"I can't come now," Fanny complained.

"You move out," Alick said. "I'll bring Fanny."

Sarah hesitated and, overcoming her indecision, rushed into the cabin to take Vesta in her arms and return to the horses. Alick took Vesta until Sarah was mounted. Braun, mounted with Israel sitting in front of him, waited for Sarah.

"We do a canter," Braun called, leading the way north.

After they had gone for some time and dawn was breaking, Sarah called out to Braun to stop. She could go no further without Fanny. Braun cried that they could halt at the next stream they saw because the horses needed to drink. Presently they came to a stream that ran between two small rises and passed beside the lane. Braun reined up his horse at a spot where it could step through the trees to reach a small pool of water. He dismounted, lifted Israel to the ground, and helped Sarah dismount by holding Vesta. The sun's rays began to light up the sky.

"Alick is taking too long," Sarah said. "Something must have happened. I want to go back."

"Not yet, m'am," Braun said. "The horses need to be fed so we do it now. We wait. Have patience. He will come." Braun took out the feeding bags, filled them partially with oats from the saddlebag, and, waiting until the horses had had their fill of water, put the bag in front of them. Sarah drank from the stream and watched Israel kneel as she did and take the water in his hands and bring it to his mouth. Walking downstream she bathed Vesta, all the time listening for the sounds of Alick's horse and praying that nothing had happened to him.

Braun began examining his rifle, and, immediately, he cursed in German. "Wiler spiked the barrel," he said to Sarah. "If I had to use it, I could have fired no shot." He took his long knife from a pocket in his boot and began working away at the barrel to bring out the material that had been stuffed into it.

After a few minutes of sitting on a rock, standing, and pacing, Sarah announced that she could wait no longer. "Please, Mr. Braun, keep Israel and Vesta safe while I go back."

"No," Braun shook his head. "I go back. You stay with your children."

"Please, Mr. Braun. I'm too worried to stay here. I must find out what happened." She mounted her horse.

Braun tried to reason with her. "Alick is very capable. He will be here soon. Do not worry."

She spurred her horse back along the trail but had gone no further than a hundred yards when she saw Alick with Fanny galloping towards her. She gasped with relief and turning her horse rode with them back to Braun.

Alick, seeing her concern, told her that he had stopped at a point along the trail where a lesser trail crossed it. He smoothed out any sign of horses' hooves passing along the main trail for about twenty yards and rode his horse along the lesser trail to mislead any persons tracking them. He rode this trail for a while and then crossed through the woods at a spot that he knew would lead him back to the main trail. A tracker would not know which direction he took when he entered the forest. The time it would take them to figure out the truth might discourage them from continuing the pursuit, he said.

Sarah hugged Fanny when Alick lifted her to the ground. As she watched Fanny run to join Israel by the stream, she told herself that she had to have faith in Alick, that she had to control her emotions because she might frighten her children and cause a misstep that could bring disaster on them. Alick, taking his horse to drink from the stream, fished for oats in his saddlebag to feed it. Braun, brandishing his rifle, declared it working again, and he winked at Sarah as if to say that he had been right not to worry.

As soon as Alick's horse had eaten its oats, the party set out at a fast pace. Braun looked truly worried now. His discovery that Wiler had spiked his gun brought him to a sharp recognition of the danger they were in.

Sarah, too, became more anxious the more she thought about their situation. She recalled now that Wiler had been looking at her rather closely during the evening meal, although he pretended to be busy at the stove. She wondered if he had guessed that she was partly Negroid. Probably he had because he had been in the country for years and knew the tell-tale signs of racial make-up whereas Braun, a newcomer, would not have known. Alick's frequent travels on the trail may have raised Wiler's curiosity and, being an opportunist for money, he probably guessed that she and her children were worth the one hundred dollar reward each that was the going rate for bringing in runaways. His small band of robbers would be acting on the side of the law if they refrained from robbery. They would earn four hundred dollars and the gratitude of the slavers by having Alick consigned to prison for years. The problem for them was Braun, who believed they intended to rob him and would put up a fight. By now Wiler would have realized from their early departure that they suspected him and that Braun might have fixed his spiked gun. Would Wiler and his men pursue them still? Sarah glanced back at Alick riding behind her and saw by his self-absorbed expression that he thought the same way and was planning for a defense against them.

The sun was bright and the sky clear of clouds on the warmest day of the spring. The flat ground gave way to rolling hills, which they climbed at a slower pace but still with an urgency. Israel cried to be let down to make his toilet. Alick called out instructing Braun to stop in the little valley ahead of them. Patches of snow clung to the ground. Braun dismounted and took down Israel who looked to his mother to help him.

Alick pointed to a slight path cut into the woods that led to the crest of the highest hill in the area. "It will take me a few minutes," he said.

Sarah nodded and led Israel and Fanny into the trees off the side of the trail. Braun tethered the horses and sat down with Vesta in his lap. Alick climbed the path on his horse, ducked the limbs of trees and guided his chestnut mare, a beautiful animal, which he trusted absolutely, up the old trail that had not been used since the Indians left this region. A few minutes later he came to the summit and, tethering his horse in the trees, he crept out to a ledge that overlooked the flat land they were leaving. He could see for miles, and, because the trees were not yet in foliage, he could make out the lines of the trail here and there. He stayed crouched low so as to keep anyone approaching from seeing him. It took him a full minute to detect movement in the far distance. He could not detect figures, merely the semblance of dots. But they were coming quickly. He ran back to his horse and returned to where he had left the others.

Braun was with the horses, which he was patting and encouraging, while he held Vesta in one arm. Sarah and the other children were still in the woods. Alick told Braun what he had seen. Visibly shaken, Braun asked if they could reach Cleveland before Wiler's men could catch them.

"Not with the children," Alick smiled. "We've got an hour or so to ride, then we'll make a stand." He saw Sarah emerging from the trees with the children and waved for her to hurry. "Don't say a word to Mrs. Kinney."

Sarah sensing their urgency did not need to be told that they were being pursued. She mounted and rode close to Braun to take Vesta from the big man's arm. Braun, looking very serious, mounted his horse, took Israel, whom Alick lifted to place in front of him and led them away at a gallop.

They rode over the rolling hills until the sun fell to half-way in the west. Alick called to them to stop at a particularly steep rise, then quickly transferring Fanny and then Israel to sit in front of Sarah, he told Sarah to continue until she came to a fork in the road. She was to take the right fork for about one hundred yards, then go deep into the forest on her right and wait for him. When Sarah asked what he was going to do, he said, "Stop them," and, giving Sarah's horse a swat on the haunches, watched as she galloped up the hill and out of sight down the other side.

"She's got courage," Braun said, wiping his brow.

"Her horse will have enough wind to make it there," Alick said. "Take a position, on the side of the road. Leave our horses in the trees. Hurry."

Braun nodded and followed him up the rise and into the forest just over the crest, where they tethered their horses and left oats on the ground for them to eat. Taking their guns, they took up positions at the top of the rise behind bushes beside the rutted road, which had been made wider at this point by the numerous efforts to bring wagons up it.

"Their horses should be weakening, considering the detour I sent them on," Alick said. "They'll have been pushing them pretty hard to catch us. I'll give them a shot, then you hit the man on your side."

"Understood," Braun said nervously.

Alick was good with a gun as he had done a lot of hunting for food and had been in battles during the last war. He could kill a man. He knew that Braun had never fired at a human, but the sound of his gun would be a deterrent. Within minutes he heard the hollow sound of horses' hooves. Four riders dashed round a turn in the trail and raced their mounts up the rise. Alick aimed his pistol at the first rider and fired when he was half-way up, hitting him in the left shoulder and watching him spin off his saddle to fall in the path of the second rider whose horse swerved to avoid the man and inadvertently threw its rider. A blast from Braun's gun hit the third rider in the ankle and wounded his horse, which screamed and dashed after the two riderless horses up over the crest of the hill. The fourth rider turned his horse and galloped back down the hill as Alick speedily reloaded his gun with powder and tamped it ready for another shot. As the unseated horse-man was running back down the hill, Alick shot him in the leg, then, shouting to Braun to keep the other from coming up the hill, he ran to the crest and watched the two riderless horses careening far along the trail and the wounded rider clinging helplessly to the back of his wounded animal. He worried that the wounded rider would catch up to Sarah and her children but decided to stick to his plan to make their pursuers retreat. Turning round, he ran down the hill past the first rider, whom he could see was unconscious, to the man he had hit in the leg. Groaning with pain, the man rolled back and forth, and, when he saw Alick approaching, he cried out in terror. Alick grabbed him by the shoulder and threw him flat on the ground. He searched him for a gun but found none. His heavy frightened breathing made Alick look at him closely. He was a boy.

"Where's your gun?"

"Don't have one," the boy whimpered.

"The others?"

"Just two have guns," he said. "We weren't goin' to hurt you."

"Wiler?"

"He's waitin' back in the cabin."

"If you follow us, I'll kill you," Alick said. "Tell your friend to get you back to Wiler. The other fellow may be dead."

Alick started back up the hill and saw Braun taking a gun from the body of the unconscious man lying on the hillside. "Is he dead?" he asked.

"No," Braun called. "He can be saved if he does not bleed to death."

"Hear that?" Alick shouted back to the boy, who, propped on his elbow, watched them.

When they reached the crest of the hill, Alick turned to look back along the trail. The fourth rider had tethered his horse and was running towards the foot of the hill. He had a rifle at the ready. Alick took Braun's rifle and fired at him to scare him into the trees. The wounded boy began shouting at him to help him. Alick returned Braun's rifle to him and led him to their horses.

"Wait a few minutes to see what that fellow does," Alick said. "If he helps his friends, let him be; if he comes after us, shoot him."

Alick spurred his horse onto the trail in pursuit of Sarah.

Sarah, by then, had ridden quite far but her horse was tiring and began to slow its pace. She heard the shots faintly and worried that Alick was hurt. Presently two riderless horses came clambering up from behind her. She moved off the trail to let them pass.

On the trail behind her, the wounded horseman, hobbling about on one foot, stanched the wound in his horse's side with a clean shirt he kept in his saddlebags. He was examining his foot on the side of the trail when Alick rode up. Springing to his feet, he tried to run, but Alick brought his horse alongside and grabbed him by the collar. Alick saw that he was in his early twenties, and, although surlier in expression than the boy, he was terrified.

"What did you want with us?" he demanded.

"It was Mr. Wiler. He said we'd get the reward money for the slaves."

"They're not slaves," Alick hissed. "You fool. Tell Wiler he made a costly mistake. And don't delay," he warned. "You'd make a tasty meal for a cougar."

The tall heavy frame of Braun leaning forward on his galloping horse appeared then and drew up beside them. Still holding the boy by his collar, Alick half-lifted him over the ground to the wounded horse and helped him mount into the saddle. "Better change your ways," Alick suggested. "Tell Wiler I'll settle with him when I come back."

"But he swore they were slaves," the young man cried. "It weren't our fault."

Alick swatted the boy's horse on the flank and watched it start with a jump and then painfully make its way back along the trail.

Braun stared in amazement at Alick. "Slaves?"

"No, they're wrong," Alick laughed.

Braun looked after the wounded rider. He sensed that Alick was hiding the truth. Surely, he thought, only the large reward for capturing runaway slaves together with an ideological conviction could have caused these young men to have risked their lives pursuing them. If Alick was lying, of what further deceit was he capable? Braun kept his face expressionless to conceal his apprehension as he rode behind Alick.

Alick called back to him. "Can we catch Mrs. Kinney? Does your animal have enough in it?"

"Just," Braun said, patting his horse's neck.

Alick urged his horse into a run. Braun, fearing that he was being used to help slaves escape and pondering his moral position, followed glumly. They closed the distance between them and Sarah within a half hour. She had come to the fork in the road and was riding slowly up the right lane when Alick called out to her. She swung her horse about happily, and, with the children waving, returned to follow the other lane towards Cleveland. Braun took Israel back on his saddle but looked at the little boy differently. Alick placed Fanny on his saddle. A few hundred yards further along, they discovered the two runaway horses in a clearing off the trail where they were drinking in some marshy ground. Alick rode over to them and took their reins. They let him lead them onto the trail at a slow pace and onto the next rise where he suggested they spend the night.

Alick picked a bluff overlooking the way they had come. Braun took their exhausted horses to a stream in the woods while Sarah clothed the children for the cold night and Alick cut pine branches from the forest to make beds for them all. Sarah, more apprehensive than ever about the dangers ahead, prepared dried meat and Braun brought fresh water from the stream. Fanny looked after Vesta while Israel helped his mother lay the pine boughs and then ran over to Alick to throw sticks on the fire he was building. They worked quickly without saying a word as the sun was falling behind the horizon and the dark cold fell upon them.

Tethering their horses near the little encampment, Alick mentioned something about a lucky star and ate his meal in silence while he looked at Sarah and her children with an admiring half-smile. Too tired to talk, they retreated into the pine boughs, watched the fire leap within a circle of stones that Alick had constructed around it, and fell asleep, the distant howls of wolves faintly resounding in their consciousness.

Braun, however, could not sleep. Ingrained in him since his youth was an obedience to the law. That he should be helping slaves to escape, regardless how unwittingly, troubled him deeply. He could see the Negro aspects of Sarah's physiognomy and traces of Negro ancestry in her white children now that he suspected them. They had put his life in danger with thoughts only for their own safety. Alick became a desperado in his mind, far worse than Wiler or any of the town wardens and sheriffs who upheld the law by capturing runaway slaves. If Alick suspected what he was thinking, he might kill him. The sweet children, the dutiful wife anxious to join her husband and her faithful servant suddenly looked devious and threatening. What hurt him was that he had become fond of them at the very time that they were lying to him. But what could he do? What should he do? He could wait for an opportunity to warn a sheriff. The return of the family to their owner would salve his conscience for any part he had in the escape. He admitted that being in the country for just a few months and witnessing none of the mistreatment of slaves that was reported in Europe—stories that he thought were exaggerated—made him a bad judge. Moreover, Alick could cause him trouble. The man was fearless and resourceful—a match for any sheriff. He felt uneasy about betraying him. Alick could be hanged. There was no doubting his dedication to Sarah and her flight from slavery. Yet Braun believed in a smooth-running, law-abiding society, which if slavery were integral to it, then slavery had to be respected. He was in a dilemma. His head ached with indecision. He calmed his mind and willed himself to fall asleep.

13

Sarah awakened to the crackling sound of the campfire. Alick was feeding the flames with branches. Braun was preparing breakfast in a pot near-by. The first streaks of dawn were just touching the sky. She glanced at her children to see that they were still asleep, then stood up and walked into the woods. Braun called after her that there was a stream to her right. She located it and washed herself, the cold water chilling her to the bone. When she returned, the food was ready. She awakened Fanny and Israel and brought them to the fire, where Braun handed them bowls of porridge. Sarah let Vesta sleep on; the poor child had withstood the punishment of the journey without complaint.

"You look rested, lady," Braun ventured to break the silence.

"Yes, Mr. Braun, so do you," Sarah smiled. "I hope we have a nicer day today."

"We can go slowly," Alick said.

"What do we do with the horses we have from those thieves?" Braun asked. "Turn them over to a sheriff?"

"Don't talk of what happened," Alick warned him. "Keep the law out of it. We don't want to be drawn into a long legal proceeding."

"Understood," Braun nodded and thought how disinclined Alick was to meet the law.

"I'll take the horses and deal with those boys personally," Alick said bitterly. "You can never get settlers here with the likes of them causing trouble."

"With enough settlers, the thieves will disappear," Braun predicted.

"This country is pretty complex," Alick said. "What's right and

125

wrong is still being sorted out, but more settlers will bring peace, I expect."

"Are we gonna have peace today?" Sarah asked anxiously. "Any more trouble?"

"No, Mrs. Kinney," Alick laughed. "No more trouble expected. But for the unexpected, that's another question."

"Come children," Sarah called and took them by the hand. "We're goin' to wash up to prepare us for the unexpected."

Braun remarked on Sarah's self-control when faced with danger. She was the calmest lady he had ever met. Her love for her children moved him. He wondered what could have driven them to escape, to risk the terrible penalties.

Alick finished packing the saddlebags, and, after throwing dirt on the fire, approached Braun with a curious look. "Are you feeling all right?"

Braun snapped out of his reverie. "Yes. I was thinking of differences in this country from my own. It will be hard for Germans to adapt but some will be glad to be rid of restrictions—especially the lower classes who will be colonizing here."

Alick looked askance at him. "I guess you have a sort of slavery there."

Braun agreed. "It takes different forms according to the country, but we all obey the laws of property."

"Humans are not property," Alick said sharply.

At that moment Sarah returned with the children and they all mounted and set out on the trail. with Alick holding the reins of the two riderless horses. Braun, taking up the rear, divined that Alick's alluding to slavery meant that he had been reading Braun's thoughts, or was he imagining it? They rode in silence, broken by the sudden cry of the children at colourful birds that sprang forth from bushes and trees and by the fitful cry of the baby from time to time. About noon, Alick stopped suddenly and raised his arm. He turned his mount about and lifting Fanny under her arms set her on the ground.

"There's men ahead camped by the trail," he said in alarm. "Bounty hunters." He glanced at Sarah. "Get back in the woods till I return."

"I'll come," Braun offered. "You'll be safer with two."

Alick reflected a second. "Good. Here, Mrs. Kinney, take these horses to the base of that big tree over there."

Sarah, hushing her children's questioning, seized the horses' reins and rode with Vesta into the woods, followed by Fanny holding the hand of Israel. The words "bounty hunters" terrified her. Dismounting she gave Vesta to Fanny and tethered the three horses to the branches of the tree. Taking the sleeping Vesta in one arm and holding Israel's hand with the other, she took her children deeper into the woods while Fanny happily ran ahead to blaze a path through the underbrush. Their helplessness overwhelmed her. If Israel and Fanny could ride, she would have used the horses to flee their danger. How hopelessly vulnerable they were hiding behind bushes from men who could pick them out of the woods like berries off a bush. She crouched with her children as if playing a game while she pictured Alick and Braun confronting the bounty hunters.

Two bounty hunters were so intent on punishing two runaway slaves, they did not see Alick and Braun approaching. A young black man, spread-eagled against a tree, his arms outstretched and bound by the wrists to branches and his ankles bound, showed deep lash wounds on his back from which blood ran down to his waist and into his ragged trousers. The young woman was lying with her knees drawn up and her arms bound behind her back. She was naked and sobbing piteously. From the cunning and amused expression of the man near her, it appeared that he had just finished raping her. The other man, a bull whip in his hand, turned to stare angrily at their visitors.

Braun's face revealed the horror and revulsion he felt, but Alick looked unconcerned. Braun noted that the prisoners were black-skinned whereas the bounty hunters were brown, the same colour as Alick. If Alick had not called these brutal men "bounty hunters", he would have thought them murderous brigands.

"Where did ya get him?" Alick asked with a friendly smile. "Cleveland?"

"Hell no! We got them in Canada," the man with the bull whip shouted as if he were challenging Alick. "What's it matter to you?"

"We're lookin' for a couple," Alick said.

"These are ours. Bin trackin' 'em for three months. The little bastards were livin' in a cabin thinkin' they were free," the man laughed, giving another lash to the Negro, who groaned.

"Didn't you get stopped?" Alick asked as if surprised.

The man with the bull whip rubbed his fingers with his thumb to suggest that they bribed the authorities.

"We never been stopped yet," the other man cried hoarsely and chuckled.

"So, we can steal 'em out of Canada then," Alick smiled. "Sounds easy. We're movin' on." He spurred his horse and signaled to Braun to follow.

"Good huntin'," rasped the hoarse-voiced man as he took the bull whip from his friend and told the woman to stop crying or he'd whip her.

Turning a bend in the trail, Alick reined in his horse and said to Braun, "What do you think?"

Braun, his face ashen, muttered, "Beasts!"

"That's slavery," Alick said grimly. "That poor man and his wife will be tortured worse by their owners."

"Can we save them?" Braun asked.

Alick looked him in the eye. "Mrs. Kinney and her children are escaping slavery. I could not tell you before, but I need your help now. Once these hunters see her, they'll know she's a slave. They'll kill us to get her." He paused to let Braun consider his words. "You can go on alone and leave this business to me."

Braun was tempted to flee and take ship from Cleveland out of this violent land, but, seeing Alick's determination, he could not desert him. He was obliged to protect Sarah and her children from these violent men. All his concerns about property collapsed when confronted with the inhumanity he witnessed. "I am by your side," he said.

Alick nodded as if he expected no less. "If we don't kill them, they'll kill us. They're thinking now that we'll come back, but later. If we catch them before they have the slaves ready to walk, we have a good chance. Besides, we have to go back for Mrs. Kinney."

Braun looked frightened. "What do I do?"

"Stay behind me, keep your rifle ready, and shoot whoever shoots at me."

"Understood," Braun said, taking out his rifle.

As Alick suspected the hunters were hurriedly trying to leave as he rode upon them. The male slave, freed from the tree, had his hands tied by a rope held by one of the hunters as he mounted his horse. The woman could not stand and, despite the frantic threats of her captor, who wanted her to run behind his horse, she collapsed, delaying them.

Alick, pistol at the ready, saw the mounted man swing round with a short rifle aimed at him. Just as the man fired, the slave pulled sharply on the rope, which the man held in his other hand, and the shot went wild. The man's horse reeled at the noise and threw its rider who fell on his back. The other hunter dropped the rope holding the woman and spurred his horse, but Alick was upon him quickly and fired into his back at a short distance. Braun rode upon the first man as he struggled to get up, and, swinging his rifle, clubbed him with the butt end. The slave leaped on the fallen man, pulled a dagger from the man's belt and stabbed him through the heart. Running to the woman still stretched on the ground, the slave enfolded her in his arms and together they wept while Braun watched, commiserating with them from his mount standing stock-still in the long grass. Alick, loading his pistol as he rode, caught the other man's horse when it came to an obedient halt near to Sarah's hiding place.

"Mrs. Kinney!" Alick called.

Sarah, clutching Vesta, crept from the bushes apprehensively. Isaac, laughing, ran ahead of Fanny who was trying to catch him. Sarah untethered the horses and led them onto the trail followed by the children still playing, oblivious of danger. Lifting Fanny and Israel to Alick, who sat them in front of him, and giving him Vesta to hold, she tied the riderless horses to the saddle of her horse, and nervously rode it after Alick. They found Braun kneeling beside the slave as he cut the rope binding the slave's hands. Regardless how accustomed Sarah was to violence, she dreaded coming upon the dead. Her poor children, she thought, when could they ever find peace?

Sarah dismounted and, leaving Vesta and Israel in Fanny's care, went to the woman and coaxed her to stop sobbing. Alick, lifting one of the bodies by the arm, asked Braun to lift the legs; they carried him

129

deep into the woods, and, returning for the second body, carried it to the same place. They stripped them of their clothes and boots and gave them to the escaped slaves. Alick said that wild beasts would devour them during the night. He picked up the short rifle dropped by the hunter and gave it to the Negro.

"Keep this. You and your wife ride with us."

The slave, stunned by his good fortune, nodded humbly.

Sarah, reviving the woman, helped her dress in the hunters' clothes while Braun brought the hunters' horses to the male slave, whose name he learned was Fields.

Alick, hurrying to leave and urging the Fields to mount, led the way along the trail. After an hour, Mrs. Fields seemed on the verge of toppling off her horse. Alick led them into a narrow valley to a stream out of sight of the trail where they camped for the night.

"We'll get to Cleveland tomorrow," he told Sarah. "More traffic, so we have to be careful."

The Fields went directly to the stream to wash the blood from their clothes and bathe their bruised bodies. Braun and Alick lit a fire and gathered branches for bedding. Sarah prepared their meal using the food she found in the hunters' saddlebags. The horses grazed the new grass. During the night, the dead bounty hunters haunted Braun's dreams and he awoke several times in a sweat to hear the soft rippling of the stream in the darkness, broken now and then by the gruntings of beasts prowling the forest. By morning, the Fields seemed transformed; their eyes shone with expectation and there was energy in their movements.

Sarah tried to restore Mrs. Fields' confidence in herself before they left. She regarded the Fields as an object lesson. Even a supposedly safe haven in a slave-free country did not guarantee freedom permanently. She harboured that fact at the back of her mind and resolved never to slacken her alertness for danger.

Field looked like a cowboy in the clothes of his former bounty hunter and his wife, dressed in shirt and trousers, could pass as his boy-helper. Although the slim Field winced with pain from his wounds when he moved abruptly, he took the reins of the riderless horses cheerfully

130

and brought up the rear of the line moving at a moderate trot. His wife, trying to appear relaxed in the saddle, rode in front of him. Occasionally they met riders and farmers driving carts on their way to outlying farms. Sarah saw by the looks on the farmers' faces that they regarded this array of armed riders as formidable, and she smiled in reply to their exceedingly polite greetings. The sun rose to its meridian when they rode past the cleared acres of farms on the outskirts of the village.

Cleveland, incorporated as a village in 1815 and just emerging from its log cabin stage to stone houses in 1820, was a major port of departure for runaways. Alick told her that hundreds of escape routes led to it; slaves arrived in wagons under bales of hay, or came alone with no guide other than the north star.

Sarah felt a surge of relief as they rode over a plank road leading from the outskirts to the village centre and log cabins gave way to houses. Many lots were cleared ready for dwellings. Stumps littered the landscape. Pigs wandered freely in the streets, which were largely made of mud but a few were lined with logs. Carriages and wagons driven by men intent on their business passed by them and pedestrians hurried along the streets. They came to a hill overlooking Lake Erie. Sarah gazed over the seemingly limitless expanse of water with wonder. As they approached a large house with a sign "Inn" hanging from it, Braun took his leave. He turned over Israel to Sarah and kissed her hand. He thanked Alick warmly for his company and his wisdom. "I might be dead if it was not for you," he said.

"Likewise," Alick smiled.

Braun shook hands with the Fields and wished them well, and they, nervously looking about them, smiled slightly at him.

Sarah and the children waved to Braun as he watched them ride west towards the Cuyahoga River. A narrow floating bridge of whitewood timber that crossed over to Ohio City was pulled aside to let boat traffic move up river. As they waited for it to be drawn back, Alick pointed to the Trinity Episcopalian Church, a whitewashed structure standing back from the river and high on a hill. Sarah looked at it with tears in her eyes. Again the kind expression of the Reverend Joseph Doddridge came to her mind, and she hugged Israel close to her with one arm and held Vesta tighter with the other. Whatever hardship lay before her was many times better than what she left, she thought. A sense of promise infused her with new energy. She smiled at Fanny, seated in front of Alick. Fanny, seeing the joy in her mother's eyes, clasped her hands tightly and held them under her chin in an expression of hope.

The bridge swung back and they crossed over. It was mid-afternoon. People were in the streets: men in homespun cloth with sheepskin overlaying the seat of their pants for longer wear, and women in brightly colored calico frocks, with bonnets looking like a parson's wig, and stout cowhide shoes. They showed no interest in Sarah and her children as it was a common sight to see immigrants move through the town's streets bound for elsewhere. As Sarah approached the Church, she saw a tall, thin man in clerical robes run down the road to greet them. He was young and intense and his face beamed with pleasure.

"You are safe! Praise be to God! I was worried," the young man confessed to Alick as he helped Sarah and Fanny dismount.

"Some trouble we shall speak of later," Alick smiled. "This is Mrs. Lewis and her children. Mrs. Lewis, this is the Reverend Chains."

"So good to see you," Chains cried happily. He reached up and took Israel down off the horse. "And you, young man, must be tired."

"We saw robbers," Israel said. "We run."

"So would I," Chains laughed.

Alick introduced the Fields. "They want to be on the boat for Canada that leaves in a half-hour," he added.

"We heard about you!" Chains exclaimed. "Where are your captors."

"We left them in the bush," Alick said quickly. "We must go now quickly."

"Oh Alick!" Sarah cried, and reached up to clasp his arms. "I thank you with all my soul. Stay safe. I'll pray for you."

"I hope you have a wonderful life in Canada," Alick said, moved by her emotional farewell.

Fanny blew him a kiss and Israel, leaving the minister, ran up to Alick and thrust out his little hand which Alick, reaching down from his mount, smilingly shook. Alick was touched, and, as he turned away, his eyes glowed at Chains as if to say that these people were special.

Sarah clasped Mrs. Fields' hands and smiled at Fields, who, impatient to depart, called for his wife to follow Alick to the stables at the back of the church, to leave off the riderless horses before going to the Cleveland docks. The minister cradling Vesta led the way through the front door of the church, a long, log cabin with a huge fireplace at one end near the altar, to a small room with tables and chairs. He explained, since most Clevelanders were pro-slavery, for safety reasons they would have to wait for nightfall before going to a safe house in the country.

"News of your escape has reached this place, I'm afraid," he said sympathetically, "thanks to the Wellsburg papers. We think that your owner won't look for you this far north for some time. So we're making arrangements, which I have begun."

"Can we leave for Canada?" Sarah asked hopefully.

"On no, my dear Mrs. Lewis. The ships are watched. We have to wait." He lay a hand on her shoulder to comfort her. "But take courage. You have come far and have only a little way to go."

Sarah bowed her head as she prepared to meet setbacks and difficulties to come, but, thankful for the young man's concern, she raised her head and smiled at him to show her gratitude.

"We keep runaways here for another reason too," Chains explained. "Many are traumatized by slavery and have to be taught to be independent and to find themselves as men and women. This can take time. But, in your case," he smiled, "I see you can fend for yourself."

"I can try," Sarah said. "I've been acting like a white woman. Do you want me to continue?"

"We want you to be yourself," Chains said. "That depends on your surroundings, I know, but you don't have to pretend anymore. Just be yourself."

Sarah felt a burden fall off her shoulders at Chains' words. She knew who she was but she had little contact with herself in the past several years. She did not know if she ever again would find the true person in her. After her servile positions where she would take any submissive attitude to escape punishment for herself and her children, she wondered how she could become more assertive in the world she was going into. She knew that she had to think and fend for herself from now on; all that took a confidence and a courage that she would have to develop. Hearing bursts of laughter from her children playing between the pews of the church, she hushed them and quickly took Vesta from Chains as the infant began wetting her clothing.

The children were hungry. Chains kept them occupied by teaching them the alphabet. When Chains left to arrange for the disposal of the horses left by Alick in the church stables, he warned them to remain as quiet as possible. Vesta began to cough. Sarah worried that their next refuge would be cold and clammy like the church. Eventually Chains returned accompanied by a man in his thirties with a sensitive face.

"This is Thad, Sarah. He's a farmer," Chains said. "He'll keep you safe."

Sarah felt comforted right away by the man's warm personality. As they stood talking, Thad noticed the cough and pale look of Vesta, and, taking a closer look at her, he suggested that they leave immediately in his carriage. Chains assured Sarah that he would see her in a month, if he was certain that no one was on the look-out for her. Sarah feared that with every day she remained in Ohio the risk of being caught increased, but she told herself to trust in these people because they were putting their welfare and perhaps their lives in jeopardy protecting her.

Thad's farm was about half an hour away on a high point of land overlooking Lake Erie. He told Sarah that he was giving her a cabin in the woods several hundred yards behind his house where she and her children would be safe. He and his wife had lived there while they built their house.

A long winding trail led from the road to his home. Thad stopped the carriage by the stables behind the house and led Sarah and the children directly to the cabin, light from which Sarah could see winking at her in the dark. When she entered, the warmth from the fire and the comfortable furnishings gave her the impression of the home that she had always wanted, and, suppressing her surprise, she took the hands of Thad's wife, a tall slim woman with black hair whose name was Susan. Sarah sensed an empathy between them, and, feeling

134

secure at last, she sank upon the nearest chair to let out a sob of relief and all her pent-up tension. Fanny and Israel stood awkwardly watching their mother's crying until Thad stepped to them to steer them by the shoulders to the meal on the table near the fire that Susan had prepared. Susan, taking Vesta, comforted her. In a few moments Sarah regained her composure and went to a small mirror by the sink to look at her face and begin washing away the tears and the grime from the long trip. Thad whispered to Susan what he suspected about Vesta. Susan quickly poured some hot water from the stove into a bottle, which she wrapped in a cloth and inserted next to Vesta's body. She felt Vesta's forehead and carrying her to a cradle in the room mixed cold and hot water in a vessel. She washed Vesta, dried her, and suggested that Sarah give her milk right then. As Sarah fed Vesta, Thad left the women to put away his horse and carriage. Susan said that Vesta had measles, and the other children were bound to get the disease.

"Just as well," Sarah said resignedly with a twinkle in her eye, "that we're stayin' in one place for a month."

During that month, the children recovered from measles without ill effect. Sarah rejoiced in the warming spring, the greening of the trees and the flights of colorful birds which migrated over Lake Erie via the long arch of land that reached far out into the lake from the Canadian side which people called Long Point. The cheerful singing of the birds and the restful time she spent with Thad and Susan made her optimistic about the future. Susan, who had lived for a time in Canada, said Sarah could meet prejudice there, but it was scattered and minor. She told of black settlements where freemen organizations had purchased blocks of land in which Sarah might find employment and there were Negroes who had bought their own land or had received grants for services in the Revolutionary War and the War of 1812. A large settlement of blacks was at Sandwich and some were dispersed eastward along the Detroit River to Amherstburg. These runaways had come from the States in the Southwest to cross the Detroit River because of the short distance between the shores. Many came from Kentucky and started growing tobacco in Canada where the soil was particularly good for the plant. The Reverend Chains, Susan said, usually tried to find work for runaways in that region first.

Thad came in the evenings after supper to amuse Fanny and Israel with learning the alphabet. By the end of a month Fanny had learned to read a bit and was writing. Israel was slower but he knew the alphabet. Sarah was pleased by the progress of her children and began to notice changes in herself brought about, she thought, by her friendship with Susan. The years of dependency that had formed her way of thinking and kept her feeling inferior and incapable of developing herself seemed to drop away from her spirit. She began to find through her acceptance by Susan a new confidence in herself and a certain pride in the way she looked. Susan taught her to dress well and gave her some of her clothes. Although Sarah knew the table manners of white households, she had no reason to maintain those standards at her own table. Now, all that was changing. Susan gave her a reason for improving herself and for encouraging her children to learn. Sarah understood now what self-dependence meant.

When Thad came with a warning that two men had been asking questions in Cleveland about an escaped slave and her three children Sarah's fear of capture gripped her more strongly than at any time during her flight because, having tasted freedom, she understood better its loss. The men moved eastward along the lake after a week. Since Samuel and his men had no idea in which direction Sarah had gone, they visited ports at random along the Erie shore in hopes of catching some lucky lead. After six weeks as summer approached, the Reverend Chains asked Thad to bring the Lewis family to his church early one morning. Sarah was giddy with expectation but her sorrowful departure from Susan, whom she would never see again, was the most emotional moment of her escape. The children were unhappy at leaving; not only had they enjoyed the freedom of the woods in the spring, but they knew they would miss the gentle Thad who taught them interesting things. Thad hugged them when they said good-bye. A short, cigar smoking, quick-talking fellow, Alfred Benoit, was entrusted with escorting Sarah and her children on a lake boat from Cleveland to The Ferry, across from Detroit. There was almost no time for introductions. Chains waved to Sarah as Benoit sat with her and the children in a large carriage driven by a well-dressed driver, giving the impression of a monied family taking an outing. They crossed the narrow Cuyahoga River and were soon at the Cleveland wharf. Benoit gave instructions to the driver to take Sarah and the children aboard the vessel, its high sails flapping in the breeze from off the lake, while he went to the purser standing on the wharf to discuss details such as when meals would be brought to their cabin. Sarah, controlling her excitement, entered a small cabin with a window looking out on the deck. Fanny and Israel excitedly sat on the bench by the window, and Sarah sat back on a settee with Vesta. In a few moments Benoit stepped into the cabin and smilingly suggested that she and the children stay there for the voyage. He would be on deck should Sarah need him. The captain, he said, was aware of their presence and would be of help should any difficulties arise. The day was sunny and warm and there was a good wind, which meant that travel would be swift. Within minutes, the gangplank was raised. The drift of the ship into the lake felt like a release, as if cords of rope about her heart and mind were falling away and disintegrating.

Sarah watched passengers walk on the deck and stand by the railing. The sights and sounds from outside intrigued her children, who begged to run out free with the children they saw from their window perch, but Sarah, fearful that their antics might draw attention to them, refused to let them go. At noonday, a steward, dressed in a white coat, knocked on the door and handed a tray of sandwiches and coffee to Sarah when she opened it. As Sarah and the children were eating, Benoit came in to see how they were getting along. He said that they were now in Canadian waters and, if the winds remained strong, they would be on shore in a couple of hours. Sarah felt like laughing for joy. She called to her children and put her arms about them in silent prayer. Benoit, pleased by the happiness, winked and nodded and went back on deck.

To make herself and her children presentable to fit the occasion of entering a new country, Sarah left the cabin with the children and asked a steward passing on deck where she would find the rest rooms. He led her down some steps and along a hallway to the ladies' rooms in which Sarah encountered the most beautiful surroundings she had ever seen. The marble of the sinks and the rich look of the polished wood and the upholstered furniture were like a fantasy. She took the children into a cabinet where she encouraged them to make their toilet while she bathed Vesta in the sink and then washed herself. As she regarded herself in a full-length mirror, the clothes she was given by Susan, although not new, transformed her from a menial to a lady, she thought.

When they returned to the deck, she sought out a deck chair where she sat with Vesta while she watched Fanny and Israel run along the deck and make friends with a few other children who were playing at hide and seek. This was an act of self-assertion, something she could never have done before. She felt that she was entering a free world, that she could now become a true person and expect to be treated as everyone else was treated, with respect. She looked over the blue waters, felt the warm sun on her face and hands and breathed in the soft breezes that filled the sails and carried the ship along to her goal. Looking back over her escape, she remembered with what hope she had begun it, a desperate hope and a faith in the wisdom of the Reverend Doddridge and George Brown. Whatever happened to her from now, she owed it to those men to do as well as she possibly could and she owed it to her children whose patience and obedience had made their escape easier. As some passengers walked by her chair engrossed in conversation she automatically bowed her head to escape detection, and then, angry at herself, she looked up and stared straight before her. She saw a low-lying strip of land in the distance. And slightly to the left, the sun was sinking and getting brighter and redder as the ship, passing between Bois Blanc Island and the Canadian shore, came into the Detroit River. Sarah could see people in the streets of Amherstburg going about their business and the cabins and log houses and the spires of the Churches. Benoit came to stand at the rail beside her and pointed out certain buildings in Sandwich, the public buildings, the mansions of the wealthy merchants, and the large quarter where runaway slaves had congregated. It was in that quarter that she would find her employer, he said, a black man named McGregor. He owned a tavern and served settlers from miles around. In fact, his tavern was a popular meeting place for traders from other parts of the country.

Sarah would be cooking for him.

Sarah looked at Benoit in surprise. "Did Reverend Chains do this for me?"

"Indeed, he did," Benoit smiled. "But I helped. I've known McGregor for some time."

Sarah welcomed work at which she was talented, but felt uneasy about working for a black man, an escaped slave like her. She had always cooked for whites and depended on her skill and her light skin to retain her position as a household slave. How would this McGregor receive her? She suppressed her doubts and thanked Benoit for giving her a good start in her new life.

The harbour swarmed with small craft. There were sailing vessels of all sizes moored along the river. The passenger boat docked alongside a long pier extending into the river. Benoit helped Sarah and her children off the ship and escorted them into the first carriage in line awaiting the departing passengers. They drove along the shore over rough mud streets to McGregor's tavern, a low-lying log building, to which a two-story cabin was joined. It was dinner time, and, as Sarah entered, she saw men and women, blacks and whites, sitting at tables, eating, while waiters ran balancing trays of food to some destination in that crowd. The noise of human voices rising in exuberation was unlike anything she had experienced. A heavy-set man of about six foot five with skin as black as coal moved from the bar as soon as he saw them enter. He approached them with a broad engaging smile and held out his hand to Benoit, who allowed his small white hand to be enveloped in it.

"Mrs. Lewis," the man said happily. "I need you worse'n a cart needs a wheel."

"This is McGregor," Benoit said to Sarah. "I'm leaving you with a good man." He nodded good-bye with a polite smile.

McGregor nodded in return and looked first at Vesta in her arms and then down at Fanny and Israel, who were holding onto Sarah's dress. "You got nice white kids, Mrs. Lewis," he said, sounding surprised, and reached out to caress Fanny's cheek. "You got a first name, Mrs. Lewis?"

"My name is Sarah. I'm ready to start when you want me."

McGregor nodded amiably. "Tomorrow morning at five o'clock will suit me. Take your kids to the kitchen and we will take you to your room after you eat. As I said, I need a good cook, Sarah. Glad to have you." McGregor beckoned to a mulatto girl in her teens to take Sarah and the children to the kitchen. "Feed 'em well," he laughed. "They's come from a place that underfed 'em for years. Ain't that so?" he asked Sarah.

"That's so," Sarah smiled, and, pushing the children before her, followed the young girl to a back room of the tavern.

The girl led them through the kitchen, where two women huddling over a stove fussed about meat that was smoking, to a small room leading off the back. There Sarah put Vesta into a chair and let her arms hang to relieve them of the pressure of having to carry the baby everywhere. Fanny and Israel sat at the table and hungrily watched the girl put meat and bread on their plates.

So, Sarah thought, this was to be the centre of her life. McGregor seemed pleasant but she sensed that he would be demanding as an employer. What she would be paid and how many hours a day she worked were questions that seemed of no concern to him. Perhaps that was how the system worked, she thought. Perhaps all these particulars would be revealed eventually. After all, she was new, and, if Susan had not schooled her in the wage system, she would have been ignorant. She wondered if McGregor was taking advantage of her in supposing that she was so happy to be free that she would accept work on any terms. Susan had warned her not to exchange feudal slavery for wage slavery. But then, with the smell of good food in her nostrils and the happy laughter of her children in her ears, she began to rejoice in her new station in life—a free woman. The words sounded sweet. She repeated them to herself and, then with sudden resolve, went to the table to eat the dinner that awaited her.

The room she was given on the second floor of the cabin was as small as any that she had known. But she looked on it as a beginning from whence she would create her individuality and her own property. As soon as it was dark, she went to bed with her children and watched them sleep as she listened to the voices drift up from the tavern below. Presently all sounds ceased and she fell asleep.

Rising early was natural for her. She made an impression with her cooking, and soon McGregor's Tavern was attracting more clientele as word got around. She worked till the mid-day meal was finished, then had three hours to herself before she prepared the evening meal. The dishes and cleaning up were done by two young mulatto girls who also had escaped. All the runaways she met in Sandwich had interesting stories to tell but they were careful about concealing who had helped them, if anyone. Sarah had had the most help, she thought; many of the others had come through the wilderness, eating berries, stealing from settlements, traveling only at night, experiencing narrow escapes from suspicious farmers or pursuing slavers. Sarah began meeting both white and black customers at the tavern when she brought in their food, and she marveled how easily they got along. As for the welfare of her children, she left Vesta and Israel in Fanny's care. Fanny took her responsibilities seriously, but, when the fall came, she begged her mother to be allowed to attend a school that a black preacher had opened in the settlement. Sarah kept Vesta with her in the kitchen while Fanny went with Israel to the schoolroom for two hours every morning. When she saw the happy look in her children's eyes, she praised God for bringing her safely to this new land. For this reason, she was reluctant to speak to McGregor about payment for her work. McGregor seemed to imply that the board and lodging he was providing for her and her children was sufficient.

It was not until she met Benoit by accident one afternoon that McGregor had to deal with the matter of a wage. Sarah was walking down to the riverside to watch the boat traffic and look across at Detroit, so peaceful and pretty in its wide boulevards and tree-lined streets yet full of hidden danger, as if a sleeping serpent might awaken and shoot its venom into unsuspecting citizens. Benoit, walking towards her, doffed his hat and asked about her work; only then could she bring herself to ask about payment. Benoit looked astonished, and then, smiling, he assured her that he would look into the matter. The next day, McGregor, displeased, came to her after breakfast was finished. His tall hulking figure, which when combined with his menacing, glowering look, intimidated the rowdier patrons of the tavern, towered over Sarah like a tree.

141

"You don't think I give you enough?" he asked. "You got cause to complain?"

Sarah knew that if she was to survive in her new surroundings, she had to be assertive. Now was not the time to back down. "You're not paying me," she said. "I can't buy new clothes for myself and my children. I can't save money for my future."

McGregor nodded, sourly acknowledging her words. "Mr. Benoit said you spoke to him. You have problems after this, you speak to me. Do you understand?"

"It's not that I'm not grateful to you, Mr. McGregor, but I do good work and I don't see any reward."

McGregor cleared his throat. "I was just testing you to see how'd you work out. You're doing okay. So now I'll pay you. If you do better, I'll pay you more. That okay, Sarah?"

"That's just fine," Sarah smiled. "Will that include back pay?"

McGregor frowned, then throwing back his head, he laughed, "You're catchin' on fast. I'll give you somethin'," he said, "but don't press me on it."

Sarah watched him retreat from the kitchen in a more humble manner than he entered it. She was proud of herself.

With the small earnings she received, Sarah was able to buy a few clothes for the children and the few items that Fanny needed for school. Her cooking became well known. After six months, McGregor increased her payment a little. Sandwich was the centre of commerce in the region. All ships traveling down the Thames River through Chatham and into Lake Erie stopped there. It was a major port for trade along both sides of Lake Erie. The roads inland were in very poor shape so that all commerce went by rivers and lakes.

Sarah began making friends in the community. She could dress for church now. When she visited the farms of people she met in the church, both white and black, she no longer felt ashamed of her clothes. McGregor hired a cooking helper for her and this gave her more time to herself eventually. But she had to be careful. Bounty hunters could trap runaways at any time and take them bound back to the States. There were no police to prevent such kidnappings, although it was against the law. Groups of vigilantes watched out for the Americans and rescued runaways from their clutches, but they could not always be successful. Sarah worried about her children, and, aside from attending school, made them stay close to the tavern. The swarms of people coming and going in such a busy port made the spying out and capture of people easier than in a quieter place. For this reason, Sarah and her benefactors did not let news of her whereabouts go back to her relatives in Virginia.

She knew little about the communities forming outside of Sandwich and Amherstburg and considered moving to them beyond her capabilities. She met men who came to eat at the tavern but cared for none of them. Although still beautiful and desirable, she had a brood of children who few men would want to support. Many men, however, wanted to share her bed, but she could not be bribed with money or presents. Her sexual appetites were strong, but she controlled them until one evening, when a waiter did not come to work and she had to take food to the tables, she encountered a young Scotsman. The attraction between them registered immediately. She knew better than he that their meeting would be consequential, if she allowed it to develop. He ordered a large dinner and remained drinking beer after the other diners had gone. Sarah felt his eyes follow her when she returned to the kitchen and sensed that he was trying to work up the courage to proposition her. She guessed that he was at least ten years younger, but he was so good-looking that she could no longer drive thoughts of love from her mind. When McGregor locked the doors to the tavern and informed the young man that he would have to leave on finishing his beer, the Scotsman seemed surprised that he was the lone patron. McGregor, retiring, instructed Sarah to show him out the back door. Mr. Campbell, he said, was a guest at the tavern and could find his way to the separate entrance to rooms on the second floor. At the sound of the name, Sarah let out a little gasp and went cold. She was alone with the stranger now. Was he from Virginia? His accent sounded as if he were newly arrived from Scotland. Suspicious, she went to his table and, smiling with all her charm, asked if he were from the States.

"Not been there," he confessed.

"Passing through?" she asked.

"No, I' won't be doin' that," he smiled. "I'm stayin' a night or two. Just tradin'."

"Tradin'?" she asked quizzically.

"You see, I run a store, a merchant post really. I'm sort of seein' what I can buy down here. First time in these parts."

"Where you from in Scotland?" she laughed flirtatiously

"Greenock, a port on the south side of the Firth of Clyde. Why d'ye ask?"

Sarah, greatly relieved, said, suddenly serious, "I knew some Campbells but they came from Ireland. You have no connection then?"

"We're almost a different race of men," he laughed. "Where do you come from?"

"I'm Irish," Sarah said. "You ready to go now?"

Campbell stood up and held out his hand. "Duncan Campbell's my name. What's yours?"

"Sarah," she smiled, taking his hand and feeling the animal attraction flow through her arm and to her heart.

"I'll see you at breakfast then," he said.

Sarah nodded and led him to the door. He went into the night and turned, rather awkwardly to say, "I'm pleased to meet you, Sarah."

Sarah smiled and closed the door. He was very young, she thought. He had little experience with women; that was obvious. But he was lovely. Since he was just staying briefly and lived so far away, perhaps they could make love once, just once. She went to her room with a lightness in her heart and knew that she would make love with this young man.

She did not see him at breakfast as she was too busy in the kitchen, but when she went for a walk to the dockside on the warm summer day, she heard her name and turning saw him running to catch up to her. He was smiling as if with joy at seeing her.

"May I walk with you?" he asked. "It's a beautiful day."

"But are you not doing business?" she asked as if surprised.

"Just finished. Do you see that sloop?" he pointed along the wharf to a ship with yellow and green markings. "It's carrying vegetables and fruits for me, and some tobacco. I saw you walk by and decided I'd enough business for one day."

"I don't have long," Sarah warned. "But come along and we'll make the most of our time."

Conversation was easy with him, Sarah discovered. He was very bright, very quick. Their hands brushed occasionally and he put one hand against her back when guiding her through a narrow passageway. By the time he walked her back to the tavern, both of them sensed an intimacy that demanded further expression. Campbell stayed late again after dinner, but this time, after McGregor left, Sarah went out the door with him and around to the entrance to the second floor and up the stairs, hand in hand with him, to his room. Their love-making was vigorous, and, when Sarah left him near morning to go to her room, she understood that they would be making love more than once.

Her children were asleep when she returned. Fanny had looked after the younger children, and, wise beyond her years, had understood her mother's absence. There seemed to be a settled peace upon them all. No word need be said, but the intimation implied that they had reached a new plateau in their new life, a sense of belonging, a commitment to each other that was being confirmed by Sarah's ebullience and inner strength, which had been revitalized by her experience of love. Sarah hesitated to call it love because she knew that it could not last, that their relationship could not be permanent. Some day she would have to tell Duncan Campbell that she was an escaped slave.

Campbell did not return for a couple of months. It was in late November 1821 when they slept together again. Sarah taught Duncan how to make love; he was a quick learner as in everything he did. He prolonged his stay for more than a week and insisted on sleeping with Sarah every night. His passion was powerful. He admitted that he had never known anyone as lovely as Sarah and he thought she was younger than she was. When he met her three children, he was taken aback at first, but, so strong was his desire, that he disregarded her past life so long as she was not engaged with any other man then. He left before ice formed on the lake. He felt that the winter that separated them seemed the longest and bleakest that he experienced after coming to Canada. Sarah, too, yearned to see him and toiled away at McGregor's Tavern throughout the long winter with just the hope of spring and the returning Duncan to maintain her happiness. That Duncan should have the identical surname as her former owner amused her. She had been so hated by James Campbell that it seemed ironic that she could be so loved by Duncan Campbell.

Fanny was learning quickly at school, and Israel, although slow at school, was growing fast and seemed talented in working with his hands. Israel helped McGregor in a workshop that the innkeeper kept near his tavern and in which he spent several hours every day. McGregor was gentle with the children but inclined to be overbearing as a supervisor in the tavern. Sarah worked hard and resented McGregor's interference in her cooking. He was so obsessed in the orderly running of his restaurant that he harried his employees to perform quickly and faultlessly. The result was that staff left him for other situations that they found in the new settlements along the Thames River. He came to depend on Sarah and feared losing her. Sarah kept her affair with young Campbell hidden from him lest he claim that it was interfering with her job performance. Also, she suspected that he would have been angered if he knew that her lover was a white man. McGregor looked upon his blackness as a racial distinction and seemed to claim the allegiance of anyone with negritude in their background, however small. Sarah's white children could not be helped; they had been born before McGregor knew her; but Sarah, under his supervision, would have to show favour to a black man and eschew attentions from a white. Such thoughts would not have disturbed Sarah if her affair with Duncan had been brief as she intended. But her longing for him during the monotonous days of the long winter not only surprised her but complicated her future. Eventually, McGregor would catch her out and she worried that he would dismiss her, regardless of her value to his business. There were many runaways looking for work. Hundreds came over the river on the ice at night from Detroit to The Ferry and sought out protective associations for help. Sarah knew that she could not find as good a position as her present one. She almost hoped that Duncan would lose interest in her but rejected such thoughts helplessly as soon as she had them.

Finally the spring came, the ice in the lakes melted, and shipping resumed as the large sails caught the warming winds and scudded across the waters bringing traders to Sandwich and more escaped

146

slaves from the States. Duncan appeared again in early March and took a room at the tavern. He saw Sarah that evening when he looked into the kitchen. She was bending over the stove. He called to her and, when she turned to see him, the old excitement was still there. He said just one word "Tonight?" and she nodded beaming happily. As he started back into the dining room, McGregor came up behind him to bar his passage, and, smiling, asked if he could be of service.

"Just giving the cook my preference for a meal tonight," Duncan said quickly, "but it's you I want to see, McGregor." He motioned for them to sit at the bar where Duncan under six feet and, as an eighteen-year old, just beginning to fill out, would not have to look up to McGregor. "We're makin' a fine brew in Bird Town. I brought a bottle with me for you to try. You're goin' to like it."

McGregor raised a hand as if to reject the suggestion. "There's plenty of drink bein' made here. I got no end of supplies."

"But this is a different taste. It's goin' to bring in customers. And I've got good whisky too, but can't give you any yet. The American ports are swallowing all we can produce."

McGregor rounded his eyes as if impressed. "Well, if the price is good, we can try it."

"I'll give you the bottle tomorrow. I'm stayin' three days, so we've got time to come to an understandin'." Duncan stood up. "That cook of yours, Sarah, she can turn out a good dish."

McGregor laughed. "Glad you like it, Mr. Campbell."

As Duncan sat at a table and awaited his meal, he sensed that McGregor was slightly suspicious of his designs on Sarah. He would have to be more circumspect in future, he told himself. His desire to see her again had led him to go to the kitchen door, something that a gentleman would never do. He ate his meal while contemplating Sarah's nakedness beside him that he would experience again after the long winter of abstinence. Surely, he thought, McGregor as a man could understand his need and would not thwart him. But he detected a presence behind McGregor's black eyes which served as a warning. He wondered if he would have to take precautions when Sarah visited his room.

Sarah, too, noticed McGregor's aggressive attitude to Campbell and wondered what her boss was thinking. That night she went to her room and stayed with her children longer than she usually did. She watched from her window to see if McGregor was standing in the street bathed in light from a three-quarter moon. Just as she was satisfied that there was no one in that cold air, she saw a movement in the doorway of a cabin opposite. The tall, bulky figure of McGregor moved slowly into the street and entered the tavern's side door to his apartment. Sarah decided to wait a while longer. Moreover, she was troubled by the fact that she had not had her periods for three months. There were emotional times in the past when she failed to have her monthly menstrual period, and, at first, she dismissed any thought of being pregnant, particularly as she had taken precautions against it. But she could ignore the fact no longer, when the other symptoms of smells and certain foods made her nauseous. She intended to keep it secret from Duncan for fear that he would not see her again but wrestled with whether to tell him now. If McGregor dismissed her, she would need Duncan's help. But then she would have to tell him the truth about herself. How would he react to having a child who was part black? There was a world of difference between him and the fathers of her children in Virginia. Duncan was like a George Brown freed from the bonds of the society in which he lived. But there would be social consequences for a young businessman hoping to make his way upwards. Although she grieved having to give up Duncan, she prepared herself for his rejection yet hoped for his help in finding her another place. When she finally went to Duncan's room, she was still undecided whether to tell him.

Duncan was sitting on his bed when she entered his room. He looked worried. "Did McGregor try to stop you?" he asked with concern.

"He didn't see me," Sarah smiled, "though he was watchin' for me."

Duncan came to her and embraced her. He began removing her clothes but she stepped away and stared querulously at him.

"What is the matter?" he whispered. "Don't you like me?"

"I like you, foolish man," Sarah said seriously, "but I'm afraid."

Duncan shook his head. "McGregor can do nothing. I'll see to that."

"I want to leave here," Sarah said. "I'm tired of the pressure he puts on me. I do most of the work and he pays me little."

Duncan studied her for a moment. "There is somethin' else, lass. What is it?"

Sarah bowed her head and decided to tell him everything. She took his hand and made him sit on the bed beside her. "I'm having your child," she admitted.

Duncan looked stunned. His mouth opened to say something but he made no sound. He put his hand to his face and slowly rubbed his forehead.

"I'm sorry." She looked at him sympathetically. "I don't want you to feel responsible. I'm to blame and I'll raise my child on my own like I've done before." A tiredness crept into her voice as she said those words. She wondered how she and her children could survive. "But I think that I'll lose my work here." She bowed her head and tears came to her eyes. "And after what the Church's done for me."

"Don't feel guilty, lass," Duncan said, caressing her shoulder. "No one's to blame. You have my help, I promise you that. Every problem has a solution, at least, that's what I know. So cheer up." He took her in his arms and kissed her.

They fell onto the bed and began caressing and loving one another. Their cares seemed to melt away and they found solace in one another. For the moment, as they made love, only the present mattered. Sarah knew that Duncan loved her, and, whatever solution he promised, she felt secure in his love. But he was ten years younger.

As they lay in one another's arms after making love, Sarah began talking of her background. "I haven't told you this, Duncan, but I was a slave."

"I know," he said gently. "I know, I know." He kissed her on the cheek. "I heard that after the first time we were together. You know, I move around in this community in doin' my work. Also, I know that the fathers of your children were white."

"I love my children, though they was forced on me," Sarah said proudly. "They are all I have in this world, and I am all they have."

"You are a good lady," Duncan said.

"My husband was a black slave," Sarah admitted. "Mr. Lewis was a good man."

"Was?" Duncan asked, sitting up and looking at her in the dark. "Is he dead?"

"I think so," she said with a sigh. "They were after him. He could have died in the forest. I ain't had word for years about him."

They continued talking about the past. Duncan said that he was from Bird Town, a village east of the Long Point, and worked for Montreal merchants. From what he said, Sarah gathered that he could be recalled at any time to Montreal. He had no property of his own and little means to help her, but he would do something, he promised. Meanwhile, he would conclude his business tomorrow and take a ship home on the next day. He would not see Sarah until the next time he came. "Don't doubt me," he said, when he saw her brow cloud with doubt. "I may have to return to the big city to make money, but I'll help support you."

Sarah was buoyed by the sincerity of his tone. "I'd rather have you than money," she said with a thin smile, "but I'll hope for the best. I couldn't have got this far without hope."

They kissed lightly on the lips when they parted. Duncan returned to his bed but failed to fall asleep. He was thinking of having a child who was black and how he could disguise that fact in his community. Duncan was a practical man. The only libertine moment in his life had been his relationship with Sarah and that had called on a romantic notion in his soul that he had never experienced. As he thought of the situation he was in, he knew that he could not desert Sarah. She was too good a woman for him to let down. But he also knew that he could not allow this indiscretion to ruin his life. He tossed and turned as he worried over his future. And the more he worried, the more depressed he became. Finally sleep came in the morning, and he was able to face the next day with his sharp business mind intact.

Duncan put all worries aside as he dealt with the merchants he had come to see. By the close of the business day he had accomplished all that he thought would take him two days, thus he was ready to leave early the next morning. It so happened that he had made acquaintance with Mr. Benoit on a previous visit, and, in the meantime, having learned that Benoit had escorted Sarah to Canada, he arranged to eat dinner with him in McGregor's Tavern. After discussing the economic conditions in the American and Canadian port towns, Campbell spoke of the large number of escaped slaves that were proving so beneficial to the Canadian economy. Benoit looked defensive and his eyes darted about suspiciously. Duncan went right to the point. What was Benoit's assessment of Sarah's character? Benoit, taken aback, looked at Duncan for a moment before he understood that Duncan was genuinely interested in the woman rather than in Benoit's role in helping fugitives.

"I won't ask why you want my opinion," Benoit said with a glint of humour in his eye. "But from what I have observed and have heard from high circles in the Methodist Church, she is a woman of worth."

At the mention of the church, Duncan realized that Sarah was better connected than he supposed. "She's the reason why I stay at this tavern," he said laconically. "I wish there were some way to bring her to Bird Town. I miss good cooking."

Benoit laughed. "McGregor would rather give you his right arm than Sarah. But I think she might want a better place to work. There are too many bar fights and raucous goings-on here for a lady as nice as she is."

Campbell changed the subject abruptly to Bird Town and asked about the reputation of his partner William Bird in the American ports. Benoit confided that the merchant owed money, but that was not surprising because the chances of running a competitive business in a hamlet was doomed to failure. Duncan's face fell, and, Benoit, seeing this, quickly suggested that if a merchant wished to be successful, he would invest in the surrounding countryside for additional income. Duncan reflected on the wisdom of Benoit's advice.

The Scotsmen running the Montreal firms which sent Bird dry goods, expecting a better return on their investment, dispatched him, fresh from Scotland, to look after their interests. Bird harboured an ill-concealed resentment and made it difficult for Duncan to know the true state of the business. Now this bad news upset his plans for caring for Sarah. With bankruptcy staring him in the face, he would be scrutinized closely by his Montreal employers, who, if they found out about Sarah, would surely dispense with his services. The region's first settler Aaron Culver, had told him that the farmers pinned their hopes for the community's development on his industry and intelligence. Aaron might help him. Bringing his relatives and slaves to Upper Canada from New Jersey to land granted to Americans who remained loyal to Britain during the Revolutionary War, Aaron farmed on the heights on the east side of the Lynn River, while his sons and cousins made farms farther south to form a triangle of land called the Gore. From the trail running north-south through the hamlet, blazed through the centuries by the Neutral Indians, the Culvers cut short streets down to their corn and grist mills on the river, which worked to meet the demands of new settlers arriving from the United States and Europe. Duncan knew that to succeed he had to be as helpful as he could to the Culvers, but he was uncertain of Aaron's views on escaped slaves. After Upper Canada outlawed slavery, allowing owners to retain for a number of years the slaves they already owned, Aaron's slaves remained on his farm. They were all free when Duncan arrived, and, on warm evenings, he liked to hear them singing, accompanied by banjos, carried down from their log cabins on a hill overlooking the Lynn River.

That night, he tossed in his sleep, worrying over his abilities and his resolve to commit himself in the long term, even if his employers forgave his indiscretion. No doubt he would lose the respect of the righteous families that farmed near Bird Town, if he brought Sarah to live with him. Perhaps he would have to return to Montreal and leave Sarah to fend for herself. Perhaps her church would help her. He groaned and knew he could not do that. He left early the next morning by ship for Port Ryerse. Although he did not see Sarah, she was in his mind and stayed there until he arrived by horseback at Bird's store.

FREEDOM

MAP OF SOUTHWESTERN ONTARIO

Georgian
Bay

Lake
Huron

Collingwood •

Barrie •

Toronto •

Lake
Ontario

Paris • Hamilton •
• Brantford

Drummondville •

• Sarnia

London •
Sodom •
Scotland •
• Otterville

St. Thomas •
Simcoe •

• Port Stanley
Port Dover
Port Ryerse •

Lake
Erie

• Sandwich

N

10 0 10 20 30 40 50 60
miles

14

Sandy McPherson was alone in the store when Duncan walked in. The same age as Campbell, McPherson was wandering through the Great Lakes, fleeing his military father in Halifax, and accompanying goods up the Lynn River when Bird hired him as his accountant. People called him Sandy because of his hair colour. "Hello Duncan," McPherson cried out cheerfully on seeing him. "What was it like being in civilization?"

"Where is Mr. Bird?" Duncan said, fixing his eyes on him as if he was guilty of hiding the man.

"No one knows," McPherson said, shaking his head sadly, "although lots are ready to give an opinion."

Campbell looked at him impatiently. He found the young Irishman's indirectness exasperating and attributed it to his literary tastes—Latin poets.

McPherson explained that Bill Bird had gone by horse to Port Dover and disappeared after spending the night at an Inn.

"Into thin air?" Duncan asked sarcastically.

"Someone saw him riding along the shore road three days ago," McPherson ventured with a suggestion of hope in his voice. "He could be visiting friends, or, you know, he could have been killed."

Campbell looked at him askance and stomped into the back office. He reappeared less than a moment later with a piece of paper which he handed to him. On it was scrawled, "Can't deal with the goddamn debts. I'm sorry. Bird."

"He's skipped it?" McPherson suggested.

"He's flown the coop," Duncan said with a wry smile. "We won't see him again, and we won't find his body. I think he's in New York State and taken his horse with him."

"What are we going to tell the creditors?" McPherson asked, thinking of the precariousness of his employment.

"Not one word," Duncan said. "Not one word," he enunciated again, but, this time, fiercely. "Bird, for all we know, went on holiday and will be coming back. By the time people realize he will never come back, I hope to clear these debts. But if the creditors make a run on me now, we're ruined. Do you understand, Sandy?"

McPherson nodded glumly.

Duncan decided to inform Aaron Culver right away.

Without a successful core business, the hamlet could not attract new settlers and businesses. Instead of lands increasing in value, they would decline as the hamlet became a backwater.

When Duncan came to him in a depressed state and declared that he could be recalled to Montreal, Aaron was alarmed, more for the fact that he was losing his one hope to create a viable community than for Duncan's emotional state.

"You'd be makin' a huge mistake leavin' this land of riches, my son," Aaron said patiently. Tall, muscled, his face wrinkled, his black beard streaked with white, Aaron spoke with authority.

"But I'm practically penniless," Duncan complained. "If I fail in the store, I'll be in debt for life. I have no land."

"Land?" Aaron's bushy eyebrows shot up. "There's plenty of that. I was fixin' to give you ten acres right here by the river. It would give you a stable feelin', Duncan."

Campbell looked shocked. "That's valuable property you're giving me!"

"On condition, of course, that you stay and help me develop this place," Aaron said quietly. "I can't run my mills no more. You can have the major interest in them if you run them for me." He looked at Duncan with a satisfied expression.

Duncan smiled faintly. "You are making it hard for me to leave, Mr. Culver. But I can't accept your gifts. I'm not worthy of them."

Aaron, mystified, looked at him closely. "There's somethin' botherin' you, son. Tell me."

Duncan shook his head. "No, no. I just have to think it over. I'll come to you tomorrow and give you my decision."

"You know, son," Aaron said compassionately. "We need you in this community. Remember that."

When on the next day Duncan came to his farm, Aaron expected him to accept the offer without further discussion. Smiling broadly as if about to welcome a prodigal son, he gaped in amazement when Duncan broke down in tears. "My dear boy," he said, putting his arm comfortingly about Duncan's shoulders and leading him to a sofa in his study. "You can confide in me. Let me help." Whatever Duncan was hiding, Aaron was prepared to wrench his problem out and deal with it.

Duncan, wiping his tears and composing himself, apologized. "It's kind of you to want to help, Mr. Culver, but I'm beyond help." Suddenly, weakening under Aaron's fatherly sympathy, he decided to confess and take the consequences. "You see, I made a woman pregnant and I must support her and the child."

Culver smiled benevolently, relieved that it was not a real problem. "Well," he said, as if the matter were of no concern, "the offer I made you yesterday should give you the means."

"You don't understand," Duncan looked at him guiltily. "She is a former slave."

Aaron, who had children by his own slaves, concealed his surprise with a shrug. "So you want to support her. You are a good man, Duncan. Tell me about her."

Duncan gave him the bare facts.

"Ah, I see. You think your career is ruined. But I think you can grow to be a pillar in this frontier community. No one need know about it. This woman, Sarah, can work for my cousin Joseph who needs good help in his Inn. Then, when the time is right, you can make other arrangements. What do you think?"

Duncan looked at him as if he was scarcely able to believe what he heard. "Then you think it will be all right?"

"I am a good judge of character, Mr. Campbell," Aaron smiled genially.

Duncan embraced him. "Then I accept," he cried. "Oh Lord! This is wonderful! You'll like her, Mr. Culver."

"Think of it as the beginning," Aaron said. "Which reminds me, now that Bird is gone, I want to call this place Simcoe, after our first

Governor who banned slavery. What do you say?"

"Good name," Duncan laughed with joy. "Good choice."

In the next weeks Duncan winnowed away the debts of the business from Bird's personal debts and revived the store's good credit while the debtors of Bird failed to get a resolution because there was no further word of the man.

A buoyed Duncan wrote to Benoit in Sandwich to inform Sarah that she would be coming to a farm run by Joseph Culver, a first cousin of Aaron, whose land was at the south end of the Gore and near the Methodist Church. Sarah's happiness could scarcely be contained, but she managed to keep the secret from McGregor and, for a time, concealed her expanding waistline, all the time hoping for word from Duncan that she could board ship and sail for Port Ryerse.

When McGregor noticed her pregnancy, he stormed angrily about it. Benoit came to Sarah's defense. His appearance in the tavern made McGregor understand that Sarah would have help in finding other employment, and he calmed down, fearful of losing her. Finally, in the early spring of 1822, arrangements were made for Sarah's reception at Joseph Culver's farm. Quietly, with Benoit's help, she left the tavern with her children in tow early in the morning before breakfast and boarded a sloop in the harbour. The anchor was raised, the sails unfurled, and Benoit stood on the wharf waving adieu to Sarah while rehearsing in his mind how he was to tell McGregor of her departure.

The boat from Amherstburg glided into the docks at Port Ryerse on a strong breeze that tossed her hair about her head and her expectant eyes ready to grapple joyfully with a new life. McPherson, sent to bring Sarah Lewis and her children from Port Ryerse to Joseph Culver's farm, thought that she had a very fine figure and carried herself with a sense of distinction. Her face showed character and beauty at the same time. The high yellow quality of her skin and certain movements of her head and hands were the only traces of her Negro ancestry, or they could have been Irish traits because her maiden name was Kinney. But he knew she was an escaped slave, which is why he was surprised by her strong spirit when he first saw her. There she was with three little kids and a fourth just waiting to be born.

The bright spring day and the cool breeze off the lake and the colourful blossoms in the orchards and the fields sprouting crops made the land seem like paradise to Sarah. Her children caught her enthusiasm and gleefully cried out at the sights of the wide expanse of green farms and the pretty-looking farmhouses snuggled under a copse of trees. Considering her condition, she took the bumps and drops in the road without a complaint as if they were gentle taps after what she had been through.

Simcoe was seven miles inland from the lake shore and more secure from pursuers and bounty hunters than Sandwich. Joseph Culver's farmhouse was just off the main route that took traffic inland as far as Brantford and the Six Nations Indians. Joseph Culver was much younger than his cousin Aaron and, back in New Jersey, he had been an ardent abolitionist. He took part in building the Woodhouse Methodist Church which stood across the road from his property and served the settlers scattered throughout the region. Joseph, unlike the bearded Aaron, was shaved and had an engaging personality. He helped Sarah and her children alight from the carriage, and, picking up Vesta, now too heavy for Sarah to carry, led Sarah and McPherson over paths winding into an orchard behind his house to a cabin at the north end on the border of the forest. This was to be her home: one large room with a loft for sleeping, clean, airy and furnished. Sarah sat down at the table with a look of wonder. Joseph told her about the crops he raised and pointed to the cabin that could be seen across his land as belonging to his married daughter, Charity. He had given Sarah bed sheets, he said, and put vegetables and fruits in her cupboard for the next few days. He would give her all she needed until she found her feet. He pointed to a weaver's wheel by the window and said there was a great need for clothes and sheets, and for sewing and mending. Culver ran an Inn for travelers, called Poplar Inn because of the row of poplar trees that grew in front of it. Sarah would find plenty of customers there. Sarah, excited, wanted to start work in the morning.

"You look to be carrying a big load," Joseph cautioned. "Give yourself and your babies a rest."

A girl servant from Joseph's house entered with a tray of chicken breasts and salad and a pot of tea. Joseph returned to his house to take his mid-day meal with his wife. Sarah was overwhelmed. The change

159

from a smoky, hot kitchen in an often rowdy tavern to the fresh country air in a verdurous landscape seemed miraculous. She felt that she had taken a large step on her way to independence. McPherson left her admiring the large wood stove while Fanny and Israel playing near the front door happily waved good-bye.

As the days passed Sarah became resigned to not seeing Duncan. Perhaps he would come when she gave birth, she thought. Culver's wife came to her cabin with her daughter Charity Rusling quite often to see what help she needed. Sarah enjoyed their company and depended upon them in many small ways. William Rusling, Charity's husband, came by a few times. He had been a wild young man, often drunk and completely irresponsible, until one day he returned to his father's home in New Jersey and turned over a new leaf. He came back even more religious than the Culvers and married Charity to whom he was devoted. He wrote poetry and sometimes read a new poem to Sarah and her children. He left some books for Fanny, who taught Israel to read from them.

Sarah wove for most of the day and into the night. She made blankets and winter clothes. The Culvers had merino sheep to provide the wool, which reminded Sarah of the flocks of merino sheep that grazed on the hillsides in northern Virginia. Sarah, who had not been this large before her other births, worried about the difficulty she might have. There were no doctors in the region so that the settlers had to provide their own medicines from herbs and remedies that they learnt from the Indians and that were handed down within families. Mrs. Culver brought the mid-wife Mrs. Stacey to examine her. When Sarah began having birth pains, Fanny ran to Mrs. Culver, who immediately sent for Mrs. Stacey. The large, heavy-set Mrs. Stacey arrived by carriage within the hour and began instructing Mrs. Culver to prepare linen and hot water. Charity took the Lewis children into her cabin and kept them amused with games. Since it was a hot day in early August, the children wanted to play outside. Charity led them to the stable, and, with Vesta walking unsteadily beside her, she hitched her horse to a runabout, and took them to Port Ryerse to wade in the water on its sandy beach.

The birth was protracted and difficult but by evening a girl was born, followed a few minutes later by a boy. Sarah was exhausted but ecstatic. The infants, perfectly formed with a slight hue of brown in the skin, could live their lives as whites, Sarah thought gratefully. On her way home Mrs. Stacey stopped by Charity's cabin to ask if she would mind the children for the night to give Sarah much needed rest. As a precaution, Mrs. Culver stayed the night in Sarah's cabin.

The next day Sarah asked Mrs. Culver to plant a poplar seed in a corner of the orchard to mark the births as something special this time. Born free, her children would not know slavery and the fears and humiliations that tortured her mind. Mrs. Culver took the seed, which Sarah had saved, and planted it in a spot that Sarah could see from her cabin window. News of the birth spread quickly. Duncan Campbell looked pleased when he learned of it but made no comment. McPherson went to see Sarah a few days later. She was weaving at her wheel. The twin babies were lying in a crib by the open window. Her spirits were high.

"You look beautiful," he said. "Having babies is good for you."

She laughed. "It's not babies, it's freedom that makes me look good."

Sarah offered him tea, but, as she had much work to do, he left, saying that he would report to the people in town who were interested. A look of meaning passed between them.

Business was improving under Campbell's direction. The corn and grist mills hired more workers. Campbell chafed at the fast growth of Wellington village on the high ground north of Simcoe; the competitive enterprise of its settlers made it a going concern of small industries and stores. A wooden bridge spanning a small swamp connected the two settlements, but for some weeks in the year the swamp overflowed it and made passage impossible. Campbell began draining the swamp and buying up land for the day when, he claimed, Simcoe would be the major town in the area. His store was on the main thoroughfare which took the name Norfolk St., and along it Campbell built a tannery and a blacksmith's shop.

Sarah, disappointed that Duncan made no effort to see her, surmised that he did not want people to connect him with these children born out of wedlock. But she knew he would come to her one day.

Wanting to share her joy, she sent word of the births through the churches to her sister Nell in Virginia. When her message reached the Campbell farm weeks later, the slaves rejoiced, calling her escape a miracle. Henry and Molly were elated too, although they felt truly abandoned with their mother somewhere in a huge land to the north and their father missing in the forest. The slave boys on the Campbell farm, however, wanted to memorialize the good news. They cut the date "1822" into a large tree. Every time slaves saw it, they thought of escape and freedom as a real possibility. Henry, as he grew older, came to take pride in his mother, and the mark on the tree reminded him of her courage.

Sarah quickly regained her strength, but the baby girl, ailing, died within a few weeks. Sarah, though despondent, refused to see it as a bad omen. God wanted her little girl, she said, and had the right to take her as long as He left her a strong son. The Culvers buried her on the farm. Sarah named the boy John. He was healthy, happy and easy to care for. With the demands of work and caring for her children, Sarah had little time to travel the three miles into Simcoe—not that there was much to see—but she did want Duncan to know his child. She came into the store with John in her arms when he was about six months old. Duncan, who was in the back room, heard her voice and came out right away. He smiled and went up to Sarah, who looked at him affectionately. He spoke to her as if she were a stranger but in a friendly and inquiring manner. He patted the little boy's head, and Sarah, impulsively gave him John to hold. Flushing slightly, Duncan took the child and held him awkwardly in his forearms for a moment before returning him to Sarah.

Sarah came to the village more frequently after this first visit. She advertised her weaving business to new settlers buying up plots of land that Aaron Culver made available. The various communities throughout the region grew slowly owing to the swamps that separated them and the inadequate roads and bridges between them. From the Gore to the lake shore, however, there was plenty of traffic. Industries developed in the ports. Country schools began operating. Sarah sent Fanny and Israel to be taught in the Methodist Church near Joseph Culver's property.

The months fled by as Sarah adjusted to her new life and weaned John. She was accepted by the people as one of them, and, when Charity Rusling gave birth to a boy seven months after John arrived, Sarah took part in the celebrations and was always welcome to visit. For the most part she was very content, and, although the weaving was hard work, she rejoiced in the fact that she was paid for what she did. On occasion, however, she thought of her two young children at James Campbell's. She received news from the Reverend Doddridge only rarely, but life moved slowly on the farms and his reports said little more than that they were well and growing, and, strange to say, James Campbell allowed them to attend a school. Age was mellowing the man.

At the close of two years with the Culvers, when John was walking, Sarah received her first visit from Duncan Campbell. It was in the fall, and the leaves were in bright colours and pumpkins were in the fields. Duncan asked McPherson to accompany him. Sarah was sitting on a bench before her cabin and sewing a shirt as they walked towards her. She was wearing a summer dress that she had made. Her older children were skipping rope and John sat on the ground and laughed at their antics. Duncan stopped suddenly, struck by the scene, smiled and stepped quickly forward when Sarah rose to greet them. She was in her mid-thirties at this time, but looked ten years younger, about Duncan's age.

"Mrs. Lewis," Duncan said affably, "forgive us for interrupting your work."

"Not at all," Sarah said pleasantly, "I was looking for an excuse to stop. Will you have tea with me?"

"Thank you, we will," Duncan smiled, relieved that she was not angry with him.

They followed her into her cabin as the children stopped playing to stare at them curiously.

Duncan remarked on the neatness and cleanliness of the cabin. He and McPherson sat at the table while Sarah heated water. Sarah was a bit excited and suddenly ran to the door to call to Fanny to keep an eye on the small ones for a few moments.

"Keeps one busy," Duncan smiled.

"I get little time for anything else," Sarah said, "but Charity helps me and so does Mrs. Culver. My work gets done."

Duncan cleared his throat. "It's about work that I've come," Duncan said seriously.

Sarah looked surprised. "Have you something you want sewn or made?"

Duncan shook his head. "Not at the moment, but that is something I will need, come to think of it. A bachelor is not the best maintainer of clothes. You can see that from looking at McPherson's garments," he smiled.

McPherson tried to speak but Duncan held up his hand to quiet him.

"I want to ask you, Mrs. Lewis, if you would consider working for me as a cook."

The water started boiling, and Sarah lifted the kettle off the fire, which gave her a moment to think over the offer. "As a cook!" she cried. "Well, that sounds good to me, but how am I to go the three miles to your home every day and look after my children?" She poured the water into a teapot.

"I'm not making myself clear," Duncan apologized. "I'm told I am too abrupt sometimes. What I mean is that you and your family can move into the farmhouse that I just finished renovating. You would be my housekeeper. At the same time, I would expect you to cook for my millhands."

Sarah came with the pot to sit at the table. "How many hands?" she asked.

"Four or five," Campbell said dryly, "And McPherson here. But only for the mid-day dinner. They will get their own breakfast and supper where they live."

"That's a lot of responsibility," Sarah said, trying to sound non-committal despite her excitement.

"You will have help," Duncan said encouragingly. "And I'll pay you well."

Gales of young laughter sounded from outside.

"Are you sure that you can put up with the children?" she asked with an amused expression.

"I like children," Duncan said. "And we have McPherson to look after them. You like children, don't you, Sandy?"

"I'll do my best," McPherson said cheerfully.

Duncan explained that if he was to keep his workers from drifting away to other jobs, he had to provide good meals, which they were unlikely to find elsewhere. Moreover, he liked to eat well and had been suffering from his own cooking.

Sarah poured the tea into cups. "May I give you an answer later. I want to discuss it with the Culvers who have been so kind to me. Mr. Culver depends on my work for his Inn."

"Of course, you may," Duncan took a sip of tea. "They will miss you, but then you are free to do what is best for your family," Duncan said, with an emphasis on "free."

"There are many advantages," McPherson interjected. "First of all the work would be easier than weaving all day. And soon there will be manufactories making clothes faster than you can. We get clothes and blankets from across the lake. They're cheaper than what you can make."

Sarah listened closely. Baby John ran into the cabin, fell, picked himself up and stumbled toward Campbell. He seized Campbell's leg and held it tightly.

"Johnnie!" Sarah cried, embarrassed.

"No, that's all right," Duncan said and, reaching down, picked John up and sat him in his lap. He let John explore his face with one hand and to grip his lapel with the other.

Sarah looked pleased and watched with fascination at the liberties that Duncan allowed John to take with him. When she took John away, John howled in protest. Duncan was visibly moved. Sarah put the struggling boy on the floor where he rolled about.

"He misses his sister," Sarah said wistfully. "They were so close for the first weeks."

Duncan nodded but said nothing.

"The grave is just near-by," McPherson ventured.

"Would you like to see it?" Sarah asked suddenly.

Duncan nodded in agreement, swallowed the rest of his tea, and stood up.

"I'll watch John," McPherson said.

"She was a sweet girl. I think she had a defect when she was born," Sarah said as she went out the open door.

When she and Duncan stood looking down at the gravestone, Duncan in a quiet voice told her that he was very sorry; he had not known that the girl was ill until after he heard of her death. "I want to make sure my other child stays healthy," he said. "I'll take good care of you, Sarah. I could not have done anything sooner. Won't you come with me?" He looked pleadingly at her.

"I will," Sarah smiled. "I thought that you wanted to forget me."

"I think of you often," Duncan admitted. "But I had to prepare the ground, you know. I had to have a reason for a housekeeper."

Sarah laughed and reached for his hand. "You will go far, Duncan. I shall do what I can to help."

Looking relieved, Duncan grasped her hand and squeezed it gratefully. When they returned to the cabin, they were smiling.

Campbell's home, a big farmhouse built after the Americans burnt the buildings in the area on a marauding sweep in 1814, sat on bank of the Lynn River south of Aaron Culver's home. The kitchen was large with a great hearth for cooking. Duncan, who prepared three rooms in the back for Sarah and her children, lived in the front of the house. Sarah was the only live-in servant at first. Duncan hired girls to come in to clean the rooms every so often; some of them were married to the men who ran the mills. The grist and feed mills were a short walk south along the river and a barn-like structure near-by served as living quarters for the mill-hands and other employees who ran Campbell's businesses. There was a kitchen in these quarters. She might prepare the meals in Campbell's home, carry them across the river to the big barn and reheat them, but mostly she cooked the meals in the big barn. Sarah was popular with the men, who were a rough lot. Since she came on the scene, the men tended to stay on rather than wander off to other opportunities. Sarah enjoyed her popularity with them.

To the outside world Campbell's relations with Sarah were that of master to servant. On many evenings Duncan invited her and the children to come into his living room and play cards by the fire. The crusty martinet that Campbell seemed to many of his associates in town was transformed into a genial, fun-loving young man on those occasions.

Sarah did not expect that Duncan would make love to her. She was grateful to him for saving her from bleak poverty and hardship and thought he helped only because John was his son. She was surprised, therefore when, after two weeks of living in his home, he suddenly put his arms about her and kissed her long and hard with a passion that she thought never to experience again.

"That, lass," he said earnestly, "is what I've been missing for too, too long."

Sarah smiling with delight rounded her eyes at him. "I thought it was my cooking you liked."

He laughed and seized her again. "I've been missing both, but thinking of you the way we were. I love you, Sarah. Tonight, come to me, will you?"

Sarah rested her arms on his shoulders and looked him in the eye. "How could I ever refuse you, Duncan. I love you. And you are the father of our son."

"My love for you," he said, as if clarifying a point, "has nothing whatever to do with duty. I planned and worked hard for this moment when we could be together again."

Sarah smiled and pecked him on the cheek. "After the children are in bed, I shall come," she said sweetly.

A loud knock on the front door forced Duncan to pull away and respond to the call to business. Sarah sang to herself as she returned to the kitchen and prepared the evening meal.

Duncan became a model of respectability in the community, a trader, businessman and land speculator. He kept his private life concealed from everyone. That he and Sarah became intimate was no surprise to McPherson because she was very attractive and Duncan's sexual drive, once awakened, could not be suppressed for long.

Sarah understood Duncan very well. Aside from her husband Henry Lewis, Duncan was the man she felt closest to, that is, the only man she loved in the sense of commitment. But Duncan was more than Henry Lewis: he was a man of position and a promising future, a man who could protect her and her children and a man whose love for her,

167

although secretive, was nonetheless intense. Duncan's education and business acumen entitled him to the highest rank in this little society, which, in the early years was very limited, but, with the influx of immigrants, became greater over the years. He was appointed a magistrate with the title "squire" setting him apart from yeomen and trades people.

Sarah stepped partly by accident, partly by intent into the white world because she knew that it was better for her children. At Sandwich, Fanny and Israel suffered from the slights of some blacks because of the lightness of their skin. Sarah, as a slave, experienced the resentment and sometimes violent quarrels between blacker-skinned farm slaves and lighter-skinned household slaves in the slave quarters. Sarah learned quickly that one had to use whatever advantages one had to the best of one's ability to survive in this factious world. Her beauty had made her a victim, but now it brought her rewards.

When they moved in with Duncan, in 1824, Fanny was thirteen, Israel was ten, Vesta was five and John was two. Fanny helped her mother look after the younger children and took part in the cooking. Sarah's children continued to receive the rudiments of an education in a red-painted schoolhouse that Aaron Culver built across from Campbell's store. Sarah was proud of their ability to read and write. Her children met black children in Culver's school because he encouraged the children of his former slaves to learn. In the early years in Simcoe, skin colour was unimportant; later, as the society began forming social strata, a distinction was made. Although Sarah brought her children up to disregard the opinions of others and to be pragmatic about life, their environment had subtle influences upon them that she could not have foreseen, let alone control.

In the summer evenings she listened to the songs and string music that drifted down from Buttermilk Hill from Culver's former slaves. It reminded her of the rare occasions in Virginia when the slaves could gather together for jamborees. She clung to this part of her heritage, and, when the Negroes moved off the hill into the village proper, she made friends with some of them. She hoped that her children would do the same, and all but John had black friends. John, knowing no other influence but the "white" atmosphere of Campbell's home, was very selective of the friends he made.

As for her children Henry and Molly, Sarah trusted her sisters and God to look after them. Although they belonged to another life, she felt an invisible bond passing through the wilderness and connecting her to them, whom she loved all the more because they were deprived of a mother's love. She would have been happier had she known that at about the time she moved to Duncan Campbell's house, Henry Lewis Sr. reappeared in the slave quarters of James Campbell's farm.

Henry had come to see Sarah and his children. He was forty years old now. His strong lithe body and weathered face told of years of solitude and fortitude. His eyes measured men, classifying them, warning them not to mess with this black man. His black hair was graying at the sides. His carriage was confident and his manner was attentive and thoughtful. He had heard that his long-time pursuers had given up looking for him. His Kentucky master was dead, and the expense of searching for him had cost the family far more than his worth as a slave. He was a nomad who lived by training horses and doctoring humans and animals with the secrets of herbal medicine that his Indian patron had taught him. His reputation for healing was known in various parts of Ohio, but he had wandered for so long that he could not settle down in any place for long. He had a wife and a child in the Indian village in Logan County to whom he sent money through the banks when he could not return to stay with them. It was mid-morning when he rode over the rise to the cabin from which he had fled twelve years before.

As his eyes swept over the familiar surroundings warily, for he had always to be on guard, he felt a thrill of expectation. He expected to find Sarah looking the same, but he could not visualize his children, who, he thought, must have grown to be unrecognizable. Henry Jr. was seventeen and Molly fourteen. He dismounted and looked in the door. No one was there. He walked with his horse to the large barn where the field slaves lived and, knowing that they would be in the fields until the noon-day meal might bring some of them back to the barn, he let his horse graze and stepped into the stables. He saw a young man scrubbing down a large black horse in a stall and walked over to watch for a moment. When the young man stopped to look at him, he recognized his son. He felt a leap of joy and his eyes blazed, prompting the young man to ask if he needed anything.

"Yes, I do," Henry said. "I need my son, Henry Lewis Jr."

The shock on young Henry's face broadened into disbelief and then, unable to remember his father's features but recognizing his manner and seeing the expectation in his father's eyes, he cried out in joy and ran from the stall to embrace him. Both men cried and hugged one another, as if they had gone through years of sorrow and darkness and stumbled into happiness and the light. The word "Dad" had been in young Henry's mind unspoken for so long that it seemed strange coming from him, but it was also joyous.

When they had recovered and could talk, Henry asked his son about Sarah.

"She's in Canada," Henry Jr. said proudly. "Escaped with the others."

Henry's eyes opened wide in surprise. He had not dreamt that such a thing was possible, but as his son told him of the beatings and troubles Sarah had to endure, Henry fought to control his surging anger. "And Molly?" he asked. "Did she escape?"

Henry Jr. shook his head. "She works in the master's kitchen. She'll be out tonight. We have our own cabin. Come with me, Dad, and you can settle in with us."

As they left the barn, Henry gave a short whistle and his horse trotted up to him. He took its reins and followed his son, whose strong body and arms reminded him of himself at that age. There seemed to be no one about until, as they came to the last cabin on the hillside, Candor MacDonald appeared driving a calèche toward the barn. Candor smiled when he saw Henry whom he recognized immediately.

"About time you paid us a visit," he shouted as he drove by.

Henry looked at his son questioningly and the young man smiled. "He and his brother are our friends," he said. "The old massa can't bite anymore. He lost his teeth."

Henry laughed and, clapping his son on the shoulder, followed him into the little cabin to find a place to spend the night.

When Henry met Molly that evening, he found a girl who was

almost as pretty as her mother, but who acted strangely with him. Having no memory of him, she resented him for deserting her and her brother, that, although she knew it could not be helped, festered in her soul as a consequence of her enslavement. She went back to the main house to bring more food to the cabin. Like her mother, she had become close to Margaret Campbell. She came and went in the household with confidence; the feeding of an extra mouth for a short time would not be noticed.

As the three of them talked and ate by the candlelight, Molly studied her father. His suffering was lined into his face. She began to understand his nomadic life, his fears and his struggles. She listened to his voice and began to love its mellow tone. His sense of humour, she thought, was like her own. He seemed to be enjoying his children's company and responded to their queries about his life with amusing stories. Despite his hardships he seemed to laugh at fate. He was darker than his children and had to be constantly on the lookout for someone or some group prepared to capture him and sell him into slavery. Whatever tensions he had been under, however, seemed to drift away in the presence of his children, to whom he now confessed his pain at being separated from them and for having to neglect them. Molly had tears in her eyes and, going to him, threw her arms about his shoulders. She felt a sudden compassion and a relief within her, as if she had lost a sense of guilt that she had carried with her for years because she was blaming her parents for deserting them. Henry Lewis Sr. had come to them when he could because he loved them, and this realization made Molly overcome her resentment and rejoice in really being wanted. Her father held her in his arms and promised that from now on he would come to them as often as he could. He did not like to stay long in a slave state. Every hour was a risk. But he needed them, he said, as much as they needed him. It was hard being without a real home such as he had with their mother for a few years. To make a living he had to be on the move, to be a traveling herb and horse doctor.

"There's always gonna be sickness," he said, "and there's always gonna be young horses to be trained. You just have to find them, cure them, and move on to find them again."

Henry Jr. listened to his father with fascination. "Take me with you, Dad. I love horses and I could help you lots."

Henry shook his head sadly. "It's too rough a life, my son. You're better off here where you're fed regular. And who's goin' to look after your sister?"

Henry Jr. blushed and he looked at Molly apologetically.

"We've all got our responsibilities," Henry said. "Remember we're family even if we don't live together. You see, son, I love freedom as much as any man, but I paid a price for it. When you and my daughter get your freedom, you get it on different terms. Make sure you're ready for it. Meanwhile wait it out here till you're ready."

Henry Jr. sensed his father's loneliness and his need for them to be in one place where he could find them. "You're right, Dad. And I guess I couldn't get away with you anyway. They got people on the look-out for runaways all up and down the river."

"Mrs. Campbell treats us well," Molly said to her brother. "We got little to complain about."

Henry Sr. chuckled. "So the old man ain't what he used to be."

"Massa's got rheumatism and he's slow gettin' around. He's just as mean but he's learned a lesson with momma."

"Your momma had to do it," Henry Sr. said sharply, as if he were remembering his own breaks for freedom. "Nothin' angers a white man more than havin' white slaves who ain't afraid to challenge him. He must of hated those white kids to sell them down river."

"I didn't understand it then," Henry Jr. admitted, "but Fanny and Israel were despised by a lot of us who said they had slaver's blood running in their veins."

"No fault of them," Henry Sr. said. "Your momma had more white than black blood, but I married her. There's some people you just can't please. They live by outward signs and tokens. They don't have real inner lives. You know what I'm talkin' about?"

"I know, Daddy," Molly said, glad to have an opportunity to enter the conversation. "It's like the law that keeps us slaves. People follow it without thinkin' about it."

"Yeah, that's right. And it's gotten worse in my life. They think of black and slavery together now."

"Well Dad, as mulattos, I guess we're still here because old massa thinks we're black enough to remain slaves," Henry Jr. said with a smile.

Henry Sr. laughed. "You just keep growin' and gettin' stronger, then someday you can get away to Canada too. Maybe there skin colour no longer counts for anything'."

When they went to sleep that night, the three of them had the happiest feelings that they had known for many years. It was as if the reappearance of Henry Sr. had reminded them of their essential humanness, expressed through the bond among them.

On the second evening together they talked of the days when they lived on Brown's Island and of Sarah, whom Henry still loved but knew that he could no longer join because she had moved into the white world. He confessed his guilt to his children at being unable to protect her and them. Even now, he stopped the conversation occasionally by raising his hand and listening for sounds outside the cabin. He slept fitfully that night, awakening several times to listen in the dark. At dawn the next morning he kissed his children good-bye and rode down the slopes, across the river via Brown's Island and into Ohio. Henry Jr. found out later that only the MacDonald brothers knew that he had been there so discreet were his movements.

15

Sarah loved the gentle climate of the land north of Lake Erie. Winters were not severe and the springs were glorious. In summers, the days were warm and the nights cool and the autumns brought forests of bright colours that lit up the countryside. She enjoyed Duncan's farm because she directed others in the work to be done. She made certain that her children had chores to do and learned to work hard. Although illiterate, she had a good sense of finances and took an interest in Duncan's work.

Sarah lived a life in two camps. She was friendly with and accepted by the gentry of the community; at the same time, she was on good terms with the working class both black and white who accepted her as one of them. As the village multiplied rapidly in population and new housing sprang up to accommodate immigrants, Sarah clung to her associations as an anchor for her emotions and ambitions. She always dreamt of owning her own house and land and being independent and free of servanthood. But in the late 1820s this seemed a long way into the future.

She admired those blacks who built their own houses on the west side. Most of them had been slaves and trained as artisans with skills in brick-making, carpentry, plastering, construction, which they put together to help each other construct a home. Once they started building, Culver's former slaves drifted down to live among them, but they were not as talented nor as hard-working. Sarah came to know a tall, copper-colored man with a lively mind who arrived in Simcoe shortly after she did. Richard Plummer was a free black who left Kentucky because prejudice against the coloured population became unbearable to a sensitive man like him. Plummer shopped in Campbell's store and while talking with Sandy McPherson they discovered their mutual love of literature. On handling some merchandise, McPherson made a quip from the Roman poet Horace and Plummer followed it with a quote from Lord Byron's *Don Juan*. McPherson, agreeably surprised, quoted a passage from Virgil's *Aeneid*, which Plummer matched with a passage from a Shakespearean Sonnet. At that moment Sarah entered the store and put a box of her home-made pies on the counter.

"Cassius," joked McPherson, who saw Plummer watching Sarah display the pies, "I perceive you have a lean and hungry look."

"Can't be helped," Plummer laughed and introduced himself to Sarah.

Sarah liked Plummer's forthrightness and supreme self-confidence. This time she talked just long enough to sell him a pie and return to her kitchen; thereafter, she often met him on the street reciting passages from the liberator Wilberforce and others to small crowds, or preaching to larger crowds on the commons on Sunday afternoons on any subject. Eventually he was in demand as a speaker at events which supplemented the income he made as a tailor.

The hamlet of Simcoe throbbed with energy and enterprise: a few wooden houses by a narrow river surrounded by a wilderness of trees of all kinds—ash, oak, maple, pine—muddy streets, a swamp with narrow bridges over it, and roads that were often little more than pathways to other hamlets to the north and south and to the mills cutting wood and grinding corn and wheat in every community along the rivers and streams, and then the timber crews hacking away at the forest and the huge tree trunks floating down the rivers to the great lake to supply the needs of the British navy. From its mills and distillery on the Lynn River, Simcoe shipped grain and liquor to Port Dover for loading on ships for distant ports. The citizens built boardwalks along the sides of the streets, often ankle-deep in water, and constantly hauled in gravel from pits in the countryside to build up the road levels. The common stretching to the west of the village's main street began to fill up with stores and houses after the Post Office opened. The crown lands were sold off in lots so that a new common was laid out to the west of it as far as the eye could see to the rising heights in the distance. The village's many beautiful old trees kept it like a tree park for decades. But there were bears and wolves just outside the hamlet, and, in winter, wolves would eat human flesh. The struggle for survival hardened the people and many took to the drink that local distilleries supplied. Bill Rusling caught their state of mind in one of his poems that Sarah used to recite when watching millhands careen along the pathways of the settlement in the dark of a cold, snowy night: "I had lost all my pleasures, they had fled like a dream/ And from no point of heaven could happiness beam/ The cup of strong poison in madness I drained/ And nought but confusion and anguish I gained." She sympathized with them because the only amusement available was the occasional dance. Fiddlers would make the music. All the women for miles around would be required for partners. Sarah was always in demand, not only for cooking but for dancing, which she did with lovable gaiety. Her daughter Fanny was in her early teens and popular at these dances, but she had the proud look of her mother and commanded respect even at that age. Outdoor religious meetings in a cleared area by Water Street hosted hundreds of people to hear itinerant ministers shout out brimstone

175

and fire by the light of blazing flambeaus stationed at the four corners of the field. There were celebratory dinners for the gentleman class of people that Duncan Campbell hosted on St. Andrew's Day in November when government officials, large landowners, ship owners, and the more educated people would drive or sleigh in from Port Dover, Port Rowan, Long Point, Big Creek and the like for a feast of lamb, beef and pork. The bagpipers would come out for that day, which being at the end of November, was getting cold to the hands, and many a finger would have to be warmed by the big fires before the stirring sounds of Scottish lament would fill the old barn.

Sarah was kept busy preparing for these feasts. She did such a good job that she got offers to cook in other places, but she would not desert Duncan. She took pride in being his companion. She also felt secure with him; he would not allow bounty hunters to interfere with her or her children. She gloried in her freedom running Duncan's household. No one spoke down to her or ordered her about. Her tendency to act in a humble manner before white persons, which characterized her when she arrived, was replaced by a commanding personality as she gained confidence running the farm. She decided what to cook, how much to cook. She won the respect of the mill hands and other workers in the small community. When the farmers came from miles about to have their grain ground at Duncan's mill, they were willing to part with scarce coin to buy her pastries on sale in Duncan's store. Duncan took no commission from Sarah so that she began to save. Soon Vesta and John attended the red wooden building that served as a school and meeting house across from the store. They were good learners, but John was particularly bright, which pleased Duncan.

Duncan gave Sarah the satisfaction of helping him develop this backwater into a thriving village. Simcoe's rival, Wellington, soon faded in importance and, owing to better bridges spanning the swamp, became a section of Simcoe. Because he had Sarah, Duncan concentrated on his ambitions without distraction. He loved her, but like many industrious people, he took for granted the help that she gave him. Duncan's reach was wide. He began several businesses including a wagon and blacksmith shop and hired enterprising young men such as Thomas McMehan, fresh from Ireland, and Thomas McMicken as blacksmiths. They all came to know Sarah and her family and formed friendships with Fanny, Israel and Vesta. In 1829, Duncan got the break that he and Aaron Culver had been wanting. The conservative alliance that ran Upper Canada acceded to their wishes to place a Post Office in Simcoe, and Duncan was made postmaster. It marked the development of the village because settlers from miles about had to come to Simcoe to mail and receive letters and to deal with the government offices that came to it because of the post office. As postmaster, Duncan was at the centre of communication and learned of the new industries and the valuable lands in which he could invest. When Duncan became the Commissioner for Crown Lands in the area, he grew rich through land transactions and providing mortgages to new settlers, who moved into the houses that developers built on the Crown lands they took over. He soon joined other prominent men in the District calling for a Bank in which they could put their wealth. The elite in Toronto and Kingston formed the Bank of Upper Canada, which, by taking the province's share of the exchange and general business away from the Imperial Government, increased its capital and used the legislature to defeat attempts to form other banks. It loaned money only to government members and their friends. But Duncan's group worked with conservative politicians in the bigger settlements such as Ancaster and Hamilton to find support for their own organization. The growing power of these men, whose connections brought them wealth, began to cause resentment amongst those who worked hard but seemed to encounter legal and political barriers to their progress. The growing legislative power of the Reformers, called Radicals by the Conservatives, became evident when their own Commercial Bank was encouraged to develop. Angered, Duncan and his group pushed harder for their Gore Bank.

Sarah's wizardry in the kitchen, as guests called it, gave her a special place in the community. People looked forward to invitations for dinner from Duncan. Sarah began to be included in Duncan's circle of close friends in after dinner discussions while the scullery maids washed the dishes and prepared the kitchen for tomorrow's meals. At first, Sarah listened politely and responded only when asked directly her opinion, but, when she heard of the disaffection among some of the settlers, she quickly joined in with Duncan in condemning those people who would criticize a government that had given her a refuge. She, of course, had no dealings with the autocratic Family Compact which ran the province. She had not had to contend with Clergy Reserves taking up huge swathes of land and cutting communications between settlements and stifling economic growth. She knew only the sentiments of conservatives like Duncan Campbell and Aaron Culver, who benefitted in land grants and business opportunities from their close association with the elitist power structure in Toronto. Moreover, when she talked with her friends in the black community, she heard their fears that these reformers were largely American settlers, who wanted to bring in an American style of government and reinstitute slavery. Regardless of how passionately the Reform leaders such as William Lyon Mackenzie spoke against slavery, those thousands of escaped and emancipated slaves in the province mistrusted them because they knew that any American influence meant the undermining of the British principles that they had come to depend upon.

The lively discussions were an education for her and served to introduce her to the more interesting members in the community. For instance, George Kent and his wife Sarah, who came from England in the early 1830s, through their connections were given the Crown Land in Simcoe that stretched westward from Duncan's property. Kent intended to lay it out in plots. The Kents were pleasant people who took an interest in other people's welfare. They helped to give Sarah a sense of her own worth and took a special interest in Vesta, who was a prepossessing girl just entering her teens. And there were the carefree men such as Captain Alex McNeilledge and Captain John Hall, who had seen the world in all its guises and now owned grist mills in Port Dover and shipped on the Great Lakes, whose connections with Duncan were both through business and friendship. They paid their respects to Sarah whenever they came to Duncan's farmhouse, and she enjoyed their salty mannerisms and speech. Sarah remained close friends with Mrs. Joseph Culver, whom she called Phoebe by this time. Sometimes, after services at the Methodist Church, Sarah and her children went to the Culver farmhouse for a Sunday mid-day meal.

Yet there was one person with whom Sarah formed a particular friendship. She was the strongest-willed woman that Sarah had known.

They met by accident while shopping in the open market, to which the farmers brought their produce from the outlying farms. This woman, tall, lean, and with a determined expression, was selling flowers in addition to the vegetables from her farm. No one else sold flowers. The very idea of buying flowers for decoration was unusual in this spartan community, and the bright colors and cheerfulness of the display in early summer caught Sarah's fancy. She decided to brighten Duncan's household with a bouquet or two and began asking the woman questions about planting flowers and making her own garden. The woman was enthusiastic in giving advice and soon they began to like one another. The woman said that she lived with her husband on several acres of land on the flats on the heights to the north-west. Her name was Lucinda Landon. For a time their meetings were at the market only, but in time Sarah persuaded Duncan to invite the Landons to dinner. They were from the States and held political views different from Duncan, but they were careful not to express them clearly, and, consequently, met with Duncan's approval. Since it was awkward to invite Duncan and his housekeeper to dinner, Sarah was rarely included in reciprocal invitations from Duncan's friends, but Lucinda would drop by the farmhouse to visit Sarah and stay for long chats and sometimes Sarah would borrow a horse and buggy from Duncan's stable and take her children on a visit to the Landon farm on the western heights.

Returning from one of these visits on a snowy evening in a sleigh that skimmed the hard snow behind the drum beat of the horse's hoofs, Sarah saw a figure standing by the side of the road and hailing her. Concerned, she drew the sleigh to the roadside and stopped alongside the figure who approached her with arms outstretched pleading for help. Sarah made out the features of a dark-skinned Negro whose eyebrows were caked with ice and whose drawling voice came out in a low moan.

"Please, please, I need hep," he said. "Mah woman and chillun..." he turned and pointed across a field at the forest.

"Israel!" Sarah said, "bring that man into the sleigh. Fanny, come with me."

As Israel stepped down and guided the man carefully into the back of the sleigh, Sarah seized a couple of blankets and, with Fanny behind

179

her, walked across the hard snow in the direction which the man pointed. A cold wind chilled her to the bone and she thought of the man's wife and children freezing together. Within a few minutes, she entered the darkness of the woods, and seeing no one, shouted out, "Halloo!"

As she heard no rejoinder, she told Fanny that they should walk along by the side of the woods and shout out every so often. Fanny held up her hand implying she heard something.

"Here, over here," cried a voice feebly.

Walking in the direction of the sound, they came upon a woman and two children huddled together at the base of a tree. A short distance in front of them was a stream, the surface ice of which they had broken so that they could drink the water. Sarah knew at a glance that they were too listless to save themselves. The cold was lulling them to death. Quickly pulling the children to their feet while Fanny tried to get the woman to stand, Sarah cried out encouragingly, "Come with us. You'll be warm soon."

"I can't," the woman moaned. "Just help my chillun."

Sarah asked Fanny to take the children to the field and watched her struggle with the children, propped up by her shoulders as they hobbled slowly away. Kneeling and putting her arms under the woman, Sarah inched her off the ground to a point where she could put her shoulder under one of the woman's arms and stand up with her. Then tightening her arms about her, she dragged her slowly out of the woods to the field where Fanny sat with the two exhausted children.

"Get Israel to drive the sleigh here," Sarah shouted to Fanny as she furiously rubbed the hands and arms of the woman.

Fanny ran lightly across the snow, and, before Sarah had time to turn her attention to the children, the sleigh approached swiftly. Vesta and Israel jumped out to take the children into it and Fanny helped Sarah drag the woman into the front seat. They all climbed in, squeezing into the little room that was left, and Sarah galloped the horse to the Campbell farmhouse.

The Negro was recovered sufficiently to help his wife into the back of the farmhouse while Sarah's children carried in the black children, whose clothes were thin and ragged, useless against the cold.

The children built a fire in the hearth and Sarah heated water and made coffee and hot soup. All four of the rescued had frostbitten fingers and toes. Fanny retrieved blankets and asked them to take off their frozen clothes and wrap themselves and sit near the fire. The children scurried away looking for dry clothes while the family slowly revived and wrapped themselves in the blankets. They looked abject and conscious of causing trouble. Sarah, bringing them pans of warm water in which to bathe their frostbitten feet and fingers, tried to reassure them that they were going to be well-looked after. Gradually as the warmth took effect, the black children, both boys, fell asleep where they were sitting by the fire, and the adults appeared to recover from hypothermia that would have killed them had they remained much longer in the cold.

"We thank ye," the man said. He was about thirty-five years old. "I had to stop ye. We were dyin'."

Sarah gave them the hot soup. "Do you come from around here?"

The man and woman glanced at each other before the man replied. "Miles north of here," he rasped. "Worked a farm for some years. Never got paid." He looked angrily at the floor. "Then we got thrown out."

The woman let out a sigh that went straight to Sarah's heart.

"We was promised land, our own land, and we got nothin'," she moaned. "We got nowheres to go."

"You are welcome to stay here," Sarah said. "Just forget everything but getting well. Not everyone's like the folks who pitched you out."

Gradually Sarah won their confidence and they told her that they were the children of slaves of early pioneers. Since the law of emancipation allowed their owners to keep slaves for nine more years, the parents of this couple died in slavery.

"But wasn't the pressure to free slaves too much for those trying to hold onto them?" Sarah asked. "Weren't they all free despite the law within a few years?"

"Not for us, M'am," the man replied. "We was not usual, I guess. Anyways we were born free but our daddy and mammy being slaves, we were really slaves, do ye see?"

Sarah nodded and looked at her children who were sitting around

181

them and listening in awe.

"We should've been paid when we started work, but we weren't, and we didn't know what was right," the woman said. "Until our parents passed and we heard about our rights from an itinerant preacher."

"We was promised pay," the man said grimly, "but never got it."

Sarah smiled. "You'll get it here. Children, bring the mats for our friends to sleep on. You sleep tonight in the kitchen. That all right?"

They nodded eagerly. "We's so tired, we can barely keep our eyes open," the man said.

As the children dragged mats into the kitchen, Duncan Campbell came in behind them. His face wrinkled in distaste, he spoke angrily. "What's this I hear, Sarah, we're giving refuge to the homeless?"

The Negro couple got to their feet and bowed nervously to him.

"They almost died," Sarah said.

"I see," Duncan muttered. "Well," he said to the Negro, "you're welcome as long as we can find the room. Come, Sarah, it's bed time. We'll deal with all this in the morning."

Sarah commanded her children to go to bed immediately and, bidding the couple good-night, followed Duncan to his bedroom.

"We can't be giving shelter to whoever needs it," Duncan said as he undressed. "We'll be eaten out of house and home in no time."

"But we have no choice," Sarah said calmly. "It's a matter of life and death."

"Look, Sarah, dear, as more and more immigrants arrive, there's goin' to be lots of homeless. You work very hard, cooking for my workers and me, cleaning the house, bringing in the food. You can't be looking after homeless."

Sarah put on her nightgown and snuggled up to him in bed. "As you say, Duncan, we can talk it over in the morning." She sensed that Duncan on his own would not have offered his home to any stranger, dying or not. If he had known slavery, then his compassion for people would be more evident. But his love for her compelled him to humour her wishes. That thought gave her a sense of self-satisfaction.

The next morning Duncan asked Sarah to remove the people from the house as soon as possible. He had no idea where they could go, but he did not want them living on his property for any longer than was

182

necessary.

Sarah said she understood. She instructed Fanny to do the cooking while she went into the village to visit Dick Plummer in his tailor shop. She agreed that her visitors had to find a way of supporting themselves, but they were not the only ones, according to Duncan. There would be many homeless in hard times. Surely their community could do something for them.

When she entered Plummer's shop, she found him deep in conversation with Isaac Dorsey, a young light-skinned black, who with his brother, came from Virginia, south of the Panhandle. She had spoken to him a few times but they never talked of Virginia other than to say that they never wanted to see it again. Dorsey had a reputation for great intelligence; he impressed for whomsoever he worked with his industry and general knowledge. The men drew apart and looked at Sarah with curiosity as she walked up to them.

"You men heard of homeless people?" she asked.

"Hell, yes," Plummer said. "I been homeless."

Dorsey laughed. "We've all been homeless, Miss Sarah. Why do you ask us?"

"Cause, I got homeless people in my kitchen and Duncan wants them to leave."

The men looked at her blankly.

"There's got to be many more homeless, dying on the roadways and in the fields less we do something about it," Sarah said. "We got to find these people jobs and places to live."

"What about your church?" Plummer asked.

"I'm going to my church about the family I have now, but it can't help the dozens that need it. We need to find them jobs with farmers, or in town if they got talent."

"I see," Dorsey said quickly. "We have to set up a place for the homeless to go to, somewhere that can help them."

"Save their lives," Plummer nodded. "Like a society or somethin'."

"We'll need donations to run it," Dorsey said, warming to the subject. "It can be a good thing for our people. The runaways and all those in trouble. Let me go to some of the good white folks in town. See if we can start something." He rubbed his hands enthusiastically. "Thank you, Miss Sarah. You have given us a wonderful idea. Dick will let you know how we do."

Sarah beamed with pleasure. "You be sure to tell me soon, Mr. Plummer. I don't want this to go by the wayside as just another pipe dream."

"No, no," Plummer promised and walked her to the door. "You can ask Duncan to contribute. That would be real helpful," he smiled.

Sarah found a place on Joseph Culver's farm for the grateful family on the following day and saw them from time to time when they came into the village with new clothes and a changed attitude. She learned from Plummer that a group of whites and blacks were starting the Wilberforce Society to help the poor and homeless. She persuaded Duncan to contribute only after he learned that other whites were serving on its board.

Sarah was well-known in the growing community and, owing to Duncan's great success which garnered respect for her as his mate, she grew in self-confidence. Her children went through primary school and knew how to read and write and add and subtract. Fanny worked alongside her mother in the kitchen until she left home in her late teens. She had her mother's good looks and, as she admitted to her mother, she felt that she would have a better chance in life if she went out on her own. Sarah encouraged her to separate herself from the black side of her background. Moreover, Fanny's chances of finding a marriage prospect in the village of Simcoe were slim. The roustabouts who worked the mills, tanneries and the small manufactories were not of her liking. She wanted a sober, serious family man. Since the Talbot Road had been put through from the Western Regions to Simcoe, there were opportunities in the settlements being rapidly developed in the West. Duncan found her a position at an inn in Otterville to the northwest of Simcoe. The forests of white pine in that region were being cut, and the river through Otterville made it a convenient place for mills. Migrants were coming from all over to the place, and many of them were young men seeking a livelihood in the West. Sarah bid her daughter a tearful farewell because with the difficulty of travel she knew that they could not meet for months.

Israel, at fifteen, hired on with one of the logging teams and became one of the roustabouts that Fanny abhorred. He disappeared for weeks into the forests with logging teams and came back to the village looking for a good time in the taverns and inns that sprang up as the village developed or he would drift down to Port Dover or Port Ryerse and drink in the taverns there. Often provoked into fights, he became proficient with his fists. Sarah lost nights of sleep worrying about him. He seemed destined to spend his life as a labourer as he refused any clerical and craft work that Duncan offered him. Sarah recognized the mean streak of his father James Campbell in him. He liked combativeness and enjoyed the free, hard-working life of a logger. He was kind to his mother, however, and accompanied her to church whenever he was home.

The government set up grammar schools in every region, but the tuition cost more than a labouring family could afford. Therefore, Vesta learned to sew and make dresses in the way her mother taught her. Vesta had darker skin and was considered coloured by some. She was a kind-hearted girl with an open and engaging personality. Sarah felt more protective of her than of her other children.

John was a good-looking boy with startling brown eyes that seemed to transfix one with their intensity. His personality was engaging, and he seemed to be good-natured and happy. Sarah favored him, not just because he was her youngest, but he seemed to have the best chance of becoming prominent in life. She treated him as someone special, and a strong bond grew between them from the earliest days. She encouraged John to be like Duncan Campbell. The boy earned extra money, which he gave to his mother, by working under Duncan in the Post Office and in the general store. He liked handling merchandise and used to watch McPherson keeping accounts in the big ledgers with a thirst to learn. When Sarah went shopping she took him with her. They became a familiar sight in the streets. .

When he was old enough to understand, Sarah told him his origins. Of all her children, he was the most sensitive about his Negro background. He was shocked and hurt that his mother had been a slave. Although she warned him to keep his father's identity secret, he did not deny the rumour that Duncan was his father, as if Duncan's prominence made up for that real dark secret, slavery. He made friends with few schoolmates and spent his time in studies. Aside from his mother and Duncan, he confided only in Sandy McPherson, who had taken an interest in him since he was a baby, and his best friend, Theo Hunt, who knew his secrets and said he wished he had some like them. His relatives he saw as a part of his past, a past that one day he would have to hide from the outer world.

When he learned that his siblings had different fathers, he became more indifferent to them, as if their births in slavery from fathers who were slave owners tainted them. Sarah had to explain to him how this came to be. They spent many evenings talking over the past and Sarah's helplessness against oppression. Her fortitude and perseverance nurtured in him a deep sympathy and admiration for her. Sarah spoke to him as she could not with her other children. John had understanding and wisdom beyond his age. Vesta was the closest to him when very young, but after childhood they had little in common.

In schoolyard snow-ball battles, when the black children would take on the white children, John aligned himself with the whites. The blacks regarded the whites as newcomers to the American continent, and they traded racial insults as they stormed one another's forts and snowballs struck their mark, but these divisions were part of the game and had no bearing on their friendships. In time, however, class and racial distinctions became sharper as the village took on the dimensions of a town and the early settlers and richer immigrants banded together to control municipal affairs. Certain immigrants from the minor gentry and retired army officers formed select groups in some of the towns. John, although friendly with all, kept his distance from the working man.

When John was twelve, Duncan sent him to the best school in the region, a grammar school in Vittoria, a near-by town, run by Methodists. Although there were a number of schools forming in Simcoe and down along the Lynn River, Duncan thought that the dedication of the teachers in Vittoria far exceeded the talents of the underpaid and often inebriated local men, who, recruited from the United States for the most part, quietly inculcated inflammatory ideas in the heads of their charges. Campbell gave John a horse to ride to school, which demonstrated his confidence in his abilities and his special affection for him. John had a sense of fun and enjoyed sports, but he was totally unlike his half-brother Israel, whose wild drinking and uninhibited behaviour disgusted him.

Israel came home rarely. When he was nineteen he turned up one summer day with a yellow-haired, good-looking sailor whom he introduced to his family as his best friend, Job Seaman. Job was full of life. He captivated Vesta, who, at fourteen, was well-developed for her age. They went out dancing at the local tavern that night and came home in the early hours of the morning, Israel and Job hanging helplessly on the steady arms of the spirited Vesta, who guided them to their beds and went to her own with romantic thoughts of Job. From then on, Job turned up at the farm frequently and reported to Sarah the doings and whereabouts of her wandering son. Job sailed on the Great Lakes and knew the ports of call, which he described to Vesta as if they were fabulous lands of adventure. It became very apparent to Sarah that love was growing between the two. She knew that she could not dissuade them, and Vesta looked happier than she had ever been. She counseled Vesta to be cautious and wait until she was older to commit herself, but she could not help feeling joy when she saw them together. Their love was pure and genuine in contrast to her own experiences. She thought back to the days when Henry Lewis was courting her. She was sixteen and proud to attract the attentions of a good-looking man whose strong mind and body declared him to be special. She thought that he was free and that in time he would be able to free her. How deceived she was! Henry's helpless fury at being led away in chains stayed with her on nights that she could not sleep. His imprisonment reflected her own condition and a state of being for the coloured race. It had taken her years to overcome that nagging despondency that she was doomed. The Reverend Doddridge had told her that God would help her. As she watched her lovely child fall in love with a charming rascal, she prayed to God to help her child. Deception, disillusionment and betrayal could stalk blissful lovers like a wolf stalks the deer.

Meanwhile in Virginia, Henry Lewis Sr., whose name Sarah so proudly carried and clung to as a sign of respectability in a world where respect was often difficult to find, came every two or three years to James Campbell's farm to discover how his children were faring. In his travels about Ohio and Pennsylvania he met escaping slaves many times and helped them as best he could. He had seen them captured too and taken back south under armed guard. He knew the safe places and where danger lay. Roads had been built through the wilderness leading to towns on the Great Lakes from which ships could be found to carry hideaways in barrels and trunks to the Canadian shore. Often, runaways would take small vessels but this was dangerous because a storm could arise within minutes and swamp the boat or send it back to the American shore. Desperate men and women made rafts to paddle across thirty miles of water and some floated on doors and other flotsam like shipwrecked survivors. Henry was in Salem attending to sick horses in the stable attached to the main hotel when he struck up a conversation with a slim coloured man whose horse had been ridden too hard and needed to be saved.

"He's gonna need rest," Henry said, applying a concoction of cooked herbs under the animal's nose to soothe its breathing and settle its lungs, wheezing like bellows caught in spasms. "Were you chasin' somebody or tryin' to lose them?"

The slim man laughed and asked Henry what the concoction was.

"Secret," Henry said. "My job's hard enough without me encouraging competition. Besides, I got to at least know your name if I'm goin' to tell you what you're goin' to do for your horse if you want to keep him."

"Go by Alick," the man said laconically.

"I heard of you," Henry smiled. "Active on the trail in the cause."

Alick nodded, looking at him warily.

"I been helpin' too in a way. I know quite a few of you folks now. I got two children in the Panhandle may want to escape someday."

"If it ain't too bad there," Alick said, "tell 'em to stay put. Most of our people are finding communities in Ohio to hide in and it's getting harder and harder to make a living."

"What about Canada?" Henry asked, thinking of Sarah.

"Have to be self-sufficient to survive there. Most find work in the free states as free men. Though, I guess you heard that Ohio is taking away our rights as citizens this year." Alick spat on the floor of the stable and wiped his foot in it to smooth out the mucus. "My job's getting difficult."

"Hope you'll be around for some time to come," Henry said wistfully. "If my children are lookin' to escape, who can they contact? I'm askin' just on spec."

"Captain Wells plies a ship on the Ohio. He's efficient and can get them to Wellsville. From there they have to find their own way." Alick stepped back and turned to go. "But if they're being treated okay, tell them to stay put. What's their name?"

"Lewis."

Alick nodded. "Keep it in mind. Knew a Mrs. Lewis once, but had to call her Mrs. Kinney for the journey."

"Wait," Henry said firmly. "I'm treatin' your horse for free."

"Why's that?"

"Mrs. Lewis is my wife."

Alick stared at him sympathetically, shook his head sadly, and muttered, "Pretty woman."

Henry watched him walk away and pictured him protecting Sarah on the trail in a way that he never could. He decided to visit his children soon because he had not been feeling well. Henry was in his mid-forties and the stresses from his mode of living appeared in his craggy and lined features. His Indian wife understood his passion for the open road and raised their son largely by herself, although Henry came home at the important times in the boy's life. He regarded his responsibilities to Henry Jr. and Molly as emotional. If a person were on his own as a slave, he would soon have the spirit crushed out of him. His children had been luckier than most because their early years were passed with loving parents whose spirits were strong and independent. He himself knew little of his past, but Sarah had told her children of her Irish heritage and made them proud of who they were. But the grinding years of hard work and subsistence living with no hope of reprieve from a sentence that seemed a natural law destroyed the soul of the strongest people. Recent slave rebellions in Virginia had brought greater repression on slaves and even on the free blacks. He felt its repercussions in a free state like Ohio. Fear and suspicion raced through the white population like a fire through a dry forest. As a consequence, Henry worried about his enslaved children.

On his last visit he learned that Henry Jr. had responsibilities which required him to oversee the shipping of goods on the flatboats stopping at Hollidays Cove and to travel to Wellsburg where sometimes he called on his Aunt Fanny and Dick Dawson. Where he was well-known, he would be relatively safe, but encounters he had with white strangers could be perilous. Although intelligent and even-tempered, he had not the experience of his father in dealing with dangerous situations. On the other hand, Molly could analyze a situation immediately and make good decisions. The two had grown very close over the years because they could depend only upon themselves. Their Aunt Nell Grady lived poorly on a small farm and rarely saw them while their Aunt Fanny saw only Henry Jr when he came to Wellsburg on Campbell business. Together, they would survive, Henry thought, after he was gone from this world, but the vagaries of slavery might push them apart. If James Campbell died, and the old man was close to ninety now, the auction block could send them to different parts of the country and then individually they would be crushed. These thoughts brought Henry Lewis Sr. back into the Virginia Panhandle to see his children.

Hollidays Cove bore no resemblance to the quiet, bucolic village that gave him refuge when he fled his servitude in Kentucky. When he climbed the hill to Campbell's farm and looked down at the river and at Brown's Island, he was transported back to those days when he loved Sarah. He recalled her looking up at these hills with dread and remarking that she felt evil eyes were watching her. The whirring sounds and rhythms of the present industrial activity may have distracted the observer from that evil but, if one had experienced it, one could always detect it. It was late afternoon when he led his horse into the area of the slave cabins and tethered it outside his children's cabin. He went inside and stretched out on his son's bed. The aches in his body seemed to fire up and then to slowly extinguish. He closed his eyes and opened them immediately or so it seemed, although he had been sleeping for an hour. Two white men stood in the doorway and were looking at him. One called his name.

Henry jumped to his feet in alarm and his hand was on his knife when a voice he recognized spoke calmly to him.

"Sorry to waken you, Henry, but we saw your horse and wanted to talk to you."

Henry recognized the MacDonald brothers. John, the older brother, was talking.

"Good Lord!" Henry cried. "You gotta be more careful the way you wake me! Come in and sit down." He pointed to the other bed.

The brothers went to the bed and settled themselves on it.

John smiled. "You know that old James was in court with his brother Alexander?"

"Fightin' again," Henry laughed.

"No," Candor said, "James was supportin' his brother against his brother's wife. His brother threw her out into the cold without a cent and she went to court asking for restitution."

Henry shook his head. "Feel sorry for her."

"So does our sister who supported the wife against Alexander and as a consequence also against James. "

"She did! Never thought anyone had the guts for that," Henry said, amused.

"Since James hated his brother, people here are surprised he'd go to his defense, but since it's against Alexander's wife, we guess it's a case of blood bein' thicker than water."

"It's a case of the men keeping the women down," Henry laughed. "He's a mean-spirited man. Is he after doin' harm to your sister?"

"We can protect her all right," John said. "She began disagreein' with old James when he sold your wife but never opposed him openly till now."

"There's a big division in the household," Candor explained, "and old James's slice is gettin' smaller and smaller by the day. He's gettin' meaner and likely to do somethin' irrational."

"You mean that my children are in danger?" Henry asked in alarm.

"Don't you worry," John said quickly. "We've got control here to a point. We're just warning you to be careful this time. We've taken

191

away his gun, but we can't guarantee he won't find another."

"Did his brother lose the case then?" Henry asked in surprise.

John shook his head sadly. "The judge agreed with the wife but said that to rule in her favour would only encourage other wives to bring actions against their husbands."

Henry nodded. "I could've told you that from the first. Well, I'm not goin' to stay long. Just see my children and find out how they're doin'"

John and Candor stood up and, wishing Henry well, they went to the door. Candor looked back as he went out and said, "Old James may not last more than a few months. We'll look after your kids."

When they went, Henry mused on the brothers who were unlike most white men he had ever known. Whites either tended not to see slaves or to notice them only when they needed them. But these men actually took an interest in his children. Candor MacDonald's remark on James Campbell's health could be taken as a warning that things were about to change on the estate. Henry regretted that he could do nothing to help his children. He had impressed upon them the importance of learning, both letters and a trade, as well as they could. At the very least, he had seen them into their twenties. He began thinking back to their childhood and revisiting scenes that seemed to spring from his memory as if they had happened in the past week. There had been good times with Sarah and their children, moments of such joy that they came to him with such emotion that he seemed to float with euphoria. The Sundays after church pic-nicking on the Island and teaching the children to learn the songs of the birds that flew through the area in the springtime. How he treasured those moments of laughter and innocence! All gone too soon. As he lay on his son's bed, he thought of his salvation by Kokataw and the Shawnee. His mentor had taught him true freedom, a mixture of resourcefulness and tolerance. When Kokataw died, Henry supported Kokataw's wife by hunting and helping her cure with herbal medicines. She died from pneumonia soon afterward, but she imparted what she knew to Henry, who, whenever he returned home, taught the knowledge to his son. His life, he thought, had not been a waste. He had cured people and horses for years and tried to help people out of desperate situations. If he had remained a slave, he would have died a useless carcass years ago.

His daughter woke him up. She placed her hand on his forehead and was gazing lovingly down on him. He studied her young, pretty face and her concerned smile, and, despite himself, tears began to roll down his cheeks. Sitting up, he wiped his eyes with the back of his hand, and, taking his daughter's face in his hands, he kissed her.

"I've been dreamin'," he said hoarsely. "Rememberin' when we all were young. Times, I guess, you were too young to remember."

"You rest, Dad," she said apologetically. "I shouldn't have wakened you."

"I am rested, daughter," he smiled. "The old man is all right. Nothin' wrong with me. Where's my son got to?"

"Henry's at Miller Campbell's," she said. "He's bringing back the grain." And when her father looked curiously at her, she quickly explained that the miller was James Campbell's nephew who ran mills on the river.

"You doin' all right, Molly?" Henry sat her on the bed beside him. "Got a boyfriend?"

She giggled. "No one serious. Besides, I don't have time to get to know anyone. Massa keeps us runnin'."

"And Henry Jr.?"

She shook her head. "He goes into the Cove some nights. I don't know where he goes." She paused. "We don't want anything permanent because we plan to escape someday."

"When the old massa dies?"

She nodded. "In a year or two. When nobody will go after us too hard."

"A fellow I met said that Captain Wells runs a boat on the river and helps escapees," Henry whispered. "Tell Henry to get in touch with him when you're ready."

"I'm scared to try it," she admitted. "But since mother did it, we figure we can do it."

"Your mother had help," Henry cautioned. "You got to plan it in detail. Start thinkin' of it now and find out all you can about the routes you can take. If I can, I'll find someone to come here and talk to you about it."

"You can, Dad?" she said incredulously.

"I can try," he smiled. "I meet folks who are in the business of helpin'. But, my dearest girl, don't go until you've got it all figured out. Even then, things can go wrong. It's better here where you're known and treated with some respect than to be sold down river where you have no respect and where you'll be workin' in a cotton field all day."

She sighed. "We want to be free so bad, like you and Mama. I call myself Mary now 'cause Molly is just my slave name, like Mama who hated the name Sal. We miss Mama. We want to see her again. Do you think we can?"

"Yes, my dear Mary. You will see her. Just make it your goal and you'll get free. You get nothin' without workin' for it. That sounds overworked as advice, but it's the best advice I've ever known, and it has to be said over and over again until you really know what it means." Henry put his arm around her shoulders and gave her a squeeze. "Think of it this way, the sooner you are free, the sooner you can get married."

She laughed and pushed him playfully away. A loud bellowing sounded from the farmhouse. They froze to listen. The rasping voice of an old man was complaining at something. The shrill voice of Margaret MacDonald Campbell answered him. There was silence.

"The massa's gettin' too much for her," Mary explained with a sigh. "And he's gettin' too much for the rest of us. I'd put arsenic in his soup if I could get any."

"The brothers told me he could be dangerous. You be careful now."

They heard footsteps approaching the door. Henry jumped to stand against the wall. The door opened and Henry Jr., looking weary, stepped into the room. He looked puzzled at Mary's beaming face, and then catching sight of his father, he broke into a smile and they embraced. Henry Jr. insisted that his father sit on the only chair in the room while he and Mary sat on the beds. They talked about themselves and what had happened to them, and about the events in the Panhandle such as the death of the Reverend Joseph Doddridge, the success of Philip Doddridge as a debater in the Congress, about George

194

Brown starting a democratic Methodist Church separate from the Methodist Episcopalian, about Dick Dawson's failings as a farmer, about the slaver Samuel, who sold his slave auction business to become an overseer in the south, and about the changes in the Cove. Mary left them to wait on table in the farmhouse, and Henry Jr. left his father to attend to his evening chores in the barn. Later in the evening they talked by candlelight until tiredness forced Henry Sr. to fall asleep on Henry's bed, and Henry Jr., blowing out the light, wormed his way onto a narrow strip of the bed that remained to him.

During the night they were awakened by gunshots. Angry shouting erupted from the farmhouse and then died away. Henry Jr. murmured that it was Old James shooting at shadows, and they fell asleep immediately.

16

In the autumn of 1834, Job Seaman, returning from a voyage, staggered to his small cottage in Port Dover and collapsed on his bed with stomach pains. His neighbour saw his distress as she was returning to her home, and, coming to the open door, she called out to him. Job knew from watching others die in the ports along Lake Ontario that he had cholera and asked her to get a doctor if she could. She ran with the news to the houses huddled about the harbour, and one of Captain McNeilledge's sons rode like the wind along the river road to Simcoe. It took him some time to find the doctor, who was visiting patients. Meanwhile word of the disease spread rapidly.

Unlike Asiatic Cholera, carried in by immigrants, *Cholera Morbus* was an acute enteritis that sprang up in towns and villages along the main waterways and roads where its bacteria could hide. Severe vomiting and cramps killed victims within twenty-four hours if medical aid was not given within two hours.

In Simcoe, Israel was loading grain on a riverboat to run it down to Port Dover when the crew stopped work, retired to a near-by tavern for a drink and waited for Duncan Campbell to decide to continue or delay the shipment. Israel was arm-wrestling when an old sailor whom he knew came to his table and looked at him sympathetically. Israel grinned up at him and cocked his head questioningly.

"It's Job Seaman who's brought the cholera," the sailor said softly.

Shocked, Israel stared at the man's lined face. "Where is he?" he asked incredulously.

"In his home."

Israel stood up, looked in dismay at his companions, and ran to Campbell's blacksmith establishment. He seized reins and saddle from a hook, adjusted them quickly on a horse waiting to be led to a stall and galloped away before the blacksmith was aware of what he was doing. He reached Job's cottage in Dover shortly after the doctor and waited just inside the door where he saw the doctor apply mustard to Job's abdomen. Job saw him, and, while trying to give him a bright smile of welcome, his face suddenly seized up, and he vomited with such violence that Israel feared he would bring up his internal organs. The doctor refused to let Israel come closer to the patient and exploded when Israel wanted to take his friend's hand.

"Do you want to die?" he shouted. "Now clear out before you infect the rest of the population."

Job spoke in a broken voice. "Tell Vesta I love her. If I don't get out of this, I leave her that clock." He pointed to a standing grandfather's clock in his room. "It's been in my family. Israel, make sure she gets it. It's all I have of any value." He smiled.

Israel nodded, tears rolling down his cheeks. "You get well, my dear friend."

Vesta learned from Israel that Job was deathly ill but the authorities were preventing travel between the villages. She and Israel went to the Methodist Church and prayed for Job to live, and Israel swore that, if God allowed Job to live, he would not take another drink. Job died that night. Since the contagion was spread by corpses, Job was buried immediately without a funeral.

Job's clothes were burnt and his cottage sprinkled with chloride of lime. Within a few days Israel and Vesta took a wagon to Port Dover and fetched the clock that Job left her. Vesta stood on the sandy shore in front of Job's cottage and looked out at the great expanse of lake. Its calm waters reflected the sun's bright rays on a warm October day seeming to speak to her of the sunny, happy personality of her lover.

Israel, slumped in thought on the wagon seat, roused himself and walked over the sand to put an arm on Vesta's shoulders and guide her back to the wagon. They arrived at the farm in Simcoe as the sun set.

Sarah had a meal with Vesta's favourite foods waiting. She helped Israel carry the clock into Vesta's room. For Vesta the clock stood for the fleeting nature of time. Her moments with Job came back to her when she was alone in its presence.

Israel was never the same. He was sullen and seemed to resent the world around him, except for his mother, to whom he turned over his earnings from his mill and lumber work. About mid-way through November when he was cutting lumber several miles north of Simcoe, a great ash toppled the wrong way and crushed him to death. His body was returned to Simcoe. Sarah had the funeral in her Methodist Church. Her friends the Ruslings, the Landons, the Kents, Duncan Campbell and all the men who worked for Campbell and admired the family attended. Some of Israel's mates stood at the back of the church. Fanny came all the way from Otterville to comfort her mother.

At first Sarah plunged into despondency. She felt that she failed Israel, who was easily tempted to throw in his lot with hard-drinking rowdies. Israel, affected by the attitudes of others, believed that since his mother had been a slave, he was inferior and he adopted a belligerent attitude to cover his feelings. He was accepted among the millhands and lumbermen as an equal, but could not overcome the resentment he had for the patronizing tradesmen and gentry whom he encountered as he grew up on Duncan Campbell's farm. Duncan had not helped, she thought. He had no sympathy for Israel and made no attempt to understand the boy who resented any attempt on his part to advise him. Israel loved the carefree and challenging work in the forest and on the rivers and admired the happy freedom of Job Seaman, whose close friendship had meant much to him. Sarah sensed that

Israel would die young, but age twenty was too young. She put the money he gave her into a strong box that she was secretly saving and planned to give him when he married. Now that money would have to find some other use, perhaps to start her son John in business.

Duncan sympathized with Sarah and gave her a new dress and new shoes to cheer her up, but for real consolation, Sarah sought out her closest friend, Lucinda Landon. But Lucinda could spare only a few moments of kind attention. Her husband was dying of cancer, and the time she had after nursing him, she devoted to running the large farm with her seven-year old son Zebulon. Young Zebulon, who sold kindling wood to the houses and farms, was a favorite of Sarah's. She and Vesta asked him in for cookies and a glass of milk when he went on his rounds. Lucinda's philosophy was to allow children to discover themselves, and, since their friendships were integral to themselves, they were not to be interfered with. She, being practical, applied to take on wards of the state, orphans with nowhere to go, and brought them up as her own children. They went to school and worked the farm as if it belonged to them. That was the way that Lucinda treated children—as if they all belonged. Sarah took strength from Lucinda's example.

The calamity of Israel's death superseded her worries over Vesta's poor chances of marrying. When she saw Vesta's happiness at the prospect of having Job's child, she understood her daughter's need for a living memory of her first love. And when a baby boy arrived in the late spring, she shared Vesta's joy and proudly showed the baby off to her friends. Vesta was fifteen and eager to experience adulthood. Sarah taught her to make her own dresses and found that she had a talent for making clothes, which were more interesting than the manufactured garments coming from Buffalo. With a son to support, Vesta applied herself to turning out dresses that the ladies of the region would buy.

Vesta liked young men and spent time in the taverns with them. Sarah hoped that she would find a husband among the workers employed in the new businesses: tinsmiths, harness shops, dry-goods stores—offering competition to the established businesses of Duncan Campbell. Duncan's major competitor, the enterprising young Leonard Sovereign, on moving to Simcoe married one of Aaron Culver's daughters and opened a dry-goods store, which bought in bulk and sold a variety of goods at low prices that competitors could not match. Young Europeans and Americans flocked to the foundry that made iron vessels, the lumberyard, the grain elevator, the mills by the riverside and Duncan Campbell's distillery. But Vesta showed no interest in them; rather she became close to Jimmi, a young mulatto, whom Sarah thought pleasant but unmotivated. He seemed to just want to hang about and escape work anyway he could. Vesta, falling in love with him, overlooked his shortcomings that her mother pointed out.

Taverns and hotels multiplied in the town to accommodate the workers. One of them run by a newly arrived American called Life Henry became a dangerous place for the colored people. American bounty hunters went there and plied unsuspecting Negroes with drink in order to smuggle them back to the States with little or no resistance. Vesta heard the talk and spoke to her boyfriend Jimmi about it, but he thought that he could take care of himself. He and his friends met there for drinks before Jimmi dropped in to see Vesta after her work was finished for the day. He did odd jobs around town that gave him enough to live on, but it was Vesta's generosity that kept him in drink. When he did not turn up one evening, Vesta began to worry because Jimmi may not have been reliable in some matters, but always kept his appointments and never let her down. She told Sarah that she was going to the tavern to look for him.

Life Henry was at the bar when she walked in. He was a charming man in his thirties, smooth-faced and pleasant in expression. He turned away from a couple of patrons to come to Vesta, whom he knew was Jimmi's personal friend.

"Where's Jimmi?" she asked anxiously. "He should have come to me an hour ago."

Life Henry shrugged. "Saw him here earlier. Have a drink and relax. He'll turn up."

Vesta turned away to go to some young men whom she recognized were Jimmi's drinking buddies. One tall, lanky young man had been at school with her. He told her that Jimmi had gone out with a man who was offering him a job.

"He sounded like an American," he said.

199

Vesta's eyes jumped in alarm. "Jimmi's been kidnapped. I just know it!"

They laughed at that, except for two of them who, being mulattos, looked as if they were considering her suggestion seriously.

"That's happened before," one of them said.

The others stopped laughing.

Vesta implored them to help her. "They could have bound him and be carting him to Port Dover right now," she cried in exasperation.

"Come to think of it," one of them said, "that guy seemed suspicious. He asked me about the black people in Simcoe and then started complaining about them, saying things like they're no good for working and you can't trust them. Strange that he'd want to hire Jimmi."

Vesta's school friend jumped up in alarm. "We'd better get down to Dover quick. I got a wagon and horses outside. Coming, fellas?"

The others, alarmed now, hurried after him out the door. Vesta looked back to see Life Henry looking sharply after them, and, when his eyes encountered hers, he suddenly beamed a bright smile.

"He'll turn up, Vesta. Don't you worry."

Vesta glared at him. Calling to her school friend to wait, she ran to his wagon and climbed aboard as he lashed the horses and they raced along the road to Port Dover.

One of the boys said that Negro families he knew traced their sons to Port Dover where witnesses said they saw them in the company of other men taking fishing boats onto the lake, but it was at night and hard to make out the parties. They were spirited across the lake to Erie, Pennsylvania, then to the deep south and never seen again. Once in the States, a prisoner flanked by armed bounty hunters had no chance to flee.

When Vesta and her friends reached Port Dover's docks, they jumped down and ran to the fishing boats tied to the wharf. They called Jimmi's name in the darkness. The boats were empty, except for the last in which a light came from the cabin. A man appeared at the cabin door, a knife in his hand for cleaning fish.

"Have you see anyone on the docks?" Vesta cried.

The fisherman, a swarthy young man with an indifferent look, gazed at her quizzically and then up at the young men on the dock staring down at him. "Somebody pushed off about five minutes ago," he said.

"What did they look like?" Vesta's school friend asked. "Was there a tall, colored man with them?"

The fisherman thought for a couple of seconds. "Yeah, I think there was. There were two men sort of holding him up. I think he was sick."

"That was Jimmi!" Vesta cried desperately. "We've got to go after them."

"Can we take your boat?" Vesta's school friend asked.

"Well, I don't know," the fisherman said. "I got work to do."

"We'll pay you," he shouted disgustedly and jumped onto the ship's deck, followed by the others. "Unfurl the sails," he said as he took up the oars and set them in the water.

The fisherman attempted to protest, but, seeing their determination, he kept silent and watched as they took over the running of the fishing boat and steered it into the lake. The boys pulled in the oars as a strong wind caught the sails.

After an hour of swift sailing under the moon and stars, some of them began wondering if they were too late or if Jimmi's captors were taking him to a port other than Erie, but Vesta said that she was positive it was Erie because it was the closest.

Vesta's anger and fear kept the young men urging the ship to its fastest speed while the fisherman sat watching dejectedly. Finally they saw harbour lights at Erie. Drawing into the harbour, they detected a fishing boat, only a couple of minutes ahead of them.

"That's the boat!" Vesta said. "I'm sure that's the boat!"

Nursing the sails to catch all the energy they could glean from the wind, they watched three men climb onto the dock, one of whom seemed to have his hands bound behind his back. The two men put the third into a carriage and climbed in behind him. The coachman shut the carriage door as Jimmi's rescuers came alongside the dock.

Vesta shouted, "Jimmi!" in a vain attempt to stop the coach from going, but, hearing the shout, one of Jimmi's captors yelled at the coachman to get moving, and, as the coach lurched forward, he sent a rifle shot in the direction of the boat. By the time Vesta and the young men jumped onto the deck, the coach disappeared into the darkness, and there was no conveyance to use in pursuit. Vesta spent three days in Erie making inquiries after Jimmi, but there was no sign of him. She returned disconsolately to Simcoe with two of the young men who had stayed with her. It took Vesta a long time to get over the loss of Jimmi because she truly loved him. The colored people of Simcoe complained to the town magistracy. But the handful of policemen had a wide area to survey and could never respond to an alarm quickly enough to prevent a kidnapping that was efficiently planned.

There was no proof that Life Henry was connected with the disappearances. Regardless of how dangerous Life Henry's tavern seemed, the young colored people kept patronizing it because they liked the atmosphere and thought that nothing could happen to them. But the episode sent alarm bells ringing in Simcoe among the older blacks who had endured slavery.

While Sarah tried to console the heartbroken Vesta, Fanny visited her with news that Sarah found disconcerting. She had fallen in love with an Irishman from Quebec named William Powers. He was her age, but he had no money and could not marry her for some time, he said. He was a house painter. He migrated West to get from under the oppressiveness of the Catholic Church and the Chateau Clique only to find that the élites in Upper Canada were smothering the workingman and farmer just as ruthlessly. He joined a group of dissidents who talked of reform and read the journalism of William Lyon Mackenzie. Sarah warned Fanny to keep Powers from doing anything foolish. Were reformers not fronts for the Americans, who, having failed to take Canada by war in 1812, expected to take it over from the inside by revolution? Fanny tried to convince her mother that the reformers were not betraying the country and would not bring slavery to the Canadas. Sarah, however, thought that Fanny was so besotted with love that she could not see the stark reality that lay like a threat behind the growing unrest.

"If those people get control here," she said sharply, "you'll be called black, not white, and they'll take away everything I worked hard to give you children."

"Oh Mama," Fanny sighed. "Bill says we'll all benefit when we get rid of the oppressors, and I agree with him."

"Don't forget that the oppressors as he calls them freed this country of slavery. If we had a democracy like he wants, then the majority of people would still have us enslaved. I don't trust democracy. It's the tyranny of the ignorant over the enlightened, as Duncan says."

"But Mama, look at the men who are wanting reform—they're all good men and you know that because you've seen some of them—like good people who help out the black community here," Fanny argued.

"It's not the good people I worry about, it's the forces that come up from nowhere and take over despite the good people," Sarah said worriedly. "We've got enough settlers from the States here who will come to power with the Reformers and change the laws. All it would take to force us back to Virginia is a law saying that Americans have the right to retrieve their slaves from Canada. There's nothing that your friend could do to save you then."

"I have met the leader in the West and he hates slavery," Fanny protested. "He's Dr. William Duncombe and Bill goes to his meetings."

Sarah gasped in alarm. "Squire Campbell thinks this Dr. Duncombe is a dangerous man. He's taking us into civil war."

Fanny shook her head as if implying that further argument was useless. She put an arm over her mother's shoulders and kissed her cheek. She hoped that William Powers really knew what he was doing.

Sarah like Duncan could not understand people such as Dr. William Duncombe, who brought great benefits to the colony in the medical and administrative fields yet preached reform. Since Duncombe lived near Burford, a town north of Simcoe that lay on the stage route to Paris, he came into contact with Duncan Campbell in the course of local business. Duncan remarked to Sarah that Duncombe's radicalism was owing to a dispute over land with the Legislative Council. This governing body refused to give him a patent to some land formerly occupied by a settler named Mallory, who had been a traitor in the War of 1812. Duncombe had plenty of land and influential friends, but, as Duncan explained to Sarah, it takes little sometimes to earn a successful man's enmity.

Sarah took satisfaction in Simcoe's reputation as a loyalist town because of its settlers from the British Isles and its blacks. Its loyalist numbers increased as many runaway slaves found their way to Simcoe and built houses in the southwestern part of the town. In the rural areas, however, disaffection was strong. Farmers coming to Simcoe to grind their grain and get supplies voiced their anger at the tight controls over land and licenses that the ruling group used to get richer. Arguments over politics in the hotels and taverns became heated after the men had a few drinks. One of the most hated men was Duncan Campbell. His name was blasphemed in many a tavern. No one contradicted the farmers, who thought they had been victims of Duncan's lending policies and his Crown land dealings. Duncan's employees, on overhearing these angry outbursts, reported them to Duncan, but he just smiled. He was made Colonel of the local militia and often called drills to make certain that his men were ready for any military emergency. Astride his horse, his solid short body taut, his square face determined, and his russet hair tousled he shouted orders to his men to march and halt. The community formed two orders of militia: one with men under forty and one with men over forty. Militias were formed in all the villages, and, as clamour for political reform grew louder, the militias were trained all the harder. Not all the militia men were as staunchly loyal as their colonels and captains. Generally there was the feeling that reform should be brought in by political means rather than by armed force. This had been the thinking of loyalists during the American Revolution; it remained the thinking of their offspring.

Bill Powers was in Brantford talking to a resourceful young man whom he had met in the course of journeying from town to town offering his services as a house painter. Powers was over six feet tall with blue eyes and reddish hair. His muscular frame and strong face reflected his tenseness as he spoke of the poverty in the villages in the west that he had traveled through. His listener hung on his every word, his dark eyes flashing with anger at times, his mouth twitching with a tart remark, and his thin body writhing as if feeling the pain of frustration and impotence of the farmers and artisans whom Powers described.

When Powers referred to the Doctor, he meant Duncombe whom he had just visited in Burford to the west of Brantford. The young man, Will Mathews, had not met the Doctor but he was enthusiastic about him. On Duncombe's return from a mission to England on behalf of the people, word spread of his humiliation when his delegation of reformers was rebuffed by the Colonial Secretary because the Attorney-General of Upper Canada had reached him first with a message to ignore the Doctor. Mathews, who arrived in Brantford from Ireland three years before, empathized with the rude awakening that the doctor felt. His complaints over the lack of resources given to the towns were met with indifference by the elected officials. It had been a revelation to him how corrupt the government really was—that the Legislative Councilors would take the profits from the sales of Crown Lands and divide it among themselves and the members of the English government rather than invest them in the country was reminiscent of his native Ireland. But Mathews, a bootmaker, who led artisans and workmen in street fights against Indians, blacks, and Scottish Presbyterians known as Covenanters, meant to make his weight felt on a larger scale than the village of Brantford. He saw Doctor Duncombe, William Lyon Mackenzie, Dr. Thorpe and the other leaders of the reform movement as opening the way for him to enter provincial politics. By joining the town workers with the farmers, a strong opposition to the Tories could be created, which was the reason for William Powers meeting with Mathews to persuade his city gangs to support the Reform movement. No reformer considered violence as a method at this time. Mathews was needed, not because of his propensity for violence, but for his leadership of disaffected persons who followed his orders unquestioningly.

Brantford was growing rapidly with new industries. The sudden mixing of peoples with differing ideologies inflamed passions over small issues that grew out of proportion under economic and social pressures as workers competed for jobs. These pressures were exacerbated by the official disregard for these cauldrons of activity while the oligarchs taxed them largely for the benefit of the provincial capital and its bureaucracies. Mathews' men resented the blacks and Indians who prevented them from reconstructing their homogenous type of society which they had left behind in Europe. If Mathews had his way, he would deport all the blacks to the States, but he was careful not to say this to Powers, whom he regarded as a well-meaning but idealistic character.

"You needn't go on with all that description," Mathews interrupted Powers. "I've seen it first hand for years. What we want is action. We've got to change the situation. Years of talking reform have got us nowhere when the boys in power don't even listen. The good Doctor has got to give us more than talk."

"There're too many reformers who don't want violence," Powers warned. "The citizens here are not ready for revolution."

"But by George! that's the only way for us to go," Mathews shook his fist. "Think of the help we'd get from the Americans. Why! they'd be here in hordes helping us set up a Republic."

"There's a time for that," Powers smiled, "but not yet, and I hope, not ever."

They were startled by a banging at Mathews' door and the shouts of men outside. Mathews jumped to his feet and swung open the door to reveal two young men bleeding from the face and with their shirts torn.

"They're fightin' down at the Big Tavern," one of them cried. "We need you to negotiate."

Mathews looked questioningly at the other man who nodded in agreement. "Some of the boys got in a fight with Indians. We got the worst of it. The Indians got them surrounded. They're holdin' on till you can get there."

Mathews turned to smile at Powers. "Behold the peacemaker. We make promises, they make promises. We go home. Next week it's the same thing. God! we need a revolution."

Powers accompanied him into the street. "Revolutions are more bloody than street fights, though," he warned, "just think of the opposition—British regulars with cannon rather than braves with tomahawks."

"Ah!" Mathews waved good-bye to him and followed the young men down the street. "You're a poor excuse for an Irishman," he shouted back.

Powers shrugged and walked to his lodgings. The difference between himself and Mathews lay in their goals, he thought. Mathews sought physical confrontation to effect change because it activated him whereas he himself wanted change, preferably through reasoned argument, to bring improvements. He had a strong feeling, however, that physical confrontation was going to be required from all reformers, regardless of how fervently they hoped to avoid it.

17

In 1836, before the troubles began in Canada and in the early days of the economic recession, a seemingly happy-go-lucky young coloured man walked up the hill from Hollidays Cove onto the farm of James Campbell. He stopped an old Negro, who was coming in from the fields for lunch, to ask where he could find Henry Lewis. On learning that Henry was at the neighboring farm getting wheat ground but was expected back soon, and having the old man point out the road that Henry would be taking, the visitor walked out along that road for several hundred yards until he found a cluster of pine trees by a stream running under the road. Here he stretched out on the grass under the shade of a tree and waited. In about an hour, he saw a husky-looking coloured man driving a wagon loaded with grain coming slowly along the road, and, as the wagon came even with him, he gave a short loud whistle. As Henry looked startled at him, he cried, "Henry Lewis Jr., I assume."

Henry pulled his horses to a halt and said with some annoyance, "What do you want?"

The visitor stood up and said with a bright smile, "You! I want you!" He strode up to the side of the wagon and stretched out his hand. "I am George M. Smith and I'm here because your Dad sent me."

Puzzled and surprised, Henry grasped the man's hand. He saw that the fellow was cocky, good-looking and about his own age, thirty.

"Get down and we can talk in the shade. I've got some news. I don't want anyone overhearing it. Understand?"

Henry stepped down from the wagon and cautiously approached

George Smith.

"You got nothing to fear from me," George said. "I'm not in the grain stealing business. I steal people, not things."

"What do you mean by that?" Henry asked as he sat on the grass facing George.

"You're someone's property, aren't you? Well, I've been appointed to steal you and your sister. Your Dad told me that you wanted to get away to freedom."

"Ssh!," Henry said, looking round at the stretches of grass, the fields and trees about them. "You never know if anyone's around."

"Well, you see," George said humorously, "I've never been a slave so I don't appreciate the finer points of etiquette that you slaves observe."

Henry looked at him with astonishment. "If you don't tell me what you have to say, I'm goin' on."

"You heard of the Underground Railway?"

Henry nodded. It was a term that had been in use for a couple of years and had passed through the slave quarters in Virginia.

"I'm a conductor," George said, suddenly serious. "Your Dad Henry died a couple of months past." He paused to allow Henry to absorb the news and watched quietly as Henry struggled to control his emotions. "He was at peace with his Indian family," George said quietly. "He met me about a month before he passed on and asked me to get you and your sister to Canada. He was a good man, and I said I'd do it. So here I am, good as my word."

"We're ready to go," Henry said quickly. "Old James Campbell kicked the bucket not long ago, and we were hopin' Dad would come again before we risked it."

"Can you go in the evening?" George asked. "In three days?"

Henry nodded, looking uncertain.

"Come to the wharf at the Cove at 9 p.m. I'll meet you and we'll go on Captain Watts's passenger vessel. He'll land us upriver in Ohio and we'll go inland from there. Dress warmly 'cause the nights will be cold, but don't carry much, if anything, to avoid raising suspicions. You think you can manage?" George looked quizzically at him.

His eyes lighting up with expectation, Henry sighed with relief. "I never thought this day would come. Mary and I will meet you on time. She'll have finished her kitchen duties by then."

They heard the sound of carriage wheels rolling over gravel and the crack of a whip. They jumped to their feet and with a nod of assurance George stepped quickly away into the trees. As Henry climbed onto his wagon seat, the overseer of a neighboring farm drove rapidly by him and shouted, "Get a move on, nigger. When I get you, life ain't gonna be so easy." He laughed gleefully as he lashed his horses and sped away.

Henry heard the words as a threat, but not with the sinking feeling of a trapped man that he would have been before meeting George M. Smith. The auction of Campbell's slaves was not for another month, and, by that time, he and Mary should be far away in the Ohio wilderness, he thought.

When he told Mary about their father's death, Mary left their cabin and went for a walk in the dark. She pictured the man whom she had come to love on his first visit to them after years of hiding from his pursuers. Her resentment at being deserted by her parents had been quickly overcome by his forthrightness and kindness. He had endured all sorts of misfortunes and hardship in being free, which made him special for her. He stood against the system and proved that man could be above it. He showed his love for his children and remained for her a reminder of her worth as a person. The fact that he cared for her and came to see her despite the dangers was sufficient to awaken the love for him that she had buried in her heart. And now, like a miracle, he had sent a guide to bring them to freedom just when they had to escape. His death too seemed to say that she need not hesitate to flee because she would not be deserting him. She stood on the crest of a hill and looked down at the darkened valley below and the moonlight on the Ohio River and she cried.

Returning to the cabin, she spoke with Henry about their flight. Where would they go? to their mother? Yes, to their mother, but they were adults and had to fend for themselves. They could not burden her. But how could they begin a new life with no possessions? Trust in providence. And would they be pursued like their father was hunted? Henry considered the question at some length. He reasoned that the

MacDonald brothers would not want to pursue them, but that James Campbell's children would be affronted and definitely track them down because they would not want to lose their value. Farming had become more competitive. Newer farms and newer ideas surrounded them and undermined their profits, and the industries in the towns along the river were getting an ever-increasing share of the wealth generated in the region. Slaves had become more valuable to their owners since their mother's day. The Campbells would want to sell them and reject any suggestion from their mother Margaret and the MacDonald brothers to save them.

Henry planned carefully how they would leave the farmhouse and what route they would take to the wharf to board the ship. It was summer but the nights could be cold in the forest. Fortunately they were leaving at night and could wear warmer clothes without looking conspicuous. He dropped by Grady's store in town to tell his Aunt Nell that he and Mary were going to see their mother. Nell, alive with excitement, urged him to be cautious and promised not to utter a word to anyone, not even to their Aunt Fanny, until they were safely away. During the three days they had to wait before they could escape, they pretended that they were devoted to the family. Mary was particularly attentive to Margaret, intimating gratitude rather than saying it. Margaret made up in many ways for her mother's absence, teaching by instruction and example. But Mary dared not risk the slightest suggestion that she might be leaving. She and Henry had some value for the family, and she could not be certain that ownership would not win out over sympathy in Margaret's case.

Mary noticed Margaret's relief after James Campbell died. Over the years, if it had not been for her brothers, Margaret would have broken down, but their steady support and timely interventions saved her from violent and humiliating situations. When she cleared away the dishes after supper on the third evening, she smiled at Margaret, who, unaccustomed to be smiled at by her slaves, looked blankly and then smiled in return as if she detected some kind thought on Mary's part.

Mary, sensing that she was behind schedule because the dinner had taken longer than usual owing to unexpected guests, told the kitchen help to wash and put away the dishes. She almost ran to her cabin where she found Henry impatiently waiting with a small bundle of their clothing in hand. Mary quickly changed into a pair of sturdy boots, which she had been given to wear in the muddy barnyards when she gathered eggs and did other farm duties. Neither of them said a word as they struck out under cover of darkness over a back path down the hillsides into the Cove.

Few people were out on the streets. If either of them spotted someone, they would alert the other and take another route to avoid contact regardless of who it may have been. When they arrived at the wharf, they were reasonably certain that no one had seen them. A man moved from the shadows of one of the boats anchored there and stretched out an arm to direct them to the ship they were to take.

Henry recognized George Smith and whispered his name for the first time to Mary as they quickly followed him up a gangplank and into the hold of a paddle-wheeled steamer. There were other figures in the hold that they could barely discern in the dim light from the moon. Smith, whispering that they were runaway slaves from further south, left them to go on deck. The motor turned over and presently they were in midstream heading north.

The group in the hold were silent but the air was full of tension. Someone had sighted the vessel run by an association of slave owners, who paid for a vigilante crew to capture escaping slaves. But because Captain Wells ran the best passenger service on the river and the respectable citizens who used his transportation service resented delays and unnecessary searches, it was unlikely that his boats would be stopped. The slave owners as a result put most of their funds into patrolling the shore near the important towns and in spying or sleuthing in those towns.

After what seemed like hours, Captain Wells, having taken the ship above Wellsville, Ohio, anchored it off a rugged section of shore. A small boat was lowered and Henry and Mary were directed to climb into it with the others. Smith signalled for Henry to take one of the oars while he took the other and quietly they rowed to a spot on the shore that Smith indicated. They waded ashore in shallow water with Smith pulling the boat by its painter after him. A man waded out from shore, took the painter from Smith's hands, and whispered to Smith that all was well. When they climbed up on the bank, Henry looked behind to see the rowboat moving in the gloom back to the passenger ship.

Smith whispered to the group that they were to follow him in single file and say no word. He told Mary and Henry to take up the rear. The moon having disappeared under clouds, it was so dark that none of the features of the group could be seen, just their figures, tall and short, slim and fat. The smell of fear from their bodies was recognizable in the night air. As they walked rapidly along an Indian trail into the forest, the older members of the group became distinguishable by their heavier breathing. George Smith did not slacken the quick pace until they had walked for some hours. Then, when they came to a small clearing, he pointed to some logs on the ground and whispered that they were to take a rest. He touched Henry on the arm and indicated that he follow him into the forest. They walked for less than a minute when they came to a brook and a small pool of fresh water. Smith took a bucket from a bush, filled it with water, and taking a wooden ladle from the bucket gave it to Henry to drink.

"Look in that bush, Henry," he said as he took a drink.

Henry felt through the bush's branches and felt a parcel, which he pulled out. It fell open to reveal apples. Henry picked one up and began eating it.

"Just one each," Smith warned.

Henry looked round him at the tall trees looming above him in the darkness. "You pick this place?"

"I know what you're thinking," Smith said with a smile. "What a place for an ambush!"

"I was thinkin' it could be a perfect trap," Henry admitted.

"I check it out before every run," Smith said. "I can see any disturbance, any blade of grass stamped by a foot that does not belong to any of us."

Henry nodded as if impressed and watched Smith fill the bucket with water.

"We'll give them time to drink this and rest for five minutes before we move on," Smith said. "We've got to stay in the woods all the way, at least for a while. It's too dangerous to go into the towns and villages the way folks used to do. There's people on farms that will help us, but in some regions you won't find anyone."

They returned to the group and passed around the bucket from which people ladled the water to drink. Mary spoke to a young family of four: parents in their thirties with two teen-age children. They had come from Kentucky, guided through the forest to the Ohio River and then by Captain Watts' ship up the river. The constant whippings had finally put the resolve into them to escape and search for a better life for their children. Mary found them pathetic in their hopes for a utopia, which they equated with freedom. They were uneducated and unfit for fending for themselves in the world they were entering. But maybe they would survive, she thought. Maybe desire was stronger and more resourceful than ability.

When dawn filtered through the trees, the group was still walking. They walked all that day with short rests to feed on the berries they found in the forest and to drink from the streams and relieve themselves. Near the end of the day, Smith allowed them to find pine boughs to stretch out on and sleep for five hours. Then in the darkness they moved onward, Smith pointing to the northern star as their guide. About noon the next day, Smith called a halt. The exhausted band sat heavily on the ground. They were aching for nourishment. Mary was surprised that some of the older people whom she expected to fall by the wayside were more vigorous than she was. No sooner had they stretched out when three white men came out of the forest. A shock of fear shot through the group, but Smith held up his hand in welcome and gave a small cry of pleasure.

The men were rangy and bearded. Mary saw that they had kind eyes and felt relieved. They brought with them food: bread, meat, cheese, and apples, which they began distributing to the people.

Smith shook hands with them all and turned to address the group. "These men are conductors and we'll split up after this into small groups. We've all got to go by different routes into the towns on the lake shore 'cause the slavers are watching out for us in full force nowadays." He surveyed the group with a humorous expression. "Some of us are going to fit into coffins and go by train, others are going to be good servants to white masters and we'll go by carriage. Others are going to keep tramping through this forest. These men are going to decide who does what. Do everything they say. Remember that their lives depend on you as much as you depend on them." He stepped among the group and sat down.

The three white men, having given out the food, consulted among themselves while the band ate. Henry looked up at the treetops swaying in the summer breezes. He thought of the meticulous planning that had gone into this escape and how this scene was being repeated in forests throughout the northern states. He looked at George Smith and saw a smiling happy fellow who was covering his apprehensions with bravado and self-confidence to give courage to his followers. He gave silent thanks to his father for sending George Smith to him and Mary, otherwise they might have stumbled into the many nets laid in the forest and the "friendly" towns by the slave catchers and be trundled in chains back to slave country and a certain sale to the southern plantations. But regardless of how well-planned, happenstance and bad luck could end it all in tragedy.

One of the rangy white men approached Mary and suggested that she go with the family with whom she had made friends. They would be put into coffins and be shipped by train. Mary looked balefully at Henry and shook her head.

Henry stepped up. "My sister goes with me," he said firmly.

The white man cocked an eyebrow. "But can she keep up?" he asked George Smith.

George looked at Henry as if asking for confirmation.

"Yes," Henry said.

"I will," Mary promised.

Smith looked at her admiringly. "If you're tired now, be prepared to be doubly tired tomorrow 'cause we're walking," he smiled, looking down at her well-built figure. "And Henry and me aren't carrying you," he added with comical exaggeration.

Mary laughed and the group giggled. It was the first moment of relaxation they had felt, and it came over them like a sudden upset to their equilibrium. They began laughing and laughing until even the white men were laughing with them at this incongruous suggestion. Gradually as the tension evaporated, they stopped laughing, and, rest-ing contentedly on the ground, they ate the meat and bread and drank the water from a pail that the white men had produced from somewhere. Just as the group was coming together, Mary thought, it had to be broken up to survive. No one among them was over fifty and most would be in their twenties. Most were dark skinned. Henry and she were the lightest skinned mulattos, like George Smith. She looked at their conductor with curiosity. He was easy with himself and others, a man of supreme confidence, which was so unlike colored folk she knew. She guessed that he had never been a slave, that he had been educated, even well-educated by the sound of his speech. One of his parents had probably been white and given him the advantages of a cultured upbringing, which showed in his gestures, although he was doing his best to conceal it. She liked him and felt confident under his guidance. By contrast, the white men seemed slightly nervous, as if the responsibility they were assuming might prove too great. They had to arrange for all manner of escape and subterfuge. Perfect timing was needed for success.

Two young black men joined Mary and Henry under George Smith for the trek through the forests to Lake Erie. Their names were Jeb and Ross. Jeb was eighteen, slightly built and light on his feet. Ross figured that he was about twenty-five; he was strongly built and stood just under six feet. Jeb was fairly mild in manner whereas Ross had a constant angry expression as if he were prepared to kill anyone who stood in his way. Mary thought that he must have suffered much which, instead of cowing him, had created a person capable of extreme violence.

The oldest white man, who had a long white beard and seemed the very essence of patriarchal rectitude, told the group that they had to go. The group stood up, stretching and rubbing arms and legs, and broke up into smaller groups as the white men had arranged. Mary watched them form behind one of the white men and leave on a path going westward. The young family with whom she had spoken turned and waved to her before they disappeared into the trees. George Smith told his four followers to move out behind him on a trail heading due north. "We can't stay long in one place," he warned. "We've been here too long already. I'm setting a fast pace," he added, looking at

Mary. "You all have to keep up with me. I'm showing no mercy."

Mary smiled, and Henry, looking on, was amused because if there was one thing he was certain about his sister it was her stamina. Within a few hours of walking, the small band fell into a walking order naturally: Smith led followed by Ross, Jeb, Mary and Henry. Occasionally they heard voices in the distance when they moved into the thick underbrush and waited until the forest returned to its customary brooding silence. They walked until the small hours of the morning when Smith called a halt for sleep and a meal. While his charges slept on the ground, Smith took a narrow path to the east for about twenty minutes when he came onto a ploughed field at the end of which loomed a barn in the starlit darkness. As he approached the barn, a dog barked but fell silent at the sound of Smith's voice. Smith rounded the barn and gazed up at the windows of a farmhouse. There was no cloth in the windows, thus he assumed that the area was safe. He went into the barn and found a bag to the right of the door in which were eggs, bread and cooked chickens. Snatching up the bag, he passed back through the door, and, glancing again at the windows of the farmhouse, saw a face in one of the windows. He waved and moved swiftly across the field and into the forest.

Smith found his charges were sound asleep and concealed the bag of food in the crotch of a tree. He sat down at the base of the tree and, trusting that no animal could smell the food and disturb him, he fell into a deep sleep. The birds wakened him with their singing at dawn. He looked round at the bodies strewn on the ground near-by in the pale light filtered through the trees and thought of the miles they had to travel. Mary Lewis was sleeping near her brother. He had to admit that he admired her spirit. She was not the adventurous sort but she could overcome hardship without complaint. He stood up and saw that the bag of food was still in the tree crotch. Possibly the smell of human was stronger than that of the food and had kept the animals away. He shook off the effects of the cramped position in which he had slept and gathered some wood for a fire. Within minutes he started a small blaze and the others, hearing his movements, awakened joined him. He laid out the food in individual lots and held out a tin for Ross to get water. When Ross hesitated unsure of which direction to go,

Smith laughed and pointed to where he would find a stream. The others fell on the food hungrily. Ross returned with water and Smith passed the tin to the others who drank from it in turn. Smith was the first to speak, his voice sounding conspiratorial.

"We're getting nearer the great lake," he said. "We'll be getting closer to settlements. Don't talk unless it is absolutely necessary. Keep alert. Don't panic."

"Where we goin'?" Ross asked suspiciously.

"To a farm," Smith said quickly, "where we can sort things out and you can look for work."

"We won't get work," Ross snorted. "Nobody's hirin'."

"Things are better near Cleveland," Smith said. "We'll keep you in food at any rate, Ross."

"Can we get over to Canada?" Jeb asked in a high-pitched voice. He sounded like a child, Mary thought.

"You got somebody to go to there?" Smith asked.

Jeb shook his head and looked at the ground.

"Can't get employment there," Smith said. "Better to find work here, then go there with cash to buy land. Wait a couple of years. That's what we're telling people. Just be patient and keep out of sight. We can get jobs for you, I think."

"I can't stay," Ross said angrily. "They'll be lookin' for me. I'll take my chances in Canada."

"Look here," Smith said calmly. "Americans are talking about invading Canada to help the Canadians to overthrow their government. I can't explain it more than that. If you float in there, chances are you could be mistaken for an invader. We're telling folks to stay here till the whole thing blows over. We'll get you a place where bloodhounds can't find you," Smith smiled at Ross, but Ross looked doubtfully at him.

"It's true," Henry spoke up. "I heard that settlers are leaving Canada for the States 'cause times are so bad there."

"This is my third escape," Ross said sternly in a soft southern accent. "You can't know what I been through. Even had an iron lock on my head after the last time. I'll kill myself the next time."

"We'll make sure they don't catch you again," Smith said. "Trust me." Then with a look at Mary to see if she was ready to go forward, he pointed north. "We'd better start goin' again if I'm to keep my promise."

Mary stood up and took her place in file as the band set out. About mid-day it started to rain, but Smith insisted that they keep up the swift pace he was setting. At first the trees caught most of the rain but then blasts of it came along the forest floor with a strong wind that, beating at their faces, slowed them down. It was only when they heard gunshots that Smith threw up his hand to halt. They stood listening for a minute until they heard shooting that was nearer to them. Smith led them off the path into a huge thicket of bushes and trees and told them to slide under the bushes and be quiet. He went back to the path and walked along it stealthily, as if he were hunting the hunter, whom he suspected was making the noise. By instinct he stepped behind a large tree just as a hound dog rounded the path in front of him. The dog, sensing his presence, stopped and sniffed and waited. Presently two white men carrying rifles came up to it.

"What is it, Rex?" asked the older man who could have been the father of his fellow hunter.

The dog began to bark at the tree at which point Smith stepped into sight.

"You're not hunting people, are you?" he asked with a grin. "Had any kills?"

The men seemed startled. The young man lowered his gun at him. "Who are you?"

"I'm on my way to Cleveland. Heard the shots and thought I'd better make sure who you were."

The older man quieted the dog and was holding him by the collar. "You'll find a deer about a hundred yards up the trail. We're planning to pick it up on our way back."

"If the bears don't get it first," Smith joked.

"If you heard our guns, the bears must have," said the older man with a wry smile. "You're walking alone, are you?"

"No," Smith said. "My wife is back aways waiting to see if you were honest or villains. If I didn't come back she would know you were villains."

The hunters looked disconcerted at this. Smith noticed that they ceased to be suspicious of him and tried to appear casual. "We hunt in these parts since we live a few miles over," the young man said.

"Well then, I'll walk back with you to where my wife is. Will you hold onto that dog. My wife is terrified of dogs, especially hunting dogs." Smith led them back along the trail.

"You met many villains?" asked the older man, holding the dog by its collar.

"A few," Smith admitted. "We learned to be careful, you know." Smith was thinking quickly. These men would know that he was not a slave because of his manner, but if they saw any of the others they would suspect that they were slaves. Yet if he did not produce a wife they would become suspicious again. He could not tell if they would turn him in for a reward. He suspected the young one would, but not the older one. The rain worked to his advantage. These men wanted to keep moving rather than stand in it. Smith led them just beyond the point where his charges were hidden and shouted out, "Mary!", at large as if he had no idea where she had taken refuge. "It's all right, Mary, you can come out. They're just hunters. They won't hurt you."

The three of them stood waiting. There was silence. "It's all right, Mary, my dear. The dog won't hurt you."

The dog began to growl and then bark. The hunter yanked at its collar to keep it quiet. Then Mary appeared coming towards them through the trees. She stopped about ten yards away.

"She's afraid of the dog," Smith said. "If you gentlemen don't mind moving along, we'll be on our way."

"Come, let's go," said the older man. "We're wasting time. Good-day to you," he said to Smith and nodded at Mary before turning down the trail and pulling his dog along after him.

Mary walked to Smith and stood with him watching the hunters disappear over a ridge. Then walking with Mary back to the thicket, he called softly on the others to come out. "Stay quiet," he warned as they stood up. "We'll walk through the underbrush for a bit, then cut back to the trail." He led the way.

"I was gonna run for it," Ross admitted.

"Then you would have got us all caught," Smith said sharply. "I had to get the dog out of the way or he would've sniffed you out."

They came back onto the trail and, noting that the rain had let up, they proceeded with lighter hearts. Smith was glad of the rain because it kept people from moving about as they would have on a sunny day. But that evening, when they stopped to rest and eat the remainder of the food he had saved from their previous meal, he announced that henceforth they would travel only at night and hide in the forest in the day.

"There's a lot of settlement from now on, and I don't know if it's friendly or not because it's recent," he explained. "It's better to go slow and get there than risk not getting there."

The rain stopped in the night. As they continued along the path, watching for stumps and branches in their way, they felt their wet clothes drying on their bodies. Mary was sensitive to the strong smells that made everyone of them more and more distinctive. Being the only woman she slept a distance from the men during the day, but it was the smell of her companions which made her grateful for the distance. She thought Smith noticed her aversion from the amused way he looked at her.

For two days of walking along faint trails, past prickly bushes, over sharp rocks and through dark forest where animals watched and darted through the underbrush, Smith led the group deeper into the wilderness. On the third day when the sun was high in the sky and beating down warmly, they came upon a large pond, fed by a spring. The water was cool. Smith suggested they wash their clothes and themselves before they went to sleep. He went to a large oak tree and, reaching up into a hollow, brought out a bar of soap.

"Ladies first," he said, handing the soap to Mary. "While you use the pool, Mary, we'll scrounge up some branches for bedding."

Mary looked at him gratefully, as if he had just given her a treasure, and, taking the soap, tired as she was, ran to the pool, knelt and raised the water to her face. It felt divine. She undressed quickly behind a large bush and waded into the water, soaping herself as she went. She heard the men breaking off branches and dragging them into piles for sleeping upon. After washing herself, she scrubbed her clothes and beat them on near-by rocks until they were clean, then stretching them on the rocks in the hot sun, she crawled naked onto the grass and let the sun soak into her bones.

She awakened from sleep to hear George Smith asking for the soap. He was at a distance, out of respect for her nakedness, but she thought that he could see her. She reached for the soap and on her knees threw it to him. He caught it and bashfully laughing, he apologized for disturbing her. "There's a place over there," he nodded, "where the pool bends out of sight. The men will bathe there. How does it feel?"

"To be clean again?" she smiled. "Like I've gone to Heaven."

Smith laughed and disappeared. She could hear the men splashing and shouting faintly through the trees and drifted into sleep. In the late afternoon Smith came to her and she awakened to see him naked. Smiling, she opened her arms and he fell to the ground beside her. They kissed passionately and made love. For Mary, it was the first time she had made love and she was twenty-six. It was the most symbolic act of her new-found freedom that she could imagine.

In the evening when the sun waned in the sky, the party finished the last morsels of food they had with them, supplemented by wild strawberries and raspberries that Henry and Jeb under Ross's guidance had gathered. It was enough to keep them from hunger. Just as the first animals, deer, elk, wildcats and bear began appearing to drink from the pool, Smith led his party back to the trail in the twilight and ever onwards to the north.

Mary walked directly behind Smith now. The others felt the closeness between them and smiled among themselves at the romance. Henry was disconcerted but said nothing to Mary. He saw her happiness but worried that she would be hurt when George left them. Smith, he sensed, was a ladies' man and unlikely to feel committed to his sister. Jeb, his thin long face wreathed in smiles when George and Mary conversed together at rest stops, regarded love in others as entertaining. The angry-looking Ross became sexually awakened and began to look at Mary in meaningful ways suggesting that she share her favours with him.

Mary frowned at Ross and pretended to be absorbed in the difficulties of the trail. Ross, walking behind her, whispered suggestively whenever Smith went ahead to scout the way. Smith could tell from the worried look in Mary's eyes and Ross's manner that he was going to have trouble, yet he said nothing in the hope that Mary could resolve the problem. In all his years of conducting he had not crossed that line of detachment into familiarity with one of his charges. That he had allowed his desire in Mary's case to undermine his judgment meant that she was special to him, he thought. He worried that his action threatened the cohesion of the group and could lead to capture. Ross was stronger than he was, and Ross had an air of meanness that, if challenged, would lead to a physical confrontation. When Ross playfully slapped Mary's haunches causing her to look in fright back to her brother, Henry barked at Ross to walk at the back of the line.

Ross snorted at him. "You ain't my boss man. I kin walk where I so please. And what I see in front of me, pleases me," he smiled wickedly.

"Walk at the back," Smith said calmly. "Don't make trouble."

Ross seized Mary's arm. "Then she walks with me," he growled.

As Mary cried in pain, Ross let her go with a contemptuous smile. Smith stepped between them and pushed Ross away.

"Who you think you are?" Ross sneered angrily and brushed George aside with a sweep of his arm. "You ain't the only man who can fuck!" He ran to Mary who was trying to walk away, and seizing her about the waist began to half-carry, half-drag her toward a thicket of bushes.

Smith stood transfixed by the sexual urge that transformed Ross. Henry's shout of alarm and the blur of his body rocketing past him to grapple with Ross acted like a switch to propel him into action.

Ross held Henry off with one arm while continuing to drag Mary with the other until, confronted by Smith, he let Mary fall and thrashed at his assailants as if they were slavers. The nimble-footed Jeb picked Mary up and ran with her stumbling and falling to a small clearing where he left her to return to help subdue the maddened Ross. Mary, trembling with fear, crawled to some bushes and curled up behind them.

Ross bloodied Henry's face with his fists which he used like clubs, and with one hand gripped George Smith by the throat. Henry held onto one of Ross's arms and tried to strike at his face to force him to release his stranglehold on George who gasped for breath. Jeb, expecting to witness the deaths of the two men, picked a thick branch from the ground, and, running with it struck Ross with all his might on the side of his head. It hit him above the right ear and bounced back to roll off his shoulder as the big man's knees buckled and he fell unconscious in a heap in the long green twitch grass covering that area of the forest floor. Smith bent over, supporting himself with one hand on his knee while the other smoothed his throat as he coughed and sucked in air. Henry fell on his knees beside Ross and listened to the man's breathing.

"Well," he said to Jeb, "least ways you didn't kill him."

"We got to leave him," Jeb said hurriedly, "before he comes round."

"He's not goin' anywhere," Henry smiled and felt a rivulet of blood run from the side of his mouth down his chin and onto his neck. He looked round at George still clearing his throat and massaging it softly with both hands. "You really started somethin', didn't you!"

George shook his head and choked out, "Where's Mary?"

Jeb pointed to the clearing. Henry started to go but George seized his arm. "Let me," George said, his eyes pleading with him.

Henry shrugged and looked at Jeb. "If Ross starts to wake up, hit him again. I think there's water a little ways off so's I can clean myself up." He walked slowly away in the opposite direction.

George came into the clearing and called Mary's name. She stood up and ran to him. They clasped in a long embrace. "It's all right," George said softly. He stroked her back and whispered, "I heard of sexy women, but didn't know they was this powerful."

Mary began to laugh. "Guess I got to be extra careful—mind who I give the stare to."

They walked back arm-in-arm to where Jeb stood over Ross. "Where's Henry?" Mary asked in alarm.

"Washin' his self," Jeb said. "He'll be back in a minute or two."

Mary thought Jeb had soft eyes. She had heard the expression "the eyes of a poet" and decided that if Jeb had been able to write, he would be a poet.

"We gonna leave him here?' Jeb asked Smith. "He can look after his self once he comes round."

"No," Smith said. "He's my responsibility." He went down on one knee and felt the side of Ross's head where the stick had hit him. There was blood on his hand when he removed it. "Best we build a fire 'cause night's coming on." He swung the small bag that he carried on his back to the ground and pulled out a metal basin. "Get some water, Jeb, and we'll clean his wound. If we're lucky he may be able to go again in a few hours."

Jeb took the basin reluctantly and headed in the direction that Henry had taken. He found Henry standing naked in a stream and washing the blood out of his shirt. After drinking as much water as he could, he filled the basin and cried out to Henry, "Ross is goin' with us."

Henry nodded and smiled. He slapped his wet shirt on a rock, and, since darkness was falling, he dressed hurriedly and followed Jeb back to the others, his wet shirt dripping down his back.

Ross was sitting up while George cleaned his wound when Henry reached them. Jeb and Mary were building a fire. No one spoke a word. When George had finished with Ross, he fished from his knapsack some apples which he kept for emergencies and handed them to everyone, who munched them while gazing into the fire and ruminating on their private thoughts. Mary thought she saw an expression of contrition on Ross's face. George was right to care for him, she thought, because it made him aware of how dependent they were on one another.

When they had sat in silence for some time and the night sounds of the wilderness had grown more intense, George asked quietly, "How you feelin', Ross?"

"Got a pain," Ross said. He smiled suddenly. "And I caused pain too," he added apologetically. "Sorry, Mary. I got worked up."

Mary nodded at him but kept her face expressionless.

"We got time to make up," George said. "Can you walk?" he asked Ross.

Ross stood up, held his head for a second, and took a few steps. "I'll keep up with you all," he said with determination, "but I'm takin' the back of the line."

"That's a good man," Henry said. "Let's go." He helped Mary to her feet and took the water remaining in the basin to kill the fire.

They set off with George Smith leading and Mary, Henry, Jeb and Ross following in that order. The long trek through the frightening hisses, shrieks and cougar-like breathing in the darkness concentrated their minds on survival, and soon they forgot the tension and enmity that brought them to the brink of tragedy. Ross fell behind occasionally, at which times George would slacken the pace until he caught up with them. Ross's head throbbed in pain, but he forced himself to continue until morning arrived and Smith rewarded them with a few hours of sleep on the ground. When they awoke to continue, Ross said that the pain was almost gone.

Within two days they reached the outskirts of Cleveland. Smith led them to an isolated farmhouse. From the barn there came a colored man beaming at Smith and calling out to his wife in the farmhouse. He embraced Smith and looked joyfully at the runaways. He was of middle height, round-faced, and enthusiastic in manner. His wife came running from the house to embrace Smith and then turning to see the others she went to Mary and put her arms about her. "Welcome!" she sang.

"I won't introduce you," Smith explained to his charges, "because we don't want to burden you with something you have to keep secret. Friend!" he said to the farmer, "I'm leaving two men with you, Jeb and Ross." He looked at Jeb and Ross, who were surprised. "You'll be either working for them or their friends for the time being until we decide what's best," he said to them. "It's been a pleasure guiding you." He put out his hand. Jeb and Ross shook it as if still unsure of what was happening to them. "Henry and Mary, we'll go further into the town. Come, we can't waste time. The Reverend's going to be at a certain place at a certain time and we can't afford to miss him." He patted the farmer on the back, waved to his wife and signalled to Mary and Henry to follow him back along the trail.

Mary turned round to see Jeb and Ross being taken into the farm-house. Jeb happened to look back at the same time and waved to her. She waved back and realized that in that gesture she sensed for the first time the hope and goodwill that only a free person could feel.

The three of them were too ragged and dirty to enter the town. Smith was accustomed to his beard growing during his conductor trips and being clean shaven afterward, but Henry had never had a beard; it made him feel itchy and unkempt. Smith led them to the outskirts of

Ohio City, where at nine o'clock every morning, the Reverend Chains went for a long walk in the forest near his home. If there were runaways to be helped, he could be reached at a point in his walk where he stopped to meditate and commune with God. It was here that Smith stepped from the forest to hail him. In the sixteen years since Sarah Lewis met him, Chains had grown stouter but still had a tall, rangy look, and a clean-shaven boyish face. To an observer, the Reverend appeared to be greeting a parishioner. Smith told him of the brother and sister waiting in the forest and their need for work. Chains nodded and whispered that he would meet them at the same place at nine in the evening, when it was still light enough to see one another and find their way to whatever destination Chains had selected. The Reverend continued his walk while Smith went in the opposite direction until he was far enough along to step into the forest and double back to Mary and Henry.

"It's going to be all right," Smith told them. "He knows a place that needs servants. Just get some sleep now. You'll be eating soon." He smiled at the thankfulness he saw in their faces.

For almost two weeks of hiking they had been pursued by fear. No one mentioned it, but it was a part of them, as if it had been born in them. It was fear that gave them the energy to accomplish the feat of passing through a wilderness with little food and absolute faith in their conductor. For Mary and Henry, the promise of seeing their mother again gave them determination. That they would have to wait some months near Cleveland before getting to Canada was a disappointment, but one they dealt with as they did with so many in their short lives. At least, they had stayed together and could depend on one another for moral support. These last few hours in the wilderness they passed in a state of subdued joy. Smith told them about the independent nature of the people who lived along the Great Lakes and what to expect with regard to their colour. Whereas Southerners needed to know everything about their neighbours and their community and kept all coloreds under surveillance, in the north people tended to mind their own business and usually thought of coloreds as free people who were farming and working as they did. There was always that element looking for opportunities to make easy money that the fugitive slave laws offered.

One had to be alert and watch the movements of strangers. Both black and white bounty hunters came through Cleveland and other lake ports looking for prey, but the abolitionists often thwarted them. Over the years some rather complicated procedures for protecting runaways were developed. But there were cases of betrayal. Man was always open to temptation. And so they passed the day, talking and dozing, until as the sun was setting the Reverend Chains appeared. Smith hurried his charges to Chains and introduced them quickly. Chains put his hands warmly on their arms and said that he had found a farm where they could hide for the first weeks. Smith shook Henry's hand and embraced Mary.

"Aren't you coming with us?" Mary asked in disbelief.

"Not a good idea," Smith smiled. "But I know where I can find you. Look for me someday." He stepped away and hurried back into the forest.

Mary and Henry felt less secure and looked disconcertedly at the Reverend.

"He's a good man," Chains said. "He's risked his skin many times, with the result that he's known to our enemies. He cannot be seen with you for your own sakes. Please follow me and we'll be in a safe place in less then a half hour." He led the way along the path to a road where a covered carriage pulled by two horses was waiting. There was a plump white man sitting on the carriage seat and holding the horses' reins. He smiled and nodded at them as they approached. "He'll take you from now," Chains said, holding open the carriage door. "I will see you soon."

Mary and Henry got into the carriage with a sense of unease. When the carriage rolled away, Henry said that they had no choice but to trust the Reverend. They were well hidden from view and traveling rapidly as if on an errand. Henry held Mary's hands to calm her and occasionally peeked outside the window to see the changes in the landscape they passed through. The land looked increasingly cultivated. At the close of twilight, in that gray light before darkness, the carriage turned off the main road and up a long lane to a farmhouse on a hill. When the carriage stopped, the driver thumped on the carriage top with his whip. Henry and Mary descended and saw a middle-aged man approaching them as the carriage drove off. They could not make out his features clearly in the dusk but his voice and his manner indicated that he was a gentleman. He asked them to come with him and led them to the barn behind the house. He lit a candle by the doorway and led them up some stairs to a loft at the back of which was a furnished area with two beds, wash basin, a table set with food for an evening meal and candles, which he lit with the candle he was carrying.

In the candlelight their host's features became illumined. He had a gentle face, with clever but kind eyes, and an expression which showed his concern for their welfare and a reassurance that they would be taken care of. He pointed to some clothes hanging in a wardrobe and suggested that they wear new clothes on the morrow. He would leave them now to enjoy their dinner, and, unwrapping a parcel which he carried in one arm, he placed a bottle of red wine on the table.

"Where are we? and what is your name?" Henry asked suddenly, overwhelmed by the kind treatment.

"My name is John Alwyn, Mr. Lewis. If you or your sister desire anything during the night, please knock on our door and we shall be pleased to oblige." He nodded a good-evening with a smile and left them.

Mary went to the washbasin immediately and poured water from a jug into it to bathe her face, arms and hands. Henry took the covers off the plates of food, which were still hot and had been placed there obviously just before they arrived. He listened to the sounds of crickets from the outdoors as he looked over the table laden with food. He thought that he must have reached freedom because this was how free men were treated. Mary came to stand beside him and looked at the same scene. She suppressed the hunger biting at her stomach and the desire to throw herself upon the food in order to enjoy this moment with her brother. Could these good people who arranged all this, Henry said aloud, could they have known how much such consideration would mean to slaves coming into freedom? He and Mary bowed their heads and gave thanks to God, and, as they prayed, tears of wonder and gratitude ran down their cheeks.

The next morning Mary and Henry after a deep sleep awakened to a bright summer day and dressed in the clean clothes which John Alwyn indicated that they should wear. Their movements were noticed by the Alwyn family because when they were ready to go out, a servant of the family arrived with a breakfast tray and set it on the table. She said that Mr. Alwyn would meet with them shortly. Just as they were finishing their breakfast, Alwyn climbed the stairs to the loft and, cheerfully greeting them, asked if he could sit with them. After eliciting some details about their journey north, Alwyn offered them room and board with a sum of money per month for their services. Mary would work in the kitchen and Henry would join the other hired men who brought in the harvest and tended to the many orchards on Alwyn's estate. In that way, Mary and Henry would save money for their future life in Canada and help him out until the late fall. When winter came, he would find jobs in Cleveland for them. In the spring he would hire them back. And so it was in this fashion that these two escaped slaves spent two years near Cleveland and went undetected by the bounty hunters looking for them. During that time Mary did not encounter George M. Smith once.

18

The Upper Canada Society for Emancipation in Cleveland alert for spies who might upset rescue plans, preferred that members meet in small groups of fifteen to twenty persons. Men such as the Reverend Chains, John Alwyn, and Alfred Benoit spoke happily of bringing new members into their group and of the monies they raised for the cause, but in recent months reports of the forming of political lodges of American sympathisers with Canadian Reformers began to worry them. They sent George Smith along the frontier from Detroit to Buffalo to calculate the extent of their strength. Smith found that these lodges had sprung up in all the major towns, that great numbers of unemployed men, who roamed the roadways after the financial breakdown of American business, were joining them as much for the charity they extended as for the revolutionary sentiments they expressed. And, what was truly threatening, the professional rich were donating large sums of money to them on speculation that, when Upper Canada was democratized, they would be in a good position to pick up the spoils. Moreover, the Sons of Liberty had lodges in western Upper Canada with men domiciled every ten square miles; when the Canadian patriots rose up, a rider could carry the news quickly to his neighbouring lodge; then the Americans would invade from Detroit. Surprise and rapidity of movement were their watchwords. Could reformers be persuaded by Americans to reintroduce slavery into Canada and could the so-called American Sons of Liberty by their superior numbers gain control of the Upper Canada government? The Society provided funds for Smith to go to the areas of greatest disaffection in Upper Canada to discover the real state of affairs.

Thus it was that Smith was farming in Southwold Township near the village of St. Thomas in west Upper Canada in the spring of 1837. In his travels about the area he saw small groups marching with rifles and training for an uprising. A big man with a barrel chest, and a warm and gentle disposition, he quickly made friends with the farmers who came to barn meetings. The intensity of their determination surprised and impressed him. At a barn meeting in Otterville, he encountered Dr. Charles Duncombe. Under middle height with a handsome, cheerful face and an engaging personality, Duncombe kept the farmers in a state of excitement and anger at the unfair and corrupt measures of the government and their own impoverishment as a result.

"Greetings! Glad to see you out!" said a wiry little man with a serious face. "We don't see many black folks holdin' our opinions."

"That's cause a lot of them don't have farms like I do," George said and stuck out his hand.

The farmer said his name was Avril Brooks. "I'm from New York State. I hear you're from Michigan, right?"

"You're hearin' right," Smith smiled.

Dr. Duncombe, passing through the crowd, put his arm through Brook's arm. "Will you have a good turnout, when I come to your area next month, Colonel?" Duncombe had a clear baritone that carried to all corners of the room.

"More converts every day, Doctor," Brooks smiled. "Just hopin' George Smith here will be one of them."

Duncombe grasped Smith's hand warmly. "Welcome! I can tell you're a farmer, Mr. Smith. Suffering like the rest of them?"

Smith nodded. "Clergy reserves cut me off from my neighbours—costin' me too much to get my crops to market."

Duncombe smiled. "If I can help in any way, get in touch with Bill Powers, that tall, dark man you see over there," Duncombe nodded at Powers who was looking down at the men around him as he listened. He moved away to greet a crowd of farmers eager to shake his hand.

Avril Brooks smiled wryly. "My lodge elected me colonel. It's secretive because we don't want the government to know our business."

"How many lodges are there?" Smith asked.

"I can't tell you," Brooks looked serious. "There's one near you in St. Thomas. Their Colonel is very suspicious of newcomers. I'll tell him to get in touch with you, but he likes to be pretty sure of you before he even approaches you. He doesn't even allow his members to come to meetings like this in case they are seen by an informant and cause the lodge some trouble."

Smith smiled. "I guess you know more about the boys in power than they know who's against them."

Colonel Brooks nodded and turned away to speak to a group of men in earnest discussion. Smith saw Bill Powers striding by him and, throwing out an arm, stopped him.

"The doctor said to speak to you," he shouted above the voices and introduced himself.

Powers said he wanted to talk to him but had to meet a friend for lunch, would he come along? Smith, taken aback, recovered quickly and agreed. They mounted their horses and rode into Otterville while they talked of the complaints of the people against the government.

"These things have been goin' on for years," Powers said. "We may have to fight to get rid of the oligarchy, but first we've got to have a sort of protective force the next time we have an election. The oligarchy is so corrupt that it encourages hoodlums to keep the reformers from voting. Trouble is, that frustrates the people even more. Can you handle a gun?"

"Yes, I can handle a gun," Smith smiled. "I hear that I can join a lodge."

"I know nothing about those lodges other than they're unnecessary," Powers said abruptly.

"That's strange. I thought the doctor liked having those lodges."

"The doctor is diplomatic but he tries to make clear that if there is a rebellion, it has to be by Canadians. We don't want Americans to risk their lives for us. And we don't want undue American influence on the government we set up."

Smith nodded as if agreeing with Powers, but he was nevertheless pleasantly surprised by the man's forthrightness. Perhaps, he thought, the blacks had nothing to fear from a reform government. "Looks though as if you've got to accept American fighters since all these lodges are set up to respond at a moment's notice."

Powers laughed. "They're just getting organized. Besides, the American government's got troops along the border to quash any attempts at invasion. Maybe in a year or so the lodges will be capable of helping us, but I hope it doesn't come to that." He led Smith through the main street of the village to a house set back in a field. "I hope you are hungry. My girl makes a good meal. Someday I hope we can get married."

They dismounted and tied their horses to a post. A woman's voice called out from the house. Smith looked up to see a woman standing in the doorway. She was very pretty and looking at him with great curiosity.

"Fanny," Powers called to her. "I've brought a new friend to share lunch with us. He tells me he's hungry."

Fanny Lewis smiled and held out her hand to grasp Smith's hand. "A friend of Bill's is always welcome."

"I'm unexpected," Smith looked apologetic.

"Never mind that," Fanny laughed. "I always prepare plenty because I never know how many will be with Bill. That's the way it is with politicians."

"She's making me out to be more than I am," Powers smiled. "I'm more of a troublemaker than a politician."

Powers took Smith to a room off the hallway where he could pour water into a basin and wash his face and hands. Alone and looking into a mirror Smith felt uneasy, wondering whether Fanny could perceive that he was not a reformer. She was not likely to be so enthusiastic about the cause as Powers. She might detect an ambivalence about it in another person. When he came to sit at table with them, he felt that Fanny was sizing him up.

Powers said a short grace and passed a bowl of chicken legs to Smith. Fanny helped herself to salad. They were silent until everyone had food on their plates.

"George is a free man from Michigan," Powers said. "Not a runaway."

"Aren't you lucky!" Fanny said quickly.

"Nothing's sure in Michigan," Smith said.

"Things are no better here," Powers said bitterly. "That is, economic-wise. The panic south of the border came here with the crooks that robbed you all and brought your factories and banks to a standstill. 'Fraudulent endorsements' the papers call it. That's fancy talk for thievery by the rich."

"That's not the worst of it," Smith interjected. "The British refused to give them more credit, so they blame England for the depression. The swindlers you talk about are financing groups of unemployed to invade Canada."

" I knew it!" Powers cried emphatically. "It's because they're anti-British, not because they love us Canadians and want to bring us freedom."

"Not all of them," Smith smiled. "Lots of Americans really believe you're suffering under tyranny."

"Oh, it's tyranny all right," Powers said. "People here are afraid to speak out because there are government spies, but we have legitimate complaints and the oligarchy is afraid of us. But I don't think that the Family Compact has any idea of the opposition it's stirred up."

"Speak of tyranny," Fanny scoffed. "Do the Americans never think of their tyranny to the Negro? I came from Virginia, Mr. Smith. I was a slave and witnessed such tyranny that makes the Family Compact look like angry nursery maids by comparison."

Smith looked astonished. "You! a slave!"

Fanny nodded. "My aunt after whom I'm named can pass for white and is the slave of a coloured man."

Smith nodded. "We are fighting against that too, Miss Fanny, believe me," he said sympathetically. "It's gonna take time, although it may take a war to do it."

"One war at a time," Powers said with a smile. "First we have to get rid of the Family Compact."

"Here," Fanny said, raising a jug of red wine, "take some of this and we'll toast to that."

Smith drank the wine in a toast although he felt hypocritical doing so. He noticed that Fanny was watching him closely, knowing that blacks were resolutely opposed to the reformers. He wondered if she could see through him. He decided to broach the subject straight on. "You know that blacks in Canada like the status quo," he said to her. "But you support the reformers."

"Just like you," Fanny said. "But I don't hate the men in power here. They brought the country stability and gave the black people a refuge. But their time is passing. They got too corrupt, too rich, and the kind of men who got into their ranks are not the same who started this country. That's why I'm for reform, Mr. Smith. But I'm not for Americans coming here to help the reformers. I don't trust the unemployed and those fraudulent endorsers."

"You are giving me insight into the situation here," Smith said kindly to her. "I thank you for putting it like that. I'm getting my bearings here now."

"Fanny's right to caution you," Powers said. "The black communities could see you as an enemy, like those black bounty hunters who befriend escaped slaves and then betray them to kidnappers."

Smith wondered if Powers really trusted him. "It sure is a dilemma." He shook his head. "My skin colour puts me with the blacks but my farming profession puts me with the reformers."

"You have to decide for one or the other," Fanny suggested. "Me, I'm for reform."

"And how do the blacks see you?" Smith asked quickly.

"It was never about skin colour," Fanny said. "We were all who we were. It's just this politics that's dividing people, and the new immigrants bringing their prejudices with them. Besides, I'm a woman, and where I'm from they know I love a white man."

Powers laughed. "That sin excuses all others. Funny how some people who don't show prejudice get upset when black and white live together. I guess it would be worse for us if Fanny did not pass for white."

"It's the mind set that comes from slavery," Smith said. "If we could get rid of slavery, the whole colour problem might go away."

"Don't be too sure about that," Fanny warned him.

"The problem is oppression," Powers cried angrily. "Slavery in the States and a stupid oligarchy here."

When it was time for Smith to leave, he promised to be in touch with them again soon. "I like the doctor," he said, "because he's courageous and he's for the people."

"That's what's needed here," Powers agreed, clapping him on the shoulder, and watching while Smith rode out of sight. He turned to look questioningly at Fanny.

"There's something about him—a whiff of danger—a sense of the world—that doesn't fit the humble farmer," Fanny said. "He's not working for the government, but he's got an agenda, I think."

"Is he for us or a'gin us?" Powers asked with a frown.

"He's a good man," Fanny said. "And he's for us up to a point. He looks like he's observing right now—as if he hasn't convinced himself."

"I'll take a chance on him," Powers said. "We need all the men we can find. Anyway, I like him."

"I wish my Ma was here," Fanny said wistfully. "She'd size him up right."

19

Sarah was sizing up her own situation and came to a conviction that she had reached another stage in her life. For the past months she had not slept with Duncan and for a couple of years their sexual encounters were less frequent. Duncan's business interests took him away to government offices in Toronto for weeks at a time. Sarah regarded herself in the mirror and resigned herself to the tell-tale signs of aging—the lines in her face, the wisps of gray in her hair, the rough-ened hands from cooking and washing and cleaning—work that gentle-ladies never thought of doing—and her progress or decline into her late forties, whichever term suited her mood for the day. She suspected that Duncan met young ladies in the cities and towns which he visited. As an eligible bachelor, he was invited to all of the great social func-tions and met important people and their lovely daughters. He used to tell her about these grand balls, the wines and foods, and the funny incidents, but for some time he stopped relating his experiences and demurred replying to her questions. She sensed a coldness growing between them. Duncan's progress into the better class of society left her and the muddy little village of Simcoe in his past. She served her purpose, she thought, and it was time for her to leave his life, which had brought her so much joy and satisfaction, lest she become bitter. On a Sunday afternoon, when the Kents were visiting Duncan, she left her work in the kitchen and joined them with her own mug of tea as she often did with close friends.

"The streets have all been laid," George Kent was saying. "We've divided up the lots and many have been taken." He stopped to smile at Sarah. "Good-day, my sweet lady. I see you have provided us with your tasty cookies. You know how much I love them, don't you?"

"You spoil him, Sarah," Mrs. Kent said with an admonishing look at her husband. "Sometimes I think if Mr. Campbell did not have you, Mr. Kent would do all that he could to bring you into our household."

Duncan smiled benignly at George Kent. "You do understand, George, that without Sarah my household would fall in pieces, like Humpty Dumpty."

"I hope he pays you what you are worth, Sarah," George said jokingly.

"The squire's been good to me," she smiled, "but I've been thinking of going into business on my own."

The others looked surprised.

"How's that?" Duncan asked frowning. "Your own cooking business, do you mean?"

"Yes, squire. Vesta is wanting to have a dress-making business in the village. She finds it difficult to work from the farmhouse here."

"Dear little Vesta," Kent said. "Well, that can be arranged. We're erecting houses on the lots as I guess you've noticed. She can rent one."

"And Mr. Kent will give her a rent she can afford, won't you, George?"

"For a nice girl like Vesta, she can have her pick. She has a good business head, Sarah. I'll do everything I can for her. Just send her to me."

"But," Duncan said quizzically, "you said you wanted your own business."

Sarah hesitated. For years she worshipped Duncan and did all that he asked with love and admiration. His acceptance of her meant that she had grown in her sense of self-worth over the years, but to separate from him took a resolve and confidence that she never expected to have to call upon.

"Perhaps this is not the time to discuss it," Mrs. Kent said tactfully.

"Yes," Sarah said. "Vesta and I want to start together. She is too young to work on her own. I have saved some money and Israel left me money." Sarah looked at George Kent meaningfully.

"Well then," George said. "You think it over, my dear lady, and come see me. I need tenants for the buildings we are constructing and you would be a perfect one."

"I hope," Duncan said with slight embarrassment, "that Sarah is not serious. I'm not ready to lose her just yet," he smiled at Sarah.

Sarah perceived an ambivalence in Duncan. He recognized suddenly that their relationship had come to a separation, but he needed her to run his household. "I'll give you plenty of notice, squire," she said. "I have to see to the kitchen." She stood up and said good-bye to the Kents, who smiled kindly at her to hide the discomfort they felt at Duncan's unease.

Sarah heard them return to their discussion of laying out the town and marvelled at her temerity in broaching the subject of her leaving Duncan. His reaction confirmed its inevitability, she thought, and she took satisfaction from the fact that he would truly miss her. A few years ago she could never have had the courage to announce her independence, but now she knew that it had been at the back of her mind all the time.

That evening, Duncan came to her and said that he understood her reasons for wanting to be on her own. He thanked her for all she had done for him and hoped that he had not appeared ungrateful.

"Both of us have to move on," he said philosophically. "But, remember, you can count on me. The village is thriving now, so you ought to make a successful business, but, if there are hard times, I am always willing to help." He stretched out his hand and Sarah, tears in her eyes, took it and pressed it to her chest.

"You need to develop free of me," she said. "I'll just drag you down, squire. You helped me more than you could understand. And, we'll see each other over John's future, won't we?"

"We will," Duncan assured her. "That boy will go far and I'm here to guide him. Don't you think twice about that," he smiled, and stepping to her, he kissed her on the cheek. "Good-bye, my dear Sarah. Our time was a good time. I shall never forget it."

He left her with a sad smile, but Sarah was happy to hear what he said. Their son kept them together, she thought, if only to discuss his welfare. Thoughts of living in her own home liberated her in a different way from slavery. At last she was stepping out of servitude into independence.

George Kent built houses on his land grant west of Norfolk St. and now rented one to Sarah. It was a modest wood frame house on two lots facing Norfolk St., a bit removed from the centre of the village but opposite Duncan's property and close to the road called Union St. that ran east-west, branching north-eastward up the hill through Aaron Culver's farm to meet the major routes.

Sarah was very proud of her house. Duncan gave her some furniture and let her have discounts on furnishings from his store. She raised chickens, had a couple of hogs, a cow, bought a horse from Duncan's stables, and planted her own vegetables. The ground about the house was extensive. A ravine ran in back of it. George Kent rented a couple of other houses on the same lot, but they faced Kent St., which was becoming a busier and noisier section because of the taverns and shoe and tin workshops that developed just south of the lot. Opposite Sarah's house, across Norfolk St., was a section of forest on Duncan Campbell's land. Duncan left it wild as a deer park. Sarah took her grandchild across the street to watch for deer.

Sarah set herself up as a cook for hire. Duncan had to hire Sarah to cook for special functions because the maids, who replaced her in his household, could not make food taste as good as she did. Vesta worked out of Sarah's house as a professional dressmaker. John, who was attending school, and Vesta's small child lived with them.

In addition to cooking, Sarah took in laundry as it complemented Vesta's business. She laundered the clothes in spring water in the ravine. It was hard work, but she was strong and hardy in middle age. The economic downturn in 1836 affected everyone, but Sarah established good relations with the town gentry through Duncan Campbell and received their business. She saw the poverty of some people and the anger of others toward the government. The anger was not just over the injustice of land grants and corruption in the bureaucracy. People blamed the greed of the business elite that used government to consolidate its wealth through public works. Sarah followed events through hearing the discussions of Duncan with his friends and from her young son John who was fascinated by politics and economics. John told his mother what he learned: that as the fur trade ended when she arrived in Canada, the ensuing timber trade with Great Britain brought wealth to the merchants, professional men and bureaucrats; they leagued against the rural population expanding quickly from an influx of poor immigrants, who were brought as ballast by the timber ships on their return voyages from Britain. With the enormous increase in Canadian wheat exports in the 1830s, the newly rich called for inland improvements: bridges, roads, canals, railways—demands met by the proliferation of American banks and the expansion of credit. But the collapse of the railway boom in England and the passage of the English Corn Laws, which stopped the import of Canadian wheat into Britain, caused a glut of timber and wheat forcing down prices in Upper Canada. Sandy McPherson said that the Canadian commercial class, trying to construct a new commercial empire by free trade with the United States, beggared the Canadian government by having it grant loans to construction projects, which failed when sources of capital for Upper Canada dried up. When crops unexpectedly failed in Lower Canada and the North-West States, wheat from Upper Canada supplied them and prices rose; but scarcities developed and bread riots erupted in New York City. The United States government, fearing inflation, refused to honor paper script for public lands and insisted on payment in gold and silver, thus bankrupting western banks as anxious depositors withdrew their money. Likewise, the Canadian governing class refused to relieve the hardships among the farming class and opposed an expansion of capital by the issuing of bank notes as legal tender. Protest marches and riots by farmers became increasingly frequent. Sarah heard the verbal abuse directed against the gentry such as Duncan Campbell and his friends. The division between the two camps grew starker and more violent.

"Things are very bad," Sandy McPherson said to Sarah when she dropped off her homemade pies at Duncan's store. "All the industries are laying off. I don't know if I can sell these pies nowadays."

"Reduce the price," Sarah said. "Maybe to half."

McPherson shook his head doubtfully. "It's no use your baking them, Sarah. You're working for nothing. Take Leonard Sovereign. He's been getting our business cause he undersells us by buying cheap in bulk, but even he is looking scared."

"There's a lot of angry people," Sarah said grimly.

"Some robberies," McPherson whispered. "Keep this to yourself, but Duncan has hired an armed guard to sit in the bank. He thinks some men are desperate enough to rob it."

"A lot of our black children don't have shoes," Sarah said, "and whole families go hungry but nobody I know wants to break the law."

McPherson shrugged. "Duncan is getting more and more anxious. He mistrusts practically everybody. I hate to say it, Sarah, but wealth has made him different. He thinks he is part of a vulnerable elite against the great horde."

"He'll change again, once we get past this bad time," Sarah said confidently. "He's a good man at heart."

"I wish I had your optimism," McPherson grinned. "I need to talk to you more often, or listen more to Richard Plummer," he laughed. "I wish you were a man, I would conscript you for our regiment and listen to you say that there's going to be no violence."

"I can't say that, Sandy," Sarah said stepping away. "I feel like a piece of driftwood being tossed about by the course of events."

"That sounds nice. Sort of poetic. I like it, Sarah."

Sarah looked askance at him, and, with a wave of dismissal, she left the store to walk home. She looked down the streets and at all the buildings that comprised the town and thought back to the muddy little street and handful of houses that she knew not so long ago. Was this great surge of energy, ambition, and creative activity to be destroyed by sudden fury, by blind violence, by the refusal of men to understand one another? Perhaps if all men had endured slavery they might hate intolerance and violence as much as she did and recognize that force could change nothing.

Captain Duncan Campbell gave drills daily to his Norfolk Militia, comprising Sandy McPherson as his lieutenant, two other officers, three sergeants, four corporals, and eighty-seven privates—ready for action. Mercer Wilson, a twenty-four year old man from Scotland, who was appointed a judge at the Court of Requests, was directed to form the Volunteer Cavalry, and Colonel Joseph Ryerson, an early settler at Port Ryerse, organized the 1st Regiment when the authorities sensed that the dissension in the country was becoming dangerous. A few blacks from Simcoe joined Wilson's Cavalry, but most of them joined the black regiments guarding the Niagara and Detroit frontiers, where there was more likelihood of action against American invasion.

The smooth-faced, energetic young Wilson, despite the influential background of both his father's and mother's families and his easy access to the men in power, could not earn sufficient to pay for the needs of his family. His command of the Cavalry brought him additional income which helped him pay off some of his debts. Sarah knew him through Campbell, and he always stopped to speak to her when they met on the streets of the village. She liked his gentlemanly manners and his concern for her welfare now that she was in business for herself. He could not afford to bring her his laundry, but he recommended her to others.

"Hello, Mrs. Lewis," he called out from behind her one day. "Can we talk for a moment."

Sarah knew his well-modulated voice and turned to face him. "Yes, Justice?"

"I need your advice, if you don't mind." He caught up to her and lowered his voice in confidentiality. "It's about the command I'm building up."

"I don't know about military things, Justice. I can give you recipes to feed your men, but that's all," Sarah smiled.

"You are the best judge of character that I know," he said seriously. "And the best cook," he added with a smile. "You have been here much longer than I have and know most of the persons well. What do you think of Henson Johnson and Dick Plummer?"

Sarah frowned, uncertain of what he was asking. "Henson Johnson is the finest, most honest man in Simcoe and Richard Plummer is one of the smartest. Why do you ask?"

"They want to join my cavalry unit. Both can ride, they say, and Plummer says he's had experience fighting Western Indians."

"You can believe them," she said. "They are good men. Richard is a friend and the best public speaker I've ever heard."

"So I believe," Wilson smiled. "I heard him recite speeches out of Shakespeare's plays. He sounds very educated."

"Richard was never a slave," Sarah said sharply, as if defending him. "Mr. Johnson was born into slavery but was freed by his master when he was young, so I heard, but he's quiet and never speaks about himself."

Wilson thanked her. "It's a responsibility getting the right men. I think they will fit." He turned on his heel and plunged into deep thought as he strode away.

Wilson was sensitive about introducing Negroes into his company who were, after all, volunteers. He had three light-skinned blacks already, and they seemed to be accepted, but Plummer was copper colored and Johnson was jet black. He shrugged and thought that if any of his men objected they could join one of the other regiments. Since coming to Canada he had heard some whites talk disparagingly of blacks and Indians, but they were likely to be reformers, not loyalists. The very fact that Negroes were willing to fight alongside loyalists against the white reformers would give loyalists confidence in their cause, he thought. Then there were bull-headed Tories like Allan MacNab who needed no assurance that his cause was just. Wilson knew the man only through hear-say, but his public escapades and outspoken behaviour in the Assembly against reform had stamped him as a man who could accept only one side of an argument. How enlightened the reformer Duncombe was by comparison! He dominated debate in the Assembly on social issues; his recent report advocating lunatic asylums and treating insanity as an illness was revolutionary; his education report which was rejected by the legislature would some day be adopted, Wilson thought. What a pity that he and good men like him were driven into the arms of the reformers! Wilson had sympathy for them, but he himself could never take the drastic step of challenging the authority of the state. It was the state that gave him meaning and would provide for his family.

Wilson stopped by at Henson's blacksmith shop and came up to Henson who was shoeing a horse. "What a beauty!"

"He is, ain't he?" Henson said in a deep rich voice. "As black as I am," he smiled. "What's up, Captain?"

"You and Plummer will ride with us," Wilson said emphatically. "We are drilling tonight on the Walsh wild lands, starting at seven. I have weapons for you."

Henson nodded.

"There's all sorts of rumours of rebels training north of us, so we've got to be ready."

Henson drove a nail into the horse's hoof. "Understood, Captain."

Wilson left him with a wave of his hand and went to the new courthouse beside which Plummer was one of the men building the jail. Since Plummer was high up on the scaffolding, Wilson gave him a shout and an okay sign. Plummer gave a whoop. Wilson spoke to one of the white workmen on the ground and told him when to bring Plummer to the drilling exercise. Wilson felt satisfied that his troop was complete. He thought of his father and his uncles commanding British troops in India; they had fought bloody battles in hand-to-hand combat. What would they think of a civil war between political factions? He felt certain that they would never have let the situation drift so far out of control. This could be a tragedy or a farce. One thing he was certain of—he had to make his regiment put on a good show so as to make would-be rebels think twice before risking their lives. His regiment could be depended on for absolute loyalty, he thought, whereas the other militia regiments were full of moderate reformers who were either not bold enough to rebel or disapproved of violent means. If loyalists did not react strongly and show that they had the situation in hand, they might be overwhelmed by these moderate reformers, who would take courage from the success of the rebels and join them. Wilson hurried into the court house as he was late for a hearing on a case of petty debt—a common complaint of increasing frequency in these hard times.

20

George Smith had just harvested the last of his wheat when one sunny morning in November a mild-mannered white man knocked on his front door. He invited Smith to the next meeting of the St. Thomas lodge, and, leaving directions, quickly departed. Delayed by a sudden rain storm, Smith walked into the lodge after the meeting began. He figured there were close to fifty men present. He listened to a stout farmer recite stories of farms forfeited and businesses closing. The anger in the audience seemed to mount with every succeeding disaster and with every account of human tragedy. Hearing his name called out, he walked with ten other men to the platform where a young man arranged them in a line facing the audience and stood with a book open before them. He read off the four degrees of trust and then swore the men to the first degree which required them to be brothers to their fellow members and maintain secrecy. After the men swore one after the other to the oath, Colonel Alfred stepped from the audience on to the platform.

Smith took great interest in this man. Alfred was about six feet and looked to be in his sixties. His eyes were dark, but his hair was fair with some white strands. His sideburns were turning white. His movements were athletic and quick. He shook hands with each of the inductees in turn and stood talking with each one before moving on. When he came to Smith, he looked deeply into Smith's eyes. His hand-grasp was strong. He gave him the secret passwords that he would need to remember on his level of trust. When the meeting adjourned, the members came forward to greet the inductees. Smith shook hands with numerous men, most of them farmers, and listened to their views of the political situation in the country. They had differing ideas on the type of government they wanted, but they were united on toppling the oligarchy. Smith eventually found himself face to face with Colonel Alfred.

"Where are you from in the States?" Alfred asked casually.

"Michigan." Smith sensed that he was being checked out by a master.

"What part?" Alfred looked interested.

"On the shore of Lake Huron. But I've been traveling since I was a boy," Smith smiled. "Got the wanderlust."

"You also got a good education," Alfred said. "Were you sent over to Canada for any particular reason?"

"Sent?" Smith looked puzzled. "I just came to get away from the colour problem."

Alfred stared at him blankly. "I ask because we get Americans settling here who think that the province will become a state and they'll be in on the ground floor, they say. You don't have any ideas like that?"

"I just want to live a good life and settle down with a wife," Smith laughed. "I'm with you against tyrants because they make the good life impossible."

Alfred smiled, held out his hand and warmly shook Smith's hand. "Welcome. I wish more of our black immigrants had your faith in our cause."

Smith shrugged his shoulders. "It's a matter of perception. Slavery is a god-awful experience. Those who have not experienced it can't understand."

"Since you do understand," Alfred paused and looked at him sideways, "would you go into the black communities and talk to their leaders about our real aims?"

"Whatever you want me to do," Smith said eagerly, although inwardly he hated the idea.

"Just try in the township," Alfred smiled. "We'll watch how you do and give you help when you need it."

"I'll start right away," Smith said, relieved that Alfred seemed to have approved of him.

Smith, feeling a tap on his shoulder, looked round to see Avril Brooks smiling up at him. "Good to see you, George. Looks like you're fittin' right in."

"What are you doin' in this lodge," Smith asked, although he suspected that Brooks had sponsored him.

"Duty," Avril said proudly. "And I wanted to see how you'd make out," he winked.

Brooks took him by the arm and led him to a group of settlers whom he wanted him to meet. They were immigrants from various states. Smith sensed that some of them had been slaveholders by the way in which they looked at him. A couple of them avoided shaking his hand and moved away. He thought that he recognized one hard-faced man across the room whose slaves he had helped to escape. On his way home he resolved to get close to these men to discover their true intentions, but events overtook him.

When the scorched earth policy of the Lieutenant-Governor in Lower Canada provoked the disaffected French-Canadians to rebel prematurely in November 1837, the Lieutenant-Governor of Upper Canada sent British Regular troops to help out, and, seeing their opportunity, Upper Canadian reformers under William Lyon Mackenzie rallied radical farmers to capture Toronto. Owing to poor communication, the rebel forces were easily dispersed by loyalist citizens with weapons from the Toronto arsenal.

News of Mackenzie's uprising reached the Western districts with glorious but false stories of rebel victory. Dr. Duncombe and the Malcolm brothers gathered a rebel force to join with Mackenzie's men in Toronto from where they would create a new government representative of the people.

Bill Powers was quitting work after a long cold day under the dull December sun when he heard a rider shout out the news of the rebellion and the order from Duncombe for all men of liberty to join the doctor in the village of Scotland. Scarcely believing what he heard, he rushed to the central street of Otterville and heard the messenger shout out the good news of Mackenzie's victory. Caught up in the joyful enthusiasm, Powers ran to tell Fanny the good news and ready himself to march through the night. Darkness fell as he armed himself and gobbled the food which Fanny insisted that he take before leaving. He gave her a long kiss and joined a group of other men with rifles, who welcomed him with cheers as they set out to the east for Scotland. Months later when he accompanied Fanny to Simcoe, he told Sarah of his experiences as if they were a nightmare.

A half-moon provided enough light for the men to see the pathways that led them through the forests. At every settlement along the way, they shouted the news and welcomed the men and boys who joined them. Rumours that Mackenzie's government was in place and was sending rebel forces to help the French-Canadians in Lower Canada swept through the files heightening their enthusiasm. They encountered groups of armed men from Sodom, Norwich county, the bastion of disaffection. who told of a large rebel force marching out of London. Powers heard that with messengers spreading the call of rebellion throughout the towns and villages to the south, the rebels would have a force of thousands. By dawn Powers' group came into a large clearing where they found a couple of houses, firebrands alight and oven fires blazing as men fashioned pikes over anvils. A genial old man, clean-shaven and bright-eyed, stood with pikes ready to hand off one to any man who had no weapon. "Ten minutes to Scotland!" he shouted every so often.

Powers marvelled that they had met no opposition. Where were the Tories? Perhaps not awakened to the events that were overtaking them? He looked forward to hearing from Duncombe all the news. It had happened so unexpectedly that he knew that Duncombe had not had time to work out a plan of attack. As he entered Scotland village, merely a cluster of log houses and a few stone ones on a rise of ground, he saw that tents were pitched in a field and the community hall was lit up and swarming with rebels standing in groups drinking coffee and eating. Powers stopped one of the women who was rushing between their homes and the hall carrying pots of coffee.

"Have you seen Dr. Duncombe?" His voice was shrill, betraying his emotion.

The woman turned and pointed to a cabin at the end of the road. "He's busy," she said.

Powers nodded his thanks and hurried to the cabin. He knocked and waited, wondering if Duncombe would still use him as an aide. The door swung open and there stood the giant form of the commissary for the rebel forces, Orismus Clark. Frowning, Clark was about to turn him away, when a gleam of recognition came to his eye, and he turned to Duncombe and Eliakim Malcolm studying a couple of maps at a table. "Bill's arrived." He reached out and pulled Powers by the shirt collar into the room and shut the door. "It's bloody cold out there!"

Duncombe raised his arm in greeting. "Join us, Bill. We need your advice."

Powers stepped eagerly to the table and sat in the chair vacated by Clark. "How many men do you expect, Doctor?"

"We'll only know that when they arrive. I brought 100 from Sodom, Eliakim has 60 from Burford, you must have come in with over 100, and we're waiting for reinforcements from St. Thomas and points west. Doan's Spartan Rangers will bring in 200. We need Doan's expertise in battle."

When Powers looked questioningly at them, Malcolm, his long prematurely white hair pulled tight in a knot behind his head and his large eyes dancing with excitement, explained that Colonel Doan had been a brilliant commander in the War of 1812.

"They'll be here by tomorrow, the 13th," Duncombe continued, "but we must begin operations by the next day, Thursday, if we hope to take Brantford and Hamilton. You have this good contact in Brantford, the bootmaker, don't you?"

Powers nodded. "William Mathews. He hates the Orangemen," he added with a smile.

"But can he neutralize them?" Duncombe asked.

"We can ask him to try. If he gets control of the town and holds it till we get there, it will save us a load of trouble."

"Exactly," Duncombe said. "Will you go to him? Tell him we'll march on the 14th and be in Brantford by noon."

"I'm worried about the Indians," Malcolm said suddenly. "Dr. Kerr can raise them at a moment's notice. They'll follow him anywhere."

"All the more reason for swift action. A reformer has been jailed in Hamilton, I hear, so the spies have been reporting on us," Duncombe said angrily. "Orismus has plenty of donations of hogs and calves, so we can feed ourselves for a couple of days, but after that we have to live off the land."

"My men are setting up the fires," Clark said. "We'll roast meat all day to get ready for the march."

"Eliakim," Duncombe said. "Let's get those with military experience to drill the men. We're going to be facing well-drilled militia with plenty of ammunition at their disposal. Allan MacNab will be stirring up the Tories in Hamilton and spoiling for a fight, if I know him," Duncombe laughed.

"The men have been marching all night," Powers interjected. "They need a sleep."

"After the noon-day meal, which our big friend Orismus will provide," Malcolm said, standing and patting Clark on the shoulder, "they shall learn to obey orders."

"No small feat," Duncombe warned.

As Clark and Malcolm left the cabin, Duncombe suggested to Powers that he go to Brantford to alert Mathews.

"After a strong cup of coffee," Powers said, "and with a good horse."

"Take mine," Duncombe offered. "She's the white beauty who will see you through any danger."

"Why did you pick now to rise up?" Powers asked. "Was it because of news from Toronto?"

Duncombe shook his head. "I would have waited for word from Mackenzie first if I'd had a choice. There was a warrant for my arrest. I had to move now."

Powers stood up and shook Duncombe's hand enthusiastically. "I feel victory in my bones," he said and quickly left the cabin on a mission that he knew was his most dangerous.

Duncombe's white stallion carried Powers swiftly past the groups of rebels drilling in the fields and hollow at the near-by village of Oakland. A light fall of snow covered the ground and the brisk chill in the air drove the tiredness from his eyes. The dirt road took him over the rich farmlands that gave promise of a great nation to be built when the Family Compact was defeated. He sensed that he was a part of a movement which would be honoured for generations to come for bringing liberty and prosperity to the people. The fear of democracy that moved people to defend rigid, conservative rule stemmed, he knew, from the excesses of the French Revolution. The madness that lay just under the surface of the mass of people could break into the most horrible and degrading spectacles if a strong hand did not control events and channel unruly outbreaks along harmless channels of expression. His father had been typical of the previous generation who, petrified by the continuous, irrational massacres initiated by the mob and sanctified by a state, allowed military minds and opportunistic methods to consolidate power and rule over them. Now, this generation had to break this irresponsible power even if it meant the death of many of them. Powers' thoughts of Fanny and fear of never seeing her again mixed with apprehension about his mission to stir up the Irish Catholics and reformers to seize control of Brantford. Lost in thought, he barely noticed that he was nearing the bridge over the Grand River, which led into Brantford, when he heard the crack of rifle shots. Coming over a rise he saw a man leaning low over a horse and galloping towards him. Behind him men at the bridge were tamping powder into their rifle barrels. As the fleeing horseman grew closer, Powers recognized a medical man from Oakland who was a friend of Duncombe. He reined in his horse. The doctor seeing the white steed, thought he was Duncombe and cried out to turn and flee with him. Powers turned and galloped alongside him, at which point the doctor, seeing that he was not Duncombe, looked very alarmed and tried to veer away.

"It's all right," Powers shouted. "Dr. Duncombe sent me on a mission. I have his horse."

They rode together into the next valley and came to halt behind a cluster of trees.

"They were government militia," the doctor said between gasps for air. "I persuaded them I was visiting a sick patient and put them off guard. Looks like the Tories have got control of the town."

Powers looked at him in disbelief. His hopes, so high moments ago, collapsed, leaving him with a baneful expression.

"You can't get in there," the doctor warned him.

"I'll make it because I have to," Powers said. "You tell Dr. Duncombe. He'll have to prepare for the worst." He brushed his heel against the stallion's side and rode swiftly down to the winding river bank. He looked behind to see the doctor galloping toward Scotland.

The river wound behind a hill separating him from the men on the bridge, and he could cross without being seen. He dismounted and led the horse into the river; the coldness cut him to the bone. Letting the horse take the lead, he held onto its saddle while it swam and clambered up the other side into the shrubbery. The water turned to ice on his clothes. He had to get warm soon. Racing through the woods, he came to a path that led him into the town. There were bunches of men with rifles standing in the main street. He rode to a side street and reached Mathews' house without difficulty. Mathews happened to be on the watch at a window and ran to let him in. Without a word he took Powers to the hearth in his living room and set out dry clothes for him. Powers stripped off his wet clothes caked with ice while Mathews went outside to tend to the horse, dry it down and take it round to the back of the house out of sight of prying eyes. When he re-entered the living room, Powers was dressed in Mathews' clothes, which looked absurdly short for him and brought a twinkle to Mathews' eyes.

"You're safe now," he said. "No one could recognize you."

Powers laughed.

"You know that the town militia was alerted by MacNab and all the Orangeman are out in full force. MacNab is marching from Hamilton with 600 men," Mathews said ominously.

"How's that possible?" Powers exclaimed. "Mackenzie's controlling Toronto, isn't he?"

"Mackenzie was defeated. It's all pretty pitiable." Mathews looked glum. "They got their messages crossed. It was a fiasco. Everyone's on the run, every man for himself."

"God!" Powers cried and sat down heavily on a chair. "When will MacNab get here?"

"By tonight," Mathews said. "I told my men to get to Scotland any way they can, but, you know, a wise man would just stay put at this point. There's a feeling that the whole blasted game is lost."

"If we get the three thousand men that the doctor expects, we're far from being lost," Powers said.

"Well, in any case, I'm coming back to Scotland with you. I'm a marked man and the sooner we leave this place the better," Mathews sighed. "Do you know that Kerr is leading the Indians?"

"Dr. Kerr? I thought he was a reformer."

"Yes, but not a revolutionary. That's what we're up against. By moving fast, the government's got the moderates to fall in line against us."

They were interrupted by a knock at the door. Mathews looked out the window, and, seeing a friend, went to answer.

Powers heard the door open and a hoarse voice telling Mathews to get away because the militia was going round to the houses of known reformers and arresting them. Mathews came back to Powers, still warming himself before the fire, and threw him an overcoat while he struggled into another one.

"You heard?" he said, and seeing Powers nod, he led the way to the back door. "My horse is saddled. I know a way to get out of town, so follow me close." He disappeared while Powers mounted Duncombe's white stallion. He reappeared in a moment on a chestnut mare. He cantered his horse down an alleyway and, looking sharply about as he came into the street, he signalled for Powers to come up with him. They rode side by side until they reached the town's out-skirts at a distance from the bridge where the cliff fell off precipitously and the river ran shallow among rocks. Silently Mathews led the way down a small path and across the river which did not come higher than the horses' forelegs. They were free now to inform Duncombe of the great danger they all faced.

George M. Smith was caught up in the same excitement, although he wished that there were some way that he could avoid it. Men awak-ened him in the middle of the night and soon had him dressed and walking with them through the darkness. He carried his own rifle which he had used formerly against western outlawry and continued to use to hunt deer and smaller animals. His lodge leader, "Colonel" Alfred, walked beside him.

"Don't like this," Alfred complained. "It's all too sudden. We didn't plan for this."

"Got to strike when the iron's hot," Smith said, trying to sound enthusiastic.

"You don't really think it's hot, do you?" Alfred said, as if he detected a reluctance on Smith's part.

Smith paused and thought quickly. "I agree with you. I think we could use our American brothers."

"They just are not ready," Alfred said angrily. "We needed another six months."

"How many we got with us?" Smith asked.

"About fifty from the St. Thomas area," Alfred said. "And Doan's mounted rangers of thirty or so will be coming from Sparta."

"We got enough then," Smith said, "that is, if Mackenzie really got control of the Toronto district."

Alfred lapsed into silence. Smith thought that his last words had disturbed him. Just the slightest doubt seemed to dampen his spirits. He felt the same about all the men. Their bravado came from the news that their side was winning easily, but, when they actually had to face troops trained to kill, he thought that their present state of optimism would desert them. He began to feel uncomfortable in the presence of men who were risking their lives and depending on his help while he was working for the other side. His activities of spying on the slavocracy and rescuing escaping slaves seemed noble by comparison. Now he felt disgusted with his hypocrisy. If only he could lag behind and disappear into the woods, he thought, but to know the result of the rebel rising he had to stay at least until they marched on Brantford.

The men were walking in single file along well-worn paths and breaking into song every once in a while to boost their spirits. They had been walking about three hours and were passing through a hamlet in the wilderness where they called out for the men of the place to join them, but in vain. The few houses, caught in partial light from a half-moon, were eerily quiet. Smith thought that if there were rebels in the place they must have left with earlier marchers. He sensed an uneasiness that was disconcerting. Surely women folk would have lit candles and looked outside to see them pass.

As they climbed through a narrow defile up a rise, the sharp crack of rifles and sudden flares of gunpowder came from both sides of them. Some of the men stumbled and fell, the others fell onto their hands and knees. Before they had time to bring their rifles to bear on the woods on either side, more shots resounded through the trees and more men fell groaning. The rest ran along the path and into the woods. Smith ran directly into the woods and stumbled over one of the ambushers who was lying on the ground trying to reload his rifle. He hit the man on the head with his rifle butt, got to his feet and ran as hard as he could into the forest. Since the defile was almost black, the ambush was not as successful as it should have been. The targets were hardly visible, and even at such close range, the shooters could not be sure that they were hitting men or trees. Most of the rebels got away unscathed, but four were too badly wounded and lay groaning on the pathway and a few others, although wounded, managed to escape.

As he ran, cut by bushes, swatted by branches, and tripped up by tree roots, Smith heard the shouts of pursuers, but presently all was quiet as the Tories must have realized that pursuit in the darkness was folly. He came to a stream and sat on a rock beside it to bathe his face and hands and wipe away the blood from his scratches. He heard a crashing in the bushes near him and seizing his gun he pointed it in the direction of the sound. A tall man rounded a tree and tripped, stumbling forward for several steps until unable to gain his balance, he flopped face first into the stream, with the sound of a slap. When he pulled himself up and looked round to see where he was, Smith recognized the sharp features of Colonel Alfred in the faint light from the moon.

"Good evening, Colonel," he said cheerfully. "Strange that I should meet you here."

Alfred ducked and was going to roll away until, recognizing Smith's voice, he stopped and sat up. "Damned Tories!" he cried. "Damned, damned, treacherous asses!" He stood up and brushed at his clothes although he was unable to see what he was brushing.

"Makes you think our opposition may be stronger than we planned for," Smith suggested.

"All the more reason for us to get to Scotland," Alfred said angrily. "The boys that got away are going to have to get there on their own. Are you with me?"

"Where to?" Smith said, looking round in the darkness. "Should we not wait for dawn, Colonel?"

"Don't need to," he said tersely. "This stream will take us to a path north of here. From there I can find the way. It's better we go in twos and threes from now on, anyway."

"Makes you think about how many other ambushes are bein' set up," Smith said glumly.

"Makes you think about the whole damned business," Alfred said sarcastically. "We could be going into a guerrilla war. It's times like this where we could have used American help. Blast it!" He struck out along the side of the stream.

Sighing, Smith stood up, picked up his rifle, and trailed after him. He listened to a pack of wolves howling in the distance. This little adventure was becoming more dangerous than rescuing slaves, he thought.

When Bill Mathews and Bill Powers reached the rebel encampment, they found the men huddled in groups and arguing apprehensively. The doctor from Oakland had warned them of the militia organized to defend Brantford, sending them into a state of uncertainty. Duncombe sent scouts out in all directions to find out the size of their opposition and from where it was coming. Seeing Duncombe and Eliakim Malcolm addressing a score of listeners in front of the community hall, Mathews and Powers reined in their horses. Duncombe broke off what he was saying as he watched the men dismount and approach him.

"Brantford is full of Orangemen," Mathews shouted. "Colonel MacNab is bringing in at least six hundred militia from Hamilton and Kerr is joining them with over a hundred Indians."

Duncombe seemed to rock back on his heels as if hit.

"How's it possible?" Malcolm demanded to know. "I can't believe that!"

"Mackenzie was routed," Mathews said. "He's on the run."

"No!" Malcolm shouted in disbelief.

The men about them began to murmur in dismay. Other men nearby, sensing the importance of the discussion, came to them asking questions. For a moment there was a hubbub of noise. Malcolm and Duncombe excitedly exchanged words and Duncombe turned away in disgust.

Mathews looked apologetically at Duncombe. "I couldn't ask my men to take over the town. It would have been a fool thing to do."

Duncombe cleared his throat. "This changes the complexion of things. What do you think, Powers?"

"Reformers are being arrested in all the towns and probably men we could have counted on are going over to the loyalists to save their skins." Powers shook his head. "We've committed ourselves, though. We've got to show them that we're not cowards. How many have we got here?"

Duncombe deferred to Malcolm who looked embarrassed. "Just four hundred."

"What?" Mathews cried in astonishment. "Where are the thousands you expected?"

Malcolm shrugged. "Didn't come."

Duncombe broke in. "There's worse news. Tories are organizing in all the townships and some are ambushing our men preventing them from reaching us. And then again," he smiled sarcastically, "there are men who don't have the courage of their convictions."

At that moment they heard a shout from a rider dashing across the field. The men turned to watch one of Duncombe's scouts gallop up to them and jump from his horse. He gasped for breath while they waited for his news. "Hundreds of men coming out of London and points south, marching up through St. Thomas."

"Ours?" Malcolm asked hopefully.

The scout shook his head. "Tories, bein' led by Colonel Askin."

Malcolm visibly paled and Duncombe frowned impatiently.

"They'll be coming at us from the south-west and the north-east," one of the men cried out. "We can go either to the north-west or south-east."

"Going to the north-west takes us back to Sodom," another man replied angrily, "and that would be retreatin'."

"We're not quitters," another man shouted.

"So," Duncombe cried, raising his hand for attention, "if we go south-west, or more like south, through Simcoe, what can we expect?"

"There's lots of sympathizers down that way, the other side of Simcoe," another man shouted. "I just know they'd join us if they had the chance."

"If we could add a couple of hundred men to our force," Malcolm said, "we could take on MacNab and win."

"There's all those blacks in Simcoe to consider," Mathews warned. "The blacks in Brantford are with the Tories."

"But we should strike at Brantford before MacNab's men reach it," Powers objected. "We'll be wasting our time taking Simcoe because meanwhile MacNab will be in Brantford and releasing the Indians on us."

The men began swearing at the thought of the Six Nations Indians, their faces painted and their tomahawks in their belts, coming softly through the woods.

"All right," Duncombe shouted for attention. "Our scout will be coming back from Simcoe soon. After we hear from him, we'll call a meeting and decide." He stepped away into the community hall with Eliakim Malcolm.

Mathews and Powers followed them into the hall while the men dispersed into small groups and discussed their options.

On the south side of the village George M. Smith and Colonel Alfred walked in from the wilderness. Their clothes were torn, their faces and hands badly scratched and bleeding, and they looked exhausted. Some women, waiting with cups of coffee for newcomers, went to them with coffee and made them drink. Both men relished the heat from the drink and sank onto a log to rest and enjoy being looked after by feminine attention. One of the women brought a pail of hot water, soap and a wash cloth and began wiping the blood off their faces and hands. The steam from their coffee cups circled in the cold air as they relaxed and looked at the rebels engaged in making arms or drilling in small groups in the field near-by or huddled in heated discussions. A young woman brought Smith a coat to replace the shredded surtout that he was wearing. Smith smiled warmly in thanks and put it on slowly. The cold was gradually draining from his limbs and he was beginning to feel more normal. He watched Colonel Alfred help himself to a third cup of coffee. The man was as dedicated to liberty as he was, but in a different fashion. How strange it was that both of them wanted fervently for the same thing but were on opposite sides! But he was naive. The forces behind the American patriots, the financiers and the hordes of opportunists in their ranks, would take over the province. It would happen because the rebels would need American strength to subdue the loyalists. Poor Colonel Alfred had no idea of the catastrophe he would be bringing upon his people and, although he himself hated slavery, he would be dismayed at how quickly Upper Canada could revert to slavery. Smith gritted his teeth and steeled himself to continue to get as much information as he could before he melted into the woods. His mentors in Detroit must be worrying at not hearing from him, he thought.

Approaching them, looking thinner than usual, was Avril Brooks. He was glum and said waspishly, "So you got here finally."

"What's going on?" Colonel Alfred asked, ignoring the implication that they were laggards.

Brooks informed them of the approach of Askin's troops from one direction and MacNab's from another, and the disaster of Mackenzie's attack on Toronto. "There are more Tories out there than we thought," he added bleakly.

Smith felt his heart jump with delight, but he kept his expression placid. He noticed the distraught look on Alfred's face. Alfred buried his head in his hands.

A horseman galloped in from the south close by them.

"That's the scout from Simcoe that we've been waiting for," Brooks said. "Let's go to the hall to hear what he has to say." He started away without waiting for them.

Alfred did not move but Smith, anxious to get more information, quickly stepped along behind Brooks.

They found Duncombe, Malcolm, Mathews and Powers talking to the scout in the hall. Smith smelt the dampness of men's bodies, some of which had not been washed for days. A few men were standing at a distance and watching them but most were not aware that the scout had arrived with news. Smith caught the end of the scout's report on the forces in Simcoe and of the reinforcements coming from Port Ryerse and Port Dover. He noted that Malcolm looked cast down by the news. He plucked Powers by the sleeve, and Powers, turning, smiled at him in recognition. As Powers stepped away, taking Smith by the arm,

Mathews scowled at Smith with a look that Smith had encountered thousands of times. Looking blankly at him, Smith filed in his mind that the man was a racist.

"Don't mind Mathews. We've got to take help from whatever quarter it comes," Powers, observing the interaction between them, explained.

Smith smiled. "I hope Mathews knows that."

Powers laughed. "He won't bother you. We've got a more serious problem right now."

"Yes," Smith nodded. "From the looks of things, we could be outnumbered."

"By four to one," Powers said. "But I don't care. I'll fight regardless."

Smith made a moue. He looked round the room at the men watching them, some worried, some suspicious, some wary. "You may be on your own," he said.

Duncombe suddenly stepped out from the group and raised his arms. "We have to talk to everyone," he cried. "Assemble outside. Call everybody together."

The huge form of Orismus Clark went quickly to a bell rope that had been rigged up by the front door to a large bell suspended from the roof. He began to ring the bell with an incessant fury, transferring his fear and impatience to the whole body of men, some of whom began running in from the fields as darkness began gathering in the trees ready to fall on the encampment. Some men on the porch, where Duncombe stood facing the men and women who gathered to hear him, lit torches and held them aloft. Duncombe signalled to Clark to cease ringing. He stepped to the edge of the steps and surveyed the hundreds of listeners with a genial smile.

"Mr. Clark has prepared a wonderful meal for us all. He is anxious to have you eat it," Duncombe shouted.

The crowd cheered and Clark blushed.

In the twilight Duncombe waited for stragglers to reach the mass and quiet settle over them all. He felt a huge responsibility for these men. He was careful to hide his worry about controlling this force itching to battle for rights and justice, which, these men felt, they had been denied for years, if not decades. He pretended that they were still strong enough to effect their goal, despite Mackenzie's defeat and the bad news coming in from Lower Canada of the routing of rebels there and the devastation of their villages. To make the choice either to oppose the Tories or disband and go home, he had to consider the women and children of the villages and towns from which these men came. If they fought the Tories and lost, then their families might be chased into the freezing forests, their homes burnt, their food stocks destroyed, their young women raped. And the horror of being attacked by Indians would bring back nightmares of the Indian wars, which older residents had experienced. These thoughts stirred at the back of his mind as he informed his listeners of the facts. Two armies were advancing on them and a third could be organizing at Simcoe, which, together with the failure at Toronto and the wholesale desertion of their cause by moderate reformers put them all at a grave disadvantage. He could not be a ruthless commander and lead his men to certain death for a cause. He was a medical doctor and spent his life trying to save lives. He had no heart for the slaughter that was certain to take place, nor did he want to see the loyalists killed. He had thought that with Mackenzie's victory, just the show of armed force would be enough to bring about the reforms that his country needed. He had been abused of that idea and now regarded his naiveté as a danger. But he would let the men decide. He dare not decide for them to retreat and surrender their dreams. He put forward dispassionately the different avenues of action which he had discussed with Malcolm.

George Smith during the talk inched his way to the back of the crowd. Duncombe's clipped accent became pronounced when making a speech, reminding Smith that the doctor had migrated years ago from Delaware. Night fell and he could see just the forms not the faces of the men around him. He listened to men shout out defiantly that they should march on Brantford. There were Scottish accents, Irish accents, German accents, several English accents, all urging a fight to the finish.

"But MacNab's troops are there now!" someone shouted. "They'll be here tomorrow morning and so will the Indians."

"And so will Askin from the south-west," someone added.

261

Sections of the crowd broke into arguments among themselves. Duncombe called for order and waited a while before he obtained it.

"We can't be divided," he said. "A group wants to attack Brantford, another group wants to attack Askin, others want to retreat to Sodom and regroup there because MacNab cannot drag his cannon through the woods after us and we'll be able to fight with better advantage. As your commander, I choose the last option"

There were hoots from many men in the crowd.

"But you decide!" Duncombe cried, his short, athletic body tense with emotion, his voice conveying his resolution. "We're not cowards, you say. We want to show the Tories that we can fight. Then can we all agree that we march on Simcoe?"

Many of the men cheered.

"We can demonstrate our courage in battle, and if there are sympathisers to our cause south of there, we can hold that part of the country till we get strong enough to persuade the Tories to grant us our demands."

Some of the men, unable to face the reality of their position, cried "No!, No! We march on Brantford," but the majority shouted out their agreement. Some among them thought that if they could control the country down to Lake Erie and the Niagara River, they could get help from the Americans who would send fighting men to join them. If all else failed, they could escape across the border to the States.

Duncombe, realizing that he had struck on a theme that most favoured and allowed them to test their courage, now asked them to give him their verdict. As voices shouted out questions, some hoarse and bold, some demanding, and some querulous, Smith slipped into the darkness. He passed by the fires over which women roasted cattle and prepared the food that the rebels would soon be devouring. His stomach ached for food as he looked at the scene, but he walked determinedly by it, and, as he came to the last shed, he saw that a horse had been tethered to it with its saddle still on its back. It seemed that the last scout had not had time to unsaddle it before the meeting began, and he had left it for later. Unobserved, Smith mounted the horse and walked it quietly down the road toward Simcoe.

A short way along the road he turned along a concession line to avoid the sentries which he could barely see on the roadway ahead. Cutting through farmers' fields, crusted with snow, he brought the horse to a canter until he reached a cluster of trees when he dismounted and led the horse through the dense shrubbery back to the road. He had heard that there was a considerable black community in Simcoe; it would turn out to oppose the rebel advance. But he had no clear idea of the loyalties of the townspeople in general. From the way Avril Brooks talked, it seemed that the settlements along Lake Erie were ready to rise up at the first sign. He galloped through the night, the stars lighting his way, and trusted that he would not be mistaken for a rebel and shot by a militiaman guarding the town. When he felt that he must be nearing Simcoe, he slowed his horse to a trot and, peering through the darkness, caught a movement off the roadway. A deep voice demanded that he halt and identify himself. Smith cried out "I am a friend," and pulled his horse to a standstill. He held his hands in the air.

Slowly a horseman detached himself from the woods at the roadside and moved his mount towards him. Smith could make out the man's rifle held in front of him.

"I've come to warn Simcoe of a rebel attack," Smith explained.

The horseman said nothing but rode alongside him and reaching over lifted Smith's rifle from the holster on the saddle.

"You ride ahead into town," the horseman said.

Smith recognized a Negro timbre to the man's voice and realized the man was black, in fact, so black that he could barely make him out in the darkness. Somewhat reassured, he added, "I've been spying for our side."

"Tell that to the Captain," the man said crisply. "Just ride quietly."

Smith said not another word as they trotted toward a number of torches pinpointing the blackness in the distance.

21

Sarah had just fixed up her house on the outskirts of the village when the troubles descended on her. Her young son John was the only man in her house and he was inexperienced with a gun, but she refused to move to a safer place. Rumours of a rebel uprising frightened the townspeople into running about to their neighbours and seeking out weapons, some of which had not been fired for years. Some people in town looked happy at the news which disconcerted the loyalists. Who among them was a rebel? Whom could one trust? The militia officers were frustrated as they could not move against the rebels in their midst until the rebels were identified. Wilson's cavalry roamed outside the town and watched for suspicious movements.

Campbell, suspecting that he was marked for plunder by the rebels, told an employee in his blacksmithing shop to scrape away the manure in the hen house on his farm and dig a hole that could take a couple of big trunks. When the young man returned to meet Duncan in that section of the Post Office reserved for the business of the Gore Bank, Campbell showed him trunks full of bank notes and boxes of gold and silver and watched his eyes glaze over at the sight of such wealth. After dark, they quietly drove them to the farmhouse, put them in the hole and spread the manure over the top to obliterate any signs of digging.

Duncan confided in Sarah what he had done because, he said, if he died in the fighting he wanted someone he could trust to know where the treasure was buried.

Such was the tension in the town that in the night a wagon full of weapons that Campbell had ordered from Port Dover was surrounded by militia ready to shoot what they thought were rebels. Fortunately one of them recognized the voice of the driver.

As militiamen lined up to collect their rifles and gunpowder under the flaming light from dozens of flambeaux, George Smith walked into the hall accompanied by a determined-looking Henson Johnson. Thinner and taller than the barrel-chested Smith, Johnson directed Smith to where Captain Wilson was chatting with Duncan Campbell, and, seeing Wilson look at him with surprise, he announced that he had caught a rebel trying to infiltrate the town.

Smith smiled with amusement. "I've just come from the rebel camp, but I'm no rebel," he said.

"Silence until you are spoken to," Campbell said sternly.

"I'll handle this," Wilson said quietly. "Come over here where we can talk," he said to Smith and led him to a small table with chairs against the wall. "Sit."

Smith sat and Wilson drew up a chair to face him. "Where did you find this man?" he asked Johnson who stood behind him.

"Riding on the main road from Scotland," Johnson said.

"What did you want to tell us?" Wilson asked Smith.

Smith gave his name and explained his connection with the rebel camp briefly. "I came here to warn you that they'll be attacking Simcoe before anywhere else. You better be ready."

Campbell came up to listen at that moment. "Who gave the order?"

"Dr. Duncombe let the men decide. I don't know when they'll be here, but I think early in the morning," Smith said, looking as sincere as he could.

"My men are scouting them," Wilson said to Campbell. "We'll know when they get close." He looked back at Henson Johnson. "Good work, Private Johnson. Put Mr. Smith in jail for the time being." He saw Smith frown. "One of our people will be round to question you on the strength and morale of the men at Scotland. Thank you for your information."

Johnson prodded Smith to stand and go with him. Smith sighed and, casting a glance round at the Norfolk militia and the many arms that were being distributed, he asked if he could eat.

"Feed him," Wilson commanded Johnson. "Make sure he's well treated."

Campbell stood behind the young, wiry Wilson to watch Smith walk in the direction of the town jail. "Do you believe him?" he asked.

"Absolutely," Wilson smiled. "But he stays in prison just to be sure. Anyway, it's for his own good. If we lose tomorrow, his rebel friends won't think he's betrayed them."

"Lose?" Campbell cried. "Perish the thought. I'm checking on our defences now. Coming?"

Wilson shook his head and motioned to the long lines of militiamen still waiting for gunpowder.

Campbell's men laid tree trunks across the road leading from the north into Simcoe at the bridge that crossed Patterson's Creek. The creek was narrow but nevertheless acted as a deterrent to advancing troops. The water was ice cold and Campbell's men had the advantage of firing down at the invaders who would have to climb its banks. Moreover, a large swamp stretched to its west preventing an attack there. As a second line of defence, Campbell placed some troops on the road just north of his property and Sarah's house. If the rebels got through the first line, the second line defenders would cut down the bridges spanning the small swamp between Wellington district and Simcoe proper. Rebels then would face the musket fire of the Norfolk militia as they tried to cross the swamp. Campbell was nervous but appeared calm in front of his men. As he passed Sarah's house, he saw Vesta and young John Lewis carrying trays of food and coffee to the troops that were spread out in front of it. The sight pleased him. He recalled John Lewis asking him to be employed as a messenger between the militia regiments and the various points of defence, but Campbell refused. He did not want John hurt. The boy was too bright to be put at risk so young. John, visibly disappointed, appealed to Sandy McPherson, who, taking pity on him, employed him to ride to the villages to the south with the latest news and bring back reports of unrest in their districts. Campbell pretended not to know of it, but he liked the boldness in the boy as in a way it reflected on him. A young militiaman greeted him, forcing Campbell out of his reverie and into the responsibility of engaging the enemy. He brought his horse to a gallop as he crossed the bridge leading to the first line of defence. It was going to be a long night of watching and waiting. These young men

266

under his command had not killed before, and he was certain that many of them would not be capable of it, particularly if they were being confronted with family friends or relatives caught up in the rebel cause. But he would not allow these thoughts to weaken his resolve, he told himself. If war was what the rebels wanted, then they would have it. The honour of the country was at stake.

What Campbell had no way of knowing was the irresolution in the rebel camp that Powers later told Sarah was the worst part of his nightmare. When Doan's Rangers came into the camp, Colonel Joshua Doan went into conference with the leaders. Doan was a practical man who spoke in terse phrases. The others heard of his exploits defending Canadian territory in the War of 1812. He was the only leader amongst them who had led men into battle, and, when he heard the startling news of Mackenzie's failure and the panic of his followers in the face of equally panic-stricken loyalist defenders, he smiled sarcastically and said that he would not lead his men into certain defeat and unnecessary slaughter. He adamantly vetoed the idea of linking up with American patriot forces coming across Lake Erie. He proclaimed their situation quixotic because there was no longer a realistic goal. Even if they were fortunate enough to win a battle or two, how could they contain the great numbers of loyalists and faithful Britishers without employing the same dictatorial powers that they were rebelling against? He said that the only choice left to them was to effect the best means of retreat; meanwhile he was going to bed. The other officers watched him leave with dismay for they knew he was right. Then mumbling good-nights they all went to bed, leaving Bill Powers discussing strategy with Duncombe and Malcolm throughout the night.

Powers represented that faction of young men who refused to retreat regardless of the size of the enemy. Malcolm pointed out the overwhelming strength of MacNab's forces. If the rebels moved against Simcoe, they would have to cut through the Norfolk militia quickly or they would be trapped by MacNab coming up from behind. And Askin's force would be diverted eastward to attack them from the side. As they talked, Duncombe studied the lists of names of rebels to try to assess their strength and to determine how many could be expected to join them if they were fortunate enough to break through the defences at Simcoe. He concluded that the numbers were not great enough. Before dawn he and Malcolm persuaded Powers and themselves that the best they could do was to retreat to Sodom and reorganize and make a stand. There was a chance that MacNab's men without their cannon and worn out from trekking through the forests could be bested in battle. Reluctantly Powers agreed. He felt angry, betrayed and finally ill in mind and stomach.

When Duncombe addressed the troops the first thing in the morning, he had little trouble persuading them of his decision. During the night a sense of reality had overtaken the troops, who knew that they lacked the military training to win against overwhelming odds. Numbers of them had already taken the forest paths to their homes. The men agreed to find their own way through the wilderness back to Sodom. Powers and a handful of determined young men elected to stay in Scotland to slow up MacNab's forces by guerrilla action. Malcolm warned them about the Indians who were expert at such warfare, which served only to frighten them as they knew the reputation of Indian warriors only too well.

Finishing their breakfasts in the cold morning air, the men broke their encampment and melted away by twos and threes into the trees. Powers discovered that George Smith and Bill Mathews had left during the night. Their disappearance saddened him because he thought that they were representative of the force; they symbolized in their actions the rebels who had not wanted to admit it but felt beaten after hearing of Mackenzie's failure. Few, he thought, would regroup at Sodom. He watched as Malcolm and Duncombe gathered up their papers in preparing to leave.

"We can't take our muster rolls with us," Malcolm said. "Supposing we are caught with them."

"You're right," Duncombe grimaced. "We should burn them, but we'll need them in future."

"We'll bury them," Malcolm said. "Some day we can come back and collect them."

"That's dangerous too," Powers interjected. "If the Tories find them, they'll round up all our supporters, burn their houses, and God knows what else!"

"We'll make sure they can't be found. Come, the three of us will be the only ones to know where they are buried." Malcolm mounted his horse and waited for Duncombe to mount his white steed.

Powers walked alongside the mounted men into the woods to the base of a tall oak tree that Malcolm selected as a landmark. Dismounting and taking a trowel from his saddlebag, Malcolm dug a hole, put the papers rolled in a thick paper cover into it, and smoothed the earth over them very carefully. Mounting his horse, he said, "We'll be back in better days."

Waving good-bye, Powers watched the men ride away in the direction of Sodom. The doctor's white stallion seemed to symbolize the proud spirit of the rebel leaders who did not doubt that they would be victorious one day. Powers caught sight of some women carrying the last vestiges of the encampment into their cabins. Aside from the stretches of trampled grass, no sign remained of the hundreds of men. The men who volunteered to slow MacNab's advance had left the village, expecting MacNab's main force to drive due west through Oakland to Scotland. These diehards hated MacNab so much that they elected to fight against his troops before any other and were gathering outside Oakland village. It made no sense militarily, but what did it matter, Powers thought. The point was to stand up and be heard from. A smaller force of Tories was reported to be filing through the forest of white pine from the north through Burford to cut off any retreat in that direction. Kerr's Indians were advancing on the other wing through Waterford to cut off rebels who would flee to the southeast. Powers took up his rifle and walked to a position south of Scotland. He guessed that the news of Duncombe's retreat would reach Simcoe first and thus the Norfolk militia would be the first to arrive.

Waiting in the cold among denuded trees, Powers began to think of Fanny and his love for her. He wanted to see her again. The more vividly she came into his mind, the more wretched he felt and the more foolish his lone vigil appeared. All he could be expected to do was to fire a warning shot at troops advancing along the road and perhaps hold them up for a few minutes. He could very well be stormed while he was reloading for another shot. He would most certainly be killed. As he was considering this possibility and mulling over what action to take, a company of dragoons came into view. He considered shooting at their leader, but he knew that the horsemen would be upon him in an instant. He stood still and watched them ride past. He figured that they were an advance party and would soon be followed by other dragoons. Running swiftly into the woods he decided to try to save his life. He panicked suddenly and fell to the ground expecting dragoons to be harrying the bushes searching for him and Indians prowling in the vicinity. After a minute he breathed more easily and, getting up, he stepped warily away in the direction of Otterville and his beloved Fanny.

Mercer Wilson's cavalry burst upon Scotland and scoured it for rebels. They found women, old men, and children in the cabins, but no men of fighting age. Wilson ordered his regiment to wait for MacNab to arrive. He did not know of the small group of rebels waiting to ambush MacNab's militia as it marched along the road running through Oakland.

Colonel Ryerse, having led his militiamen from the shores of Lake Erie through Waterford and meeting no resistance, continued post haste to Oakland. Ryerse could move ahead with confidence because Campbell had kept his Norfolk Militia guarding Simcoe and thereby protected his flank. When his scouts warned him of a pocket of rebels ahead, he rallied his men to engage them immediately. The rebels, seeing no sign of MacNab and realizing that Ryerse's men would overrun their position in any case, marched quickly south out of Oakland, but before they could reach the rise of the hill before the village, Ryerse's militia fired at them, dropping a few men in their front and striking fear into the others. Shouting to keep up their courage, the rebels discharged their rifles at the militia who charged them on horseback, but their firepower had no effect. They retreated into the hollow while trying to reload their rifles. In seconds the militiamen engaged them in hand to hand fighting. In the confusion some rebels escaped into the woods but most were forced to surrender. The militia, shouting in jubilation, rounded up their prisoners.

Minutes later MacNab's force marched into view. Colonel Ryerse reformed his regiment, placed his prisoners under guard and rode with his officers to the head of MacNab's column. MacNab's militia halted while MacNab rode up to congratulate Ryerse and incorporate his men under his command. Riding at the head of their troops and conversing amicably, MacNab and Ryerse led their men toward Scotland and the waiting regiment of Lancers under the enterprising young Wilson.

MacNab, expecting a battle, was disappointed at the ease of his victory. He summoned all of the troops to the front of the village hall where Duncombe had addressed his men that morning. He told them that they were short of food. None had been left by the rebels. They would have to leave their heavy equipment behind. They could not drag their cannon over the high rocky ground and through the dense forest. They had to move quickly to prevent the rebel forces from regrouping. They could rest for an hour, after which they would pro-ceed to Sodom. At that moment, Askin's regiments marching from St. Thomas came into Scotland and raised a cheer from MacNab's loyalists. MacNab dismissed his men and went into the hall to await Colonel Askin and plan a strategy for mopping up resistance in the countryside. He joked with his officers about the phantom rebels who talked a lot but were cowards when it came to fighting. He took out his report that he was writing to the Lieutenant-Governor and scribbled his latest news until Askin walked into the room. John B. Askin, grandson of a famous fur trader and son of his half-breed son who had led a band of Indians in the War of 1812, approached MacNab with his arms outstretched and a huge smile. MacNab stood and embraced him. Their bonhomie became even more demonstrative when Askin stood back and waved sheets of paper in the air.

"Rebels' muster rolls. All the names," he shouted gleefully. "One of my men found them buried outside the village. What do you think of that?"

MacNab reached for the papers with delight. "We'll round the bug-gers up," he cried. "Captain Wilson," he shouted. He liked the young man for his resourcefulness. "While we beard the lion in his den, you take your dragoons through the country south of here and see how many rebels you can round up." He gave the papers to him. "Look at these before you go; you may recognize some names." He turned to address all of his officers. "From now on we have a different kind of

271

warfare. We have to fight in the woods and we may mistake our friends for our enemies. To distinguish ourselves I order that every man wear a scarlet fabric in his hat. Our commissaries brought the cloth from Brantford and are cutting it up for you to distribute to your men."

MacNab noticed Dr. Kerr entering the room. "Do you hear that, Will? Our men will have a red piece of cloth in their hats. Make sure your warriors know that, please." He accented "please" in a humorous way that brought laughter from the officers.

Kerr nodded with a slight smile. As a son-in-law of the Mohawk chief Joseph Brant and an advocate for Indian land rights, he had disagreements with MacNab but they found themselves together against the rebels. "My warriors have brought in some refugees from the skirmish in Oakland and await your order as to their disposal," he said. "None, by the way, wears a red cockade."

The officers smiled and looked at MacNab, who appeared to be amused. "Refugees, you call them," MacNab said. "Well, I suppose we can't shoot them. Rope them together and we'll march them to Brantford. And Captain Wilson," he added suddenly, turning to look at the wiry young man studying the list of names with his lieutenant, "be sure you lock up all the rebels you find in one central place. And where will that be?"

"In the Simcoe jail, Colonel," Wilson replied. "There's no other place south of here."

"All right," MacNab said loudly to the other officers. "Feed your men now whatever they can find in this place. They won't be eating again for some time. Dismissed." He looked at Wilson. "I'll have those papers now. Our prisons are going to be crammed full."

When George Smith was put into the Simcoe jail, there were just three other prisoners, two of whom were thieves and the third was a murderer. Part of the jail was under construction, which was delayed because most of the workmen were in Wilson's dragoons. Smith joined the other prisoners for breakfast. The young man, who had murdered a farming family for whom he worked, was friendly. He was not political, he said, but he was sympathetic to all political prisoners regardless what political beliefs they held. Suspicious, Smith declined to express his political views. He knew intuitively that the man was working for the authorities to save himself from hanging. When the man insisted on asking him questions, Smith lost his temper and shouted at him to mind his own business. At noon, Smith was taken from his cell. The money which he had relinquished to the jailer was returned to him. That was a good sign, he thought. The jailer escorted him to the court house where Mercer Wilson in his militia uniform awaited him in the company of a dozen men from his regiment.

"You were wrong, Mr. Smith," Wilson said. "The rebels did not attack us but rather fled into Norwich county."

"Despite their best intentions," Smith said cheerfully. "That's good news."

"There is a man among us here who knows you, Mr. Smith. You are in luck, I believe."

Smith looked incredulously at the dragoons arrayed around Wilson. He noticed three black men amongst them and looking closer at them he thought that he recognized the tall man with the lean face and bright eyes who was suppressing a smile.

"He's the one," this man said in a well-modulated voice. "He is definitely George M. Smith, the Black Pimpernel. You remember Dick Plummer, don't you, George?"

"Plummer!" Smith cried in surprise. He stepped forward and grasped Plummer's hand. "I thought you had died." He laughed with Plummer who pumped his hand.

"This man got me to Canada," Plummer told the others. "I'm not dead, thanks to him. We got into a spot of trouble some years ago, but old George is as smart as a fox."

"Never thought I'd see you again," Smith shook his head bemusedly.

"You are obviously a veteran in the game of spying," Wilson broke in. "With your information on the rebel camp you gave us last night, we had the confidence to attack it straight on. So, Mr. Smith, you are free to go, unless, of course, you would like to join our regiment."

Smith cocked an eye at Wilson which brought laughter from the men. "I'm afraid, Captain, that some people in Cleveland are waiting news from me. Thanks for the generous offer."

"I'll give you a pass signed by me. I'm the magistrate here. It should help you get back to your people," Wilson said. "Men, you know your business. Let's get out and make a sweep of the areas we discussed. There should be hundreds of rebels on the run now that word has leaked that we have their names."

Plummer introduced Smith to the two black men standing with him while the other dragoons hurried to their horses. "Private Johnson, the man taking you in last night, is out on the hunt," Plummer said. "He asked me to say he was sorry." He smiled and patted Smith's arm affectionately. "George, I hope we can get together soon. I feel like I could talk to you for days."

Smith hugged Plummer to him and with a broad smile bade the men good-bye. As he watched them go out the door, Wilson's lieutenant approached him with a laissez-passer that would save him from being picked up again as a rebel.

"What is the fastest route to Cleveland?" he asked the young man.

"By ship," the lieutenant said advisedly, as if he were thinking of several routes, "go directly south to Port Ryerse and cross the lake or west to Amherstburg where there are ships going daily to Cleveland."

Smith left the court house with the lieutenant, who was hurrying to catch up to his Captain, already mounted and waiting impatiently to set out on the hunt. He sensed the tension in the town dissipating with the news of the rebels' defeat. Feeling the bite of hunger, he entered the first tavern he chanced upon on the main street and looked round at the tables. Only at one table at the back of the room were there vacant places, but a white man was eating his lunch alone there, and Smith, by training, avoided joining him. But the white man, a sandy-haired, blue-eyed young fellow, saw him hesitate and signalled to him to join him.

Smith, still cautious, went to the table. "You want me to sit with you?" he asked, as if he doubted the man's intention.

"There's no place else, is there?" the man said cheerfully. "The food's good here, probably the best in town. Better sit and enjoy it," he smiled.

"All right, then," Smith said affably, and, pulling out a chair, sat opposite the man.

The man pointed to the menu chalked on a blackboard. "Take the fish," he advised.

Smith saw that he was eating fish and ordered it from the girl who came to the table.

The young man stuck out his hand. "I'm Sam Tisdale," he said. "You?"

Smith shook his hand. "George Smith." He wondered if the fellow was a reformer because of his open democratic manner.

"Passing through?" Tisdale asked.

"Going to Cleveland."

"You can have a ride with me," Tisdale beamed. "And we can catch a sail for Erie, Pennsylvania, where you can take the regular steamer to Cleveland tomorrow. How's that?"

Smith nodded appreciatively. He was beginning to like this forward young man. His natural sense of caution, however, made him question the ease with which everything fell into place. "Are you going to Erie, then?"

"I'm in ship insurance," Tisdale explained. "Got legal business there. It's easier to get a ship from Ryerse for the States than from Port Dover these days. Too many rebels in Dover, I hear, so the boys are closing the port to all but fishermen." The man's frankness seemed natural to him.

"You say, anybody leaving Canada is suspect," Smith said. "Will they let you go?"

"Don't worry, Mr. Smith. I'm carrying all necessary documents. Besides I know the captain of the ship we'll be taking," Tisdale smiled. "You should worry about yourself."

"I'm provided for," Smith said cryptically.

The waitress placed a plate of fish and boiled potatoes in front of Smith, who, smelling the aroma of good solid food for the first time in days, ate with relish.

"The last thing we need is a war among neighbours," Tisdale continued. "The economy is flat, our leadership is reactionary, and our lord and masters in the old country don't give a damn. But American style republicanism is not the answer for us," he added thoughtfully while watching Smith eat. "I think our silly little rebellion will wake up

275

some people and we can get the changes we want. But you, you interest me. Why is a black man returning to the land of slavery?"

Smith swallowed and looked at him. "For one thing, I'm free, and for another, I can be useful to those that are not."

Tisdale gave him a look of admiration and held his hand out across the table. "It seems that we are in the same business, Mr. Smith. I'm glad we met."

Smith, surprised, shook his hand again and looked questioningly at him.

"But we shall say no more about it," Tisdale warned. "Let's just remember that we have a friend in one another, shall we?"

Smith nodded. "Are you from Simcoe?"

"Ancaster. An enterprising community near the head of Lake Ontario. From there I can get east to York, west to London and south to this country equally fast."

Smith, liking this man the more he listened to him, wondered how much he knew about the rebels' secret lodges and the preparations the Americans were making for invasion. As he listened to him talk about the state of the country and its politics, he realized that he was not a spy for the rebels or for the government but rather an individual who acted according to his convictions. He dared not allude to the lodges lest he betray his mission, even if it were to someone sympathetic to it. During the wagon ride to Port Ryerse, the checking of their papers by militiamen at the port, and the sail under a strong wind across Lake Erie, the two men talked, enjoying one another's company, but never again mentioning their work for emancipation. As Smith boarded the steamer for Cleveland, he reflected on his good fortune in meeting Sam Tisdale, whom he was sure to meet again, and how it complemented the information he had fortuitously gathered for his friends in the Upper Canadian Society for Emancipation. He noticed, however, that a crowd of men with rifles were on board bound also for Cleveland. They called themselves hunters. Smith kept his distance from them, but managed to approach one young man who was standing by himself and watching the sea from the railing of the deck.

"Are you one of the patriots?" he asked as he stood looking over the rail with him.

"I guess I am," the young man said.

"Going to liberate Canada, are you?" Smith smiled.

"That's to be decided in Cleveland," the young man said quietly. "They're forming the Republican Government of Upper Canada and my Dad told me to get in now so's when we take over in Canada, I'll get a good job."

"That's smart thinking," Smith said. "God knows, there are no jobs to be had here."

The young man looked earnestly at him. "You want to join?"

"No," Smith shook his head vigorously. "Guns frighten me. I couldn't hunt animals let alone human beings." He stepped away with an apologetic smile.

The young man gave him a pitying look and returned to watching the lake water slide by the boat. Smith resolved not to approach another hunter lest he be enlisted or pressed into their service. What, he wondered, would most Canadian Reformers have done if they knew that the new Republican Government was just then organizing to take over their lives.

Sarah did not sleep during the night that Simcoans expected to be attacked. Only when news came that the rebels had fled did she relax and give up her vigil at her window. Vesta and John, having stayed up until the small hours of the morning, were still sleeping. Sarah left breakfast for them to eat when they awoke. She went to the court house to hear the latest news from messengers who rode in from all directions. There, standing on the front steps with a seriousness that was unusual for one so young, she saw Theo Hunt, a schoolfriend of her son John. Theo came to her as he watched her approach.

"Hello, Mrs. Lewis," he cried. "Come to see the prisoners?"

"Prisoners? So soon, Theo?"

"They've been bringing them in by twos and threes," Theo said excitedly, his copper colored hair glinting in the morning sun. "Here's more." He pointed behind her.

Half a dozen young men, their arms tied behind their backs, walked disconsolately in front of a man on horseback who kept his rifle leveled at them.

Theo cried joyfully at recognizing one of Wilson's men. "Where'd you get them?"

"Hidin' in the fields around Normandale," the horseman replied grimly, as if he did not want to reply but felt that he had to. "Keep out of the way, now," he warned.

A constable appeared from the jail and ordered the prisoners to enter where other constables awaited them. "We got over thirty. You better not bring us any more," he said to the horseman. "We've got no room."

The man laughed. "You better make room 'cause Captain Wilson is bringing in a dozen or so and there's others in tow from the other side of Long Point."

Sarah came up to them and asked, "Anyone important? Any of the leaders?"

"Naw, Mrs. Lewis," the horseman yawned. "Just small fry, except for a member of parliament from Oxford who Henson Johnson caught early this morning as he was running for Port Ryerse."

"Alway?" she cried, remembering the man who had done good things for the local people and was always pleasant to her. "I hope he's not hurt."

"His pride is hurt, that's about it." He turned his horse and rode toward Campbell's stables on Norfolk St. where his horse could be fed. "Plenty got away, though," he added over his shoulder as an afterthought.

"You going back out?" Theo shouted after him, and, receiving no reply, turned to Sarah. "Colonel MacNab's men went into Sodom and met no resistance. So all we got to do is mop up."

"That's good to hear, Theo," Sarah said. "But I feel sorry for those young people in jail." She thought of Fanny's friend Powers and pictured him crowded into a damp prison cell with dozens of other rebels.

Since it was market day and the vendors would be putting out their meats and the vegetables they had preserved from the summer and fall seasons, Sarah walked behind the Court House and north to the outdoor stalls where she knew that Lucinda Landon was setting up her flower stand. Lucinda was the only person in Simcoe with a hothouse and remained the only source for plants and flowers during the winter.

Sarah caught sight of her tall, thin figure stooping over an arrangement of colourful long-stemmed flowers, and, feeling a rush of empathy for her best friend who worked as hard as she did, she walked directly to her stand and greeted her warmly.

"Sarah!" Lucinda threw her arms open and brought Sarah against her, "I was worried about you, being on the front line and all that."

"All I had to worry about was all those boys tramping over my front yard and comin' round for coffee and cookies every so often. Duncan was ridin' around shouting out to everybody what they should be doin', which made them more confused than ever," Sarah laughed. "If the rebels had run up against them, I don't know if there wouldn't have been pandemonium. All those tree trunks and branches across the road wouldn't have done much good against a real fightin' force. We're just lucky the rebels were as confused as our boys."

Lucinda laughed and hugged her. "The worst is over for now. A messenger stopped to get flowers for his wife. He says MacNab's troops have been setting fire to farms, charging bleaching huts and hen houses, and generally wreaking havoc on all those Quakers in Sodom who wouldn't join the militia. Teaching them a lesson, he said. I don't like it. Those people have enough resentment against us without our troops provoking them to madness. MacNab should rein his men in, but he's vindictive and stubborn. He's even let the Indians scalp a couple of rebels they found in the woods, so I hear."

Sarah shook her head sadly. "What happened to Dr. Duncombe?"

"Once he discovered he didn't have enough men left to make a stand in Sodom, he let every man fend for himself. A lot of them got a head start for the Detroit border. I suppose he's got away too."

"You'd think," Sarah frowned, "that having got the people of Oxford County behind them, the rebels would have stood and fought just to save the people from being victimized by MacNab."

"They'll be coming back stronger than ever with American support," Lucinda said in a softer voice, "and from what I've been hearing, they have a second campaign coming up soon."

Sarah gave her a startled look. "Are we prepared for it?"

Lucinda's eyes flashed with humour. "The Norfolk militia is not to be trusted to defend us. The Lieutenant-Governor has ordered the 32nd

British Regiment here to live in our houses, eat our food, and protect us. I have a feeling that you and I will be supporting British soldiers for months to come."

"But I can't afford to feed any more mouths," Sarah said in amazement. "Are you sure, Lucinda?"

"Enjoy Christmas," Lucinda laughed at Sarah's dismay. "After the New Year the troops will be billeted with us. But at least we'll be safer."

A customer came to the stand and Lucinda went to wait on her. Sarah waited to speak to her again, but as more customers came to buy flowers, she wandered to the other stands and bought the foods that she needed. She had to return to her house because people had left laundry with her, and, despite the excitement of possible warfare in her front yard, they expected it to be done quickly as usual. Her happiness at the defeat of the rebels was being dissipated by her sombre thoughts of British soldiers swarming over the town and ordering the citizens about with the disdainful attitude they habitually showed to colonials. The threat of invasion from the United States must have been greater than she had imagined, and the danger to the blacks all over Canada had become so real that she began to worry about being enslaved again. She felt again that deprivation of soul that she thought she had put behind her forever. Now as she passed black people in the streets they looked one another in the eye with apprehension. Word that the rebel leaders had got away safely to the United States, from where they would invade, swept the towns and countryside like a storm. She happened to meet Life Henry, the tavern keeper, as she rounded the corner onto Kent Street, and he, looking down guiltily, hurried away without a word. How many Americans like him would join those invading forces and put shackles on her and her children? she asked herself. If it meant housing the lordly British to prevent such a travesty, she would work to the bone to keep them fed and happy.

Down the road she observed Dick Plummer and Henson Johnson, stalwart members of her church, on horseback herding some prisoners before them. Her mood changed as she watched them. She felt confident and proud. And the same feelings of relief and joy that she knew when she crossed the Canadian border to freedom came back to her. If there ever were an invasion, the people would repulse it, with or without the help of British regiments, she thought confidently. Then dismissing from her mind all musings, she concentrated on the large pile of laundry that awaited her like a challenge.

22

Fear now possessed Bill Powers. He ran for hours through the bush as if mounted militia were pursuing him. Having had little sleep for forty-eight hours, he regarded himself as more fully awake than ever. His energy seemed to surge through him, driving him onward. He ran past clusters of retreating rebels who were trudging along as if oblivious of the danger behind them. Some of them had put their disappointment aside and were joking and laughing amongst themselves. Others were counting themselves lucky to have avoided a pitched battle, which they had never expected to fight in any case. They were unaware that Colonel MacNab had their names and had given orders to round them up; indeed, they were unaware that their names had been listed in muster formation by the rebels' leaders. Powers, however, suspected that the muster rolls had been found by the loyalists, who impressed him by their resolute appearance when they rode into Scotland. These men were sure to find the hurriedly buried rolls. Powers had pangs of guilt as he thought of it. He was not listed because, as an aide at large to Duncombe, he did not belong to any regimental formation. He veered southward, away from the main trails leading north to Sodom to which the rebels had been directed. He knew there would be no regrouping, no military action against the advancing militias. His dream of liberty was shattered. Perhaps, if the lodges kept their secrets, there could be another uprising, better planned, better executed. For the time being he had to look after himself.

Stopping only once to rest and drink from a stream, he ran back to Otterville. It was twilight as he loped to his home where Fanny was cooking by candlelight. She was alarmed when she saw him, his clothes torn by brambles, his body soaked with perspiration and shaking, his eyes startled. She took him in her arms, soothing him, forcing him to sit, and bringing him to a state of calm. Then eliciting from him all that had happened while she finished cooking their dinner and placing his plate before him, she urged him to eat and watched as his hunger seemed to enter him like a satyr and he ate all that was given him. Suddenly, as if a heavy burden had settled upon him, he stood up, walked unsteadily to their bed, stripped off his clothes and fell onto the covers instantly into a deep sleep. Fanny covered him and sat thinking of the dangerous situation they were in. She knew that many farmers, who would have supported the rebels had they won, would be only too eager to report them to the militias, if only to prove their loyalty. She could not trust their neighbours. How easy it would be to report Bill, see his land expropriated and take it over for themselves. Bill and she would have to go as paupers to the States, a land she detested. She was sure that no one had noticed him arrive in the dusk, and, if they did, she would deny it. It was too dangerous for Bill to stay in the house because the soldiers might come looking for him. The only way they could keep him out of prison and keep their land from being confiscated was for Bill to hide and for her to carry on as if she were a loyal citizen. In the morning, Bill could ride to friends in Sarnia. She could say that he was away on business. She lied down beside him, satisfied of the wisdom of her choice, and fell asleep.

Fanny, waking with a start, leaned over and shook Bill Powers. It was still dark but dawn would be upon them soon. Groaning, Bill got out of bed, washed and dressed. Fanny had breakfast for him when he came to the table.

"You can't look as if you are running away, Bill," she said. "I think you should take the horse and wagon with your ladder and painting equipment. If anyone stops you, say that you are engaged to do painting."

Bill smiled, "That's smart. I like that idea."

"The militia are out in force all over the province now. Everyone wants to prove his loyalty," Fanny said with a smirk. "But you just pretend that you have nothing to do with it and want to work undisturbed."

"Yes, but where am I going to have work? I can't say I have a job in Sarnia. It's days away, and they won't believe me. I saw in the London newspaper about a week ago that they want artisans for the new government buildings. London is on the road to Sarnia. What do you think, Fanny?"

"I think you have to leave right now for London. Hurry, my darling. Get your tools while I hitch up the wagon." Fanny put on a coat and ran to the barn.

A light snow had fallen during the night and the air was freezing, but the wind had blown the trails and roads free of snow. Powers brought his paint cans from the back of the house to the barn where he found that Fanny had hitched up their horse and put his ladder and other tools into the wagon. He set his paint cans into the back, embraced Fanny strongly, and climbing up on the wagon seat with a sigh, he drove the wagon out the door which Fanny held open, waved good-bye and disappeared into the darkness.

About mid-morning he drove past a line of twenty prisoners, tied together by rope around their necks, and accompanied by mounted militia. He recognized a few of the faces and remarked on the pain and humiliation they revealed. The militiamen did not stop him as they assumed he was on business. Thus, always fearful of being apprehended and acting as a tradesman anxious to get to an appointment, Powers came to the outskirts of London as the sun sank below the horizon and turned into the farmstead of a known reformer who would give him shelter. The man's wife came out of the house and warned him to get away quickly. Her husband had been arrested that morning and all known reformers were being rounded up and sent to the London prison. Clutching a kerchief over her head and looking about furtively, she beckoned him to bend down to her. Holding to his coat lapels she spoke into his ear. "Mr. Allen, the big stone house as you enter town. He'll help you. He's Tory but he'll help you." She turned awkwardly and ran back into the house.

As Powers drove back down the driveway he felt her watching him from a front window. Her advice to stop at a Tory's home puzzled him. The name Allen was particularly worrying because an Allen was a prominent member of the Family Compact. This London Allen could be a relative. But if he were sympathetic to the rebels' plight, any rebel under his protection should be safe. When he came to the house which was just inside the town limits, he stopped to admire its grand look with two wings sweeping to either side of a cylindrical main section, as if it were a medieval castle without a moat. His feet and hands were very cold and his body ached from the constant jolting of the wagon over many miles of muddy, rutted roads. He decided to risk putting himself at Mr. Allen's mercy and drove his wagon up the long driveway. There was no sign of movement behind the great tall windows. Powers, thinking that the place looked deserted and he would have to find somewhere else to stay, approached the front door perfunctorily, seized the large brass knocker, beat out three strong slams, stood back and listened. The wind sifted snow through the large fir trees in front of the house. Powers sensed an anticipatory quality in the air and looked expectantly at the front door. Instead, he heard a girl's voice and looking round saw a girl in her early teens with fair hair standing by the side of the house and watching him.

"Come this way, sir," she called. "Bring your wagon this way, please."

Powers, hesitated, unsure if she had mistaken him for someone else. "I want shelter for the night," he said.

"Yes, I know," the girl said quickly. "Come, please, now. Don't delay. You need help, I know."

Seizing his horse's reins, Powers led it and the wagon alongside the house to a barn at the back where the girl said that he should unhitch the horse, feed it with the hay beside the stall and come into the house through the back entrance. She left him before he could ask a question.

As he led his horse into an empty stall, he noticed several horses in the other stalls and stopped short in amazement. There in the next stall was a white stallion. He came closer and looked at its face to see a thin brown streak on its forehead. His heart gave a jump with joy. Dr.

Duncombe had taken refuge in this house. Hurriedly brushing down his horse and setting the hay for it to eat, he went directly through the back door of the house into a warm kitchen where a large fire burned in an open stone oven. He stood warming himself and taking off his outer garments while expecting someone to appear. He looked at a pie baking in a small oven to the side and imagined tasting the pastry and swallowing the warm fruit. As he was about to sit, he heard laughter from the front of the house. Walking cautiously along a hallway and following the sounds of voices, he saw lights from a room to the side. Stepping into it, he found himself in a large sitting room, well-lit with candelabra, at the far end of which were two men and the young girl talking and drinking tea. One of the men, distinguished-looking of medium height with white side whiskers on a long, intelligent face, stood up and approached him.

"Come and introduce yourself to my other guest," he smiled genially. "I'm Robert Allen, and this is my daughter Tina."

Powers shook his hand, glanced at his daughter and looked immediately at the weather-beaten face of Dr. Duncombe, who was watching him in amazement.

"Let me introduce him," Duncombe said, coming to him and taking him by the arm. "This is Bill Powers, who has been my aide and good friend." He hugged Powers to him, standing on his toes to reach the taller Powers.

"Doctor, I can't believe it!" Powers exclaimed.

Duncombe laughed. "Robert Allen is an old friend. It's natural for me to be here, but not for you. Where are you going?"

"To Sarnia. And You?"

"I shall have to cross the border there some day, but not for a while." Duncombe's eyes twinkled with humour. "I can't stay here much longer either. How is it that you found this place?"

While Powers quickly related his experiences during the day, Tina, the young girl, poured him a cup of tea and handed it to him. "I hoped," Powers added, "that I could find someone to hire me for a paint job in London."

"I shall be glad to do that," Allen interjected. "The paint in the front hallway has been peeling. I'm afraid it will take some days, but you can stay in this house. You will be safe here until you decide to move on."

"That's excellent," Duncombe said cheerfully. "But I have to move on later tonight. The very fact that Bill was directed to your house means that word will get round that you are protecting rebels."

"No, no," Allen shook his head.

Duncombe raised his arm to signify that he was not to be contradicted. "It's too great a risk for me on any account. MacNab has already prepared the noose for me, and the London prison will be the centre for the trials. Would you like to see yourself arraigned with me in the downtown jail, my good friend. No, I must leave at midnight."

"But where will you go?" asked Tina in a voice of concern and compassion.

He shrugged and laughed suddenly. "Bill, last night, I took refuge with some friends who dressed me in their grandmother's clothes and set me in bed just before there was a pounding at the door. It was militia wanting to search the house. 'Yes, but be careful of grandma. If she's disturbed, she has temper tantrums,' they said. The Captain took it upon himself to check the bedroom. He barely looked at me in my bed bonnet. One glance at this granite face of mine and he ran away."

As the men laughed, Tina said excitedly, "We can dress you as our grandmother!"

"No, my dear," Duncombe patted her shoulder to comfort her. "Best I go so that I can live to fight another day," he smiled. "Come, let us put out the dinner. Bill might be hungrier than I am."

"You two go ahead," Allan said. "Come, Mr. Powers, I'll show you the front hall." He led Powers into a high vaulting hall, very long and magnificent in its architecture and lit by a large chandelier. "This will take you some days to paint. Let us hope that the pursuit will have lost some of its urgency by then."

"May I ask why, as a Tory, you are helping us?"

"Some years ago Dr. Duncombe saved Tina's life. Beside the significance of that, politics has no meaning," Allen said earnestly. "He is a good man in a foolish cause. But I see that change has to come despite what I think. You are welcome to stay as long as you wish." He smiled and added, "So long as you don't fill me with radical ideas. Now, let us go into dinner. We have to serve ourselves as the servants went to their homes when the troubles began." He led the way to the dining room where Tina and Duncombe were helping themselves buffet style.

As they ate, Allen told them the latest news he had of MacNab's force. Sucking blankets to keep down their hunger as they pursued the rebels through the forest, MacNab's men terrorized the villages they came upon, encouraged Tory magistrates to harass suspected reformers and stole food from the silent Quakers. "They are not popular," he added in wry understatement and continued in a sarcastic tone. "Hearing that Mackenzie regrouped at Navy Island on Lake Erie and is planning to lead a force in a sweep up the Grand River, MacNab has dashed back to Hamilton for reinforcements. The drivers of the sleighs carrying his militia were so obsessed with speed that they drove their horses to death before they reached the city. And all of this frantic rushing around is based on rumour."

Duncombe shook his head sadly. "He'll bring an overwhelming number of white and Indian militia to Lake Erie and try to smoke out Mackenzie. All I can hope for is that he creates an international incident that will make the Americans mad enough to go to war. I'm itching to get back into the action." Wrapping himself against the freezing cold, he bade the Allens good-bye and walked with Powers to the stables.

As they cinched the saddle on his white stallion, Duncombe looked grimly at Powers. "Bill, my friend, some of Mackenzie's lieutenants have been captured. Our failure means their execution. If I get to America, I swear I'll bring back a scourge on these self-righteous villains. If I don't make it, I expect you to carry on the work. You are young, Bill, and your future can spell the future of the country."

Powers put his arms about the smaller man. "I promise, doctor, that your efforts will be rewarded some day. Keep safe."

Visibly moved, Duncombe mounted his horse and galloped out the open door into the blackness.

Weeks later Powers rejoiced to learn that Duncombe, after almost dying of exposure in the woods, found shelter in the hayloft of his sister's barn for several weeks, after which a friend took him dressed as his maiden aunt by sleigh across the iced-over river to Michigan. In

Detroit, Duncombe helped to organize the patriot army under an American "general", who expected twenty thousand Canadian sympathizers to rise in the Canadian countryside simultaneous with the American attack on Windsor.

When the 32nd British Regiment arrived from Lower Canada after brutally subduing the rebels there, the fierceness required to do their work settled into their character and began spending itself on the unfortunate townspeople of Upper Canada. Duncan Campbell told Sarah that Dr. Duncombe's brother, Elijah, who had nothing to do with the rebellion, had to billet 160 militiamen and went unpaid for services rendered, which even he considered unjust.

The two young Britishers billeted in Sarah's home carried all the superiority and superciliousness imbued in them through years of training in the military. Taught to regard colonials as inferior, the military took over the governance of the towns to which they were assigned and regulated the lives of the citizens. The officer class set the standard in behaviour for lesser ranks, who aped the strut and angry commands of the captains and lieutenants. The Regiment's experience of routing rebels, destroying villages and leaving hundreds of French-Canadian families starving and without shelter did shake the confidence of some in the non-commissioned ranks, who began to doubt the integrity of the men who governed them. The harsh treatment to which they were subjected, the whippings for the slightest error in discipline, and an inclination to identify with the sufferings of the inhabitants bred a hatred in some soldiers for the work they did. Such was the case of the two privates who lived in Sarah's home. Sarah's warm greeting and hospitality unnerved them at first, but gradually they came to respect her for the long hours of hard work she did and to like her for her openness and her sympathy for them.

Sarah worried over the fractures in the society of Upper Canada and was appalled by Duncan Campbell's vociferous support of the harsh practices against suspected reformers. She watched with dismay as seventy young men roped from neck to neck stumbled from the Simcoe jail along the route to London in the winter cold. Tories jeered them along the way and threw stones at them until stopped by the mounted mili-

288

tia. On the surface, aside from pockets of vociferous disdain for the authorities, the majority of the population seemed loyal, she thought. But resentment at the executions of rebels in Toronto and London and at the transportation of many rebels to Van Diemen's penal colony fomented into a powerful brew in the western townships. Later, her son John told her that pressure from the English government, alarmed at the brutal treatment, prompted the Canadian authorities to grant conditional pardons to prisoners who pled guilty before their arraignment and asked for mercy. Most rebels were released from prison when they swore allegiance to Canada and paid fines, but resentment at being held in cold damp cells, the deaths of comrades from fever and disease and the humiliation of being marched from local jails roped together through the cold for many miles for days to the central prison at London burned within them. As anger in the citizen body grew, fewer prisoners died in captivity. Sarah thanked God that others had their capital sentences repealed.

Duncan lamented the fall in property values as many settlers returned to the United States and their lands were put up for sale. Hundreds did not sympathize with the rebels particularly, he told Sarah; they went to avoid the Militia Law, which required young men to be drafted into military units. Others went because of the unchecked depredations of the military upon the civilian population or because of Tory magistrates only too willing to imprison suspected rebels on the testimony of neighbours, who may have been settling old scores and coveting their lands.

Worse than the economic depression was the nervous tension of the people, which medical authorities blamed for an acceleration in the deaths of children and old persons from scarlet fever and a mysterious canker rash. Sarah and her friends discussed events and shared the news that they learned from their husbands and sons who were called out for assignments with the local militia regiments. Meeting together helped to calm their nerves and discount some of the worst rumours. After Sarah heard from her son Henry that he and Mary had escaped from Virginia and were in hiding near Cleveland, her worry over their safety and her excitement at seeing them again gave her an extra incentive to discover the actual state of affairs.

Sarah listened to her friends of long-standing such as Charity and William Rusling, the Culvers and Lucinda Landon, but she gleaned the best judgment from a black woman of spirit, Maria Parker, who had migrated recently to Simcoe. Like most newcomers Maria kept silent about her background yet her air of quiet determination intimated that she had escaped from a brutal form of slavery. She and Sarah took to one another immediately and, whenever they could spare time in the evenings, they visited in one another's homes and talked over the latest news that Maria, who could read, gathered from the newspapers sent to the hotel, for which she worked. The newspapers came from Toronto, Kingston and Buffalo, the centres of action, and brought in their few pages a variety of views and conflicting reports that someone with an incisive mind like Maria's enjoyed parsing and reconstructing. Maria was admired in the black community for her outspokenness and her opinions, but even she had difficulty excusing the depredations of Major Tom Magrath of the Brantford Militia, who was put in charge of subduing the country south of the town to Lake Erie and from Port Dover west to Long Point on the lakeshore; a detachment of regulars from the 32nd was placed under his command. She warned Sarah that no one was safe from his suspicions. Soldiers would storm any of the taverns at any time and search the men drinking or eating there for weapons. They broke into houses and arrested people on the flimsiest of evidence given by neighbors.

Sarah awoke in the small hours of the morning to a banging at her front door. It sounded like rifle butts pounding the wood and threatening to break it down. She got to the door at the same time as John and, frightened, they swung it open only to be pushed back by large uniformed men holding torches aloft and commanding them to give way.

"What are you doing?" Sarah cried as a soldier pushed her back.

The soldiers, brushing past her, entered the rooms off the hallway.

A short, imperious man with the insignia of an officer bellowed at her. "You are under suspicion."

She recognized Captain Magrath. His bulbous nose and sharp little eyes confronted her as if she were an impediment to good order. He entered the hallway, and, taking her by the arm, pushed her into the sitting room. The cries of Vesta's child sounded above the thumping and clumping of the soldiers as they overturned furniture and stalked from room to room. John, seeing that he had been overlooked for the moment, stepped outside and ran into the road to a narrow pathway through Duncan Campbell's woods that he knew well. He could see well enough in the dark to run fast over the tree roots and through bushes without stumbling. Only Duncan could help them now, he thought.

Sitting Sarah into a chair and instructing his boyish aide to light the candles in the room, Magrath stood back to regard her fiercely.

"I don't know what you want," she said plaintively. "What have I done?"

"My men are finding out what you have been doing?" Magrath said angrily. "Now, where are you hiding weapons?"

"I don't have weapons," she cried.

"You are a supporter of the rebels, are you not?" Magrath said with a black look of accusation.

The two privates in their underclothes were pushed into the room and stood staring uncomprehendingly at Magrath.

"You two," he shouted at them. "Who are you? Explain yourselves!"

One of them sang out their names and added they were in the 32nd Regiment.

Magrath stared in disbelief until his aide said that two Britishers were boarded in the house.

"But you are supposed to be in Dover!" Magrath said angrily.

"That order was rescinded," Magrath's aide said calmly.

Magrath frowned, took a step away and then whirled round on the men. "Everyone here is suspect of aiding the rebels. What can you say for yourselves?"

The privates looked astounded and could only stare at the Captain.

"They are good boys," Sarah interjected. "They are loyal to the Crown, sir."

Magrath ignored her. "Have you seen any suspicious movement here?" he demanded of the men

"No, captain," one of the men said. "The Lewis family is loyalist.

We will vouch for that."

Vesta and her little boy rushed into the room and put their arms about Sarah, who held them tightly while still sitting. The sounds of smashing wood came from other areas of the house as the troops made their way methodically through every room and into the barn out back.

Magrath looked uncertain now, but he did not want to give the impression of being mistaken. "If we find evidence, you could be hanged," he told Sarah. "Don't try to hide anything from us." He stamped into the hallway. Sarah heard him urging his men to look thoroughly in every cabinet.

Vesta glared at the young man who was aide to Magrath until he began to feel self-conscious.

"We have our job to do, that's all," he said. "You just be patient. If you're all right, then everything will be all right."

"No, it will not," Vesta hissed. "You're destroying our furniture, our clothes, and all for nothing. You ought to be ashamed of yourselves. No wonder everyone hates you."

The aide, disconcerted by Vesta's attack, looked at Sarah holding the small boy in her arms. Without Magrath, he was vulnerable. He stared at the floor while the sounds of breaking wood and shouting men came from the back of the house.

In a few moments Magrath returned to the room. "We have found nothing," he announced, "but that does not mean that we will not. You all will have to come to the jail for questioning."

"Even my son?" Vesta cried. "What can you accuse him of?"

Magrath stared at her imperiously and then looked alarmed. "Where is the young man we saw when we entered the doorway? Where is he?"

"Whoa there!" sounded the booming voice of authority from outside the house.

Magrath gave a puzzled look at his aide, who said that it sounded like Colonel Campbell. They listened to Campbell give orders to hold his horse and heard his steps enter the hallway.

"What's doing here, Major?" he asked with the disagreeable look of a man who has been awakened from a deep sleep.

Magrath turned to stare at him with a pained look. "We are conducting an operation," he said perfunctorily, "sir."

"On whose order?" Campbell asked angrily.

"On my order. We have had reports that this house harbors rebels who are planning actions against prominent citizens," Magrath replied sententiously.

"You will find no rebels here, Major," Campbell said brusquely, his face flushed in the light from the torches. "You will give over here immediately."

"But we have just begun our questioning, Colonel," Magrath expostulated. "How can you be sure—?"

"I am. I know these people well." He called to the two Britishers. "Come here!" And when they came up to him, he asked, "Have you any reason to suspect anyone in this household of rebel activities?"

"No, sir," they answered together.

"Then, Major, dismiss your men and make sure in future that you do not indispose good people."

Magrath blushed red, and seeing that Campbell was waiting for his order to be carried out, he dismissed his men and retreated with them into the night. Sarah, carrying a torch, approached Duncan with a grateful look.

"We have to put up with these sorts of things until this fear of invasion has passed," he said gently and took her free hand. "Men like Magrath love a little power over others, I'm afraid." He smiled at Vesta, and, as he stepped from the cabin, he watched John come up running. "Good boy for warning me," he said warmly. "I don't think, Sarah, that you will be bothered again." He mounted his horse and turned towards his home. "Now everyone get a good night's sleep and you two," he called at the soldiers, who came out of the house to watch him go, "find out who made the report if you can and never let this happen again."

"Yes, sir," they replied sharply together.

Campbell galloped away, leaving the impression on the Lewis family of a benevolent and all-powerful guardian. But the incident worried Sarah. She wondered who could have spread such a lie. She discussed possibilities with Vesta and John as they tried to restore order into the rooms for the next hour, but they could think of no one person who had his eye on Sarah's property. The privates helped them restore furniture while shaking their heads at the broken pieces that they knew that Sarah lacked the money to replace. Whoever it was, they said, they had influence with the ruling powers and would try again some time. One of them, a lean young man, said that he had access to the files and would see if there had been a written complaint, although they all doubted there would be.

The suspicion, the uncertainty, the fear of a sudden action based on a falsehood, and the all-important question of an American invasion haunted everyone in the village. Major Magrath terrorized the citizens with his unexpected storming of residences, his quick arrests on suspicion, the long wait for a trial to be set free, and his overbearing manners. The loyalists tolerated his aggressiveness because they thought it intimidated rebel sympathisers and made it more difficult for rebels to prepare to help an American invasion, which was rumoured to be taking place every two weeks or so. But when one spring evening, some of the villagers burned an effigy of Magrath on the common, the loyalists spoke of him as too provocative and suggested that he be replaced by a more reasonable man.

"Trouble is," Maria Parker said to Sarah one evening at her home, "he's very careful just to pick on the poor ones like us. Note that he don't rip up the homes of the rich. I'll bet he's still in charge when the invasion comes. Then we'll all see how courageous he is." She laughed a deep throaty infectious laugh that made Sarah laugh too.

"The soldiers in my house tell me that there's been little threat from the American side," Sarah said. "Just small parties landin' to do a little stealin' and things like that, you know, setting fire to Tory property and trying to stir up a war between Britain and America."

"Ah now, Mrs. Lewis," Dick Plummer admonished her, for he was on leave from the Dragoons. "We know there's somethin' big goin' to happen. Take the fightin' in the west, those landin's on Fightin' Island, and other places there. Sure we rallied and knocked them back easy enough, but there's so many of 'em we just have to be careful not to let our guard down. And say! how'd our colored regiment do when they repulsed the Yanks on Pelee Island? Pretty good! We've made our mark, all right," he chuckled.

"We better make our mark come the big invasion," Maria Parker said with emphasis. "Look at the Americans comin' over the river by Sarnia—about forty of them—looting and shooting, landings further up on Lake Huron where our Indians killed some of them. Somethin's brewin'. Our black boys got to do their bit."

"I guess there's goin' to be a big invasion," Sarah sighed, "and a lot of secret rebels here are goin' to join 'em."

"Don't you worry your pretty head about all those secret rebels," Plummer laughed. "Our captain has got a pretty good bead on all of them. We're just sittin' and waitin' for them to move. We know pretty well who they are."

"Well now," Maria smiled sarcastically, "we are in the safe hands of some pretty smart gentlemen, seein' as they're able to spot a rebel when all's he done is going to some meetings to hear about rebelling. Why don't you arrest them now then?"

"We've done enough of that and it's sort of come back to haunt us and give us more trouble," Plummer said seriously. "If we don't identify them as rebels, they may not become rebels, if you get my meaning."

"Don't stir up trouble," Maria laughed. "That was my husband's favourite sayin'. But I never knowed of a man who got in more trouble. Right now, he's in the regiment defending Fort Malden down there across from Detroit where any invasion is going to happen. But you tell me, Richard Plummer, just how you can be so sure you've got the rebels here under control."

Plummer looked at her in amusement. "I'm not giving away any secrets, but I will tell you one thing, ladies. From my chair I'm lookin' out the window at a tall, stick figure who's out at all times of the day and night."

The women stood up to look out the window at a man who was wandering in an open field with a stick which he used to prod the ground.

"Why that's Old Horace," Maria exclaimed. "What's he got to do with it?"

"He roams all over, picking up roots and herbs to make his medicines," Plummer explained. "He looks as if he's only interested in the ground. And he's a surly old cuss. You want to keep out of his way, right? Well, he sees things that nobody else sees. And he hears a lot. And though everyone knows he's a voodoo man and he scares the pants off me, he's a real fund of information on rebels."

The women laughed and returned to their chairs.

"I bought medicine from him," Sarah said. "It always worked for my children."

"He's smart, all right," Maria said. "My son Steve knows him and gets some potent stuff that he says will make him grow up strong."

"Right!" Plummer said, getting up to leave. "Remember, ladies, you are bein' protected by Old Horace, and, if worse come to worst, he'll put the voodoo on any invading force."

"Praise the Lord," Maria sang, "and with Private Plummer riding the range, we've got absolutely nothing to worry about, Sarah."

"Nothing except for Captain Magrath," she said.

Plummer laughed louder at that and departed.

Sarah and Maria remained talking for a while, discussing their families and especially John Lewis who was in his last months of school.

"I hate to see him grow up," Sarah confessed. "He's been a good companion. He's going to have to leave home to find work." She looked at the floor sadly.

"He's too smart to stay here," Maria said. "Give him your blessing and let him know he's doing the right thing. He'll be a credit to you in a big way some day, Sarah. You mark me well, now."

Maria's reassuring words helped Sarah to overcome her heartache at separating from her son, who was just fifteen. As the only one of her children to be born out of slavery, John embodied the freedom she had found and the promise of the future. Now, this promise was pulling him away.

He looked upon himself as white but easily a victim of prejudice if his background became known. Like Fanny, he knew that to escape detection he had to work in some place where he was unknown. Even Duncan Campbell's affection and support could not protect him from bias. Moreover, owing to the unpopularity of Duncan's conservative politics and associations in some quarters, John sensed that he could be hampered in any entrepreneurial endeavour he might wish to undertake simply by the general belief that he was Duncan's illegitimate son.

The rebellion affected him too; it made him think of the uncertainty of life, and he started to question Sarah about her feelings on being called black and a slave.

"It didn't matter to me what they called me," Sarah said. "What mattered was the way I was treated. You got to remember that, son. It's the way you treat people that's important."

He learned from some of his teachers, who were sympathetic to the Reformers, the reasons for men to risk their lives trying to change a government. He asked McPherson if he could justify hanging men who had such high principles and were regarded as truly good people in their communities. McPherson deferred the question to Duncan, who had just walked in from another room. Duncan said sharply, as if the answer were obvious, that traitors were always hanged and imprisoned to keep them from committing the same crimes again. John regarded this answer as far from understanding his question, and he turned to frown at McPherson.

"But I'm asking you, Sandy."

McPherson, a loyal militia officer, who had ridden down rebels in the woods and meadows and torn them out of their houses away from their families, whose loss of their bread earner was sure to impoverish them, in the hearing of his militia captain and employer, was expected to give a loyalist's reply.

"I deplore it," he said bitterly. "And so do many of us who put down the rebellion."

John looked satisfied. "Thank you, Sandy," he said, and without looking at Duncan, who was staring in amazement, he walked out the door deep in thought.

"You ought to be careful," Duncan said to McPherson. "You could be mistaken for a rebel."

McPherson's reply acted as a turning point in John's thinking about his home country. Together with his resentment for the soldiers billeted in his home and demanding the services of his mother and treating his family in a high-handed manner, he developed a sympathy for the republican principles of the Reformers. In fact, John saw himself as a weather vane forecasting the mood of the province.

After speaking with Duncan, Sarah came to agree with his suggestion that he find John a position as a clerk away from Simcoe. Duncan did not want the boy to work so far away that he would lose connection with his family but far enough away to give him a sense of venturing into the world. He chose Drummondville at Niagara Falls. The town was about a day's travel by stage from Simcoe, which meant that John could come home on occasion. A sharp, hard-working merchant, Joseph Woodruff, who, like many businessmen at that time, ran several operations including a tavern, agreed to take John as a clerk in his dry goods store there. Of course, Woodruff knew John's background and heard the rumours that he was Duncan's son. At first, he welcomed the boy as if he were doing him a favour, but soon he discovered the boy's talent for selling and his mastery of the stock.

On John's first visit home, Sarah took John to see Duncan in his farmhouse. She noticed that the place was not as well kept as when she lived there. Duncan appeared to have lost interest in it. His hired help did just what was necessary to maintain it, but the loving care that she gave it seemed to have been lost. Duncan sat on a rocking chair on his front porch and put down a sheaf of papers as he saw them approach. Sarah felt a surge of pride as she walked up the porch steps with her bright, good-looking son.

"Well, well, well, John," Duncan cried cheerfully and, holding out both arms to grasp John by the hands, brought him to sit in the chair beside him. "Your mother and I have been discussing your affairs with great interest. I'm glad that you like the work."

"I love it, squire," John said enthusiastically. "There is so much to learn, and Drummondville is much busier than Simcoe. We get the trade coming from the States going west to Lake Erie and east to Lake Ontario. It was a good choice to start me off."

Duncan beamed at him. "Are there still threats of invasion?" he asked.

"Nothing really serious," John said. "A few groups come over to pillage, burn and retreat right away. They seem to know who are Tories and direct their hatred against them. But the regiments are there to run them back."

"Reformers join the Americans and tell them where to strike,"

Duncan said to Sarah.

"Not reformers, squire," John said hastily. "They are revolutionar- ies, republicans. But without government support, they amount to nothing."

"You sound as if you regret they don't get government support," Duncan said.

"Yes," John admitted. "Sometimes I do because I want to see change here badly. But most times I don't because I agree with Ma that the Americans will bring change that none of us will like. If anyone wants republicanism, then they can go to the States, right Ma?"

"That's so, son," Sarah said, "but I hope you're not considering going to the States."

John laughed. "Not for a long time, but maybe someday."

Sarah listened to John discuss the state of business while she thought of the gap in her life left by John's departure. Only Vesta and her child remained to her. She had to remind herself that her life was no longer solely for her children's benefit. She had to develop interests that could vie with the interests of her children. As she listened to John talk about his life in Drummondville, she told herself that she must not live through his experiences but develop experiences of her own. She listened to John describe the adventure of living next to the majestic Falls, which he would gaze at while dreaming of identifying with its power and becoming a powerful person in his own right. There was a road down to the Niagara River at the foot of the Falls where he would catch the ferry for Buffalo on the American side. He would climb the stairs to the city and marvel at the crossroads of commerce that had built such handsome stone houses. The Erie Canal brought pros- perity to Buffalo, and the rail lines carrying produce from the Great Lakes to the Eastern seaboard had multiplied the wealth. Both the sight of the Falls and the big city fired John's imagination and encour- aged his thoughts of doing great things in the years ahead. But, he admitted, smiling at Sarah, that he felt the tug to return to Simcoe and be with his mother.

Occasionally he went to the Joseph Culver farm to look at the grave of his twin sister and to check on the growth of the poplar that had been planted when he was born. The tree's strength and straight beauty were examples for him. There was a connection between it and the grave of his sister that gave it a spiritual significance in his mind.

Sarah looked forward to his weekend visits as moments to be enjoyed fully because soon her son would be moving further away into that nebulous space from which he would rarely return. She was made poignantly aware of those two worlds, the one immediately about her and the one beyond it from which communication was rare and uncertain.

She felt the collective sense of relief in the countryside when an uprising did not take place and many citizens, suffering from the reckless attitudes of the militia, watched as the British regiments prepared to leave. Sometimes soldiers gave out chits for what they took, promising that the government would honour them some day. Sarah kept these bits of paper and hoped to be reimbursed for billeting the soldiers and for the destruction of her property. She regarded her burden as necessary for the good of the country, but she felt liberated when it was lifted.

The economy of Simcoe suffered less than more disaffected areas, where settlers migrated en masse to the United States. The fertile farmland and the great variety of crops that could be grown kept the people from going hungry, but land speculators like Duncan Campbell watched the value of their investments sink, and merchants like Duncan Campbell managed to avoid bankruptcy only by stringent measures. The conservative elite, hurt financially as a result of the rebellion, muted their calls for severe punishment for the rebels. The local Tory magistrates were eventually reined in and some were dismissed for their vindictive actions.

Sarah's faith in the wisdom of British governance returned when she learned that a more liberal faction of the English government sent out a new Governor-General to set up guidelines for reform, which even the conservatives began to recognize as desirable.

When activities were revived, Sarah was in demand as a cook. The gentry hired her for special occasions such as weddings, entertainments for friends and commemorative dinners. The Mansion House Hotel on Robinson Street, which became the better place to stay in town, paid her to supervise the preparation of meals. Her separation from Duncan

Campbell raised her in her own estimation. She had been at his beck and call for too long, she thought, and, as he grew richer and busier, he had become more demanding and aloof. Her laundry business was physically demanding, but it was her own. She felt that she had come through a very bad storm but now entered calm water that, when she looked down at it, gave back the reflection of a face that could smile despite the wrinkles. And then there arrived a letter from Cleveland. After Vesta finished reading the letter to her, she let out a whoop and danced about the room. Her son Henry wrote that he and Mary expected to see her before the year was out. She tried to picture them as adults. The bad times were gone for good, she thought. "We've got nothin' but the best in front of us, child," she laughed and embraced Vesta.

Throughout these months in 1838, George M. Smith moved along the American lakeshore, dropping in at "Hunters" lodges, and referring the information he gleaned back to the Upper Canada Emancipation Society in Cleveland. He was just one of several informants on the plans of the patriots who attacked the Canadian shore across the Detroit River and were easily repulsed because of their poor organization, incompetent commanders, and general illusion that the Canadian populace was ready to support them. When the Canadian black regiments from Amherstburg stopped the patriot invasion of Bois Blanc Island off the Canadian shore, the patriots who returned alive swore that, when they took over Canada eventually, they would return all blacks to slavery. Such threats, uttered with the venom of defeated and humiliated men, alarmed George Smith, who found that the hunters began to regard his brown skin with suspicion, as if they could no longer be sure that he was working with them.

Smith, however, was present in Cleveland at the convention forming the Republican Government of Upper Canada on September 16, 1838 and stayed for the seven days of discussions, resolutions and firm commitment to effect a general uprising in Canada. The present Chief Justice of the Peace in Cleveland and a former resident of Upper Canada was elected President of the Republic of Canada. The Canadian rebel, Donald McLeod, Secretary of War, despite tending to corpulence, was an active and courageous partisan who had been in several skirmishes along the border. He bonded well with Dr. Duncombe, who addressed the convention on the subject of establishing a Republican Bank to issue paper money. It was to be controlled by the people through delegates chosen to elect directors. Profits were to be shared by all. Funds in the bank and notes issued were to be secured by the public property of Upper Canada once it was conquered. Overwhelmed by the enthusiasm of the speeches, the idealism of the resolutions and the reports of thousands of lodges throughout villages and towns filled with members eager to engage the British oppressors in battle, George Smith sank into a depressed state that he had great difficulty in concealing from his republican friends. Only on the last day when he happened to meet with Duncombe by accident in the Cleveland Lodge did he find some hope that the whole enterprise might fail. Duncombe expressed his anger privately that of the tens of thousands of dollars promised to be invested in the bank, he had received just a few hundred. He was also angry at Mackenzie, who, after rallying men for invasion out of New York State, now objected to accepting American help. Mackenzie wrote to Duncombe that he suspected American motives and urged him to make any enterprise wholly Canadian.

"He is dedicated to failure, that man is!" Duncombe stormed. "Canadians will never be free if they remain attached to the so-called mother country, which is stealing them blind. Mackenzie is a damned colonial at heart!"

"But are not the Canadian lodges to be involved when we invade?" Smith asked innocently.

"Why yes! One hundred percent!" Duncombe said. "Of course, some of them have been disbanded. Colonel Alfred was imprisoned in London for months and his lodge had to be closed."

"What happened to our friends Avril Brooks and Bill Powers?" Smith asked.

"Colonel Brooks," Duncombe said ruefully and his face fell, "was taken. They sent him to Van Diemen's land. I hope he survives." His features brightened. "As for the others, they are working for us. Bill keeps in touch," Duncombe smiled as if he could see the dependable Powers quietly working to organize a new rebel force. "Bill Mathews lives near Detroit, works as a bootmaker, and he's active with the patriots there. Glad to see you made it out of that mess. Never mind. We'll liberate that land yet." He clapped Smith on the shoulder and moved away to greet A. D. Smith, the new President of the Republic of Upper Canada, who was leading his elected cabinet into private session.

They all looked important with their grandiose titles, George Smith thought, but actually they were grocers, attorneys, and businessmen with no experience on the battlefield. Against the thousands of loyalist Canadian militia and British regiments aligned along the border, how did they imagine that they could conquer the country? Smith blamed the hypocritical politicians for channeling the aggressions of the hordes of unemployed and impoverished workers and tradesmen, the bankrupted businessmen and bankers, and the starving and disillusioned young men throughout the Northeast away from their domestic problems and into fanciful dreams of liberating a people who supposedly would surrender their lands to them out of gratitude. He felt sickened by their talk of liberty when the blacks and Indians amongst them were deprived of it. Duncombe, although personally opposed to slavery, was obliged to share his cause with racists like Mathews. There were just too many unknown elements in such a mixture of motives for an enterprise to succeed; and, in this case, with so many forces opposing it and prepared to betray it, it would fail. He shook his head at the foolishness of it all and decided to forsake his role of informer. It was time to take Mary and Henry Lewis to Canada.

Bill Powers, who had been working at repairing and painting houses in the London area, received a message from Dr. Charles Duncombe in Cleveland. The American invasion of Canada was set for July 4, 1838. American forces and Canadian refugees would swarm across the Detroit River and attack Windsor and Amherstburg. Powers was to inform all the lodges in his part of the country and prepare to aid in a general uprising on that date. Powers was unhappy at the news. He worried that Duncombe had not understood that the campaign against the rebels in Upper Canada had seriously reduced their numbers: hundreds of those caught had sworn not to rise again, and others were turning against the idea of American help as they feared American dominance.

The trials of rebels in London, Hamilton and Toronto, elicited some sympathy from the people but generally intimidated them from making any expression of discontent with the government. Although Powers welcomed an invasion as a means of rescuing the half-dozen or so rebels slated for execution, he feared it would result in a great slaughter of young men and devastate the country economically even more than it was already. In a quandary and missing the advice of Fanny, he spent several beautiful spring days wandering the banks of the Thames River and pondering over what he should do. He recalled the stories he had heard from old settlers who remembered the American invasions of the western part of the country during the War of 1812, the wholesale destruction of property and the denuding of the countryside of all food so that the invaders, unable to support themselves, retreated while the settlers starved. No! an invasion would be catastrophic. He had to warn Duncombe of the true state of the country and stop the attack. But how was he to contact him?

By chance he walked into a tavern in a village south of London and recognized Colonel Alfred sitting alone and drinking a beer. Alfred was looking much older and thinner. Powers went to his table and greeted him. Alfred gave a start, and, looking up apprehensively, gazed at him as if trying to recognize his face. Powers said his name, and Alfred, nodding, pointed to a chair for Powers to sit.

"Are you still active in your lodge?" Powers asked quietly.

Alfred looked round and, seeing that no one was watching them, shook his head. "I'm too busy makin' a livin'," he said. "Besides I'm on parole."

"They caught you?" Powers asked sympathetically.

Alfred nodded. "I almost lost my mind, it was so bad. Freezin' cold, bad food, disease. Lost some of my friends. Died in prison. They let a pack of us out. I ain't seen the lodge since and I doubt that it's a goin' concern. Why?"

Powers evaded the question. "What would you say to an invasion by Americans and a general uprising here?"

"There'd be nothing worse," Alfred said between his teeth. "Even I'd fight against that now! Look, we got Lord Durham as Governor here now and he's talkin' reform. Things are going to change. We don't need or want the Americans. You tell Duncombe that. Trouble with Duncombe is he's so full of hatred after what he's been through, he wants revenge. He's American anyway so he really thinks the American way is a solution. To hell with that!"

"Are the string of lodges across the country still operating, do you think?" Powers asked.

"From what I hear," Alfred said, "there are militiamen ready to rise with them. But, you know, you can't believe what you hear. I don't think there's support for Duncombe anymore. He and the others are smoking a pipe dream. You ought to tell him that. Besides, the British have gone so they must know something. They have spies in those American lodges, you know."

Powers sighed. "I can't write Duncombe—could be intercepted."

"Just go to Amherstburg and take a steamer for Cleveland. They're runnin' all the time. Say you are on business." Alfred looked at him askance.

Challenged and given a clear route to follow, Powers took a stage for Amherstburg the next day and boarded a steamer for Cleveland. His fears of being stopped as a rebel sympathizer or a false businessman evaporated when he found no hindrance to his travel. Traffic across the border had resumed its customary activity as if threats of invasion and Canada's preparedness were of no concern. Landing on the Cleveland docks, Powers looked up at the town rising on the hillsides to the east and west. It was a bright day in mid-June and the harbour was teeming with ships and wagons. The patriots' headquarters was in the Miller block which he found after a brief walk along Superior Street. A couple of men talking at the door stopped him as he entered the building.

"The sign?" one of them growled.

Powers crossed his arms in front of his body, the left above the right, let them fall to both sides and pinched his coat sleeves with his fingers.

"Welcome," the man said. "Who you lookin' for?"

"Dr. Duncombe."

"You'll find him talkin' to Secretary of War McLeod. Just go up the stairs to the second floor," the man said genially.

Powers came to a large hall on the second floor. Off it were offices, from one of which issued the sounds of men's voices in argument. He stood in the doorway and watched Donald McLeod and Duncombe angrily exchange their views on the invasion of Canada for a full minute until McLeod looked up at him questioningly.

Duncombe turned round, shouted out, "Bill!", and stood up to embrace him. "What are you doing here?"

"Had to see you," Powers said and looked at McLeod.

When Duncombe introduced him to the plump gentleman with a twinkle in his eye, Powers recalled hearing of his exploits running a reform newspaper in eastern Upper Canada which the Tories destroyed and later of his leading ill-fated attacks across the Detroit River.

"We were engrossed in our differences," McLeod said, shaking his hand. "The doctor is a determined man." He paused for the doctor to smile and continued, "We have had bad news. First, some fools crossed into Canada at the Short Hills west of Fort Erie and were taken prisoner, alerting the whole coast to the possibility of invasion. Second, our treasurers embezzled our funds. God knows what's happened to our money. Third, we were supposed to get arms from a Detroit depot like the last time we invaded Windsor, but this time our raiding party was put in prison. Fourth, since the President signed the Neutrality Act last March, all the men of wealth who supported us are withdrawing their funds because they were speculating in Upper Canada land. We've lost the prestige and the energy we once had. Yet, in spite of it all, the good doctor wants us to invade on July 4." McLeod threw up his hands and glared at Duncombe.

"If we lose this opportunity, we will never have another," Duncombe said sternly. "If we are successful, the Neutrality Act will be worthless. Fait accompli."

"You know, Mr. Powers," McLeod said, "the largest segment of our financial support comes from doctors. Do you think there is something particularly aggressive about that discipline, aside from its preponderance of investment wealth, that makes it tout liberty more loudly than others? "

Duncombe made a growling sound and intercepted the question. "Maybe," he said sardonically, "but you are Secretary of War and I am not."

"Because we have members other than doctors who are more reasonable," McLeod suggested. "Caution, my good doctor, requires us to
take a new look at the prescribed cure. And what news does Mr.
Powers bring us?"

Powers shifted uneasily in his chair. He looked apologetically at
Duncombe while telling him that he opposed an invasion. As he spoke
of the unready state of the province to rise up effectively, he expected
Duncombe to brush his arguments aside, but Duncombe listened
thoughtfully and asked questions regarding the affect the new reforms
were having on the country.

Duncombe smiled wistfully at McLeod. "You're right, Donald. He
looked at Powers. "But there will be another day, and I am working
toward it. What about you, Bill?"

Powers agreed, outwardly enthusiastic but inwardly rueing the day
that he had become involved in the movement. He wanted to return to
Otterville and his beloved Fanny as soon as he could. He thought of her
while he listened to McLeod make arrangements for a meeting of the
Executive of the Lodge and the disseminating of the order to cancel the
invasion plans. Duncombe took him to his lodgings and gave him a bed
for the night. They spoke no more about the political situation in Upper
Canada, but both men felt deeply the failure of the movement:
Duncombe from the viewpoint of his disgrace and suffering endured all
for naught and Powers with mixed emotions of disillusionment at the
loss of an ideal and growing resentment at the quixotic leadership of
Duncombe and his fellow conspirators.

When no action took place, Sarah and her friends celebrated the
news in a huge party held at the Town Hall; it was as if a great balloon,
which had been ready to explode under pressure, suddenly collapsed
into a flimsy piece of rubber. Canadian spies in the States reported
that the Hunters movement was a shadow of itself and the adventurers
with their weapons and dreams of land deserted their pusillanimous
leaders for better prospects in conquering the west. The Canadians in
the rebel camp were like Bill Powers who returned to his village and his
love and took up his vocation again with never a word about fighting
for liberty. Those who were wanted by the Canadian government

307

worked in the States until an amnesty was declared when many like Donald McLeod, Secretary of War for the Upper Canadian Government in exile, returned to a village in Southwestern Ontario to work in the civil service. The irrepressible Dr. Charles Duncombe gave rousing speeches throughout New York and Ohio to raise funds for another invasion, but, aside from two or three surges of interest in the next few years, Americans realized that the majority of Canadians would not welcome their military intervention. Meanwhile, reform government came to Canada. The nation, through the give and take of political turmoil, developed its own system of democracy.

23

When George M. Smith reappeared, Mary looked at him as if he had come back from the dead. "I was afraid I wouldn't see you again!" she exclaimed.

"You can't get rid of me that easy," Smith laughed.

Henry knew that his sister loved Smith and rejoiced in their coming together again. "You've been conducting all this time, I guess," Henry said. "You didn't have time to stop to say hello."

"Couldn't," Smith said apologetically. "I get followed. I could've led your hunters right to you." He looked directly at Mary. "That's the only reason I had to stay away. You understand?"

Mary nodded and putting her arm about his shoulders drew him to her and kissed him on the cheek.

Smith hugged her and then, drawing away, looked serious. "Again, that's why you have to leave early tomorrow morning. We don't know if I was followed here, so we have to move quickly."

"Well," Henry said quizzically, "if the people hunting us have given up, why worry?"

"Because some people make a living by arresting on speculation and keeping you till they find your masters. Many times we've had to rescue friends by legal means from the local jails. It gets expensive." Smith cleared his throat. "I'll come for you in a wagon at five tomorrow morning. Be ready. We go by ship." He walked away with a wave of his hand and a broad grin.

Mary and Henry watched him mount his horse and gallop down the road.

"We're almost there," Henry said. "We can see mother soon."

"But we don't know where he's taking us," Mary said. "She could end up being miles away."

"I don't care about that," Henry said determinedly. "I'm going to see her as soon as we get to the other shore. But what are we going to do about these folks here. Shall we tell them, or is it better to keep this to ourselves?"

"George has his reasons for not telling them," Mary said. "We'd just better go and leave a note of thanks. They've been really good, so I hate going without a word. We'll have to say it all in writing."

"Do you feel as ready for Canada as I do?" Henry asked enthusiastically.

"The time spent here has made me ready," Mary said soberly. "We can fend for ourselves now. You feel free, don't you, my brother. Remember that you used to stutter sometimes when you had to talk to old James. You haven't stuttered since we've been here. That's a sign of how far we've come, I think."

Henry nodded emphatically. "We'll do well, Mary. I feel it in my bones."

In the early morning, before it was light, they stood with two small suitcases in front of the barn and listened to the wheels of a wagon approach over the cindered drive. When the wagon stopped in front of them, they recognized Smith holding the reins and slapping the seat beside him. Mary climbed up to sit with him while Henry threw their bags in the back and climbed in after them. By the time dawn had spread its pale blue light across the sky, the three of them were boarding a vessel in the harbour of Cleveland.

As the boat motored out of the harbour, its paddle wheels churning the lake water, Smith said that their destination was Port Stanley.

It was a harbour to the north-east into which many runaways floated and found refuge. Smith spoke of Southwold County, its rich soil and the great farming to be done there. And it was not very far from Simcoe. Henry's eyes lighted up when he heard this, and he could barely contain his excitement.

The sun blazed over the water as they stood chatting on deck. There was no fear of detection now. Some of the passengers were Negroes and mulattos, who mixed freely with the whites. Many of the crews on these passenger ships were coloured. He was moving into a different world, Henry thought. No other day in his life would compare to this one. He could see that Mary was as happy as he was, and more so because she was with George M. Smith again. He left them alone to talk and walked the deck to breathe in the warm breezes. As he passed below the captain's cabin, he saw the captain looking at him and he smiled. The captain beckoned to him and when he drew close invited him to climb the ladder to his cabin. The captain was a short, stocky man with a black beard and a whimsical expression.

"Ever seen the wheel?" he asked, inviting Henry to see the workings of the ship.

"Never," Henry said, enjoying the man's friendliness.

"Well then, I'll show you," the captain cried. He took Henry to a point behind the steersman where they could watch the way ahead. The captain explained the workings of the instruments which had to do with predicting the weather and navigating the ship. He showed him the knotted rope which they paid overboard to determine the speed of the vessel and invited him to sit at a table in the cabin while he spoke of the dangers of storms on the Great Lakes and his experiences with them. Fascinated, Henry felt that he was being introduced to a new experience at the same time that he was floating into a new environment. He was unaware of time until he heard his name being shouted. It was Smith's voice. Alarmed, he stepped to the cabin door and shouted down to Smith who was looking over the railing. The captain came to stand beside him and grin down at the surprised Smith.

"I'd best be going," Henry said. "Thank you for your hospitality." He shook the captain's hand.

"Good luck," the captain smiled. "But you have had luck being guided by Mr. Smith. You know that he's well known along the Great Lakes for rescuing slaves. They call him the Black Pimpernel."

Henry laughed. "But without the sword."

"Yes, but he's a mean shot," the captain said. "He's the modern adventurer."

Henry rejoined Smith, who began expostulating with him for disappearing, but by the time they returned to Mary, Smith was delighted by Henry's story of the captain's kindness.

"He's helped me many times," Smith said. "The men of the sea value independence more than anyone."

They looked ahead of them to see the faint traces of roofs in the distance where the forest had been broken to make a settlement. As they grew closer they could see log cabins and frame houses running along the shore behind a sandy beach and along both sides of a small river flowing into the lake. On either side of the clearing were cliffs as if protecting it from the elements. The ship steamed into the mouth of the river and docked to let its passengers off on a long stone wharf. The captain appeared from his cabin to watch the activity of loading and unloading and waved to Henry when Henry looked up to see him. Mary and Henry, excited, stepped ashore with feelings of wonder and reverence. Flowers in gardens alongside the wharf gave a colorful feeling of welcome. Smith, enjoying Mary's cries of appreciation at the gentle beauty of the place, pointed out the stores and taverns where they would be shopping when they came to the village.

He arranged for them to stay the night at a modest cabin at the back of the settlement and take them the next day to his farm some miles into the interior. Fearing his farm would be taken over by the government and sold to someone to bring in the crops, he asked the directors of the Upper Canada Emancipation Society to find a tenant to run it for a year until he could return. But, having heard nothing from whoever was running it, Smith worried about the state it was in and if he would have difficulty reclaiming it.

"We can room here for free," he said pointing to a log cabin, the front of which was covered with flowering vines.

The door opened to his knock and a large black woman stepped out with a wide grin and grappled Smith in her arms. He introduced her as Maggie. She hugged Mary and put her arm through Henry's to bring him into the cabin. "Welcome to your new country," she cried with pride. "You'll find lots of folks willin' to help you here. You stay as long as you want with me now, do you hear?" She took them to a long room with beds set in a row. "No other guests at this time."

"Just a day to catch our breath," George said.

"Just to drop my bag off," Henry said. "I'm heading to Simcoe. Which way is it?"

"Simcoe!" Maggie looked astonished. "There's no stage till tomorrow morning."

"I'm walking," Henry smiled. "I can't wait."

Maggie looked questioningly at Smith, who winked at her as if to imply that Henry had a love interest.

"Well then," Maggie said with an indulgent tone. "Take the Talbot Road east. It's the only one so you can't miss it."

"Hold on," Smith laughed. "You'll be walking for two days, Henry." He took a paper and pencil from his pocket and quickly sketched some lines. "Here's a route by the lake shore that at Vienna goes north then east to Simcoe. It'll save you miles." He handed it to Henry. "Maggie will tell you how to find us on the farm when you return."

Henry, gratitude shining in his eyes, embraced Mary and shook hands with Smith.

"Oh Henry, I wish I could go too," Mary said excitedly. "Tell mother that we will meet soon."

Maggie looked suddenly concerned. "Take care now." She ushered him to the door and pointed out the way. "There are bounty hunters on this side as well, you know. But you're a big strong man."

"Nobody's stopping me now," Henry laughed and set off along the narrow road leading up to the bluff overlooking the village.

His heart was singing as he strode in a fast pace toward the woman whose memory had been the centre of existence for him and Mary. Sarah's voice sounded in his inner ear again as it had for years when he was alone on the road and thinking of her. He pictured her at various times, but most of all that last night eighteen years before when she appeared and whispered her plans, and hugged and kissed them. Oh, the tears that flowed then! Henry's eyes misted when he thought of it. He had been fourteen and gone through much unhappiness, but for his mother to leave with the prospect that he would never see her again, that was a heavy burden for him. He had kept his promise to never lose hope and to look after his sister. And now he was thirty-two and had grown wise in the ways of the world and learned to read and write, thanks to Mrs. James Campbell who insisted on her house slaves being educated. He was eager to show his mother how independent he was and to see her as free and mistress of her household. He had received just scraps of information about her, actually little more than that she lived with a Duncan Campbell and was well. There was much to tell her about her kinfolk in Virginia and the death of his father. Thoughts of their joy on meeting again kept him daydreaming as he walked along in the afternoon sunshine.

Along the way, he came into clearings where cabins were being built and through villages with blacksmith shops, stores and mills and for long stretches along forest paths. The habitations he passed through such as Sparta and Vienna had supplied young men for the rebellion, and he sensed the air of defiance in them by the character of the people going about their business. Relatives of these people had been hanged or sent to Van Dieman's land on the other side of the world where they endured slavery every bit as bad as he had. He spoke to people in the villages only to ask directions every so often to make sure he was on the correct route. When the sun set, he felt suddenly tired. He heard the sound of an axe against a tree, the hollow sound announcing civilization, and presently came upon a young white man chopping a maple tree at the point that it was ready to fall. He watched as the man gave one mighty wallop and the tree fell crashing amongst its fellows. Taking a deep breath the axeman settled his axe on his shoulder and prepared to head home before darkness came.

Henry called out to him. "Hello! Can you help a traveler?" He wondered how the man would react to his skin colour.

The young man, in his mid-twenties, looked at him and then smiled. "You want a bed for the night?"

"Yes, if you can spare one," Henry said.

"Follow me. My place is off the road aways." He led the way along a path deeper into the forest and up a slight rise at the summit of which was a large log cabin. He called out to someone inside to announce his arrival. Candles were burning in the main room.

Henry took off his shoes at the door in imitation of his host and followed him into a brightly lit room where a table was set for three people. A woman appeared from a room beyond it and walked up to them.

"This man is traveling through and wants a bed for tonight, my sweet," the young man said.

The woman, raven haired and handsome, pointed to a far corner of the room where there was a bed. "Does that suit you?" she asked with a smile.

"That suits me fine," Henry said. "I'm trying to reach Simcoe and just felt tuckered out."

"You can't wander through the forest at night," his host said. "There are too many wolves. Come, I'll show you where you can wash up, then we'll sit down for a meal. You're hungry, aren't you?"

"Yes," Henry admitted. "I'm hungry."

When they returned from washing, the woman had placed hot food on the table and added a fourth place. A small girl was sitting at the third place.

"This land is plentiful," the host said, noticing with humour Henry's eyes widen at the food on the table. "I take it that you are a stranger."

"First day I've been here," Henry said.

"We want to make a new society," the young woman said. Henry figured that she was about eighteen. "We want to leave all those problems in the States behind and start anew."

"It's very hard work," the host smiled, "but we enjoy it. We are happy we came and glad that we can contribute to something new and learn from the mistakes of the past."

"That sounds encouraging," Henry nodded, "seeing where I come from."

"Being coloured you'll understand what we mean even more," his host said. "You have all the rights of any citizen here and you can develop this society like everyone else. You don't let others speak for you. You make up your own mind."

The spirit and dedication of these young people pleased Henry immensely. They told him that the recent rebellions were subtly working a change in the body politic, that most settlers, unsure of the value of those changes, took an interest in the struggle of political factions for power. It was important for the coloured man to take an active part, his host argued, because of the distinction by colour that came in with some settlers. This had to be stopped or it would set artificial preferences and barriers that would pervade this new society in unhealthy ways.

The small girl listened to the conversation eagerly and once or twice added her thoughts to the discussion. Henry became excited by what he heard and somewhat incredulous. This family, he thought, must be unique, and he said so. But both husband and wife strongly denied it, saying that their settler friends thought the same and would meet on general outings or fair days, a part of which the adults would devote to political discussion. The energy and optimism were powerful forces in Canada that directed all the people in an undertaking that promised a great country whose future had to be debated and quarreled over. They talked after the little girl had gone to bed and until Henry could barely keep his eyes open.

When Henry stretched out on the cot in the big room and the host blew out the candles, he fell directly into a deep sleep from which he awoke at the sound of cooking. He ate breakfast with the family, and, energized and enthusiastic about his new country, he struck out northward. He would come to the Talbot Road, his host told him, where, if he reached it by ten in the morning, he would connect with a stage traveling to Simcoe.

The wonder of his experience for Henry was that they took him foremost as a man and saw his colour as an appendage like yellow or red hair, but that had political significance only because others had made it so. From the slave State of Virginia, he seemed to have walked onto a different planet. Yet reason told him that he could expect to meet bias even here and that he had to maintain his vigilance to avoid insult. He came to a crossroads where the main route ran east-west and he sat on a tree stump to await the stage. A fair breeze kept the flies and mosquitoes from bothering him. His long conversation with the young settlers opened his mind to the thought that he had to believe in the oneness of man, without minorities and majorities, in order to defeat oppression and slavery. It asked a lot from a coloured man to take part in building a society where there was no bias because he must assert this principle at every turn, he thought. Would it not be easier to just submit to prejudice and work one's way around it and by doing so form one's own prejudices in return, much like religious people do?

At this moment, the stage came round a bend in the road and stopped at his hail to add him to its passengers. He arrived in Simcoe in the early afternoon. The stage dropped him off on the highroad in the Wellington section, and, as he paid his fare, the coachman pointed the way along Colborne Street into the main part of town. It was Sunday. People were strolling along the boardwalks or walking in groups to the commons where from the shouts of the children he gathered that there was a circus. Henry saw some coloured people in the crowds and considered asking them if they knew Sarah Lewis. He hesitated, however, because the excitement he felt at meeting his mother was making him too emotional, and he did not want to attract attention. By the side of a stream over which a bridge ran he saw a middle-aged white man with a fishing pole. The stream ran into a small marshy lake on the other side of which were wood-frame houses. Henry watched the man pull in a trout. As he was preparing to cast again, Henry asked if he knew where Mrs. Lewis lived.

The man nodded genially and, turning to point beyond the end of the lake, singled out a green-painted frame cottage just visible from where they were standing. Henry wondered whether this was the house of the man she worked for and whether she would be home or at the circus or visiting friends. He stood in the main street and looked at it for a moment as he tried to get control over his emotions. He decided to go to the back door, but then thought that, if he had the wrong house, he might appear suspicious. He gazed back at the small lake and at the river flowing from it through the woods across the street from the house. There were colourful song birds flying about in the trees and ducks settling on the water. This was a beautiful world, pretty and peaceful. He wondered what his mother would think of him. She must have changed and perhaps she had become a part of the white world. Perhaps she would not welcome him because he was a reminder of her days as a slave. But his heart ached to see her and to touch her skin and to see her brown eyes. There were other cabins further along the street, but there seemed to be no activity. He went to the front door which was open and knocked on the wood. He waited but there was no response. He knocked again and waited. He decided to walk to the back of the house. As he came to the back garden where plots of flowers bloomed in colours, he heard laughter from a ravine that ran behind the house. He spotted a woman with a small boy running up the hill and laughing while trying to outrun the other. He recognized Sarah and stood stock still hoping that she would recognize him. As Sarah reached the garden she looked at Henry, stopped and gave a small cry. She ran to him and they buried themselves in one another's arms. Henry kissed his mother and the tears ran down his face. She cried and then laughed with joy.

"My son, my son, at last! at last!"

"Mama, I never thought this day would come," Henry choked.

"And Mary?" Sarah asked.

"She's in Port Stanley," he said smiling. "I had to come right away for both of us. Oh mama! you have not changed much, you're still beautiful."

The small white boy pulled at Sarah's skirt. "Who? Who?" he cried.

Sarah bent down to take his hand. "This is your Uncle Henry," she said. "Now give him a kiss."

Henry knelt on one knee and the boy came to him and kissed his cheek. "Uncle Henry," he said.

"He's Vesta's son," Sarah explained. "She's at the fair grounds. Come into my house."

"Is this *your* house, mama?" Henry asked in surprise.

"I'm renting it, but I'm saving to buy it and all the land you see round here. It'll be mine soon. Oh, Henry, I am so happy here." She held the back door open for him to enter.

The little boy ran to some toys and began to play with them. Sarah led Henry to the front room where they sat together on a sofa, Henry holding Sarah's hands and Sarah looking proudly at her son. That he and Mary had escaped was one miracle, she thought, but that they had turned out well was another. Henry credited the attentions of their father for influencing their upbringing and now informed his mother of Henry Sr.'s demise. The news was not a blow. Her husband had faded of necessity into near oblivion as far as she was concerned. Yet the few years that they had spent together and the sanctity of her marriage gave him a special place in her affections. The great evil of slavery had forced them apart and eventually killed him, she thought. She had found her way into a new world where she was accepted as a person, not a belonging. She refrained from telling Henry much about her life and how Duncan Campbell had helped her to attain her economic independence. Instead she quizzed him about her sisters and friends that she had left behind in Virginia.

Vesta burst through the front door and Henry met her for the first time. She was a fun-loving girl and quite affectionate. There was a slight awkwardness between Henry and her as they tried to determine their relationship in relation to their mother. It was she who responded to the letters that he sent their mother, she said. She looked forward to meeting Mary. Yet despite her friendliness, Henry sensed that his appearance as a runaway slave had a disquieting effect on her, as if she resented his bringing the past in such reality before her. She excused herself to look after her son who was hungry.

"I saw John down the street," she said to Sarah as she went to the back. "He's rushing to catch the stage."

Sarah went to the window and called Henry to look out with her. She nodded at a boy of average height, and good-looking, Henry thought. He was parting from two other young men and, as he turned to look at the house, catching sight of Sarah in the window, smiled and waved.

Sarah blew him a kiss. "John is my youngest," she said proudly. "He works in dry-goods in Drummondville. He'll get there late tonight for work tomorrow."

"He looks like a white man," Henry said.

"He is a white man," she smiled. "He's going to be important one day. He's very clever, Henry. And he's a good boy."

318

Henry watched the boy walk rapidly toward the direction in which he came into town. He felt somehow that this boy and he inhabited two realms and that they would never meet. He understood it, but it did seem to contradict the new society that the young settlers had been preaching to him. But then that was an ideal whereas John and he lived in the reality of the present. He looked at his mother and saw by the expression on her face that she knew what he was thinking. He was sorry for her. She had to straddle the two realms and keep harmony in the family. He put his arm about her shoulders and hugged her to him.

"I can stay for just two days," he said. "Long enough to talk ourselves out. Then maybe we can plan to bring Mary. What do you think, mother?"

"I want to see Mary as soon as she can come, but I know the circumstances. Do you need money, my son?"

Henry shook his head. "We're putting our money into a farm. So it may be a while before we can come."

They heard Vesta in the kitchen.

"Your sister is cooking up a big meal to celebrate the return of our prodigal son," she laughed. "I'm so happy, Henry. Your coming makes me feel complete somehow. I worried and worried about you."

That night and the next day the family spent much time together getting to know one another and reminiscing about the past. All too soon Henry was waiting for the stage to take him west and to Southwold county where he and Mary would start farming for a living.

Sarah looked radiantly happy. Knowing that her eldest children were safe in Canada, that Fanny was in love with a man whose rebellious actions had not been discovered by the authorities, that John had a job and was learning his trade, and that Vesta and she were making a decent living: these facts made her relaxed and confident. She and Duncan would meet and talk over problems. She had close women friends who respected her for her sense of purpose and determination to overcome the effects of slavery upon her family. There was no prejudice against blacks in Simcoe, and white and black mixed socially. They were all pioneers trying to build a country together with what little they had. Some of the tradespeople were particular friends of her

319

family, and the good words that they and others in this tight-fitting community had to say about her spread throughout the township and beyond.

The village was building up quickly now. The new courthouse and prison were completed in the central square and businesses and private residences were being raised in all areas. Duncan Campbell erected a white octagonal building on his property behind the Post Office and Gore Bank. Sandy McPherson raised enough money to start a hardware business in the near-by town of Waterford but kept in touch with his friends in Simcoe.

Sarah's cooking was in demand because no one knew the recipes she did or cooked as well. Captain Hall, a wry-humored old salt, hired her for special occasions and celebrations. When Sarah told him that she hoped to be reunited with her daughter Mary, for which they had been planning for the eighteen months since Mary came to Canada, he gave her a cabin on his estate over the Christmas holidays and made sure that the food he ordered for Christmas fed both his guests and her family. The beginning of winter being unusually mild and the lake not yet frozen, Henry and Mary took a lake boat from Port Stanley to Port Dover to arrive at Captain Hall's property where Sarah, Fanny and Vesta with her little son Alex were waiting. Mary prepared herself to be calm and reserved as if to intimate that all those years without her mother's love made her free of sentimentality, but when she saw Sarah, her love broke forth like a mighty river, and she sobbed uncontrollably on her mother's shoulder. Henry cried too and turned away to cover his face with his hands. Mary and Sarah hugged for a long time. Sarah, gently rocking her daughter as if holding her as a child, sensed the years of longing expressed in their embrace and whispered that everything would be all right now that they were all together again. Only John was missing because his employer needed him for the Christmas week, one of the busiest of the year. As they gathered about their table, Sarah thanked God for their safe deliverance and for giving them a new life in a land of promise, and she prayed for Israel and the daughter she had lost shortly after birth. There was so much to talk about, so much catching up to do, that they sat up well into the night. Sarah, exhilarated, went to Captain Hall's house to prepare a breakfast and a mid-day meal, and when the others rose they continued talking, remembering things they had forgotten to tell, and asking questions about the future.

In mid-morning William Powers arrived from Otterville as a surprise. After chatting with Mary and Henry and putting them at ease, he kissed Fanny, who just returned from helping Sarah, and, pulling a small box from his pocket, gave it to her. Fanny opened it with a puzzled yet expectant look and shouted with glee. She gave the ring to Powers to have him fit it on her finger. Henry opened a bottle of wine and they all toasted the forthcoming marriage. Fanny ran to tell her mother the news. She knew that William loved her and wondered whether he would marry her because of her background, but her fears had been groundless.

Sarah returned with Fanny arm in arm to the cabin and embraced Powers. She regarded this marriage as symbolic for her; it represented what she taught her children to believe, that a person could overcome the baggage one was burdened with at birth and be recognized for oneself alone. Powers as a house painter would be able to support a family and make a dedicated father. He was the same age as Fanny, who was now approaching thirty, and with the rebellion fading as a memory in the public mind and the goals of the rebels gradually being adopted in the province, his convictions could no longer cause them trouble.

Captain Hall knocked at the door to invite them all to celebrate in his spacious home. He took Powers by the arm and put his other arm about Fanny's shoulders and led them through the snow flurries. Hall's guests stood to greet the Lewises as they entered the drawing room. Sarah was transported with pride. She felt that she was being honored by these people who knew her story and wanted to show her their support and goodwill. Hall asked his servants to bring in the lunch that Sarah had prepared and, laughing with bonhomie, gave his arm to Sarah and led the party into the next room where fiddlers were tuning their instruments. A caller stepped forward and began instructing the guests to present their partners. Sarah and the Captain led off the dance and the others formed up behind them. The fiddlers struck up a lively tune, the caller bellowed over them, and the people danced up a furore. McPherson, still a bachelor, was there and danced with Sarah as much as he could, and with her three daughters. It took him back to the dances of over a decade earlier when Sarah and Fanny enlivened the parties that the millhands used to throw. After the coming of government offices, the society gradually became stratified; the old pioneer attitudes changed and the spontaneity and joy of the old get-togethers were lost in the formal, class-based dances that replaced them. But Captain Hall belonged to the old society and liked to cockt a snook at convention, which is why everyone enjoyed themselves so much at this Christmas celebration in 1840.

Mary and Henry were impressed by their mother's acceptance in the society of Simcoe and reluctant to part from the warmth of their family which they had never known, but, after three days of partying and reminiscing, they had to return to their labours. Since winter fell quickly and the lake water froze, they went by stage back to their farm, which was covered in snow. When George Smith first brought them to his farm, they were utterly surprised to find that Jeb, their fellow runaway with a poet's eyes, had been running it for the past months. The Society entrusted it to him with the promise of finding another farm for him when Smith reclaimed it. But since there was plenty of work to do and Smith returned to the States to continue his clandestine activities, they insisted that Jeb live with them. In the course of conversation Jeb told them that Ross, their companion on the trek who had the argument with Smith, had joined the black regiment defending Amherstburg and was killed in the battle at Pelee Island. That news alarmed Mary because she could picture George Smith dying in a skirmish with patriots or murdered or arrested for his conducting on the underground railway, which had become more dangerous as southern states put pressure on northern free states to capture and return the fugitives. She and Henry spent many winter evenings in front of their hearth discussing scenarios, in which she saw the dangers, and Henry reassured her about his resourcefulness. In early spring Smith arrived at the farm looking fatigued and despondent.

"That's done it for me," he confessed. "Lost some good people on my last two trips. Some dead, some sent back in irons. Almost died a couple of times."

"Give it up, George," Mary insisted. "Your luck can't last forever."

George put his arms about her. "You and the home you got here is persuading me. Since I'm a special target for sheriffs and after the troubles I've seen, by comparison my beautiful Mary, you look good. I guess I'll retire."

"Good!" Henry sang out while Mary enveloped George in a long embrace.

"Leastways," George said with a smile at Henry, "till my enemies forget about the Black Pimpernel."

"That's not goin' to happen," Jeb cried out from the doorway which he just entered. "Just saw a family in town that owes their freedom to you and your pistols."

"Yeah, well that's another thing," George said looking down sadly. "They're saying I killed some bounty hunters—probably did, but they were going to kill our folks. So now, they've got wanted posters in all the towns."

"I know you don't like hoeing and planting," Mary said sweetly, "but it beats dyin'."

"And we need you here, George," Henry said.

George laughed. "I guess I can be domesticated. I might as well go all the way, if you'll have me, Mary."

Mary, her brown eyes twinkling, turned to the others. "Listen, you be witness now. I do believe I'm being asked to marry."

"As soon as we can," George cried, putting his arm about Mary's waist, "we're going to the town hall, and you bring witnesses."

Henry asked Jeb to get a bottle of wine. He was happy for Mary but inwardly concerned about his own future. Mary had been his responsibility throughout his life, but now he was surrendering her to a man who was closer to her than he could ever be. After Jeb poured the red wine into their glasses, Henry toasted the future of the bride and groom and smiled broadly, although he felt a shadow come across his heart.

Two days later George and Mary were married in St. Thomas and celebrated with their neighbours into the evening. After a few drinks, Jeb took Henry aside and, looking apologetic, said that he was leaving the farm.

"George is back. I was just holdin' it for him," Jeb said, his large round eyes expressive of his determination to leave.

Henry was taken aback. "We need you for the work. What will you do?"

"Goin' to a port on Lake Huron and ship out on a tradin' vessel to see the world," Jeb said, his eyes taking on a far-away look. "I got the wanderlust," he smiled.

Henry understood. Jeb wanted to experience the ultimate freedom of the seas, which Henry wanted to experience on land. He held out his hand and Jeb clasped it warmly. Henry saw George looking at them as he danced by with Mary. The planting and harvesting seasons were going to be harder without Jeb. George was no farmer. He would run the farm down, which is why Henry felt he had to stay for Mary's sake.

George proved to be a better farmer than Henry thought, and the farm supported them for a year. Mary gave birth to a daughter. In the second year, the work was harder and the rewards less. Henry felt like a third wheel. His relations with George worsened as they got on one another's nerves, particularly during the winter months. Their isolation on the farm made matters worse. Henry talked about working with horses which he had done for Campbell. George knew of people who ran a livery stable in Montreal and recommended Henry to them. Thus, after the spring planting, Henry set out for the excitement of a large cosmopolitan city and gratefully left the quiet monotony of farm life.

Mary cried when he left and George felt guilty being the cause of the rift, but then, he thought, they would do better in other occupations. He wondered if he could hold on until prices rose before selling the farm. Mary received a letter from Sarah in Vesta's handwriting. Sarah bought the lands and houses on the two lots that she was renting in Simcoe for seventy pounds and said she felt secure for the first time in her life.

"I want to be with Mama," Mary complained to George when she showed him the letter. "We'd be better off there. She'd help us."

Smith, looking out at the ploughed fields dark brown in the sun, said, as if in thought, "Then we'll go when we can, honey."

24

John Lewis, dismayed by the general unrest in Canada, which broke into armed clashes between reformers and conservatives over the adoption of Responsible government at what were termed Durham meetings, became convinced that his future lay in the relatively stable society of the United States where money could be made. There, the government sent troops to close down secret lodges when a revitalized Hunters organization joined with Hibernian societies and the Irish Repeal Association to invade Canada, because their actions were undercutting the economic recovery. John saw no prospect of advancing in Drummondville. At Christmas, he quarreled with Woodruff, who refused to increase his salary, and in mid-January 1842, Woodruff fired him because of the poor state of trade. John told his mother that he was going to make his fortune in New York City. Immigration to the States from Europe had swelled the population of the city to almost two and a half million. He was sure to prosper there.

Duncan Campbell considered him a brave young man and recalled his leaving Scotland for the New World at the same age. He recognized in John the same business acumen that he discovered in himself. He gave him a small sum of money to tide him over until he found work. Sandy McPherson too told him that he would be a credit to them all one day. Before leaving, John visited the poplar tree on Joseph Culver's farm and said a short prayer asking for help. The farmlands, covered with a crisp layer of snow, seemed to imprison his past, from which he was fleeing, to find a greater expression of himself. As he boarded the stage for Buffalo, he noticed the tears in Sarah's eyes and knew that she too had divined that he was separating his past from what he would become.

In New York he joined the thousands of recent immigrants, most of them fleeing famine in Ireland, looking for work. If he wished to conceal his background there was no better place for him to start a career. This was the melting pot or the wretched cauldron where the poor slept in the streets and huddled in basements and the lucky ones worked all day and every day in crowded, stinking, ugly conditions.

John sought temporary work of any kind while he went the rounds of the dry-goods stores and other business establishments. He wrote of his predicament to his mother who turned to Theo Hunt for help. Theo, a trader in textiles, who went to New York City on business twice a year, had grown into a friendly man with a wide smile, a bemused look, and a penchant for philosophizing about life and its unexpectedness. Sarah gave him John's post office box number, to which Theo wrote asking John to meet him at a certain time in a cafe on Nassau Street. The following week Theo went to New York City.

Spring was in the air. Trees were sprouting buds and the magnolias on the lawns of the richer houses cast their heavy perfumes at passersby. Hunt stayed at a boarding house near the outskirts, on 20th Street, and ventured into the thriving, bustling, cacophonous commercial district below the City Hall to do his business. Despite the large number of contacts he had to make, Hunt remembered his appointment for lunch with John and walked quickly over to the narrow Nassau Street with its shops, newspaper offices and small cafes. Joe's Cafe was unpretentious but comfortable. He entered it and spied John sitting at a table at the back. He went to him, a huge smile on his face, that John could not help but respond to, although his mental state hovered closer to depression than happiness.

"Hello, Johnnie. It's good to see you."

Theo shook John's hand and noticed that his skin looked more sallow, even unhealthy, which he attributed to insufficient food. John's eyes were as bright as ever and just as mesmerizing.

"Thanks for seeing me, Theo, for taking time away from your business," John said apologetically.

"You are more important. First we are going to have a good meal and chat about what you have been doing, then we can talk about prospects. Your mother said you were finding it difficult to get work."

John nodded. "Everything is possible here, but you have to get the right start. If you don't, then...." he nodded at the shabbily-dressed men lined up at the counter to buy a coffee.

"You'll do well, my friend," Theo smiled. "You are the most intelligent man I know. Once an employer knows that, he'll hire you, or he's a fool."

"You are a true friend," John said seriously. "How is mother?"

"She is doing well and looks forward to your letters."

John grimaced. "I try not to worry her, but I'm afraid I do."

"What seems to be the trouble getting work?" Theo asked suddenly.

John's cheeks reddened and he looked down at the table. "I can't give them a reference. If anyone here finds out about me, that is, my background, then I'll never get work."

A waiter approached. John fell silent. The two men ordered and resumed their conversation when the waiter went away.

"I'm taking you to see an acquaintance who runs a small textile business. He'll give you a job on my word. From there, it's up to you."

John looked at him gratefully. "Thanks. That's all I need... a foot in the door."

Theo then talked about Simcoe and the people there, the changes in the town, and John told him of some of his experiences in New York and his excitement at being in the city. They ate their lunch leisurely and enjoyed each others company until Theo, taking out his pocket watch, said that they had to be leaving if they wanted to catch his business acquaintance.

Hunt's acquaintance was willing to do him a favour but emphasized that it could only be temporary till summer when business went slack. John was made a porter's assistant, the lowest position, but it was the foot in the door that he needed. By summer when he was laid off, he contacted Poillon and Company, a large dry-goods business, whose owner he had seen several times in the course of his duties. Marcel Poillon hired him as a porter. A few months later when Theo Hunt came to New York City, he found John thriving as a clerk in Poillon's store. Poillon recognized John's abilities and knowledge. At twenty years of age, John had a promising future. He was a changed man from their last meeting. John's ambition seemed to blaze out of

327

his eyes as he talked about his work. Happy and confident, he took Hunt to lunch and regaled him with stories of his rise through the heavy work of lifting boxes of garments and machinery to exuding his charm in his work as a clerk, which was just as tiring because of the long hours he stayed in the store each day. He gave Hunt a parcel of dresses and a bundle of money for his mother, which were significant to Hunt because they showed John's determination to save in his low-paying job and help his mother. Hunt returned to Sarah with praise for her son.

It seemed that John would have remained a clerk for the rest of his days because the next step up to salesman seemed well out of reach. But an event changed his prospects quite dramatically.

Amy Poillon was eighteen when she met John Lewis in her father's store. John was 20. She noticed his fascinating eyes and how they took her all in to himself. She tried to ignore him but felt herself drawn back time and time again to pass through that part of the store in which he worked. She knew that her father would not want her to fraternize with any of his staff. He had sent her to a good finishing school and intended her to marry well. She was, after all, his only daughter and very pretty. John admired her good looks but knew that contact with her was unlikely, unless she took the first step. He could tell that there was an attraction between them and this gave him the confidence to smile at her. Eventually she smiled back at him. Then one day she stopped at his counter, which carried ladies' gloves, and pretended to be interested in a pair. He came to wait on her.

"May I help you, Miss Poillon?" he asked with an open smile.

"Yes, I think you can," she said seriously. "What other colours do these come in?" She held up a long pair of dark blue gloves that came up the arm.

"White, brown and mauve," he said seriously, "but if you would permit me to advise you, I think the blue that you are holding becomes you very well."

"Oh, do you?" she asked in surprise.

"Your blue eyes are about the same colour," he said with a smile and looked into her eyes.

His piercing brown eyes seemed to mesmerize her. She paused, looking at him in wonder, and felt unable to speak.

"I've helped a great many women but none have had the beauty of your eyes," he added matter-of-factly. "That is why you should wear things that draw attention to them."

Amy smiled, charmed. "Well then, you have persuaded me," she said quickly. "Will you wrap them for me and charge it to my father's account, please."

"Certainly," John said. "Would you like something to go with the gloves? I was thinking of the blue scarf on the next counter. That would complement the gloves and your eyes."

She laughed in appreciation. "I must tell my father what a good salesman you are. Yes, I'll take the scarf too."

"He may not be happy about my salesmanship when he realizes that it is costing him," John smiled rather wickedly.

"Don't worry about that," she said, looking wickedly back at him. "He loves to make me happy and he'll respect you for bringing me that happiness."

John nodded in slight embarrassment and walked to the next counter to select a scarf. He wondered how long it would take to get to know this young girl and whether he should take their relationship to another level where he knew it could easily go. He returned to her with the items neatly wrapped.

"What is your name?" Amy asked in a friendly manner.

"Lewis," John said, "and your father calls me John."

"Well then, John, thank you for helping me with my wardrobe. When I need something else I shall come to you."

John nodded respectfully and watched her walk away.

Amy felt his eyes following her and suppressed a thrill of gratification. She thought John had better manners than most clerks and seemed well brought up, but, of course, he was not of her class and could not meet with her on her social level. Yet he was so kind and handsome. His slightly brown skin gave him an air of mystery. She decided that she would find a way to know him better. The fact that her father would disapprove made her more determined to overcome the barrier between them. But, for the moment, she had to restrain any impulse she might feel lest it seem that she was making the advances. She decided not to visit the store for another month.

John decided that he was mistaken to think that the young woman liked him. He was too far down the totem pole to interest her, he thought. She was just being pleasant. He was unsophisticated. He was a loner by nature and mistrusted the motives of most people. When Amy Poillon came right up to his counter the next time they met, he was surprised by her forthrightness. This time she seemed more interested in him than in the merchandise. She quickly established that he lived alone and that he did little else but read in his hours off work. The new Mechanics Libraries stayed open in the evenings to serve the working man, and John took advantage of the help they provided. She evinced interest in his library and he quickly volunteered to take her. They set a date for Friday evening. She was to meet John at the library.

He was early and waited in the street, pacing and wondering if she would really come. Then he saw her, dressed with refinement and beaming with health and anticipation. They shook hands and looked in one another's eyes. When he led her into the drab library, he sensed the contrast between her life and those workers who sat at the long tables hunched over books. She was like a beautiful flower in a garden of weeds. He showed her a few shelves of books, especially the history section which was his favourite, before leading her back to the street. They walked and talked animatedly about themselves, eager to hear every scrap of information. The crowds, omnibuses, coaches, newspaper vendors, all were a vague background to the central drama of two young people falling in love but unaware of it. They reached the City Hall park and strolled its paths until they found a bench where they could sit and talk to their hearts' content. Suddenly Amy Poillon jumped to her feet exclaiming that she had to get home as it was long past the time that her family expected her. She dashed away promising to meet John again soon. He watched her enter an omnibus and the dray horses pulling it away uptown. For the first time he sensed a deep loneliness. The darkening streets, the solitary lamplighter, the dwindling number of pedestrians gave him a feeling of bereavement, as if he had experienced a loss. Such was the effect of Amy's departure upon him. He knew loneliness but it was always offset by a sense of adventure and novelty. In the beginning he missed his mother and sisters but he had overcome that sensitivity, which he regarded as a weakness. His letters to his mother were his consolation, and the occasional letters he received from Sarah in Vesta's hand helped him hold on to his past, regardless how secret he determined to keep it.

John had given Amy his post office box number. From then on she contacted him through notes, designating places where they could meet, sometimes the park bench where they had so abruptly said goodbye that first time. Amy never contacted him in the store. It was too dangerous. Suspicion could be raised by the slightest gesture or look. Already Amy could tell that her parents were somewhat curious of her long absences in the early evenings. She had used a number of her friends' names and soon began to make up names for friends she supposedly knew in school or had met at parties. Marcel Poillon did not like his daughter spending much time outside the family circle but, as he was busy with business and often came home late, he did not guess that she had begun a love affair. John took her to his room and they made love, she for the first time. He was no novice. He visited houses of prostitution. He instructed Amy in taking precautions against pregnancy. His care of her and for her made her love him more. After six months, she told him that she no longer wanted to live separately from him. She wanted to marry him. She knew that her father would never allow her to marry a clerk in his store, yet they had to be together even if it meant being ostracized by her family.

John loved her but wondered how they would be able to live, as her father would inevitably fire him and prevent him from finding work elsewhere. She had some money, she said, and she was sure that she could persuade her family to accept him after a length of time. Her ardour convinced John despite his better judgment. He did so want to believe that he could be accepted into a high class family. He could then pursue his goal to become wealthy like the rich, whose mansions he walked by on the streets up town. He would never find another girl so lovely and in whom he was so in love as Amy, he thought. The more he thought of the possibilities, the more readily he planned their elopement.

He had rarely spoken to Marcel Poillon after his initial interview when he was hired. His promotion from porter to clerk made him aware that Poillon appreciated his work and his promise, but there seemed to be no more indication of any special interest in him. When the distinguished-looking owner walked past the counters of merchandise in his inspection tours, he regarded the clerks with the same cold eye that he turned on the merchandise. He was a thoughtful man, reserved and appreciative of extra effort by his staff to improve the business. But he disapproved of familiarity with his employees and maintained an atmosphere of stern discipline. John knew that Poillon would be furious with him for eloping with his daughter, but he depended on Poillon's love for his daughter to escape harsh treatment.

On September 3, a beautiful summer morning, he met Amy at the 23rd Street ferry on the East River and they crossed over to Brooklyn. She wore a light green dress and a broad-brimmed hat of the same colour. His suit of light brown cotton he had purchased at Poillon's with his clerk's discount. His Panama hat, somewhat worn but still his favourite, gave him a sporting look.

They were married in the City Hall in a brief ceremony with two witnesses, one being a friend of Amy, the other a clerk at the Marriage Bureau. Amy sent a telegram to her parents and parted with her friend in happy tears to take a stage to a residence on the south shore of Long Island where John had arranged to stay for a week. After they enjoyed their first night as a married couple, they considered the shock that they must have given her parents and wrote them letters, expressing their love and hopes for the future, put them into one envelope and walked to the closest mail office to post it. They were young enough to think that others would rejoice in their happiness as they did.

Within a couple of days Amy received a reply from her father. Marcel Poillon told her that since she deliberately and maliciously went against the will of her parents, she was no longer welcome in their house. As for John Lewis, he was fired. Without a recommendation, he would be unable to find employment elsewhere. If he thought that he could raise his position in the world by seducing the daughter of his employer, he would find the opposite. His underhanded behaviour proved that he was incapable of trust. Poillon did not wish to hear from either of them again.

Amy broke into tears and refused to show John the letter at first.

But when he insisted angrily, she gave it to him reluctantly and watched him read it fearful of his reaction.

"Can't say we did not expect this," John said calmly as he handed back the letter.

"I put my savings into a bank account under an assumed name just in case," Amy said. "It's not that I did not expect reprisals, it's the rude, uncaring way he's done it." She broke into tears.

"It will give us time for me to find a good job. Don't cry, my darling." He took her in his arms. "Your father will regret what he's done to us. Our love is strong and gives me confidence."

They returned to his small New York apartment with boundless hope. John made the rounds of dry goods businesses but found no openings. Amy contacted old friends for help but met with indifference. She had made a huge mistake, they seemed to say, and had to suffer for it. Women who showed a will of their own were doomed to failure. Unable to control their own finances, unequal before the law, how did women expect to be treated when they broke society's rules? Amy should have known better. As for the man she married, he was an inconsequential clerk without breeding. How could she have been so misguided as to marry him?

Amy shook off these criticisms and kept up her spirits. John took some of Amy's money and gambled on the stock exchange with it. He made more money and took a keen interest in investments and how they worked or could be worked to one's advantage. This was a new world to him and one that he would not have encountered if it had not been for the circumstances of his marriage. He had learned much about commodities in the dry goods business and put his experience to work. His success for a time was such that he no longer looked for other work. He found a better and bigger apartment uptown, away from the congested streets near Canal Street. Amy made friends with couples like them, who had come to make a new life in the city. John evaded questions about where he came from and, if pressed, indicated that he might have Spanish blood in his veins. The Southern Creole was admired in New York for his resourcefulness and distinctive old-world charm, which New York merchants encountered on business trips to Louisiana. John took on some of the genteel mannerisms of that class of Southerner, just enough to suggest that he may have had a Creole background.

Marcel Poillon gradually lost his anger over the marriage and was persuaded partially by his wife's insistence and partially by John's financial success to consider forgiving his daughter. He learned from John's first New York employer that John had given J. C. Woodruff in Drummondville as a reference. He wrote to Woodruff to inquire into John's background. Woodruff told him that he was believed to be the son of a slave woman and a successful business man and that he was a conscientious worker. This information did not surprise Poillon, who as an abolitionist, was sympathetic to John's predicament, for he had guessed it, but he, nevertheless, saw the marriage as disastrous for his daughter. He gave his wife permission to seek out Amy and find a way in which she could be returned to his good graces. Mrs. Poillon soon discovered her daughter's address by consulting Amy's closest friend who had maintained contact with her. She wrote to Amy asking to see her. Amy was moved by the note. Regardless of her love for John, she missed her parents and the loving associations of her family life. But John, when he read the note, refused at first to have anything to do with her parents.

"Why should they expect us to forgive them for the way they treated us? We could have starved and be wandering the streets like beggars for all they cared."

"Please John. I miss my mother. I want to see her."

He grimaced. "I'll think it over then."

After some weeks, when he saw how deeply Amy felt about making up with her parents, he reluctantly agreed to let her meet her mother. He, however, would have no further dealings with her family.

Amy welcomed her mother to the apartment and returned with her for a tearful reunion with Marcel Poillon. The brusque businessman looked chastened when he embraced his daughter. "Forgive me, my darling girl," he moaned. "I should not have doubted your judgment. John seems to be making you happy."

"And he's not spending her money!" Mrs. Poillon said angrily to him. "He's a good businessman."

"He is a good man," Amy said as if justifying her choice. "But it's going to take time before he'll meet you again."

"Never mind," Poillon said sympathetically. "I'll do all I can to make things up to him. In time he may change his mind."

Amy met her parents frequently in the following months and spared John all knowledge of her visits. Marcel Poillon now saw John as a stronger adversary than he had imagined. He bided his time and kept Woodruff's letter in his desk drawer to pull out and peruse whenever he wanted to plan his options.

In the meantime John worked hard in stock and bond investment. He began to be known among the traders as a smart young man whose decisions were sometimes brilliant. He added the initial "D" to his name. John D. Lewis made him more distinctive. In his mind it stood for Duncan and helped give him the feeling of having roots, which he needed as he rose in the uncertain world of finance. All was going well until one of those economic disturbances hit the New York financial world and stock prices tumbled. John lost most of his money. Where he was brilliant when investing in a bull market, he was incompetent in a bear market. The strain of his losses cast him into a depressed state and sent him to bed for days.

Amy tried to encourage him, but he had lost his confidence. He feared that failure was to be his lot in life. Since he had gambled away much of Amy's money, they had nothing to fall back on. They would have to return to a small apartment and give up the friends they had recently made. In this state, John began to reconsider his relations with Amy's parents. Amy, distressed by John's failure and disappointed in their relationship, which was not as open and happy as she had expected, persuaded him to call on her father for help, and, at the same time, prepared her father for John's visit. Feeling humbled and looking distressed, John went to Poillon's offices above his store and asked his forgiveness for taking away his daughter. Poillon suppressed a surge of resentment and offered to help in as friendly a manner as he could express.

"Let bygones be bygones," Poillon smiled breezily. "I have watched you and admired your financial ability. We all suffer setbacks and bounce back again. Since my daughter loves you, I am willing to have you work for me again."

John's face brightened. "I just need a little help to tide me over," he said.

"How would the position of salesman suit you," Poillon smiled.

"That would be wonderful," John said eagerly.

"You could do very well with commissions," Poillon said, enjoying the pleasant reaction that he saw light up John's startling eyes.

"I'd do a good job for you," John cried, his voice cracking with emotion. "Thank you, Mr. Poillon. You are being very good to us."

"Don't forget," Poillon said firmly. "I love my daughter. Her happiness is important to me."

"Well, I'll do everything I can to make sure she's happy," John said.

"Of course, as you would have guessed, I checked into your background," Poillon smiled. "Your old employer Joseph Woodruff was kind enough to inform me of your beginnings in Simcoe."

John's face froze and his eyes looked frightened.

Poillon put up his hand in a cautionary way. "Don't you worry. Your secret is safe with me. But I am impressed by the strides you have made. It confirms me in my belief in the free enterprise system."

John nodded. "I know of your anti-slavery feelings, Mr. Poillon. And as you said, let bygones be bygones. I live only in the present and I think only of success in the future. America was made to produce self-made men. I promise you that I shall be one of the most successful."

Poillon was taken aback by the resolve and conviction flashing from John's mesmerizing eyes. He stood up to cover his surprise and held out his hand. "Congratulations on joining Poillon's Dry Goods Company as a salesman," he said. "Will you start tomorrow?"

"Yes, sir," John smiled and shook Poillon's hand firmly.

"You go right home to Amy," Poillon ordered, "and tell her what we've arranged. The poor girl has been suffering."

John agreed to do just that as he left, but, at the same time, he resented Poillon's inference that Poillon rather than he was actually able to take care of Amy. He disliked being obliged to Poillon for a favour which was extended only because he was his daughter's husband and he detected a quality of pity in Poillon that had nothing to do with his financial loss but rather with his origins. He wondered as he left the office how much Poillon had found out about his past and whether the wily old merchant would use it against him some day. His job as salesman, however, pleased him immensely because it would introduce him to the real trading nature of the business and bring him useful contacts. His income with commissions would mean that he and Amy could stay in their apartment and keep up with their new friends. Above all, his reconciliation with her father would make Amy extremely happy.

John, who had stopped writing to his mother during his depressed state of mind, sent off a long letter about his work as salesman for a prestigious company. He told her for the first time that he was married. But he did not say that he was working for his wife's father. Sarah showed the letter to some of her friends and as word got around Simcoe of John's progress in the business world, his story became warped into his elopement with a banker's daughter whose great wealth accounted for his success.

25

After two years of very hard work and little remuneration, Mary persuaded Smith to sell the farm. Prices had rebounded; the time was ripe. Mary dearly wanted to be close to her mother. Since George had worked as a barber in some cities in the free states, which gave him a good cover for his underground operations, he became a barber in Simcoe to do battle against the bounty hunters, some of whom he knew by sight.

Smith formed a committee of people to react when news of an abduction reached him. Citizens were eager to help because they resented kidnappers stealing away their villagers and, for the most part, they abhorred slavery. Thus Smith became friends with many in the village whatever their colour or religion. His reputation was enhanced when he was known as Sarah's son-in-law. Shortly after he opened his tiny shop on Peel Street, a black man named Harrison Hall opened a barber shop near him. Hall was a superb poker player and his shop became a meeting place for card players, white and black. Hall took over Smith's clientele whenever Smith absented himself on clandestine business.

Sarah became very close to Mary and found in her a dependability that neither Fanny nor Vesta had given her. They saw one another practically every day. In some ways Mary acted as a replacement for John. Sarah felt that she had lost her son, and, although Vesta read his letters to her, it was clear that he was anxious to keep his background secret and would communicate with her irregularly. Vesta was a dear girl but prone to trouble. She gave birth to another son, a white baby, whose father was a traveling salesman for dry-goods. Sarah distrusted the salesman whose name was Avery Shaw, and the dislike between them was clear, but Vesta took him in whenever he was in Simcoe. Mary, coming to Simcoe, therefore, helped Sarah to weather some bad emotional times.

Mary's companionship brought Sarah comfort in the face of another event: Duncan Campbell married the daughter of a naval captain. His marriage depressed her at first, although she knew that it was inevitable. Since John had left Simcoe, Sarah had less occasion to talk with Duncan. Sometimes she missed his company. He had been a saviour in her life. Her association with him had helped her build her family and become a property owner. The depth of her emotions for him seemed only to reveal themselves now, as if she had been suppressing them for years. She had no right to think the way she did, she told herself, but she felt depressed in any case. Did she regret the misfortune of birth that separated them or was it her age? was it time passing? She depended upon him for advice, but sensed that from then on she could not approach him directly unless for business reasons. Duncan felt that he had fulfilled his obligation after educating John and getting him employment. Sarah watched as he began a family of sons and daughters. His obligations to them came first. John continued to write to him every so often, but Duncan was losing interest in the early part of his life and replied only rarely. Duncan through his wife became more involved with the upper society as it began forming to distinguish itself from everyone else. In larger towns, retired English military men and remittance men organized themselves into a self-appointed elite that was recognized only by themselves. The democratic changes in government following upon the rebellions brought these people into an alliance with the dying Family Compact cliques in the cities. Failing to hold onto political power provincially, they still retained some form of control in the towns. Duncan was a symbol of success to them and as popular among his social group as he was unpopular to the growing numbers of workers. Sarah rarely saw him, perhaps catching sight of him on the street or sometimes accidentally in the post office when she picked up her mail. His wife seemed to influence him against those friends and acquaintances whom he had known for years, who tended to be "unrefined" in her view. She snubbed those she considered beneath her class.

A couple of years after his marriage, Duncan was appointed one of the commissioners to examine claims for losses during the 1837 rebellion. He and two others heard claimants from Simcoe, including Sarah who claimed the greatest loss: sixty pounds. The commissioners awarded her ten pounds. Duncan was not so strict with himself. Duncan, whose prominent position had saved him from the expense of billeted troops, claimed one pound, five shillings and received the full amount. His views on Reformers were shifting; he hired an assistant in his banking company, Henry Groff, who was an outspoken Reformer. Groff and Duncan discussed their differing political ideas, and Duncan continued to advance the young man without reservation, even after Duncan was dismissed as postmaster in favour of a Reformer in the late 1840s.

Shortly after settling in Simcoe, George Smith found himself unexpectedly in an embarrassing situation. Train lines were being laid and the roads were macadamized making travel easier and swifter. Sarah's daughter Fanny, having moved north to Norwich, where Powers found greater demand for house painting, came by train and coach to Simcoe to show her mother her first child. Because Fanny had not met Mary's husband, Sarah asked Mary and George Smith to dinner. Fanny recognized George immediately when he entered the sitting room.

"You!" she cried. "You married my sister!"

Smith looked at her querulously as he tried to place her—did he

339

conduct her to safety? was she involved in one of the abolitionist groups? did he romance her at one time—in passing?

"Don't you remember the dinner I gave you in Otterville? With my husband Bill Powers? During the rebellion?"

Smith threw up his hands, muttered "Ah!" in recognition and fell speechless.

"You were a real rebel then," Fanny said.

"A rebel!" Mary laughed. "Why Fanny, you must be mistaken. George could never be a rebel! Call him a loyalist, conservative and anything else, but never a rebel!"

Smith's face turned scarlet. He looked at Mary apologetically. "She is right!" he admitted. "For a time I was a rebel." He looked at Fanny. "I was working for the Emancipation Society, you see, so I was not really a rebel."

"You were spying!" Fanny cried angrily.

Smith nodded. "I wouldn't have harmed you. I truly liked you and Bill. But I had a job to do, and that was to make sure slavery did not raise its ugly head here."

Sarah put her hand on George's arm. "George works underground," she said to Fanny. "He cannot talk about it. He works for the good of us all."

"In that case," Fanny smiled, "you are forgiven." She came to Smith and embraced him. "It's all long ago now and forgotten anyway."

"I hope Bill will forgive me when you tell him," Smith said contritely.

"I'll make him understand, don't worry," Fanny said sympathetically. "He liked you and he wondered what happened to you the night before the force decided to abandon Scotland."

"When I see him, I'll tell him," Smith said quickly. "To think that he's my brother-in-law," he added and looked at Mary. "It's a strange world."

The memory of betraying the rebel encampment that night gave him uncomfortable moments throughout the years; his adventure among the rebels remained embedded deep within him, like a hidden shame that he could justify only by reason, never emotionally.

After more than a year of living the quiet life in Simcoe, Smith revealed to Mary why he felt restless. He wanted to enlist in the U. S. Army to fight in the Mexican War, which most people had foreseen as inevitable when the United States annexed Texas in 1845. He could leave Mary and their young daughter in the care of Sarah and indulge his love for adventure. He explained to Mary that by fighting in California, he was helping to distract Americans from invading Canada, which under President Polk they had been threatening if Canada did not cede Oregon to the United States. Mary sighed in resignation and shook her head in exasperation over his reasoning. Within the week, a happy George Smith waved from the stagecoach taking him on the first leg of his long journey to Texas and warfare in the desert.

Fanny brought her children as they were born to see her mother, and sometimes Sarah went to Norwich for a few days to be with the Powers family. Sarah loved to travel by the stage coach to the village of Paris on the Grand River banks where she caught the train. Hank Power, who drove the four-horse stage, was a good-natured mulatto who got on well with his passengers. On each of the three stopping places between Simcoe and Paris,—Round Plains, Scotland and Burford—Hank whipped up his horses to arrive at the taverns in a rush. The arrival was the event of the day. The ladies would head for the parlour and the men for the bar-room. The locals present would be easily persuaded to join them in rounds of drink, which usually were called three times before the horses were watered and readied to continue.

Sarah prospered as Simcoe, growing in population, became more colourful and interesting. She loved taking her grandchildren to the circuses and traveling shows that visited the village, and to grand parades on important holidays such as the Queen's birthday, May 24, when the citizens would restage historical events and the Six Nations Indians would put on a show of Indian dances and ceremonials. Sarah would sit with her friends Lucinda Landon and the Ruslings at these events and they would join a larger group at parties afterward. The ladies in their colourful dresses, the men dressed in red militia uniforms and riding powerful white and beige horses, all fraternized freely with one another regardless of one's station in life. They were intent on having a good time and forgetting momentarily the hard work they imposed on themselves in creating a new civilization.

That period before 1850 was the best of Sarah's life. She worked hard and felt gratified when people recognized her for it. She took an interest in the families whom she knew and commiserated with mothers whose sons, like her John, left to seek their fortunes in distant lands. When the restless blond-headed George Battersby answered the call of the California gold rush in 1849, Hank Power, driving him to the train at Paris, asked him jokingly to bring back a gold watch for him. "I will do that, Hank," George smiled. "You wait and see." Battersby's promise was humorously repeated about the village because it made people feel hopeful.

Sarah had instilled her strong individualism in her son John who rejected other people's assessment of him. She thought he was courageous to return to the country she fled. His letters, full of descriptions of the big city and his working life, thrilled her with pride at his achievements and awe at what he was accomplishing. She knew that she was right to encourage her children to be independent. Her philosophy gave John enormous psychological strength. He hid his past, not because he was ashamed of it, but because he refused to have it mark him, condemn him and hamper his career. Having tasted the bitterness of rejection on occasion when growing up in Simcoe, he was vigilant against any disclosure of his descent from slavery to his business competitors and associates. To all and sundry he had sprung up parentless into the New York commercial jungle where only performance mattered and questions of family had no meaning.

Sarah spoke of John only to her immediate family and no longer to Duncan Campbell whose new family and business interests distanced him from a washerwoman. Duncan did give some help to Vesta. When the kind Englishman George Kent died, he left land on the north side of Union Street, to the north and back of Vesta's property, to Vesta. Her property now took in over three town lots. She required financing to repair and build on it. Duncan gave her a mortgage of 15 pounds on the two lots that she had acquired from her mother. She had to repay him in three annual payments with interest. The money allowed her to erect a cottage or two and rent them to the families of tinsmiths, who ran their businesses from them. Between her residence on Norfolk St.

342

and her new property on Kent Street, there was a ravine or hollow in which Jerry Curtis, the blacksmith, kept a charcoal fire burning. Jerry kept his shop on Kent Street in front of the hollow, and, although a fierce-looking, corpulent, dark complexioned man, he could be a jolly fellow and was very popular in the town. Many of his fellow blacksmiths used to visit with him and party late into the night by the flickering glow of his charcoal pit. Sarah and Vesta, or Vesty as she was commonly called, were invited and made good friends among the blacksmiths as a result.

Vesta became well known in the Simcoe region as a good dressmaker. She fashioned her dresses after the latest styles in the ladies' magazines from Buffalo. Her companion Avery Shaw would disappear for some weeks on his salesman trips and return with an armload of these magazines. Sarah hid her dislike for Shaw. His treatment of Vesta was cavalier, she thought, and he took advantage of her good nature. He appeared on the defensive with Sarah as if he feared that she could see through him. She suspected that he had other women in other ports; but she said nothing lest she destroy Vesta's happiness. On the other hand, Vesta valued her independence in a period when as a married woman she would have had to give all her property to her husband and forfeit her business. In this way, Sarah's struggle for independence had left its mark on her children. They intended to be accountable only to themselves. That is why Fanny waited so long to marry. She wanted a man who would treat her fairly and equally and she found him in William Powers, the would-be radical, who was now making a good living as a house painter. That too is why Vesta never married. She loved Avery but deep in her soul she mistrusted him.

Sarah began to receive finer dresses and larger sums of money from New York after John became a salesman. In her late fifties, she slackened her relentless drive and began to reduce her load of laundry work, which was proving too much for her. She took care of Vesta's children when Vesta went out on the town with the slick Avery Shaw. She even decided to sell her property to Vesta, who was doing well in her dress-making business. In the summer of 1849, Vesta paid Sarah fifty pounds for the two town lots with its "houses, outhouses, buildings, woods, ways, waters, water courses, casements, privileges, profits, heridaments and appurtenances whatsoever." From now on Vesta collected the rents from the tenants she had on the land. Sarah maintained her cottage next to Vesta's house. It was a good arrangement.

Sarah's life was passing in a relatively unadventurous manner in an idyllic town facing its usual annual temporary calamities such as spring flooding, which carried water four feet high along Union Street and over her grounds. On putting her life into perspective, she thought that she had done reasonably well. All her children were independently-minded and lived as individuals, regardless of society's penchant for categorizing everyone.

Her son Henry visited her sometimes. Finding Montreal less congenial than he thought it would be, and, after several years working as a driver in a livery company, he moved to Hamilton, which was at the head of the Great Lake Ontario, rather close to Simcoe. There he found employment in a livery company and seemed to find his niche in the black community. He married a black woman, who was about fifteen years his junior, by the name of Ellen Mince. She was quite good looking and a little wild. Sarah disliked her on the one time they met and told her son that he would have a difficult time containing Ellen's high spirits and selfish attitude. Henry was a hard-working man whereas Ellen thought that money was something other people gave you. Henry visited his mother on his own since Ellen considered Simcoe dull. When George Smith returned from the Mexican War in 1848, Henry delighted in Smith's stories of his escapades. Smith pinned graphic coloured posters depicting battles of the war on the walls of his barber shop. Mercer Wilson, Sandy McPherson, the Dorsey brothers and Richard Plummer enjoyed having the Black Pimpernel cut their hair while listening to his humorous stories of skirmishes on the desert sands. Mary looked happier than at any time of her life. George was a local hero and, she thought, his enjoyment of the attention ought to make him rest for a while before returning to the Underground Railway.

Mary was Sarah's closest friend now. Sarah's friends delighted to see the pleasure they took in one another's company. In this way Sarah brought blacks and whites together when the black friends of Mary and George Smith partied with the white friends of Sarah and Vesta. Not that there was a sharp division between the communities, but it gave an opportunity for acquaintances to become friends. And those white immigrants who maligned blacks as competitors for work were inhibited from expressing themselves openly for they could not be sure but that their criticism might be offensive to those that they hoped to impress. During this period, the intermarriage between blacks and whites and the solid friendships formed over the years created an atmosphere of respect and indulgence for one another as individuals.

Mary inherited Sarah's quiet courage and determination. At their dinner table Mary countered the arguments of George Smith that his enemies were the slavers and bounty hunters in the States, not the misguided snobs of Canadian society, about whom he took an amused, sometimes ironic, philosophical view. Prejudice was a mind-set which captured the souls of the ignorant and unthinking, he said. So long as slavery existed in the States, prejudice would be strong in North America. Blacks had to work around it and preserve themselves as best they could. Other newly arrived immigrants faced the same problem, the Irish, Scottish, English, all vying for work where they could get it and all encountering bias at some time or other. She tried to persuade him to let younger men work in the underground. He should be devoting his efforts to fighting prejudice in Canada, she argued. There was little sense in trying to live with a bad situation that was going to get worse. They had to live in the present, not the future. True, life was easier for blacks in Simcoe than in some towns, but a small riot in London caused by a white woman marrying a black man and a disturbance in St. Catharines when some black militiamen were honoured for their good service in keeping the Irish canallers in check, these incidents might break out anytime anywhere. The point she was making, she argued, was that they were remaining in Canada for the rest of their lives, and no matter how much they hoped and prayed for the end of slavery in the States, it was not likely to happen for a long time. They had to demand equality in Canada now. Sarah upheld Mary's side of the argument and thus helped to spur George Smith to lead the black community in protesting unequal treatment by the local government.

The kidnappings of coloureds were rarer owing to preventive measures that Smith refashioned after his return. With an armed group of men he was able to cut parties off from reaching Ports Dover and Ryerse and take back the intoxicated victim. When news reached him too late for any counteraction before the bounty hunters had secured their victims in ships and set sail for the opposite shore, Smith's group of men, white and black, manned motorized vessels to overtake the kidnappers on the lake or to pursue them on Ohio soil, which was illegal, of course, but arguably as legal as the kidnapping in the first place. He could be absent for weeks pursuing a kidnapping party. His reputation as the Black Pimpernel was legendary; stories of his gun and sword fights on the water were repeated in Southwestern Ontario. But there were costs in men wounded in the fighting. Wanted as the Black Pimpernel for the "murder" of bounty hunters, against whom he had defended himself, he would not get a trial if caught. But Americanss never knew his real identity, and he was secure from betrayal in Simcoe, where he appeared to be a good-natured and harmless barber. That is why Smith became a hero to the blacks and abolitionist whites of Simcoe, who patronized his barbershop to the point where his barbering competition, Harrison Hall, had to find extra work as carrier of the Royal Mail for the Post Office. A genial, copper-coloured wiseacre, who faced the vicissitudes of life philosophically, Hall drove a slow old horse hitched to a buckboard and never missed a delivery.

Theo Hunt did good service for George Smith. On his frequent visits to the States he carried messages back and forth between Underground Railway operatives, and, when John Lewis became more settled in his employment, Hunt recruited him to provide information to the cause. New York received information the same way it took in goods. New York merchants were dependent on the cotton trade from the South and had to support Southern slave policies, in particular the Fugitive Slave Law, in order to keep up their profit margins. At the same time, news from the South of pursuits of individual blacks in the North went through the grapevine. John reported what he heard to Hunt who took the news back to Smith and others.

Whether it was owing to the true feelings of the Reform element, which gradually took control from the old elite, or waves of settlers from the States, who seemed to affect the general population, fears manufactured in the States about blacks, however irrational, grew alarmingly in Canada. The slave states pressured Congress to pass stronger fugitive slave laws in the free states. Black families living in the northern states had their rights taken away by law after law, and, although loath to forsake their property which they had worked so hard to maintain, they found it wiser to abandon it and seek the relative safety of Canadian soil. The Fugitive Slave Law of 1850 forbade trial by jury and testimony from the slave, and admitted untested evidence among other draconian measures. Although several states passed Personal Liberty laws to try to weaken its effectiveness, the Fugitive Slave Law was ruthlessly enforced against unprotected blacks, especially in Ohio and Pennsylvania, which caused thousands of them to escape to Ontario. The large influx of coloreds swelled their numbers in Canadian towns and brought a reaction among some of the whites who feared that they were going to be over-run by former slaves. Symptomatic of this reaction was the decision in Simcoe in 1850, following other jurisdictions, to forbid blacks from attending provincial schools. The promise of education stood like a beacon to migrating blacks who had been denied it as slaves. Now to be deprived of it again, in the land of freedom, from a people who had at first seemed so welcoming, was a blow. Whereas for years blacks assumed that they would rise from labouring jobs to skilled work and to the professions, it became apparent, with the attempt to deny them education, that they were being forced into a servitude of low wage work. The orator Dick Plummer said that blacks were suffering from slavocracy under a different name—low-wageocracy. This depressed many people whose hopes for freedom and advancement in Canada had been high. Some who had tradesman skills made money, but the rest just got by. Black children went ragged and barefoot. Many could not afford to attend school in any case. A wealthy black man fought the issue of access to the school system in the local courts and won, but since the school district lacked the money to pay, he was bankrupted paying the bills. Sarah sensed changes in attitudes but was surprised by the extent of resentment among whites. Slavery used to be grounds for discrimination, she thought, now it was skin colour.

Sarah's position in her community became ambiguous. It mattered little to blacks that her heritage was mostly Irish. Her mother had been a mulatto slave, thus they considered her black. She was respected for being an early arrival and an older person who had succeeded, but her closeness to whites, of whom she seemed to consider herself one, made some blacks wary of her. Sarah's long relationship with Duncan Campbell was common knowledge, even to the point where it was rumoured that John had been born in Duncan's home. Her so-called "white" daughters consorted with white men yet her mulatto daughter Mary was married to a leader in the black community. To some blacks, after their children were barred from public schools, Sarah symbolized betrayal. To some whites, she represented that negritude which threatened to undermine the white race. The ideologies which so divided the States were affecting the minds of Canadians, yet not on the same scale or in the same intensity. It was worrying to fair-minded citizens like the young white couple who had welcomed Henry Lewis to their farm on his walk from Port Stanley to Simcoe.

Sarah refused to be put in a box, as she worded it. She was an individual made up of different races and honored them all. She wanted the rest of the world to recognize her complexity as she acknowledged the individuality of everyone with whom she came into contact. Just as she rebelled against being a slave because her mother had been mulatto so she rejected any attempt to peg her as black. Her good looks, sense of purpose and commanding presence made her a personality that no one could ignore. She had worked hard and made the upbringing of her children paramount. Her closeness to her mulatto daughter Mary and her white daughter Vesta gave her an emotional stability in this small town of park-like beauty. With Vesta she owned hogs, chickens, a cow and two horses. The townspeople's animals wandered at liberty in and among the houses which were set a distance apart. Everyone knew one's own animals and came after them when one wanted them. The casualness and informality of the town made any attempt at discrimination hard to promote. People knew one another too well. White and black, Irish and German, all worked together to make a good community, although, as in every frontier society, there were those who kept themselves aloof and hid their poverty.

But now that elements in the community began to menace people of colour with by-laws, Sarah became indignant. Bias was not apparent in every-day living so it was difficult to understand its appearance in a law denying education. Sarah blamed tradespeople such as Life Henry for influencing the community. That smiling, hypocritical bar owner, who had been getting pay-offs from the bounty hunters, typified the Yankee sympathizer. He saw people as opportunities and profit, not as individuals. This mentality became more noticeable as the number of self-styled gentlemen increased. They invested in land through the kind offices of Duncan Campbell and resold it at large profit to new immigrants, and like Campbell they built fine houses and were on the watch as mortgage lenders for town property that they hoped to possess. These gentlemen, most of whom were sharp-dealing traders, harboured an ambition to rise to the top of the social heap on a level with Duncan Campbell and Leonard Sovereign. Sarah watched the rise of these men into positions in the courts, town councils, and professions, as the society took shape under influence from England and the States. She saw the workers and small tradesmen gradually lose their standing and their voice in village affairs. An attitude of professionalism prevailed. These "gentlemen" claimed to know alone how to run the town. The only way that the common people could control them was through the power of the vote, but the gentlemen knew how to divide the people and vitiate the vote. Turning white against black was a workable strategy and so easy to do because of the many settlers from the States who had not shed their prejudices.

The black community in the south-west section of Simcoe swelled in numbers. Blacks and coloreds had lived next to whites and still did, but the growing resentment caused the blacks to erect their own church. The better-educated blacks such as the Dorsey brothers, who ran a large farm in the south-east part of town, became spokespersons for the community. Although most coloreds were employed in menial jobs, some distinguished themselves as craftsmen and others as wrestlers and boxers. Dick Plummer was asked to speak at holiday festivals and at private black events that Sarah attended. He could bring an audience close to tears with laughter. He could influence people politically through subtle means, innuendo, and outright ridicule. The black community never forsook the politics which gave them refuge and remained conservative throughout this period of growing reformist power. But the growing black presence meant that it began forming a black agenda, which in turn alienated it from the white community of which it had been recently a part.

Mary Lewis spurred George Smith to rally a few black leaders, including the Dorsey brothers, Isaac and Allen, Jerry Curtis and Dick Plummer, to petition the town council for the raising of a separate school which the new law provided for, and, through the backroom intervention of the Minister of Education, a school for blacks was built. Such struggles for basic rights taxed the patience of many blacks whose anger was kept in check by their leaders. The Dorseys argued that blacks could not afford to alienate those whites who were helping them against the bigots. The problem was that the bigots were pushing their agenda quietly through the political system while the blacks had to work hard to reverse what was being done to them. George Smith warned the black community never to vote for the reformers and took a leading role in the Wilberforce Society.

The Wilberforce Society comprised men of marked individuality such as Mercer Wilson, Clerk of the Peace, Colonel of Militia, and rousing after-dinner speaker, Judge William Salmon and his son, Dr. James Salmon, who was known throughout the village for his kindness to the poor; not far from his home on Union and Colborne Streets was a row of shanties running to Kent St. which the doctor visited periodically to offer his help to the blacks and whites who lived there. Church ministers were members, including the "model pastor" Francis Evans, loved by all denominations; the Presbyterian George Bell, a linguist and student of science; the Methodist William Ryerson; the Congregationalist William Clark, whose church on Young and Colborne was built of mud and had a silver spire that served as Simcoe's landmark for years; and lastly the Baptist Jonathan Gundry, a small man with dark piercing eyes peering above a high stiff collar, whose combined drug and book store was a favourite meeting place for the studious such as John Lewis and his friends. Even ideological enemies such as Richard House, who with Gundry owned and edited the *Long Point Advocate*, a lively Reformist newspaper, and John Abbott, a far right Tory, who ran the *Standard*

Conservative were members. Both men warred with words—ironic, sarcastic, vituperative—all very entertaining to those who could read.

With such an array of different views and forensic talent, it was not surprising that the town's debating society, which held its monthly meetings for the public's benefit in the Grammar School on Kent St., became the centre for intellectual amusement. Here the Wilberforce Society posed questions of discrimination, racism, integrity, good citizenship and so forth. Richard Plummer, who quoted from Shakespeare and the speeches of Wilberforce and Frederick Douglass to amuse the boys in the street, became a tiger on the debating stand. Those on the other side of the colour question were first disarmed by Plummer's charm and wit and then destroyed by his incisive arguments. The Reverend Bell, whose clear and logical mind made him a dull preacher but a formidable debater, alone could best him, but only on subjects other than the colour question.

Sarah and her family attended all debates and afterwards discussed the issues with friends over coffee in one another's homes. Lucinda Landon and her son Zeb often took part and brought some of Lucinda's wards with them. The Ruslings never missed a meeting. William Rusling, as warm and friendly as always, would serve up some humorous doggerel to suit the occasion. These get-togethers made Sarah's life interesting because, unlettered as she was, she learnt a great deal and was able to speak from her life experience, which the others respected. She could cite a personal incident, stark and disturbing, which challenged the assumptions they harboured and lived by.

Such an incident brought the troubling and conflicting emotions circulating below the surface of her society into the open. She was walking on Kent St. on a spring afternoon when she noticed a cart, covered only with a thin ragged quilt, in front of a harness shop. She pulled back the quilt and gaped in horror at the body of a woman, whom she recognized as someone with whom she had a nodding acquaintance when shopping in town. She was white, the wife of Albert Rue, a black man living in a shanty on the Simcoe flats by the Lynn River. At first, she thought the woman was being transported somewhere and left there temporarily, but the flies buzzing about the body, the stench, and the fact that the stays lay on the ground as if abandoned long ago by horse or mule made her realize that the corpse had been left there deliberately. Horrified, she hurried to George Smith's barber shop. George, she knew, had talked of the woman's husband who used to alert him to bounty hunters coming upriver, when they stopped at the flats to rest. She wondered if the couple was too poor to afford medical help and too proud to beg. A black and white couple living on the fringe of society, perhaps they had been condemned by family for loving one another and sought to live for one another in solitary peace. With the barbershop in sight, she saw the young doctor Salmon emerge from it. He would be the right person to tell, she thought, and she hailed him.

James Salmon was of slight build like his father the Judge, but with a more compassionate expression. He greeted Sarah with a broad smile.

"Sarah! Why are you looking so concerned on this beautiful spring morning?" he asked.

Sarah waved her hands agitatedly. "Something terrible has happened" she cried and told him about the corpse.

Salmon frowned in alarm. "For one thing it's a health hazard," he said as he hurried away.

George was sitting on his barber chair and waiting for a customer. He dropped his newspaper and stood up when he saw the worried expression on Sarah's face. Her report about Albert Rue's wife was straightforward and simple, but the implications behind it were large and complicated. He got his hat and walked with Sarah back to the cart.

A small crowd was gathered near the cart, and Dr. Salmon was stepping away from the corpse after examining it cursorily. He looked disgusted and went to question a couple of young men who had stopped to watch. One of them seemed to agree to help while the other dashed away to his work. Salmon and the young man picked up the stays of the cart to pull it, but Smith offered his help and the young man gave way to him. Sarah followed them pulling the cart along Kent street and west on Union to the doctor's large stone house. They took the cart into the barn behind the house.

"I think she died from fever," the doctor said to Smith, "and she probably didn't have enough to eat. Do you know who she was?"

Smith nodded and, grimacing, mentioned her husband as a handyman who did odd jobs about town. "I'll speak to him. Don't send the constable. Rue is not malicious, he's just ignorant."

Salmon grimaced. "Ask him to come to the Courthouse at three this afternoon, will you please, George. My father will have to handle this." He turned to Sarah. "Thank you for alerting us. I wonder what people could have been thinking to allow the body to lie exposed in the village centre. Where were our constables?"

Sarah shook her head in pity at the cart. "What will you do with her?"

"That's still up to Albert Rue," he replied. "We need corpses for dissection to train our medical students, Sarah. Rue may be willing to donate it."

Sarah suppressed the shock she felt. Her years of slavery had taught her to hide her feelings, and she carried this ability like a character trait throughout her later years.

"I'll ask him," Smith said. "It may be best all round."

Smith walked with Sarah back to the street while Salmon went to his surgery to ask his young assistant to take a message to his father, the judge. Just as Sarah was parting from Smith to continue looking for her cow, which must have strayed westward onto the commons, the newspaper editor Richard House rushed up to them.

"George!" he cried. "What's all this about a body being found on Kent street?"

"It was not murder," George said with a smile.

"How can you be sure?" House said sharply. "Where is it?"

"Dr. Salmon said that fever killed her," Sarah volunteered.

House made a face and hurried on to Salmon's home.

"I have a feeling in my bones that this is going to be a big event," George said.

"We'll hear soon enough," Sarah said grimly. Sidestepping two hogs, which were crossing the street to sample the grass. Walking to the commons to fetch her cow and get milk for her grandchildren, she worried that this incident would tear the community apart.

SIMCOE.

LOST

26

Richard House wrote a blistering editorial about Maisey Rue's death. He charged the village magistrate, Matthew Brown, who ran a harness shop on Kent and Robinson Streets, with dereliction of duty. How could the magistrate and his several constables pass by a cart abandoned close to their work place and not inspect it? The townspeople should demand a reply. Of course, the magistrate had no reply, at least for the public. House, whose *Advocate* appeared twice weekly, returned to the subject in the next issue. He began hypothesizing that either Brown knew of the corpse but did nothing because the woman had been married to a black man or Brown regarded the poor as below his attention, which seemed always focused on the more influential citizen. These assertions brought a furious John Abbott of the *Standard* to accuse House of trying to gather black votes for the Reformers by stirring up black resentment. Resentment! House retorted, the whole town should resent the insult to a poor soul, who even in medieval days would have been given a proper burial. The issue began to heat up the body politic, *ex proprius* as it were. Richard Plummer suggested that the topic be debated. Everyone had something to say about it, had their own point of view. Although the town officials wanted the subject to disappear, the town intellectuals considered that it should be aired in public. Could Albert Rue have been insulting the townspeople, implying that prejudice had caused his wife's death? that since whites disowned her in life, the least they could do was to look after her in death? Was he pricking the conscience of the town? Albert Rue, sitting in a jail cell, admitted only to lacking the money for burial. Since he had no money, his excuse seemed plausible, Judge Salmon reasoned; moreover, his poverty excused him from paying a fine. But the judge ordered Rue to appear in court nevertheless.

Rue was a pitiful figure dressed in rags and wearing scruffy old shoes that someone had thrown out. He was in his fifties, balding, and looking beaten down by the vicissitudes of life. He said that he had been married for twenty years and that his wife was from a farming family where he first sought work after escaping from slavery through Buffalo and Fort Erie. They had fallen in love and bought a small farm. All seemed fine until drought hit them and they could not keep up the payments. Their downfall was not an uncommon story, but what made it interesting was their ability to survive by doing small services, catching fish in the Lynn River, and growing vegetables on the flatts. They had encountered some bias which made survival harder. He, being an ex-slave, shrugged it off, but she was deeply hurt and greatly offended at the slights shown them. She became like a hermit and went into town only to buy food. Rue said that he thought the town would look after her body. He himself did not want to live but would pass the rest of his days as best he could. He apologized for causing so much commotion.

All five newspapers in the area took up positions on the subject. The *Erie News*, which could be counted upon to support black initiatives, promoted the Wilberforce Society's call for a debate. Richard House and two of his writers, M. F. Foley and Dr. J. F. Clarke, whose trenchant liberal views made the paper required reading all over the province, continued to inquire into the hidden motives of the populace, which this incident did so much to reveal.

George and Mary Smith wanted Sarah to talk to Duncan Campbell and get his support for a full debate. They called out to Sarah, who was sitting on her front verandah with Vesta, her children and Avery Shaw on one of those warm, clear summer evenings. Shaw went inside to get wine for them all. Smith argued that Duncan, as a leader in the community, would give the discussion the weight it needed to be effective, but Sarah was reluctant to approach him.

"I haven't seen the squire for ages," Sarah protested. "I don't think that I could be persuasive. Why doesn't Reverend Bell or Reverend Evans go to him? They're good Wilberforce members and powerful persuaders."

"They are liberals, Ma," Mary said. "Mr. Campbell might suspect them of a political motive. You are best because you know him. He knows that you have no agenda. You can tell him that it's for the community's good."

"Yeah, but is it?" Avery Shaw broke in. "Seems like you're stirring up feelings. Better to let sleeping dogs lie. You can't change people with a debate."

"Then you miss the reason for debating," Smith said dryly. "Feelings already are stirred up. A debate will put some reasoning, some intelligence into people's thinking. That's all we want."

"We like to hear debates, don't we boys," Vesta said to her two children. "We learn from them, don't we?"

"Yes, Ma," they said in unison but, squirming to go to play with their friends, they pleaded with their eyes to be dismissed from the discussion.

Vesta waved them away with an expression of amused acceptance.

Sarah smiled, "I wonder what kind of light it will throw on the coloured question. Who is going to take my position that white is a colour just as much as black? If I agree to see Duncan, I want your promise to support the individual in man and not go on politicking for political purposes."

"That's what this issue does," Smith said excitedly. "It lets people address all those things that we have been hiding. People call coloureds black but they could just as easily call them whites, like Vesta here. That's the issue we're trying to reach. Do you see that?" he asked Shaw.

Avery shook his head. "Most people can't think deep like that. You'll just confuse everybody."

"They love hearing the debates," Sarah defended Smith, "even subjects just as difficult as this one. So I'll do it. I'll go to the squire."

Mary and George gave a little whoop and Vesta giggled.

"You could be stirring up a lot that's been lying under the surface," Shaw warned. His round face turned ominous and his dark eyes hinted at unknown things.

"What you talkin' about?" Smith asked angrily.

"He means that if you bring the forces of evil into the open, they'll start acting like forces of evil," Vesta said suddenly. "Avery is right. Who cares if an old lady's body is left on the main street for the rest of the town to bury? We don't need a race case made out of that."

"We're not makin' a race case, Vesty," Mary protested. "This is about the social condition of the poor. And the fact is that most blacks are poor."

"We don't fear things coming into the open," Smith said with a smile to Shaw. "Besides, debates help educate people."

"That's true," Sarah said. "I learned a lot from listening. I know what you're doin' is right. We have to get the town to be more caring in its attitudes. Vesty, you should remember how it was in the early days when people helped us to survive. We came here with nothing, and now look at us, with a couple of houses, lands, rental property and so on—my children educated and doin' well."

"Yes, mama," Vesta smiled with a sigh. "You're right as always. There's been a change in mood around here in the last few years, though. People are getting jealous. They don't like the fact that I own property. Avery doesn't see it because he's not here all that much. But it has to be talked about because that's one way we can keep the Yankees from taking over."

"Look here," Smith said, frowning. "We're not asking for much. If Negroes pay property taxes and support the public school system, then their children should be able to go to those schools. We want to be treated like everyone else, and that's the way it was around here for a long time. If some whites don't want their children to sit next to ours, then they should form their own white schools with their own money. It seems when we had a good Negro school going, then the whites sent their children to be educated there. That happened in Buxton, didn't it? I'm sorry, Avery, but when it comes to education, I'll do anything to keep us on an equal footing. Without an education, the black man will be kept down. That's what we're seeing here. Poor Albert Rue and his white wife. They were good people. They didn't deserve to be treated the way they were." Smith turned away, his voice choked with emotion.

Shaw looked embarrassed. "I guess I didn't realize how bad things are," he said.

"They are not bad," Vesta said. "They just are goin' bad and it's got to be stopped."

Sarah laughed. "You all are putting the fight into me. The squire's going to have to help us or else!"

They all laughed and Avery went for another bottle of his homemade wine.

Sarah came to the Gore Bank before it was open because she thought that Duncan would have time for her then. When Duncan was relieved of his postmaster duties, the post office moved to Mulkins' dry goods store on Robinson street and the former post office building became Duncan's banking and land agency. Sarah peered in the window to see Duncan's faithful clerk Henry Groff writing in a large ledger. When she knocked on the glass, Groff looked up with a start, his goatee and mustache seeming to quiver with impatience. Seeing who it was, he came to open the door.

"Sarah Lewis! What can we do for you?" he asked indifferently.

"Is Mr. Campbell there, Mr. Groff? I have something important to see him about?"

"Well, the bank opens in twenty minutes. Can't you wait?"

"It's not business," Sarah said meaningfully.

"Well then, he's in the back," Groff said, "but don't keep him long. He's a busy man."

Sarah found Duncan sitting at a desk and poring over documents strewn across its top. He was surprised to see her. Standing and coming to her where she stopped in the doorway, he took both her hands and led her into the room and sat her on a leather chair facing his desk. "Well, my dear, how are you? Nothing wrong, I trust?" He retreated to his chair.

Sarah looked round her at the bookshelves and the large ledgers piled upon them. "No, I'm not in trouble," she smiled at him. "I'm happy to see you again."

Duncan nodded as if acknowledging that he had divorced himself from his old friends. "It's my wife, you know, Sarah. She keeps me busy when I'm not away on business, which is more often than I would like these days. But I will always make time to see you," he smiled. "John wrote me a couple of weeks ago. New York is like a tonic for him. He loves the city and he's taking a leading role there. His wife seems to be a good person."

"Do you think so?" Sarah asked anxiously.

"Oh yes, oh yes," Duncan smiled. "Her father is a successful business man and John is lucky to be in the family. I knew he could make his way in the world, Sarah. Now, what did you want to see me about?"

Sarah told him of the concern of the blacks in town about a tendency to separate them from the rest of the community and of their hopes that he would use his influence to help bring attention to their plight.

"I'm not as sympathetic as I used to be," Duncan admitted. "I'm more a man of property now. 'Course I don't like to see people in poverty, but, at the same time, are they not responsible for themselves? They are free men and given the same chance as all the others coming here. If they don't fit in, then it must be something about them that they have to correct themselves. I can't help people who can't help themselves."

"You know what I'm talking about," Sarah said resolutely. "You are a fair man and I trust you and know you to want to see justice done."

"Yes, I know. The papers have been stirring up the Albert Rue case. Ever since Richard House came here, he's stirred up trouble. Well, what do you want me to do?"

Sarah smiled at the exasperated look on his face. "Just say that you would like to hear a debate on the issue. There are problems that the community should deal with now because if they are left to fester they can grow as big and ugly wounds."

Duncan sighed and pushed one of his ledgers aside as if to free himself of his business responsibilities. "You are right, my dear. I think my friends are wrong for trying to squelch the whole thing. I'm not going to make myself popular. Well, what shall I do? Support the Wilberforce Society's call for a debate? You don't want me to debate, do you?"

Sarah laughed. "No, Duncan. You'd get too angry. But you could introduce the debate and be one of the judges to decide the winner."

Duncan jumped up and took a turn around the room as he pondered Sarah's suggestion. "Yes, I think I can do that," he beamed at her. "I think I can."

She stood up and thanked him. "I'll ask Richard Plummer to get in touch with you?" she asked.

"Yes, right away," he agreed and saw her to the door. "It has been good talking with you again, Sarah," he said and his brown eyes twinkled mischievously at her.

Sarah remembered that twinkle from the first time they had met and she grasped his hand as she bid him good-bye. Although Duncan had moved far away from his past when he was struggling to build his little business empire, he did retain an affection for her, she thought, and, of course, her connection with him in the eyes of the community did help her with some people. That association had made a tough life easier. It had brought her friends and many customers who thought her dependable as a result. As she entertained these thoughts, she walked the boardwalk on Norfolk St. to George Smith's barbershop.

Mercer Wilson was in the chair. Now a colonel of the mounted militia, the holder of municipal offices and a prominent post in the Masonic Order, he was one of the professional persons in town who insisted on treating people equally. He had no airs. He encouraged the coloured people to join the Masons and was a good member of the Wilberforce Society. George looked up with a questioning expression from behind Wilson's gray head and holding his scissors up like a question mark, he paused in his telling of an anecdote.

"It's fine," Sarah said. "Squire Campbell will be present at the debate and he gives us his blessing."

"Hallelujah!" Smith sang. "We'll start organizing it right away."

"But," Wilson warned in a mild voice, "we have to shape the debate to bring out the question. In other words, don't we have to know what we are most concerned about? Is it poverty or is it being black in Canada?"

"It's both," Smith said. "The one means the other."

"Not true," Wilson smiled. "Look at the Dorsey brothers. They run my farm and I pay them well. They are richer than most people here. The opposition will hurt us by pointing to them and others like them, who are no more obliging to the poor than rich white men."

Sarah sat down to listen to the men reason one against the other. She liked to hear discussions and picked up ideas and attitudes from listening. She had discovered in recent years that she had always had a questioning mind but had no opportunity to use it. That was why she loved hearing the debates every month. They made her feel that she belonged to this society of established immigrants. It was the mental stimulus that did it, that made her feel alive and made all that drudgery she had gone through to save the coins for her livelihood seem worthwhile. It was at the debates that her mind could mingle with the best minds in the community. She knew that many others felt the same, especially those like her who were shut out from written discourse.

"I think," Sarah suggested quietly, "if I may say something, that Squire Campbell should set the question."

Mercer Wilson looked at her in surprise and then nodded quickly. "You are right, Sarah. We are too concerned with bringing out the answers we want. Better to let Duncan do it to avoid controversy."

At that moment a customer came to the door and asked Smith when he would be free to cut his hair.

"I'll be out of here in a minute," Wilson said. "He's cut enough off me already."

"I'm leaving," Sarah said, getting up from her chair. "You may have this seat."

Sarah had the graces of a lady yet a commanding presence that intimidated those who did not know her. The customer, a young, fair-haired man, doffed his cap and sat obediently in the chair she vacated.

"We'll be holding the debate next week," Smith called out as she left. "Thank you, Sarah."

"She's quite a woman," Wilson said when she was gone. "My son knew her son John, you know. Knew him in school. He's about two years older. Nice chap."

"I never met him," Smith said, pulling away the sheet covering Wilson. "He avoids the black community. When he visits Sarah he doesn't see his other relatives. He's all business. Nothing else matters."

"In other words," Wilson smiled, "he would not be debating the pros and cons of community help for the indigent."

Smith let out a deep laugh, tinged with sarcasm. "No, indeed, Colonel. No, indeed."

27

The next Wednesday evening at the Grammar School on Kent St., the townspeople came to hear a debate on the question, "Is Poverty Owing to Misfortune?" The subject was a firebrand. It was rumoured that Duncan Campbell chose it because he was a frank man who wanted to confront issues in the community directly. Duncan's fellow adjudicators, Allen Dorsey, a tall thin man of colour with a good sense of humour, and Mercer Wilson, representing the Wilberforce Society, chose six men to debate, three on each side of the issue. The last debate, which concerned Nathaniel Hawthorne's *The Scarlet Letter* and religious bigotry, had filled the auditorium. This one threatened to burst the walls of the building. Luckily, the night was warm and the windows were opened wide where spectators could perch, and, by wedging the chairs close together and allowing the audience to fill the stage behind the speakers, a couple of hundred more people were accommodated. The place buzzed with expectation. People loved the debates as a social event and, after they were over, went to the local taverns and continued to argue the points well into the night. The debates were the one intellectually unifying event. All other activities such as the many churches, which tended to restrict socializing by denomination, the town fairs and circuses, where one might chance to meet friends, and the Music Hall on Norfolk St., where one had to pay attention to the plays and operas and then get home right afterwards, lacked that sense of community which the debates engendered. For Sarah, it was fitting that the debates were held in the Grammar School where students from all groups and backgrounds made friendships and were reunited as adults. The whole audience sensed this joy of meeting old friends whether it be for long discussions or just a passing wave and smile. People came from neighboring villages such as Port Dover, Port Ryerse, Port Rowan and so on and they would stay over at one of the hotels or in friends' houses.

Sandy McPherson came from Waterford where he had a licensing business. He saw Sarah sitting with George and Mary Smith and joined them. They had just exchanged greetings when the three moderators stepped carefully through the seated audience along a very narrow aisle that allowed them to reach the stage and the chairs awaiting them. The excitement of the audience rose in a hum which got steadily louder. Duncan Campbell was not popular, but he was respected. The applause increased for Allen Dorsey, especially among the blacks and coloureds, as he walked stiffly behind Duncan, and for Mercer Wilson who seemed to bring people together by the force of his quiet personality. People trusted him, and his many kindnesses had made a good reputation for him. He remained standing and looked out at the audience with an amused expression until the clapping stopped and quiet settled over the auditorium.

"The topic tonight seems to have met with the approval of a great many of us," Wilson began. Sudden applause made him pause and wait until it died away. "Luckily we have selected speakers with loud voices whom you can hear." The audience laughed and a few cheered. "Our thanks go to Squire Campbell for choosing the subject and kindly consenting to lend his presence." The crowd applauded respectfully. "Mr. Dorsey is an old friend of mine and I am afraid I had to remind him of our long relationship on the Wilberforce Committee before he would consent to adjudicate tonight. But he is here and will lend his brilliance to our assembly." Great applause broke out and lasted rather longer than either Dorsey or Wilson expected. Dorsey was embarrassed and put up his hand to ask that the audience stop. It was apparent to everyone at that moment that the colour question was in everyone's mind. "Now," Wilson cried over the clamor, "now, let us proceed to the speakers. For the pro side we have Mr. Richard House, our eloquent editor of the *Advocate*, whose major talent is to make us think."

Richard House stepped from another room and wended his way through the crowd to the platform. He was dressed in a black suit and wore a grim expression on his round face as if he were about to enter a boxing ring. He was applauded. "For the Contrary side, we have leading off Mr. Richard Plummer, whose brilliant analyses of the plays of Shakespeare and Brinsley Sheridan we so much enjoyed some weeks ago." The tall, middle-aged black man, looking embarrassed by the praise, nodded to recognize the great roar of approval that greeted his entrance. He was tapped and patted as he wound his way to the platform to sit on the left side of the stage. "Henry Groff speaks for the question," Wilson announced. "Anyone who uses the bank, anyone who needs insurance knows Mr. Groff." Campbell's clerk, affable and beaming with delight, stepped to the platform to sit beside Richard House. "For the Contrary, we have the Reverend Jonathan Gundry." Great applause greeted this small man who was a bundle of energy as he raced through the crowd to reach the platform and then paused to use his dark, piercing gaze to survey the audience just as he did from the pulpit of his little brick Baptist Church. "Lastly for the question, there is our esteemed Albert Toms," shouted Mercer Wilson above the chatter of the audience. Toms who had come as a child with Loyalist parents fleeing American persecution, loved telling the story of being carried in a basket strung to the side of a horse. He articled himself to a legal firm in Toronto and returned to practice law. He could be found most days at the new courthouse where he offered his services to farmers, businessmen, and those facing charges for minor offenses. Toms' wily look was evident in his smile which came close to a sneer as he stepped warily through the crowd. He grew a Van Dyke beard and held himself as if he expected to be respected, which made him peculiar in this society of open approach and jocular familiarity. Nevertheless, he was welcomed with applause. "And opposed to the question we have our third speaker, Mr. William Wallace." A bespectacled man of middle height and a rather long face with a sharp nose walked purposefully to the platform and sat stiffly on the remaining chair on the left. Wallace, village clerk since Simcoe became officially a village in 1851, was as well educated as the others and as fluent. He was obsessed with the idea of adopting paper money based on government credit. His system was sneeringly referred to as "Rag Baby." The audience greeted him with good humour, certain that he would manage to introduce the subject into the debate somehow.

Allen Dorsey, after outlining the rules of debate in a well-modulated voice that seemed to entrance the listeners, announced Richard House, who addressed the audience in a strong deep voice. His serious face and black brows made him seem formidable, but perhaps it was his reputation as a writer of sharp wit and devastating sarcasm that made people read him in that light. His aloofness from everyone, the formal manner in which he dealt with people and his unending source of money by which he funded certain causes gave him the stature of a local myth.

"Poverty is caused by misfortune," he began. "What do I mean by that? Well, we meet with disasters in our life that cause us to lose our property, our work, and too often our lives. It could be illness, false imprisonment, tricky competitive business practices, autocratic state power, even radical changes in the weather, long droughts and so on. That is why we have my friend on this panel, Mr. Groff, to offer us insurance." He smiled at Groff who smiled appreciatively at him. "Mr. Groff could also be ruined," he added, "and become poor. No, poverty is just one of the many dangers we encounter in life as a mariner encounters a whirlpool. Some of us, regardless of how hard we work and how careful we are, become its victim. Some are born into it. Thus slaves are born impoverished. They risk their lives to be free, and, if they reach these shores, they are given the choice to overcome poverty with hard work or to sink back into the kind of poverty that we equate with slavery. That is, a slavery where man can move around freely but cannot improve his lot."

The spectators had expected this thinking from House, but he was an unusual man and could quickly qualify a statement in a way that seemed to reverse it. They watched him warily: those who agreed with the statement eyed him distrustfully and those who disagreed wondered it he really meant what he was saying or just leading them along.

"It was I, you remember, who made this community face up to the tragedy of Mrs. Albert Rue, left in disgrace on a busy street as a challenge to the authorities and eventually to all of you, churchgoers and

Christian worshippers." His mouth seemed to curl downwards with disgust. "You were faced with poverty, with a woman's misfortune, and you ignored her. Either you could not be bothered or you loved your metal coins too much to pay for her burial. You saw the decaying body in a cart as someone else's bad luck, not yours. Misfortune is what you saw. Of course, misfortune stood for poverty, but poverty was taken for granted and you thought no more about it until we stirred up your consciences and you flock here tonight to expiate them by finding other reasons for the Rues' poverty." He smiled suddenly. "I don't blame you because you live in a selfish society dedicated to cutting livelihoods out of the forests, streams, and fertile lands all about us. It is luck that decides who makes money and who loses it. The Rues were unlucky. They lived in a ruthless climate. Maybe, when our society learns the meaning of responsibility, the Rues would not have been so poor, maybe Mrs. Rue would have had a decent burial instead of ending up on the dissecting table."

The audience sat in shocked silence.

"Yes, the great misfortune is to be born into a society such as ours. Whom can we trust? Only those closest to us. And even then we cannot be certain. We ask for God's help and even He deserts us. No, my fellow citizens, until we learn to deal with misfortune, to lessen its impact on us as individuals and as a people, we will always run the risk of being poor, and like Albert Rue we shall be forced to throw that which is closest to our hearts onto the junk pile." Duncan Campbell rang a small bell and stopped House from saying more. There was silence as the crowd watched House return to his chair and stare about him with a challenging look.

Richard Plummer stood up. "'O world! How apt the poor are to be proud,' so the bard wrote in *Twelfth Night* and so we all know that to be true." His lithe body and strong lean face seemed to radiate pride. He spoke with a slight Southern accent betraying his origin as Kentucky, at least that was the state that had been rumoured for years to have been his home, largely because it was the only state that allowed slaves to be educated. "Regardless of our state in the world, we are proud, but it is the truly poor who bear the greatest burden, put up with the grossest insults, endure prejudice from others over the most minor things, but who become proudest of their achievements because they are made against the greatest odds. Misfortune cannot make us poor. It is only a vague, abstract name used by those who want to cloak the real reason for poverty. What makes you and me poor is other people. They may not do it intentionally. They may be thinking only of themselves and how best to become rich and get more comfort for themselves. But they are just as guilty as if they had deliberately planned to destroy another man's livelihood. And that is the message of our commerce. Get a good deal! Get the better of the other fellow! That is the root of corruption in the society that my friend Mr. House was alluding to." House shook his head with a wry smile as if to say that Plummer was misinterpreting him. "Listen to Cardinal Wolsley give his parting advice to his secretary who is to become secretary to the King in the bard's *Henry VIII* and remember that Shakespeare wrote for each one of us: 'Cromwell, I charge thee, fling away ambition: By that sin fell the angels; how can man then, the image of his Maker, hope to win by't? Love thyself last: cherish those hearts that hate thee; Corruption wins not more than honesty. Still in thy right hand carry gentle peace, To silence envious tongues: be just and fear not. Let all the ends thou aims't at be thy country's, Thy God's, and truth's: then if thou fall'st, O Cromwell! Thou fall'st a blessed martyr.'" Plummer paused to let the effect of the quotation sink into the general consciousness. "Albert Rue, a poor black man, dared to be honest and love like an honest man and marry Maisey, a white woman, a kind and gentle woman. I knew them, and I blame myself for not knowing how dire was their state. Shunned by black and white alike, they found solace in one another and their pride raised them above all criticism. Pride in poverty makes bearable many things. And yet do we not have among us by the hundreds the product of white and black, mulattos, quadroons, octoroons and whatever other names they brand us with, coloured, contaminated?" The audience laughed. "In my early years in Simcoe, no one would have shunned the Rues. Now, the corruption of ambition has slunk into our body politic like a thief in the night. Escape from slavery used to mean freedom, now we have to escape also from colour, which, of course, many of us cannot do. Though some do." Plummer looked out into the audience for confirmation and heard a man call out "Aye, aye!" Sarah wondered whether he was referring to her and her children and dreaded being pointed out as an example, but Plummer continued and Sarah thought that he was too much of a gentleman to embarrass her. "Slavery was the stigma when slaves were white and black, but today it is negritude. Why? Because the ambitious use every means to further their ends, to keep people poor, to deny them a means to educate and better themselves. Poverty is caused by man, either by the rich grinding down the less fortunate or by self-infliction in those whose spirit is too broken to fight. Poor Maisey Rue and poor Albert! Which of the two were you?" Duncan Campbell rang the bell, more urgently than he had when signalling the close of House's time. "Look in the mirror," Plummer shouted, "to see where you stand on this question!" The crowd, particularly the coloured people, applauded Plummer. Allen Dorsey stood up and quieted it with a wave of his hand.

Henry Groff, shoulders hunched, his eyes hurriedly scanning notes that he held in front of him, walked to centre stage. His voice sounded high and nervous. People guessed that Duncan Campbell had compelled him to take part in the debate. "I speak for the cause of poverty as belonging to misfortune. Lightning can strike our house and ruin us. An accident can befall our father and impoverish our family. An act of God? It depends on how you view God. I sell insurance to keep you free from misfortune, at least to make God's wrath less damning, if you like. We are not helpless in the face of misfortune. Albert Rue had the same opportunity as anyone to improve his lot in life. He chose to live on the margin of society. He chose to live frugally, catching fish, growing his food, and living in a shack on the flats, which was under threat of flooding, because he did not pay taxes on it. He did not contribute to our society. He and his wife lived for themselves. We left them alone. We respected their wishes. But when he had not the means to bury her, he expected us to do his work. The great judge Sir William Blackstone said 'Man was formed for society.' Rue and his wife ignored that fact. And when they needed help, they could not ask society for it, they could not approach them whom they had ignored. I disagree with my friend in this small point that society must be faulted for deserting them. No, they must be faulted for deserting society. We have developed ways that can keep persons from being so truly poor. We have savings banks and several financial instruments to guide us through life. Man has developed these things to help one another. Together we have found ways to mitigate misfortune." Groff dropped one of the pieces of paper he held and quickly stooped to gather it up. He looked at it while the audience waited. He suddenly seemed so familiar in that pose, bent over papers, that many in the audience smiled as they pictured him as the faithful clerk, carrying out his duty. "Now to say that colour was the cause of the Rue's misfortune, as my learned friend Richard Plummer just did, is to forget that some men are rich who are coloured. We all can point to very respectable men in this audience who meet that description. And I know because I see their bank accounts." A roar of laughter greeted this remark. Groff chuckled at his own unintended witticism. He looked over at Campbell and saw with relief that Duncan was laughing too. "They are well prepared to turn misfortune aside, that is, the kind of misfortune that Mr. House rightly claims causes poverty. These successful men have endured the same prejudice as the Rues, yet they rose above it. They cared for their families. They did not have to leave a dead relative to the welfare of the village. The Rues were the architects of their own misfortune, to use a phrase that is common and means so very much. I can say no more, Messrs. adjudicators, as I feel I have made my point adequately." There was scattered applause as he returned to his chair. Duncan Campbell leaned forward to give him a pat on the shoulder.

Jonathan Gundry rose to gaze over the assembled listeners until he had absolute silence. "With all respect to dear Henry Groff, most of us do not enjoy the security of bank accounts, whether we are white, black, red or green. Whose fault is that? Can we blame Squire Campbell for keeping us away from his bank? Is it his fault that people want to hold onto their coins to pay for their daily needs? Is it his fault that the one-time prohibition against usury acts as a deterrent in our day? Or is it that his bank is set up for land transactions, mortgages and the big money business that the average citizen will never be associated with? Our Lord Jesus Christ gave us a parable of the man who made his talents work for him and duplicated themselves as against the man who buried his talents in the earth. Investment, yes, but usury? Both can

372

make you wealthy if you are careful. Wealth brings you respect, position, and honour. Squire Campbell can attest to that. But you all cannot start banks. Like him you have to belong to a select group. Squire Campbell was helped, was lucky and was clever. Also he had an ambition that few of us do. These things set him and fellows like him apart from the common man. We have a great many drinking places in this village. We see men fighting in drunken rages. On fair days we see people lying unconscious in the sweet dreams of inebriation. As an apothecary, I feel that I am pitched against the taverns because I administer to the ailments that follow upon drinking. It is a vicious circle. People spend to get drunk and spend to get well. Few are sober. Few are those who love to borrow the books from my library. Fewer are those who emulate Squire Campbell. Do you despair like I do? You can preach as I do, but you cannot bring people to reason, you cannot make them into Squire Campbells. Since Adam succumbed to temptation, man has been drawn to vice and self-destruction. If only they can be drawn to the supreme pleasure of intellectual curiosity or, failing that, to the energetic ambitions of the upstanding gentlemen on the other side of this question? Henry Groff implies they lack something as individuals; Richard House blames the selfishness of the collective human being; but they are wrong. It is the structure of our society that is the cause of the problem of poverty. Those who sit at the top arrived there by setting the rules for those under them and determining who is to be paid what. They control their own income and who can share it with them. They choke off ambition and the sense of responsibility in the lower orders. In recent years they have used skin colour as a marker and tried to choke off access to education while gradually passing laws to further their own importance and their greed. Poverty is man-made for certain, but it is made by the men who lead our society. It is done purposefully and manipulated through encouraging the vices and keeping down any who might challenge their power." Gundry's blazing eyes seemed to brighten intensely with anger. He pulled out a handkerchief to wipe his brow and his neck behind his stiff high collar. The audience sat spellbound as the sharp enunciation of his every word seemed to knife through them. "Poverty is not misfortune, it is part of a system which only all of us together can change. Albert Rue was black and

373

poor. Maisey Rue was white and poor. The structure kept them in poverty. Albert Rue in his inarticulate way said as much to us when he left his dear wife as a sacrifice before our feet. We collectively had demanded that they live in poverty; Albert symbolized the unforgiving nature of our demand by offering her dead body to us as our due. No, a thousand times no! Misfortune does not cause poverty! The elite structure of our society, which I have seen hardening as it has been forming itself over the last couple of decades, this has brought us poverty! And we shall always have poverty until we change the structure." Gundry paused, suddenly looking exhausted from the force of his shouting and his fierce arm-waving to emphasize his points. Duncan Campbell sat up in alarm, as if breaking from the trance into which Gundry had sent him, and rang the bell furiously as if to make up for neglecting to call the time sooner. The audience exploded in a burst of applause and cries of encouragement, some of them jumping to their feet to relieve the tension they felt. Gundry, a short man, seemed to have grown to a giant in the course of his speech. He acknowledged the enthusiasm of the audience with a broad smile and returned with a tired walk to his seat.

When the last excited talking died away, Albert Toms stood up. Having made money in the timber business and taken shares in the iron foundry that developed in the region, he lent his money out as mortgages. Although interest rates were usually below ten percent, he asked twenty when he found people desperate enough to pay it. He foreclosed on several mortgages and accumulated land, which he rented. When Jonathan Gundry was condemning usury, Toms wondered if he were being criticized and glared at Gundry. He thought of himself as a practical man who only did what was necessary and legal to make a living. He favoured the banning of black children from the public schools and wanted poor children sent to special schools so that his children would not have to mix with those of lower social standing. But he was careful to make no public statements to this effect. Rather he wrote long letters to politicians on the subject. He was not a democrat, but he made full use of democracy.

"I am of the opinion, strongly, that poverty is owing to misfortune. But unlike my friends in support of the question, I do not blame society or the individual. I blame fate. I blame that mysterious, undefinable force that strikes us down and lifts us up throughout our lives. We all do our best to our abilities. I see Albert Rue as a man of limited intelligence and therefore of limited possibilities trying to cope with the variabilities in life and failing. I look at myself and say why did I not fail? and you must look at yourselves as well and ask that question. I did not fail because I was lucky in my parentage, I was lucky in my upbringing, I was lucky in my talents, I was lucky to be healthy and lucky to live in an atmosphere that respects hard work and initiative, in other words, lucky to be associated with people like you. Albert and Maisey Rue were unlucky. He was unfortunate in having been born a slave, in being uneducated, and in reaching above himself in marrying a white woman and being unable to provide for her. She was badly treated by fate, made to marry badly, and from these early misfortunes she was set on a course of destruction. Poverty or wealth is a product of the mind, and the mind is the tool of that unfathomable force that I call fate and others call misfortune. My friends on the other side of the question seem to think that certain wicked men deliberately set about creating bias against others and that the élites or powerful purposely scheme on how to control those below them. Well, have they not heard of the forces of supply and demand? If there is no demand for a man's service he will be poor. And if supply is low and can be fulfilled by a man he will be rich. Think of a scales on which one arm is supply and the other demand. Think of the force holding that scale. It is incomprehensible, just as God is incomprehensible. We will never know the reasons for wealth or poverty because fate determines which way the scales shall tip and affect all mankind by its fickleness. Are we to believe that the fine gentlemen who pass and administer our laws are secretly conspiring against us? How ridiculous! Laws are passed with the common good in mind. There may be certain groups who want favours that impinge on the welfare of their neighbours, but it is up to the aggrieved neighbours to counteract those intentions. I advise the Negroes to form their own associations and fight back against the injustices they claim to suffer. They will just be trying to right the scale. But remember success depends on fate, on luck, on good fortune. That has been my motto in life, and through my willingness to work cheerfully and accept my fate,

I believe that I have been successful. I have helped fate to help me. Others will say that it is God. Allow God to help you. That is my final word on the question."

Toms returned to his seat with faint applause. Only the very religious in the audience could have been persuaded by his argument, Sarah thought, and even they must have wondered at the message when given by a man they knew to be one of the sharpest opportunists in the region.

The village clerk William Wallace stood and walked to centre stage. He was a friendly man, and, although somewhat officious in his duties, quite prepared to help those who came to him. Up to this point, none of the speakers had been able to demolish the arguments of the other side. Those for the question had relied on the metaphysical and those against had emphasized the political, which made criticism of one another a matter of assertion rather than logic. Wallace was a pragmatic man, although given to voicing unusual ideas. The audience hoped that he could swing the argument one way or the other, but were doubtful that he could.

"Ladies and Gentlemen," Wallace said, clearing his throat and smiling slightly while his eyes flashed with humour. "We have heard from my opponents that misfortune, although undefinable, is the cause of our problems, particularly the great sin of poverty. If we are to believe Mr. Toms, we have to be one of the Calvinist elect to have good luck. Henry Groff, whom I deal with many times a week, thinks misfortune is because we don't take advantage of his bank's investment opportunities." There was a ripple of laughter. "Editor House, a man whose brilliance frightens me and who I am glad spoke well before I did and cannot come back at me," Wallace paused to smile at House, who nodded at him amicably, "he blames every man jack of us for bringing misfortune upon the world because we are just too selfish to think of anyone but ourselves. Granted that he thinks of us all when he writes his newspaper and he has roasted me often enough, but does he consider that he is part of that society causing misfortune and does he know what terrible misfortune it is to be the subject of his editorials?" The audience erupted in laughter and some people clapped. "These gentlemen would put Albert Rue standing alone against misfortune. But the speakers on my side make the point that Rue is just a member of the social fabric as we all are. The Reverend Gundry, who, although I am not of his religion, I often listen to his sermons for the sheer joy of it, points to certain elements in society who try to control it to their own advantage. Frankly, I agree with him because I have seen it happen. But I say no more on that subject. He is eloquent enough. Yet, speaking of eloquence, Mr. Plummer is our pride. I thank Mrs. Sarah Lewis for bringing me to hear him for the first time several years ago." He stopped to look out over the audience. "Sarah, are you here?" Sarah raised her hand and the people about her beamed with the pleasure at seeing her recognized. "Ah, there you are! Do you remember that evening when you took a group of us white folks to hear a man that you said was the best orator, the best informed man in the province? And we all came away from that fabulous evening agreeing with you. Do you remember?" Sarah nodded and smiled shyly. "You do. How could anyone forget? From then on, I have always tried to hear him. This evening he hit squarely on the issue of prejudice as a cause of misfortune. He is right! We all know it, although some of us refuse to admit it. Prejudice takes many forms. It is used as a tool. If we take Reverend Gundry's argument and Richard Plummer's argument together, we can see that some elements use prejudice as a means of controlling others." There came a low murmur of disagreement from some in the audience. "Of course, some of us cannot see," Wallace smiled. "That is why we are having this debate. To open eyes and minds to the facts." He paused to hear the ripple of laughter that greeted his light-hearted assertion. "But I don't leave it at what we see. I want to find the reason why. Prejudice and scheming by the powerful do not exist in a vacuum. The political structure that the Reverend outlined could not survive without an economic structure to support it. Poverty is a matter of lack of money. And what causes that? The monetary system." Some among the audience broke into laughter and others smiled indulgently as Wallace came to his favourite theme. Non-plussed, Wallace continued in a serious vein. "We are burdened with coinage which has always been hard to make and circulate and which forces us to depend on barter. This keeps us all poor in a way. True, some are poorer than others because they lack access to coins while others have better access, as Mr. Groff has illustrated so well. If we brought in paper money based on government credit, which is far more credible than value based on land or some other factor open to fluctuation and uncertainty, we could expand our wealth and bring everyone into a prosperous community. Albert Rue would not then be so desperately poor. He would have had some relationship with society through his government in the form of paper. By printing paper we bring value to everyone in the community. Rue was obliged to barter his services for food. What could he barter for a proper burial for his wife? That service was outside our system, when with the adoption of paper credit it could be part of our system. And if we were all a part of a paper money system, we would be protected against the schemes of others and sudden prejudicial treatment, at least in the short term. Think of it for a moment. The circulation of paper would make exchange easier because it would bring value to everyone. I mean paper backed by government, not the paper floated by our little banks that proves so devastatingly unreliable in economic crises. It would not bring an end to equality, but it would give people a greater part in the circulation of wealth and thereby enrich our society and the opportunities for our citizens to improve their financial position. It will not eradicate poverty, but I would bet that it would give Albert Rue and those like him the means to avoid the kind of public disgrace that Richard House called it. With freer and wider circulation of wealth we are brought closer together into one society. Our closer dependency on one another will prevent the impoverishment of one section by another to the same extent as we see it now. I know that my vision is hard to grasp, but I am sure that our leaders will see the light some day and adopt it. Until they do we are going to see more tragedies like Albert Rue."

Duncan Campbell rang the bell and Wallace walked back to his seat amidst silence as the audience considered his argument. Then as he sat, it applauded strongly as if rewarding him for expressing his views, regardless of how uncertain it was about them. It seemed that Wallace had made the strongest impression because he had tried to give a solution.

Mercer Wilson called on Duncan Campbell to render his verdict. The squire stood up square-shouldered and boldly looked over the assembly. "I came here biased in favour of Henry Groff's version but leave impressed with the others that I heard. I consider man to be the maker of his own misfortune, but in many cases he is the victim of others. Whether he overcomes adversity depends on his character but also on the extent of the power of his adversaries. I agree with Mr. Plummer that our society has been changing since the early days and, in the case of our coloured neighbours, for the worse. The liberal merchants in the Northern States have been pandering to slavocracy to keep the States in one nation, but that way leads to disaster in the long run. My advice is to persevere against the structure that the Reverend Gundry has painted vividly for us. We all can become victims of it at any time. I have felt the hot breath of Reform on my neck in recent years." The audience laughed. Campbell was still regarded as the commercial force that had made the village of Simcoe strong and often prosperous. "Mr. Wallace's plan for paper money frightens me, but perhaps it will happen some day. In the meantime, Mr. House's criticism of society strikes me as very true. Misfortune causes poverty, but misfortune can take the form of other people. Therefore I find no clear winner in this debate but congratulate the speakers for making us think." He sat down. The audience seemed disappointed.

Allen Dorsey stood up. His height and thinness and the darkness of his skin gave him a wraithlike appearance in the soft light from the oil lamps attached to the walls around the room. "I, in my turn," he smiled, "arrived with a bias for the argument of Richard Plummer but am left with Mr. Gundry's powerful words echoing in my ears. Structure! Structure! Yes, indeed, but then Richard House's charge that we are selfish fills in that skeleton of structure. We are the structure and we have turned it into a weapon against the poor. Because we are selfish. I applaud all the speakers but cannot choose a winner tonight. I consider the matter of the cause of poverty still unresolved and like Squire Campbell I cast my vote for both sides." He sat down as a quiet moan came from some of the blacks in the audience.

Mercer Wilson jumped to his feet. "A perfect balance!" he cried. "That's why we have three judges. And I cast the deciding vote and upset the balance in favour of..." he paused to look whimsically at the people sitting around him on the stage and out in the audience and up in the balcony, "the Contrary side. Poverty is owing to something other than misfortune. I won't parse the arguments. I am sure you will be doing that yourselves in your parlours or in the taverns tonight and for days and perhaps weeks to come. And I shall join you in those discussions most willingly. The deciding voice tonight, however, came from William Wallace, our advocate for paper money. He convinced me that it will relieve us of grinding poverty and raise our standard of living. It will give us faith in ourselves, in our neighbours and in our nation." The audience broke into applause and Wallace was encouraged to stand up to acknowledge the ovation. "It is late and I thank you for coming. We have tea and biscuits for those who wish to remain to socialize and talk with the speakers. If any of you would like to join the Wilberforce Society, I shall be glad to acquaint you with its goals and successes."

People stirred themselves and the clamour of talk overwhelmed all other noise. McPherson chatting with Mary and George Smith walked with them to the front of the room where members of the Society poured coffee. George thought he recognized a tall, thin, boyish-looking man of middle-age and asked McPherson who he was.

"That's Sam Tisdale," Sandy smiled. "He's just moved to Simcoe. A true activist. I'm surprised you haven't met him."

"I think I have," Smith said softly.

At that moment Tisdale stepped over to greet McPherson, who introduced him to Mary and George. A light of recognition came into Tisdale's blue eyes and he reached out with both hands to clasp George's outstretched hand.

"After these many years," Tisdale cried warmly. "I've heard of your exploits, Pimpernel, and followed you from afar. Do you remember our crossing Lake Erie together?"

George chuckled with delight and began reminiscing about their accidental meeting during the Rebellion while McPherson went to talk to Duncan Campbell, whom Sarah was congratulating for his good work. Sarah, stimulated by the talk, hailed Vesta walking with Lucinda Landon and her son Zeb.

"I think that the individual can make a difference," Lucinda was saying as she led the way out of the hall. "Albert Rue needed help and should have been modest enough to ask for it, beg for it, if need be."

380

"It isn't that he did not work," Vesta said. "He used to bring us firewood. He was a good man. He did not know how to ask for help."

"He was not lucky enough," Sarah said. "Mr. Toms was right when he said that luck has a lot to do with a person's passage through life. His wife got sick when he was at his lowest. That's bad luck."

"But he was givin' it to us when he put her corpse on the main street," Zebulon Landon said with a shake of his head. "He was sayin', you uncaring people are responsible for what you have done to us so you can be responsible for burying her."

"That's right, Zeb," Vesta agreed, "but that goes to the side of the argument that says poverty is the result of evil men in society who want to keep some people poor so they can be rich."

"I think it's a mixture of character and luck," Lucinda said. "Take yourself, Sarah. You had the character to escape from bondage and to make your way against the odds to provide for your family. There may have been luck that you met certain people to help you, but you had the courage to try."

"Not so much courage as desperation," Sarah said. "It was luck that I escaped and luck that I met Duncan Campbell. But you are an example of character winning out over bad luck, and I mean the death of your husband."

A band of young men burst out of a tavern just ahead of them and crowded over the sidewalk as they sang a rousing chorus of a song that was indistinguishable in tune and words. Sarah and her group quickly crossed to the other side of the street. One of the men cried out to Vesta. He was a tall, handsome Indian from the Six Nations Reserve.

"Who was that?" Sarah asked. "Has he been to see us?"

"No, mama," Vesta laughed. "He's a new friend. Ain't he good looking? I don't even know his name."

"Edward James or Walking Turtle, whichever you prefer," Zebulon interjected. "He's a good guy but he's got a bad reputation around Brantford for fighting the Irish."

"He can't be blamed for that," Lucinda laughed.

"Lucinda!" Sarah cried. "Remember, I'm Irish."

"But not like the roughnecks in Brantford," Lucinda said. "The whites there are a brawling, racist lot."

"That's right, mama," Vesta said. "You've been too protected in Simcoe. The world out there is gettin' more violent as we get factory workers moving into the towns."

As they reached Vesta's house, she asked them in for tea. Avery Shaw had stayed home to watch the boys because he did not like debates. He was drinking wine on the porch. Lucinda excused herself and Zeb by the lateness of the hour, and, hitching their horse to the carriage they had left at the side of Vesta's house, they rode for their home on the hill to the west. Sarah went to her cottage next door as she did not want to talk to Shaw who was slurring his words. His alcoholism was getting worse. Vesta had reached the point of wishing he would go away on a selling trip and stay away.

"The boys are sleepin'," Avery said. "I wish we could sleep."

"Together," Vesta said sharply. "Not in your condition." She walked angrily into the house. As she undressed for bed, the image of Walking Turtle seemed to hover about her in the darkness.

28

The village of Simcoe treated the debate as a catharsis. Instead of feeling resentment and suspicion, the people spoke openly about the problems of race, immigration and poverty. Instead of looking for someone to blame in the Albert Rue affair, they began looking for ways to remedy the disaffection and inequalities in the community.

The law restricting blacks from the public school system was overlooked, possibly with the quiet persuasion of the Minister for Education, and black children quietly returned to schooling with white children throughout the province, as in Simcoe, which had a very good grammar school and graduated some brilliant black students such as Dick Plummer's son, William, who became a superb after-dinner speaker.

Dick Plummer's increasing love of wine led him to strut the streets in a kilt, call himself a Scotsman, shout in his mellow voice "Caledonia!" and let his vivid imagination entertain whoever would listen to his fighting days in the clan on the heaths of the Highlands. His big day every year was August 1st when the blacks celebrated Wilberforce Day. A huge open-air feast entertained all the black community and its friends on the common. Sarah and her family, that is, the Smiths, Vesta and her children and Henry, who visited from Hamilton, came together for the occasion. Only those whites who were active in the black community either in Smith's vigilantes or the Wilberforce Society or in giving professional help attended. Generally the black community regarded it as its special day. All the Simcoe hotels and restaurants contributed and the handsomely dressed colored waiters from the Kirby House in Brantford came to show their solidarity. Dick was sober then. When the time came for him to speak, between the main courses and dessert, he stood on a wooden platform erected for the purpose and bellowed in a clear voice that the breezes carried to all assembled sitting at tables and on blankets on the grass. He told of Wilberforce's parliamentary struggles with emphasis on details that illustrated the human hopes and sacrifices. He set forth those principles of freedom that finally moved the hearts and consciences of men. Everyone listened intently as he gradually built up his argument with oratorical splendour, and, when the tension became unbearable, men and women would shout out approval. At such times Dick would digress a little and tell a story to make them laugh before soaring back to their central concern—the nobility of the individual man and his right to be free.

Old Horace forsook his wanderings through the woods and fields on this day and sat in the front row glowering at Plummer "to keep him to the point," as he said. And when Plummer finished, Old Horace broke into a large smile, as if his reputation of having a savage temper maligned him. His year-long silence was shattered by a flow of words that erupted when he turned to those sitting near him and for this day of celebration he laughed and drank with abandon. Henson Johnson and Colonel Mercer Wilson then could approach him and reminisce about the days of the rebellion when Old Horace was their best source on the state of the countryside.

Dozens of waiters then sped through the crowds handing out dessert. When all were served, Sam Tisdale was given the honour of praising Plummer for his speech. As the leading abolitionist, he reported on the current state of politics and policy with regard to blacks. His lean face and brown tousled hair gave him an ever-youthful look as he shouted passionately about the cooperation among abolitionists in the northern states and Canada and their success in exposing militant Americans planning to invade Canada. "We'll never be rid of them," he shouted, "but they'll never be rid of us either." The crowd erupted in laughter and cheers. "You've heard stories of differences among us— some want to restrict our efforts at propaganda, others want to engage in the legal system, still others form organizations to teach us how to win street fights. But when it comes to protecting our freedoms, we are united."

The leaders of the Wilberforce Society sitting at the head table applauded at this point and the black leaders, smiling, joined in the applause. Some blacks wanted a militant approach to the gangs who attacked them when they went into the larger towns like Brantford, while others feared the effects that violent confrontation would have on their communities.

Tisdale ended his speech by introducing the much-awaited wrestling match—the main entertainment of the afternoon—between the handsome Steve Parker, Maria's son, the best wrestler in the Simcoe area, against the best competitor that could be found outside the area. The broad-chested Parker was rarely beaten, and this time through nimble footwork he toppled and pinned a giant of a man from Big Creek. Sarah loved to watch Steve wrestle and presented her friend Maria with a bouquet of flowers when the match was over. It was a happy moment for them.

In the late afternoon sun, the waiters from Kirby's in Brantford gathered up the crockery they had brought and acknowledged the warm thanks of those still on the grounds when they left in their wagons on the long road back. Their enthusiastic help reasserted the close relationship between Brantford town and Simcoe village every year.

Sarah sensed that people of goodwill welcomed these expressions of solidarity. They knew that despite gang warfare between white factory workers and the blacks and Indians in Brantford, the general sentiment in the population was for tolerance and equal treatment. The rawness and unpredictability of some men could not be contained, however, and individuals could be the victims of sudden and inexplicable outbursts of hatred. The unsettled nature of growing societies needed emotional outlets. What made Sarah uneasy was that the guardians of the law could not be sure which element caused the outrage. The leaders of Reform spoke eloquently against slavery, but their sentiments for American republicanism still carried undertones of racism. The conservatives also included racists, as they were in every political movement, but the anti-Americanism coming from the early Loyalist settlers and from British rule through British institutions tended to act as a barrier of distrust of racial influences from the States..

When Duncan Campbell's store and blacksmith establishment of Norfolk St. burned to the ground, the magistrate believed that the buildings had been set alight on purpose, but he had no idea by whom. Sarah and her friends mulled over the possibilities: reformers who took their revenge for his strong conservative views, blacks who resented his well-publicized decision as a school trustee to restrict black children from a public school in another district, or people who had lost land to his mortgage and banking interests who used that method of venting their anger. This happened more than a year after the Rue debate and after the village had gone on to many more debates, many more subjects and other concerns. It is, observed Maria Parker, one thing for the general public to think one way and another for certain determined elements to push it onto a different path despite its unwillingness to go there. As the fifties wore on there were other mysterious fires.

The members of the Wilberforce Society watched closely as rebels, who had fled to the States and laid low for a couple of years, began to drift back to Canada after the early hangings and deportations had taken place and a mood of forgiveness for the past settled among the people. In the changed atmosphere some former rebels gained high political office as Reformers, but there were others such as Bill Mathews who saw opportunities in changing their allegiance to the Conservatives. George Smith became alarmed when Mathews organized his old band of ruffians and, running for political office in Brantford, became mayor by sending his men out with clubs to intimidate opponents and obstructing certain voters from reaching the polling booths, which was a fairly common practice. Smith, who championed the Conservatives, felt betrayed by the Attorney-General John A. Macdonald, who was depending on Mathews to hold the line against the Reformers in the district. He believed that Mathews was hoodwinking Macdonald by claiming to be something he was not. His friends said that Macdonald was a wily politician using whatever support he could garner regardless from where it came. This sort of uncertainty in the body politic confused issues and disturbed people like Sarah Lewis, who had always, at the back of her mind, a fear of a sudden reversal of public opinion and a return to slavery or at least a sympathy for it. John Lewis visited his mother about this time. He told her that the abolitionists in New York were growing stronger as the appeasement policy toward the South was becoming more apparent.

"They are embarrassing many of the merchants," he said sarcastically. "Trouble is, they are split along the lines of aggressive action or moderate criticism. Consequently they are divided just like the nation. But that does not mean that we are less vigilant. We watch the enemy closely. This Brantford Mayor Mathews you spoke about, Mother, he's being watched by abolitionists. One of the most aggressive is Sam Tisdale."

"Yes, son, I know him," Sarah nodded. "But you must be careful."

"Oh, I'm just a fringe character, Mother. I work quietly behind the scenes."

"And what does your wife think of it?"

"She knows nothing of my activities. It's better that she does not."

They were interrupted by Vesta who knocked at the front door of her mother's cottage with a cup in her hand to borrow sugar.

"Well, well, the prodigal son returns. Don't you look smart in your new suit?" she said.

"I have to look smart if I'm going to sell anything," John said with an amused look at his sister. "I wish I could say the same for you."

Vesta looked down at her large girth and smoothed her dress over

386

her stomach. "At least I'm keeping the human race going."

"Who is the father this time?" John mocked her. "Mother tells me that Avery left you months ago."

"I kicked him out," Vesta declared. "I haven't heard from him and don't want to hear. This child belongs to a better man than Avery could ever hope to be."

John looked at Sarah. "Sounds like she's building me up to hear bad news."

"Only you could possibly consider it bad, you and your white merchant class in New York."

"Oh, oh," John said, rounding his eyes.

"He's a gentle and handsome man," Sarah said. "He is a Mohawk Indian."

"From the Reserve?" John asked in amazement.

"Mother, would you please give me the sugar and let me return to my sewing machine. I've had enough criticism from the idle rich."

"Vesty, come on, now," John smiled. "I'm happy for you." He stepped to Vesta and pecked her on the cheek. "Though, I must say, you are unpredictable."

"You'd like him," Vesta smiled. "I wish you'd stay to meet him this weekend when he's coming to see me."

"Sorry. My business only allows me quick visits. Besides, I have a wife who's waiting for me."

Vesta took the cup of sugar from Sarah. "You are a marvel! You know, John, you may not believe this, but Fanny and I really respect what you've done."

John's face reflected a stricken look but quickly resumed a bland expression. He bowed his head jauntily. "I guess I'm my father's son," he said.

Suddenly the moment seemed strained as an awkward feeling descended on the three of them. Sarah reached out to Vesta and put her arm about her shoulders as she walked with her out the door. "I'll sit with the boys this weekend if you and Ed want to go out."

Vesta squeezed her mother's hand and called out to John wishing him a safe journey.

"And you have a safe birth," he shouted back.

When Sarah came back inside, John looked guiltily at her. "I have disconnected myself from my relatives, haven't I?" he said. "And I've done it purposely. You are the only truly emotional tie to my past that I have allowed myself." He went to Sarah and put his arms about her. "It's hard at times, ma. But just thinking of you and the sacrifices you made for us all gives me strength."

Sarah pushed her face up to kiss him. "You did the right thing," she said. "I know how hard it is to make just a little success. You need all your determination to do what you're doing. Don't let any sentiment for the past weaken your resolve. I love you, son."

John's mind shot back to his business in New York City and a restless feeling overcame him as he thought of his competition and all the money that could be made.

As John took the train to New York City, he went through his usual transformation. The devoted, indulgent son became a sharp-minded, watchful, and commanding personality. By the time he alighted at the train station in New York and hailed a horse cab in the busy street, he was completely absorbed with the business moves he intended to make when he reached his office. As a salesman for one of the biggest dry-goods businesses in the country, he made money and good contacts. He relished the freedom that the job gave him and the opportunity to make extra money in separate deals outside of the company. He put long hours into his work and saw less and less of Amy, whose disappointment with him showed in many little ways in their relationship. She had not understood why he discouraged her from making friends or refused to entertain, which she loved to do, until her father in a rare moment, when she confessed her unhappiness to him, told her of John's background. Then she understood his secrecy.

"Technically, he is still a slave," Marcel Poillon said concernedly. He seemed sympathetic to his daughter's shock. "He could be claimed by the owners of his mother and transported South."

"Oh no," Amy cried, sinking onto a chair. "He didn't tell me this!"

"I promised him that I would keep it secret," he said. "But, I thought, since you are not happy in the marriage, that you should know the truth about him."

"Oh Daddy! You were right! What am I going to do?" Amy could see the secret being whispered about New York amongst her friends and acquaintances and her ostracization. "We'll be disgraced."

"I'm afraid it could be worse. John would never be employed again."

Amy suddenly flared up in a fury. "He lied to me! He lied to me! I thought he had Spanish blood, not Negro blood."

"I'm sorry, my dear girl," Poillon said looking miserable. "I'll do anything to help you."

"But what can I do? We're married for good."

He went to her and put his arms about her. "We can do something," he said comfortingly. "We can have the marriage annulled."

"But how, Daddy?"

"Well, you said it yourself. He lied to you. You married him under false pretensions. He was not what he said he was. And the fact that he is the son of a slave, that fact alone will get you sympathy anywhere in the country."

Amy took out a handkerchief and dabbed at the tears on her cheek. "Daddy, you are so wonderful! I made a terrible mistake. But how are we going to do this? I know John very well and he will be determined to stop this. He wants me more as a trophy than as a wife, I think."

"I can get the right legal man to handle it quickly and efficiently. It will all be done quietly. There will be no discussion, no secrets bared, no reason given. But you must be absolutely sure that it is what you wish to do."

"But people are going to talk," Amy winced with pain. "I could not take that. I would die."

"You won't die. You will go on a European tour. You will live in London. You are young, attractive, and you will soon find someone better suited to you," Poillon said encouragingly. "What do you say?"

"I say yes! a thousand times yes!" Amy breathed a deep sigh of relief.

"You live with him without giving him a hint of what we are doing until I can arrange everything. I will have to keep him on in the business because he is under contract. We'll have to get his cooperation. I am sure when we explain his situation to him clearly, even the ambitious Mr. Lewis will raise no objections."

"Thank you, Daddy," Amy said hugging him. "I'll do whatever you want me to."

Amy Lewis had the same quiet determination and patience as her father. She had found John irresistible at first, but when she discovered that he loved his business more than herself and that their conversation revolved around his business affairs, her attraction for him diminished. Now that his origins had been revealed, what she had thought was of no consequence suddenly became extremely important, not only for her standing in society but for her respect for the man. His connection with slavery seemed to sully him and she found that intimacy with him was distasteful. She was not as experienced as her father in hiding her real feelings. John noticed her coldness and her forced friendliness when he returned from business that evening. He said nothing but thought to himself that her father must have told her about his background. It pained him to think that his wife would turn on him for a social blemish that was not of his doing. She could not have really loved him, he said to himself, not really. But then he had to admit that his love for her had waned after the first months of passion. She did not interest him. Her conversation dealt completely with gossip and she had not the spontaneity of the women he had known in the cafes and taverns, nor the integrity of his mother who stood for him as a paragon of womanhood. These people who condemned Sarah for being a slave were not worthy of kissing her hand, he thought angrily. He began to resent Poillon, his family, his firm, and anything to do with him. The man was a hypocrite. John had made close friends with the Coch brothers, who ran a more successful dry goods business on Cedar Street and had tried to persuade John to join their firm. John had resisted, thinking that he might be able to take over Poillon's firm someday, but, all of a sudden, he determined to make the move. He slept little that night and the next morning he went straight to the Coches' office and asked to be taken on as a salesman and given the prime customers that the Coch brothers had offered him. It was arranged that he begin work in the following week.

John said no word to Marcel Poillon but went about his business as usual. He waited for Poillon to make the first move because he was certain that father and daughter had a proposition to make to him. He knew the business mind well and, in particular, the Poillon mind. Beneath his friendly and unassuming exterior, he was upset and disillusioned. He tried to tell himself that the Poillons' reaction was normal. Being fearful of society's cruelty to those who broke its codes, Poillon was just doing the best for his daughter. But when he thought of Amy's desertion of him, he became even more convinced that no woman could compare with his mother. When he was summoned to Poillon's office on the morning of his last day at the firm, he was relieved that Poillon was finally acting. The suave mustachioed owner sat beside a large man with a stern broad face and angry eyes. This second man was Poillon's lawyer, who, after being introduced, got down to business.

"I have here a statement from your wife," he said, producing a sheet of paper. "She has taken refuge in her father's home this morning."

"Refuge?" John smiled and his eyes lit up with humour at Poillon. He glanced over the paper which stated that Amy wanted an annulment of their marriage, which had been based on a lie.

"I see," John said. "This comes as a surprise, because I understood Mr. Poillon to say that he would speak of my background to no one."

"You do confirm that you lied," the lawyer interjected.

"I did not lie. I believe I just intimated that Mr. Poillon lied to me."

"I could not keep the truth from my own daughter," Poillon said in a pique, "especially when you should have told her yourself."

"We won't argue about keeping secrets from our wives, shall we, gentlemen," John smiled mischievously. "Others may inform them of our secrets but that is usually to stir up trouble in the home." He glared at Poillon, his eyes flashing. "Amy and I fell in love. I still love her, but, it appears from this note that she does not love me. And why? Because I have a mother who was a slave. *Was!* I emphasize the word. My mother is a very fine woman. She is a beautiful woman. She is much admired."

"We are not here to talk about your mother," the lawyer said sharply. "If you contest your wife's desire to be free of you, we will take the case to court and expose you as a fraud."

"It is not that I am a fraud that concerns you," John said angrily. "It is my Negro background that is making you do this."

Poillon spoke up sharply, "No. It is the fact that you lied about your Negro background."

The lawyer put a restraining hand on his arm. "Please Marcel, recriminations and accusations are not helpful. Mr. Lewis has mentioned the subject that he knows we do not wish to be made public almost as much as he wishes it to remain secret. Let us do this in as amicable a way as possible. There are many reasons for the failure of marriages, and there is more than one reason in this case, I suspect. But the basic reason overrides all others. Do you agree, Mr. Lewis?"

John nodded. "As the world is fashioned at this time in America, I would be foolish to disagree. I can, of course, accept an annulment only if your side agrees to never say a word about my background—to anyone!"

"We will make that a condition of the annulment," the lawyer said quickly.

"That condition applies to you above all," John said firmly. "I do not trust your tribe. I must be absolutely sure that no word about me will ever issue from your mouth."

The lawyer sat back as if insulted, but seeing the emotion in John's blazing eyes, he said sincerely, almost humbly, "My dear man, I have no wish to hurt you. I swear to you that I shall never impart what I have learned about you and I shall never take advantage of this knowledge."

"If you draw up the papers, I shall go over them and sign them," John said. "I trust you to arrange this affair as quietly and confidentially as possible."

"It will be done," Poillon affirmed. "Amy is going to Europe."

John smiled ruefully. "To make the break even sharper. Well, I am going to make the break sharper yet. This is my last day with your firm. I am going elsewhere to save you the embarrassment of working with me and finding some excuse for terminating me in the future."

The relief John saw spread over Poillon's face amused him. It was with difficulty that he suppressed a laugh.

"That is a wise decision," the lawyer said, standing up and reaching out to shake John's hand.

John stood up and took the hand and looked into the lawyer's gray eyes. "I expect you to stay true to your word."

"I owe it to my client as well," the lawyer said. "Your secret is his daughter's secret too."

John took his hand away with a grateful grimace, nodded good-bye to Poillon and went to the door.

"Where will you be?" Poillon asked suddenly. "Should someone ask for you," he added quickly.

"At the Coch brothers," John said. He saw the surprise on Poillon's face that was quickly followed by concern. "You can reach me there," he said to the lawyer, "the sooner the better."

When he left, he felt Poillon's apprehension that he had joined a powerful competitor and was taking his knowledge of Poillon's business with him. As for himself, he felt rejuvenated. He was free to live a life that was answerable to no one. The so-called society of his wife was restrictive and unappealing now that he had experienced it. The real life was in the hurly-burly of the city, and his real work was in the exercise of his talents unrestricted by anyone.

John saw quickly that the Coches were not doing as well as their firm's reputation implied. The brothers had settled down to a complacent manner of running the business and overlooking problems that they seemed disinclined to fix. They had made money and were interested in maintaining the status quo, which was a dangerous position in the very competitive dry goods trade.

For one thing, their accounts were being kept badly. They fell behind in payments to dealers in the South and failed to collect from overseas traders. They made no effort to increase their distributing network to smaller retail stores in the New York-New Jersey area and as a result were in danger of losing them to the competition. John brought many of his customers at Poillon's with him, and, in order to serve them better, he demanded more action and foresight from the Coches. When he saw that the firm was caught in a rut owing to the old-fashioned ways of its complacent owners, he began talking with

393

two other men in the firm who felt as he did. John G. Haviland had been a salesman in the firm for years. A mild-mannered, round-faced fellow with graying hair, he was the main reason that the firm was still doing well. But he felt frustrated at the opportunities lost. William H. Lindsay was younger than John. A serious fellow with bushy eyebrows and a big drooping mustache that emphasized his seriousness, he was an energetic clerk who knew the business. Within six months, John persuaded them to help him take over the firm. Neither of them had the gumption nor the confidence to run a business, but with John's leadership they were prepared to combine their savings with his and buy out the Coches. First, of course, John had to demonstrate to the owners the failings of the firm and its bleak prospects. He then proceeded to prove that the business he brought the firm had revived it in the short term but could not sustain it for long. The Coch brothers reacted with surprise and resentment that their latest employee could be so bold as to challenge their many years of experience and knowledge, but, after listening to John's detailed analysis presented in his persuasive manner, they began to see that he was right and their anger at his presumption wilted under the penetrating power of his eyes. They gestured helplessly. At that point John called John Haviland into the office, Haviland having waited conveniently in the vicinity, and began to quiz him on the problems in the firm. Haviland's diagnosis was emotional with a strong undertone of frustration, but it did substantiate much of what John had been saying. The Coches might have dismissed the claims of their long-time employee if he had not been supported by John. But faced with the reasoning of both men, they resigned themselves to bringing in the changes that John suggested and admitted that the firm when seen in such a clear way would not last long in its present condition.

"It is not just your firm that concerns us," John said in a tone of admonishment. "Our careers are in jeopardy. The customers we serve are justified in wondering if we can service them properly."

"Look, my dear Lewis," the older brother said. "We want to help whichever way we can. You say what you want us to do, and, if it is within reason, we'll be glad to oblige."

"Will you?" John beamed a broad smile at the gentlemen sitting across from him. "My proposal may come as a surprise, but it is the only one that has prospect of success."

"And what is that?" asked the younger brother, leaning forward with an indulgent smile.

"Mr. Haviland and I will buy your firm at a reasonable price," John said simply.

The brothers looked shocked. They stared at one another and then at the two men confronting them. Finally, the older brother said, "Ours is an old family business. It is not for sale." He seemed to imply that John Lewis had made an improper suggestion.

"We would not take over your name," John said quickly. "With all respect, we think that the firm would have a better chance to survive under a new name."

The Coches frowned in disbelief.

"We will call the firm the Lewis and Haviland Dry Goods Company," Haviland spoke up with a smile. He was enjoying the disconcerted look of these men who had treated him cavalierly for years.

"Well, well," the older brother said, nodding, "you have been planning this little coup for some time, have you?"

"Out of necessity," John said. "Allow me to remind you that Mr. Haviland and I have the full confidence of our traders and buyers. They will come with us in any business we may set up. Since our combined contacts now comprise the majority of clients in this firm, it would be better for both you and ourselves if we could come to an amicable agreement. We ask that you think about the matter and let us know if you will sell to us and at what price. We are organizing our firm and can give you just a few days to consider, I am afraid."

The Coch brothers tried to appear calm and indifferent, but John could see that their minds were spinning. The elder brother stood up to signal that their discussion had ended. He said that he and his brother understood the situation clearly and would reply shortly. He feared John's determination and in hindsight regretted asking him to join the firm. Never in his experience had a salesman sized up the weaknesses of a firm and planned for its takeover in so commanding a fashion. He wondered if, after examining the firm's accounts, he would have to capitulate to John's demands. He and his brother could struggle with what was left of the firm after these men took away much of it, but what would be the use? He had been tired of the business for some time and his younger brother was not a good businessman. He smiled wanly at Haviland as he closed the door behind these two men who brought reality to them in such a sharp and disconcerting manner.

Within two days, John had an answer. The Coch brothers gave him a price for the firm. John made a counter offer and, after some dickering, it was accepted. The new firm Lewis and Haviland came onto the dry goods scene with an energy and ruthlessness that unnerved the competition. Most of the partners' ideas were adopted immediately. Lindsay reorganized the clerical and porter staff to be more efficient and modern in its handling of the goods. The profits that could be made as an owner surprised John who had expected a large leap in his income but not to the great amounts that he actually realized. There was much money to be made on commissions and in resale. John enjoyed making arrangements with traders which undercut other merchants and added to his coffers in the long term. He hired agents to gather the latest news on the availability and prices of commodities, and he stayed ahead of others by his quick decisions and sometimes unprincipled practices. He loved the freedom and power that money brought him. He frequented the theatres and entered into the gaiety of New York night life. It was a society that honoured him for his wealth and accepted without question whoever he said that he was. His generosity and sense of fun earned him many friends. He soon gained a reputation as a flamboyant personality who had powerful friends in politics and in the underworld. He purchased a rich bachelor apartment from which he entertained businessmen, artists, government officials and those in other fields that he felt he might need in the future. His marriage was forgotten. The Poillon family had disappeared from the social register when Marcel Poillon lost his business, largely as a result of the inroads made by Lewis and Haviland. Aside from the automatic monthly payments to his mother and his occasional letters to her, he had little contact with Simcoe. Theo Hunt visited him once a year. Their discussions centred on the slavery situation and the information that John had gathered on his trips into the Southern States to confer with traders and suppliers. Through Hunt he contributed to abolitionist societies but dared not take an active part in anti-slavery activities. He was regarded by everyone he met in business and at all levels of society as a rich and powerful white man with a hint of Spanish ancestry.

He seemed in perfect control of his life until 1855. Early in that year, he met a beautiful young actress at a dinner given by a stockbroker friend. Her name was Alexis Taylor and he fell in love with her. She was twenty-one and just getting prominent roles at the Bowery Theatre. Her voice attracted John just as much as her splendid figure and beautiful face. It seemed to speak to his heart and stayed with him when he tried to sleep at night. She found him exciting, sophisticated, and mysterious. His riches opened doors to her in her career. She got better roles and became better known to audiences. He squired her to gala events and theatre parties. They dined at Delmonico's and mixed with his rich friends. The night life south of 14th Street was one continuous party in which the guests moved from cafe to cafe into the early hours of the morning. Miss Taylor kept her own apartment and her independence. She was not happy when she told John that she was pregnant, but he was very happy and told his closest friends. She refused to marry John because as a married woman she would be less attractive to theatre-goers and feared, rightly, that managers would deny her roles. John showered her with gifts and paid for her every want as he waited for the child to arrive. He planned for a large party of his friends after the baby was born.

His enthusiasm did not distract him from his business, however, for he was capable of separating his private from his business life. He successfully defended himself in court against suits brought by business associates, who felt that he had misled them and cheated them. He forced other firms to close and took over their business. The name John D. Lewis carried respect amongst the merchants of New York and those who feared him tried in vain to find some weakness which they could exploit. When he was forced to testify in court cases, he parried questions asked about his past by his opponents' lawyers. His stock answer was that he had no living relatives. He remained suspicious of all lawyers, particularly his own, to whom he refused any information about his background. He learned to draw up his own contracts and keep his need for lawyers to a minimum. His secrecy was laid to his desire to keep anyone from knowing the extent of his wealth; no one guessed that he was the son of a slave or that he had black blood in his veins.

For the months of Alexis's pregnancy John was attentive only to her. He cut down on his socializing and his meetings with his shady acquaintances, who did the occasional work of intimidating his debtors and sabotaging his competitors. For the summer months of 1855 he took his loved-one to his cottage on Fire Island off the coast of Long Island where they played in the water, partied with neighbours and relaxed in the fresh and cooler air. John Haviland ran the business and came to the Island every second or third week to report on its state. For once in his life, John suppressed his driving desire for business transactions, for the high excitement of dealing with sharp-minded men, whose motives he divined and whom he outwitted, and indulged that tender and trusting side of him, which he had bottled up unwittingly and now unstopped and poured from his soul in an expressive love for Alexis Taylor and their unborn child.

At the close of September, they returned to the City and lived in his apartment. He eased himself back into his work, limiting himself to only half of his usual activity. When Alexis Taylor gave birth, he had the best doctors attending her that he could find. It was a difficult birth. The child was a healthy baby girl and Alexis seemed transformed when she held the child in her arms. But she was worn out from the labour and soon relapsed into a very tired state. John's happiness began to fade as he realized how ill she was. He urged the doctors to do all they could to revive her, but she passed away a few days later. John was devastated. Leaving the child with nurses, he went back to his home on Fire Island, which had been deserted by its summer residents, and mourned in bitter loneliness. He reconsidered whether his hard work and his determination to overcome the challenges that life dealt him really mattered. This tragedy was so unjust, so brutal, so soul-destroying that he wondered if he were ever meant to be happy.

It took him two weeks to purge his sadness and return to business with an angry dedication to proving himself as better than anyone. The thought that his daughter was the cause of his loved-one's death crossed his mind, but he rejected it as unjust. He loved his daughter, but he could not look after her. The child would remind him constantly of the mother and keep him in a state of grief and incapable of making decisions in business. He discussed the matter with some of his friends and decided on giving the child to a Catholic convent to be brought up by nuns. He would pay for her needs but he would not see her. He had her baptised Lizzie Barton Taylor, the name which her mother had chosen before she died, and put all thoughts of mother and child out of his mind. He re-entered the merchant world with a new energy and an increased resolve to dominate his business rivals.

29

The prospect of civil war within the States depressed trade and business and threatened the province with a slow decline, dampening the people's spirits. Simcoe reflected this general malaise: its businesses closed; shops were boarded up; the tailoring, tin-making, and carriage shops laid off their employees. The exuberant spirit that had always marked Simcoe died and left it sombre and quietly bitter. There were bright spots such as the Norfolk House. George Battersby returned from California a rich man and set up this enterprise. He brought back a gold watch for a surprised Hank Power and presented it to him on the stage ride from Paris to Simcoe. They had stopped at the tavern in Burford when George, in a thick brown beard and mustache that disguised him, called Hank into the bar room. In a loud voice he called for a round of drinks for everyone present and, stepping up to Hank, he announced who he was. As Hank shook his hand jubilantly, George pulled the gold watch and gold chain from his pocket and said that he had discovered it on the gold fields in California. Hank's eyes rounded in astonishment as George handed him the watch and claimed to everyone that he always kept his promises. For months thereafter, Hank showed off the watch to his passengers coming from Paris to Simcoe and promoted the benefits of staying at Battersby's Norfolk House.

Sarah no longer did washing. The money that she got from John was sufficient for her needs. The years of bending over sewing and then laundering and ironing in primitive conditions had worn her out physically. She felt compelled to help out Vesta whose behaviour bordered on the anarchic at times. Vesta spent liberally and often was short at tax-paying time. Sarah had to collect the rents from her tenants living at the back of the property. But Vesta was educated and kept her accounts in order. Her problem was that she trusted people too much. Sarah noticed that certain persons were eyeing the land that they lived on because it was becoming prime real estate. Vesta took out mortgages on it whenever she needed a large amount of money to pay her debts. She was able to pay them off from stints of hard work, but Sarah worried that that might not always be the case. Her concerns centred on Vesta and her children. Ed James, who preferred to be called Walking Turtle, was a carefree man who wandered restlessly in search of adventure or diversion. Unlike many of the Mohawks he could not settle down to agricultural pursuits but made money doing odd jobs or acting as a guide to hunters and fishers whenever the richer class of person decided to break away for a week or two from his banking and land interests. The son that he had by Vesta looked a lot like him and was almost white-skinned. Ed dropped by to stay with Vesta every second or third weekend, but he did not take a real interest in his boy until he learned to walk and talk. Meanwhile the two older boys were at school in Simcoe, and, lacking the guidance of a father such as Avery Shaw, who was living in one of the new villages north of Toronto, they tended to run with a wild gang of boys. Sarah tried to take care of them because Vesta was being pushed to compete in her dressmaking business against the large firms with their machines and mail-order catalogues. To bring a male presence into their lives, other than the teachers at the grammar school, Vesta relied on her friends Zeb Landon and Tom McMicken, the blacksmith, to take them to the fairs and circuses that came to Simcoe with their own children. Walking Turtle took the boys fishing and taught them the secrets of hunting, but his carefree life-style encouraged their rebellious instincts. Sarah despaired of these boys developing the talents and sense of responsibility of her son John. Recognizing this and hoping to gladden his mother, Henry Lewis on a visit to Simcoe announced that his new-born son was to be called John, implying that the child would emulate the entrepreneurship of his namesake.

Henry worked long hours in Hamilton. His wife Ellen took advantage of his absence from home to consort with a group of men who made their living by gambling at cards, at the races, and in the blood sports. She found their company exhilarating and much preferable to the stodgy responsible Henry. Their son, however, suffered from inattention. Disgusted by Ellen's carelessness and worried that his son would come to harm when left alone, he brought him to his sister Mary to be raised in Simcoe. Since Mary's daughter was in her teens and self-sufficient, Mary had the time to look after him like a mother. George Smith was pleased to adopt him as a son. Sarah, therefore, had another young grandchild to help care for. She loved this little John and hoped that his black skin would not hinder him from knowing the success of his uncle in the changing world to come. All Sarah's interest was focused on her grandchildren. Now in her sixties, she was older than most of the townspeople, the majority being young adults, either recently arrived from Europe or migrating from town to town in Upper Canada in search of work. Her close friends died. Lucinda Landon for one. This independent, strongly motivated woman, acted as a staff for Sarah to lean upon in difficult times and as an inspiration. Their friendship grew through their recognition that they were much alike. Some old friends remained such as William and Charity Rusling. William still dropped by her cottage to read a poem to her every so often.

"Sarah darling!" he cried outside her door one day. "Open and let in this ray of sunshine."

The rollicking, good-humoured and unpredictable young man she had known when she arrived in Simcoe had become a pixy-like, white-haired old gentleman with rosy cheeks and twinkling eyes. He could always make her laugh. She swung open the door and stood back expecting a rush of words as usual.

"The story I am fond of telling, about being pursued by wolves in the dead of winter and shooting some to distract the others to eat them rather than me—you remember?" He quick-stepped to the kitchen table and sat down. "Well, my dear, just listen to this." He held a sheet of paper up to read.

"We foiled the wolves when we were young
And many heroic tales we sung
Now old, we count our days
While our young friends we amaze
They think that we've escaped the grave.

The wolves no longer pursue us, friend,
No wild life left for us to offend.
On silent nights, though, when wolf's breath
Taints our sleep with scents of death,
We happily remember what we gave.

For it matters not the wolves we fooled
But the love instilled in children schooled."

Sarah clapped her hands. "Wonderful, Bill. You make me feel good. Leave it. I want Vesta to read it."

"Do you really like it?" he asked in that surprised fashion that Sarah had come to know after countless readings. "Then, I'll make you a copy." He pulled paper from his pocket and scribbled out the poem while Sarah recalled the first time he read her a poem when in her cabin on Joseph Culver's farm she sat astounded that an educated man would bother to read to an illiterate and recent slave like her.

So many young families and single people in their early twenties were arriving from the British Isles to take up work in the local industries that Sarah felt herself removed from the activities, from the heart of the village as it were. Her favourite moments were in preparing for family picnics in the vast open lands south of Stanley Street, which, although owned by the village registrar Walsh, were open to everyone to enjoy. The colourful birds, the melodies of their singing, the migrating geese in flying formation, the laughter of the children at play, and the happy talk of her daughters gave her supreme satisfaction and happiness. Sometimes she would walk with Mary a couple of miles further south to see the grave of her baby daughter and look at the tall poplar that signalled John's birth. She knew that John when he came to Simcoe, visited this tree and took confidence from it, as if it were tendering its soul to meld with his. As long as it was strong and prospering so would he, she thought, and she spoke about it to Joseph Culver. He vowed to let nothing happen to it, but he was getting old now, and his farm could soon be sold to some new immigrant who would not have such sentiments.

Sarah spent some of her time in an organization to help black refugees settle in Simcoe and find the means of earning a livelihood. The Wilberforce Society found the funding for the organization, but there were also people who did not belong to that society who helped out. For instance, Sam Tisdale was too aggressive as an abolitionist to be acceptable to some Society members, but his help in finding employment for the runaway slaves was welcomed. Sarah would canvass for old clothes and shoes, which she would distribute to these needy people. The black community in Simcoe was large now and more cohesive, as if it were forming a defense against its enemies. The abolitionist societies in Canada had disagreements with the societies in the United States over the proper tactics to be employed. Factions developed, which were embittered by jealousies and suspicions. It was really the unsettled nature of the communities, the uneasiness over the uncertainty of direction, the fears of sudden reversals of policy, that kept the workers, ethnic groups and civil libertarians on their guard. Just when one thought that the constabulary and judicial system were functioning with fairness to all, some black person accused of a crime would be returned to the States without a hearing, let alone a trial. Since the overwhelming majority of Canadians wanted no fugitive returned to the States, such incidents inflamed sections of the populace, who used the newspapers to hurl invective at the officials guilty of such practices. All blacks, therefore, had to be alert to the tricks of bounty hunters, who worked with Canadians eager to collect bounty money advertised for the return of slaves.

At this time Vesta's problems worried Sarah. Vesta was being pressed to pay taxes on her land. She could not raise rents on her properties, her business had declined, and Ed James contributed little to her household. Thanks to Duncan Campbell's indulgence, she paid off his mortgage on her property a year late. A month later she took out a mortgage on the lot which she had got from George Kent and months later she took out a mortgage on two more lots, which obligated her to pay back sixty pounds within a year. She would accept no money from Sarah other than the rent for Sarah's cottage. She was an intelligent businesswoman who could handle her affairs every bit as well as John Lewis, she said. Sarah admired her determination and had become resigned to her taste in companions. When Sarah looked back at her own life she saw it as a series of unexpected circumstances that only her determined spirit and luck brought her through. She wondered if Vesta had the luck, however, and, when her son Henry visited from Hamilton, she told him and Mary that she was going to will her possessions to Vesta because her other children could get along well enough without. This was true. Mary and George Smith were getting by tolerably well; Henry, despite the extravagances of his wife, ran a profitable livery service in Hamilton, which helped him live comfortably; and Fanny's family were well off in Norwich.

Vesta worked long hours at tailoring dresses in order to compete with the cheap manufactured clothes that Leonard Sovereign bought in the States in bulk at low prices. Sovereign flaunted his wealth by building expensive residences to the north of the village. He tried to soften the resentment of other storekeepers and win the respect of the public by financing such public benefits as the skating rink, which he built on the border of the Lynn River beside his lumber yard. The failure of competing businesses and the disappearance of their owners into poverty or servantship seemed to go unnoticed by others, who were concerned with their own welfare first. In such a competitive society, men watched and waited for the right opportunity to increase their wealth. These men were either in league with other gentlemen who were in the market for such lands or knew to whom they could sell the lands once they were acquired. These were the practices that made a part of the population rich at the expense of the other part, who depended on their work rather than their capital to make a living. The rich served a need in the community for they lent money to men like Sandy McPherson who used it to start his business in Waterford and spent years paying it back with interest. Just as McPherson made the last payment to his creditor Leonard Sovereign, there was a serious economic downturn and he sold his business to another store owner, who employed him and seemed to weather the storm. But after working for him for two years at a deferred salary of thirty pounds a month and lending him money, McPherson had to take him to court to get the seven thousand and four hundred pounds that he was owed. Thus, Vesta faced a problem common to every business in a shrinking economy and like them got no sympathy from her creditors.

Sarah's fear of losing their property intensified as Vesta worked to repay the mortgage which she obtained from Albert Toms, who had a reputation for seizing land when mortgages could not be repaid. Property was the only thing that could protect her family, she thought. Loss of land meant a loss of status in the community and the tearing away of all that they had come to love as belonging to them; it would drive them into the dispossessed, the vagrant class, seeking shelter wherever they could afford to find it; it would make all those years of struggle that brought them from slavery to respectable citizenship appear to be in vain; it could mean a loss of rights and identity, and make her family vulnerable like those Negroes being arrested on false charges and spirited back to the States before they could be brought to trial. Sarah remembered her sister telling her of their mother's Irish father, who had been one of a hundred poor contracted as servants for the New World, finding himself sold by the ship captain to thugs in some wilderness port and being driven inland into slavery. A fall into poverty led to slavery, she warned; her father's claim to be a servant entitled to freedom after seven years was ignored. But he had left a sense of injustice with his offspring, which burned and rankled through two generations until it gave her the courage to flee to freedom. Now Vesta and her children could fall back into that gaping hole out of which she had climbed. Sarah did not mention any of this to Vesta because she could see the fear in Vesta's eyes whenever they discussed paying off the mortgage and how much short they were.

Toms seemed to dedicate himself to the mortgages business and enlisted the help of the young clerks in the court house to tip him off to landowners who looked to be in trouble. These clerks, who were from England where they had learned to write in a clear full hand, signed themselves as "writers" when they witnessed legal transactions. Under Toms's influence they called themselves "gentlemen". Men training for the law had to adopt a higher form of address in order to gain the respect their positions merited, Toms explained. This lively, gregarious man, with high arching eyebrows and a Van Dyke beard, was a common fixture in Simcoe and continued to take part in the public debates as representative of the conservative side. He knew Sarah but never recognized her in public because she had been a washerwoman. He chatted amicably with Vesta whenever they met, however, and implied that she could depend on him if she needed help.

Just after Vesta was forced to sell a lot fronting on Kent Street, Walking Turtle was knifed to death in a tavern fight with factory workers from Bill Mathews' gang in Brantford. No witnesses could be found. It was termed an accident. Vesta was devastated and wept for days. Sarah tried to console her but it was only through her work that eventually Vesta overcame her grief.

Sarah thought of appealing to John for help, but Vesta was too proud to write to him, and Sarah respected his wish to have nothing to do with the "black" side of his family lest a mistake be made that could incriminate him, ruin his career. Duncan Campbell by his unfriendly manner intimated he wanted nothing more to do with her problems after Vesta was late in paying his mortgage. Moreover, Sarah felt strange about Duncan's friendship with Albert Toms who worked with him on real estate deals.

Vesta's eldest son Alexander, who was over twenty-one and apprenticed to Tom McMicken in the farrier's trade, took responsibility for the younger boys: Thomas, who attended the Simcoe grammar school and Edwin, Walking Turtle's son, who had just started school.

When Sarah felt down, she turned to her friend Maria Parker whose cheerfulness made all adversity seem conquerable. She had avoided that strong-minded lady for some weeks because she did not want to inflict her woes onto someone else, but the pressure on her mind had become too intense for her to bear on her own.

Maria lived in the black district on Chapel Street. Sarah grasped the large metal knocker and let it fall against a metal plate. The heavy thud seemed to catch her sombre mood. She waited half-hoping that no one would answer. When no one did, she was reluctant to knock again, but, forcing herself, she let the knocker fall again, sounding like a judge's gavel affirming a judgment. It was a gray morning and the streets were deserted. She felt that fate had determined that she be alone with her troubles and turned to walk away. The door opened and Maria, smiling and laughing, her large frame filling the threshold, cried: "Sarah! You just caught me with a friend!"

"Oh, I'm sorry," Sarah apologized and took a step away.

"No," Maria seized her arm. "Come in. I want you to meet him."

"I'm not in the right condition to meet anyone," Sarah said, trying to pull away.

"It'd be good for you," Maria insisted, tugging on Sarah's arm.

Sarah, sighing, allowed herself to be coaxed into the house and relinquished her coat to Maria, whose effervescent mood both surprised and began to intrigue Sarah.

"He's a wonderful man," Maria whispered. "I been seeing him off and on for months now."

Sarah looked at her. "Your husband's not coming home?"

Maria made a waving gesture as if to signify that her husband had been out of her life for a long time. "You talk to him for a while, I'll bet you'll feel better. He's like tonic to me. Better than anything Old Horace can cook up," she laughed.

Sarah caught sight of her face in a mirror and, stopping to smooth her hair and give a rub to her cheeks, she followed Maria into the sitting room.

A black man of medium height, rather portly, with a strong face and a pleasant expression, stood by the window. He stepped forward in a modest manner to take Sarah's hand and smile slightly.

Sarah heard his name as John Anderson. His intelligent eyes seemed to look right into her and his manner put her at ease. As she heard Maria speak of her enthusiastically as a good friend, she had a strange premonition that this man was to mean a great deal to her in the future. He was broad-shouldered and respectable-looking, so she could understand Maria's attraction, but it was his spirit that attracted Sarah, as if his personality gave an assurance that her worries would be resolved happily. He spoke with a slight drawl that placed him as coming from Missouri, she thought, but his self-assurance implied that he had left his days of slavery far in his past. He lived in Caledonia, a village on the Grand River on the road to Hamilton, he said. He was a plasterer and met Maria when he was working under the master plasterer, John Diggs from Simcoe. Diggs, a black, had the best reputation as a plasterer. His services were in constant demand, which required him to hire helpers, whom he sometimes sent to do small jobs such as asking Anderson to reinforce a wall of Maria Parker's house. From the moment he plastered Maria's wall, Anderson was a welcome guest in her home. This time he was in Simcoe for a couple of days before returning to Caledonia.

Maria excused herself to bring them some morning tea. While listening to Anderson talk about Diggs, Sarah felt the oppression on her mind to be lifting. She responded to his questions in an open way, which was unusual for her when discussing her past. She admitted to being upset when she heard that war between the States seemed inevitable because it would extend into Canada and take her back to the life she had been born into. The threat of retribution for escaping from her masters, which haunted her, seemed to be catching her up. But then, in response to his gentle reasoning that war was not inevitable, she admitted that she was really depressed by her feeling of helplessness against the creditors of her daughter. Her land and house marked the results of all her struggles for personal freedom and advancement in the system. She blurted this out to Anderson, who watched her with concern, and, when she stopped talking, told her that her fears were the fears of all black people. But, he said, that she could not take on the worries of war and its aftermath, she could only look to herself in her own small space.

Seeing Sarah's face reflect the torment in her mind, he asked her to listen to his own story, which worried him at times, but which he was able to discount in favour of the good that it brought him. Escaping from a vicious new master, who threatened to beat him within an inch of his life, Anderson fled north. Postbills were issued everywhere offering a large reward for his capture. After two weeks on the road, he heard a white farmer command him to stop, which he did and explained to the farmer and his sons that he was on business for his master in the south. The farmer, suspicious, took Anderson prisoner. As they walked toward the nearest town jail, Anderson leaped a fence and ran into the fields. When the younger men followed him, he doubled-back through the woods, losing them, but ran into the farmer who tried to capture him. Anderson parried the knife thrust of the farmer and, with his own knife, stabbed the farmer to the ground. He reached the border without more trouble. Two weeks after he arrived in Canada, he heard that the farmer had died of his wounds. A reward of $1000 for Anderson's arrest as a murderer was issued, which set detectives and bounty hunters searching for him. To be a hunted man who faced certain execution if returned to Missouri was depressing enough, he said, but to be called a murderer when he was resisting capture, that was truly depressing. Coincidentally, the dead man's name was Digges, and when working for the plasterer John Diggs, Anderson asked him if there were a connection. There was, he laughed, but John Diggs dropped the 'e' to differentiate himself from that large slave-holding clan in Missouri.

Sarah cautioned him about repeating his story because there were unscrupulous blacks about.

"I only tell it to friends," Anderson smiled. "And I count you as a friend, Mrs. Lewis."

"You've helped me to think positive," she said gratefully. "I'll try to see the benefits to me. But can you be sure that the bad won't catch up with you?"

Anderson smiled. "You can stay a step ahead of the bad if you try," he chuckled.

The noise of the swinging door opening announced the return of Maria with a tray of teacups and tea pot. "I hope I gave you enough time to get acquainted," she said. "But I got to watch it with you, Sarah, 'cause you are a very pretty woman."

"She is," Anderson laughed, "but I like your tea, Maria."

As Sarah laughed with them, she felt a relief come over her body such as she had not known for a long time. It was only when she heard the town bell strike twelve that the spell of good companionship was broken and she took her leave to return to her worries in the real world.

Mary saw her mother coming and ran to open the door. She fretted over Sarah's fits of despondency and noticed that news of the world at large could plunge her into despair. Her mind seized upon and exaggerated gossip to a point that Mary herself would have been terrified for her future if she had believed it. The latest news created rumours that whites would rise up to kill blacks in revenge because, according to the newspapers, as soon as two black men and a white man were arrested in Brantford for killing a sixty-year old white postal deliverer, demagogues took advantage of the angry mood to whip up gangs of Irish workers to attack black people in the streets. Bill Mathews, the mayor, swaggered about promising the death penalty.

"Have you heard the news from Brantford?" she asked when Sarah reached the door.

"No, dear," Sarah said attentively.

Thankful, Mary waited until Sarah had taken off her coat and was sitting before she carefully told her of the murder in Brantford. If she gave a little information at a time, she thought, the news would not be so alarming. Sarah had to hear it this way because she would inevitably hear it from others and become terrified. In Mary's telling, Bill Mathews promised the men a fair trial.

Sarah appeared to take the news calmly. She winced at the motive of theft and shook her head mournfully. Sarah knew of Bill Mathews' reputation as the leader of the Irish workmen against blacks. George Smith had several run-ins with him and his followers who, since they had paved his way to mayor, became more over-bearing towards blacks and Indians. The insufferable pretensions of Mathews, a highly dramatic character to begin with, became worse with the continual support of Attorney-General John A. Macdonald. As a condition for forming a coalition with George Etienne Cartier's conservatives of Canada East (later called Quebec), Macdonald's party had to establish separate schools for Roman Catholics in Canada West, and thus Macdonald needed the support of Mathews' Irish Catholics to overcome opposition from

Irish Protestant Orangemen. George Smith held his nose and continued to advise the blacks of Simcoe to vote for Macdonald's conservatives nevertheless because they more than the reformers would protect blacks from extradition to the States. He told Sarah that it was sometimes better to countenance racists in small places in order to keep anti-racists in power in the big places. Little did he guess that his philosophy was to be sorely tested in the months to come.

The politics were abstract to Sarah, who saw Mathews as bad and Macdonald as good despite their being political allies. She surprised Mary by telling her not to worry, that Attorney-General Macdonald would prevent Mayor Bill Mathews from doing harm.

"That's right, Ma," Mary smiled encouragingly. "Let us forget about the news and help me plan for supper tonight."

Sarah nodded sweetly and seemed to think of the foods they could cook, but a darkening look to her eyes betrayed her thoughts for the men arraigned for murder. Her presentiment of danger in this incident proved to be prophetic in the weeks to come. One of the murderers, the white man, turned crown's evidence against his black accomplices; at that point the black men confessed to the crime, but said that the white man shot the postal worker. The blacks were sentenced to hang while the white informer was given life in prison. George Smith lost his temper when he heard the verdict. He learned that the white was the leader and had convinced the others, who were deeply in debt, that they would get large sums from the stolen mail, yet he alone was saved from hanging—and he was white!

"Mathews is behind it," he told Mary. "The man is the worst kind of racist! He stirs up the crowd for the sake of his political ambitions."

In early June, the night before the public hangings, Smith rode to Brantford and registered in the Kirby Hotel. The town's streets swarmed with riotous white men shouting with anger and defiance. Smith was not intimidated. A tall barrel-chested man, he strode along the wooden sidewalks watching the aimless crowds and listening to the discussions that broke out on street corners. He was pleased to hear that many whites were questioning the verdict and some were questioning the confessions of the black men which were written in language that they were incapable of expressing. Others, furious that anyone would question the verdict, shouted back at them. As men went in and out of taverns, drinking with friends and arguing their points of view, a mood of belligerence invaded the night air. Smith sensed that fights would soon break out in the streets. He hurried under the gaslights to a tavern frequented by blacks. Among the thousands of men from outlying districts who drove their wagons to Brantford to witness the first public hangings were hundreds of black men.

When Smith reached the tavern, it was crammed with noisy drinkers, most of them black, and many were sitting at outside tables and standing with their beers along the front and sides of the building. When he reached the bar, Smith recognized a group of men who acted as correspondents for the Emancipation Society in Cleveland and relayed information on events and opinions from the areas in which they lived to the Society's Board. They made room for him to stand in their circle when he approached, a beer glass in his hand. A middle-aged man who ran a bakery shop was related to the two men to be hanged. They used to work off and on for him and liked playing practical jokes on him, on the customers, on anyone, so he had to let them go because they were not dependable. They were always looking for an easy way to make a living.

"Nothing wrong with that," said an older man with a thick white mustache.

The others smiled and nodded in agreement.

"It's true then that they also confessed to trying to rob a train?" Smith asked the baker.

"That's right, George," the baker chuckled. "That white man who testified against them, he's the one that had all the ideas. They were silly boys, but I never thought they'd murder anyone. God! That's so bad for us!"

Above the din of conversation, they heard a roar of voices from the street.

"Listen to that!" warned the man with the mustache. "Whitey's out on the hunt again."

Smith pushed through the crowd followed by the others into the street. Across the street under the light from a street lamp stood a wiry Irishman backed up by a large contingent of white men who seemed to dwarf him with their height. The Irishman shouted at the blacks outside the tavern, who were showing minimal interest in him. "You!" He shook his finger at them. "Obey the laws or you will end up like your friends—on the gallows. That's a warning to you," he added menacingly.

"It's Bill Mathews," the baker said to Smith.

"I know," Smith smiled. "He's had too much to drink."

"I'll hang any nigger who steps out of line!" Mathews shouted, emboldened by the quietness of the black men watching him. "The two tomorrow are just a beginning."

Some of the men behind him shouted encouragement. "That a' boy, Bill!" and "Give 'em hell!"

"Be careful yourself," Smith shouted out to him. "You'll get arrested for disorderly conduct, you drunken bastard."

Mathews stepped back as if he had been hit. He looked round in amazement until he detected Smith standing slightly in front of the men who had come out of the building with him. "So it's the Pimpernel," he said contemptuously. "Your luck is going to come to an end pretty soon. You go accusing people wrongly like that, you'll end up in jail, just as sure as I am Mayor here."

"As Mayor, your place is not in the streets picking fights with your Irish gang backing you up to do your fighting," Smith said angrily.

"You need to be taught a lesson," Mathews cried and took several steps toward him threateningly.

"By you?" Smith laughed. "Come closer then."

Most of the blacks had exited the tavern by now and stood watching the confrontation with interest. They laughed derisively when Mathews stopped advancing and stood indecisively in the middle of the street.

"People tell me you're a good actor, but you're no fighter," Smith said with a smile. "Leastways, I remember you as a rebel running from a fight with MacNab some years ago."

Mathews' face turned red under the lamplight and then became contorted with fury. "That's enough from you, nigger. Go get him, boys."

There was a collective catching of breath among the blacks as they watched scores of Irishmen brandishing clubs come from round the corner of the building behind Mathews.

At that moment a couple of constables stepped out of the crowd and confronted the advancing Irishmen. They gave Mathews a stern look and he, blinking, seemed to recover his composure. "Not here!" he shouted. "Come away. That's an order."

The men wielding clubs stopped short and followed Mathews, who walked away conversing with the two constables. The police force, although newly organized, was becoming adept at arresting street fights and riots. Its quick solving of the murder brought it a respect that Mathews did not wish to jeopardize. As the white men filed away, the blacks turned in relief back to their conversations.

"You better have a bunch of us around you tonight, George," the baker said. "That Mathews is sneaky. No telling what he'll do to get even."

Smith shook his head and was about to give a reason when he felt a tug on his arm. There grinning up at him, his poet's eyes bright and excited, was Jeb.

"That was great, George!" Jeb laughed. "You handled him like the master you are."

"Hello, Jeb," Smith snorted in surprise. "You working in this town?"

"In Paris," Jeb said. "Foreman in a plaster mill. Glad I don't live in Brantford. There's a lot of ugly feeling here!" He looked round at the others watching him. "Saw three street battles tonight and a lot of little fights. This place is real ugly."

"It builds character," said the man with the mustache sardonically.

"Well," Smith yawned. "This character is going to his hotel so's he can get up early to see the hangings."

"Kirby House?" Jeb asked and when Smith nodded, he said, "I'll come with you."

"We'll go with you too," said a couple of men behind them. "Safety in numbers," one of them laughed.

On the way to their hotel, Jeb told Smith of his adventures on the Great Lakes ships of which he tired eventually and returned to odd jobs

414

on land. Smith recognized the same wandering spirit in Jeb as in himself with the difference that Jeb tried to avoid trouble whereas he sought it out. When he came down to the hotel lobby at dawn the next morning, Jeb was waiting for him to have breakfast. It seemed to Smith that Jeb found him a protective force in a dangerous time. They went early to Victoria Park in the mid-town where the scaffold had been erected to await the executions at nine o'clock. Thousands had gathered in the park during the night and thousands more now joined them searching for good vantage points. A hum of expectation emanated from the multitude. Smith noticed few women, but the number of spectators seemed double the town's population. As they waited in the warm morning sun, Smith became reflective and stopped replying to Jeb's questions. Jeb, non-plussed, began chatting with the men near him and became more and more nervous and excitable as the hour approached. A few fights broke out here and there and constables rushed about subduing them. Finally, from the jail next to the court-house the two black men, having bid tearful good-byes to their wives, emerged accompanied by a Reverend. They mounted the scaffold and the Reverend, his voice cracking with emotion, announced that they had confessed the crime to him. A murmur of approval swept over the thousands, as if that by that act the condemned had prepared themselves to meet their maker. Smith had tears in his eyes as he watched them being fitted with white caps which were pulled over their eyes and the nooses put around their necks. The men began to sing in unison. The spectators fell silent as the men's voices soared into the morning air. Smith recognized the song as "Amazing Grace"—how they had been blind but now saw the light. The trapdoor was sprung and the men fell, their voices choked off suddenly. All was quiet as they twisted in death throes. "O Lord, if there is a Lord," Smith prayed, "put an end to their misery." But the end did not come for twenty minutes. A collective sigh issued from the crowd as the bodies stopped twitching, and slowly voices from here and there began to be heard, plaintive, sombre, and, in a few cases, shrill laughter. Smith turned to Jeb who was holding tightly onto his arm.

"Think of it as a nightmare," he said. "Then get back to work as if nothing happened."

"That nightmare's gonna come back night after night," Jeb said ruefully. "I shouldn't have come, but I couldn't help it."

"Nothing's changed," Smith said emphatically. "But there's a civil war comin' in the States. That's goin' to change a lot."

They parted with a handshake. On his ride back to Simcoe, Smith tried to imagine what a civil war would mean for black people. It might be like the hanging, and after the horror of it, nothing would change. But it could destroy the mentality that took slavery as a right. Whatever happened, he wished it would come sooner than later. He was getting very tired of conducting frightened, traumatized persons out of savagery to freedom year after year in one unending stream of black humanity. And he was appalled at the psychological paralysis that was increasingly instilled in Negroes by cruel slave masters intent on destroying any hopes emboldened by the debates over slavery. This spiritual trauma had affected the northern states and swept into Canada. Even his mother-in-law, Sarah, who had been an exemplar of independence and bold initiative for decades, was beginning to fall prey to that psychological blighting of the mind, he thought. It swept over one like the wings of a huge black bird and blocked out the light.

30

When hardship strikes, it first presses down and wears out a person, and then, like lightning, it crushes one with a mighty blow against which there can be no possible defense. One November evening, when Sarah could not sleep from worry, she thought she heard a noise against the side of her cottage, but since there was no repetition, she assumed it was a branch from a tree caught in the cold north wind that had descended on Simcoe. A few minutes later, however, she smelt smoke, and, rising to investigate, she saw flames enveloping the wooden structure. Seizing a few clothes and whatever monies she had, she ran outdoors shouting for help. One side of the cottage and the roof was in flames. She stood in amazement and fear watching the destruction of her home, her security, and her memories. She could not feel the cold, and she was just dimly aware of Vesta and her children standing by her side and then the arrival of the blacksmith Jerry Curtis and other neighbours, who stood with her to watch the fire consume the building as if it were a funeral pyre. Jerry put his huge arm about her to try to comfort her, and then only did she break into tears. The others had tears in their eyes because they knew how hard Sarah had worked to gain what little she had. The wind brought a light snow to cover the ground. Vesta's eldest son said that he found footsteps in the snow leading in long strides away from the cottage. Some of the men came to look but the tracings were faint and even then were on the verge of disappearing as more soft flakes fell upon them. Vesta took Sarah into her house for the night. The neighbours, wondering if an arsonist were loose in the night, went back to their homes and talked quietly about who could do such a thing, who would want to, especially to a respected old lady like Sarah Lewis?

George and Mary Smith came to see the smoldering ruins and George listened to Alexander, Vesta's son, recount his suspicions that someone had set the fire. Since fires did happen from natural causes quite frequently in the wooden structures and open-grated rooms of the time, there seemed no reason to suspect anyone unless there were a feud that one could point to. The citizens regarded it as just another fire that served as a warning that they be careful.

The anti-black forces were on the rise but had not and would never reach the stage where arson was a weapon, according to Sandy McPherson and the activist Sam Tisdale. The abolitionist forces, although riven by political infighting, had become stronger in defensive operations and led by the militant Tisdale, with the help of the Black Pimpernel, were so alert in Simcoe that for a southern sympathizer to resort to criminal acts would be suicidal as he would most certainly be tracked down and dealt with. However, the chicanery of some government officials was known to all by this time. They were carefully watched by a few blacks and whites, since most people had no time in the press of making a living to give it thought. It was the secretive, scheming element, with its own agenda, that worried Sarah. Who was behind these occasional arsons and what was their motive?

Sarah was cast into a gloom that neither Vesta nor Mary with all their good sense and love for their mother could dispel. Sarah regarded it as an evil portent. It worked on her mind, possessing it with foreboding. Sandy McPherson, in Simcoe on business, met her on the street and tried to console her. He reminded her of all she had come through and assured her that she would soon overcome this setback. She suddenly looked at him with alarm, and, seizing his arm, she asked him not to write to John about her plight because she did not want to distress him. McPherson thought that Vesta might have written, but then she was engrossed in her own deepening problems. Sarah told him that Vesta had caught pneumonia. Sarah thought that coming into the cold night air, scantily dressed, to help her mother escape the fire had brought it on. She blamed herself. McPherson regarded the furrows in the brow of that face he thought was beautiful and the slight stoop in the figure of that marvelously erect woman of commanding presence and he felt deeply sorry for her. As he watched her go, he wondered if she could ever recover from her loss.

Sarah wandered disconsolately in the streets, made no attempt to speak to people and did not recognize old friends until they tugged at her sleeve. She seemed to symbolize the decay of the place, now that the legal buzzards hovered about waiting for her to die.

Sarah's fears of the human vultures waiting silently in the tree of justice for the proper moment to descend soon were justified by events. Vesta's pneumonia grew worse. She could not work and had little income but enough to pay off the mortgage held by Albert Toms on her property. At Christmas, the Smiths held a large dinner at their home for their relatives. Fanny and Bill Powers and their family visited from Norwich; Henry without his wife came from Hamilton; Vesta insisted on coming with her sons to celebrate for a couple of hours, too weak to stay longer. Sarah loved to see her grandchildren together, from Henry's young son John to Vesta's and Fanny's children, some of whom were approaching their majority. The occasion marked the first time that Bill Powers had found the time to come to Simcoe and the first time that he and George Smith met since the rebellion. When the others went to bed, Smith and Powers sat up half the night reminiscing. Eventually they broached the subject of Sarah's loss.

"I asked everyone I could think of," George said, "and no one has any idea who started the fire. It was started by someone, you know."

"Who burnt down Campbell's businesses three years ago?" Powers asked rhetorically, implying that there was a connection between the two. "The fact that the magistrates could not solve a crime against the town's richest citizen means that everyone is vulnerable."

"I looked into it," George said. "No evidence of arson."

"But how could a building last for over thirty years and then suddenly burn down? It looks suspicious."

"Squire Campbell made enemies, no doubt about it," George smiled, "but no one would think that hurting Sarah would hurt him. He has nothing more to do with her. I suspect it has to do with Sarah's land."

"Someone wants it?" Powers looked alarmed.

George nodded. "It's nothing to do with her being black or whatever. When she first took that place it was too close to the swamp, had too many mosquitoes, but now the town has grown and it's prime real estate. I can handle the obvious, like kidnappings, but I can't handle real estate ledgers and secret deals, mortgages and all that."

"But if you're right, whoever it is can't get anywhere as long as Vesty has the property," Powers said adamantly.

"Vesty's dyin'," George said sadly. "I don't think she'll be with us long."

"Is it that bad?" Powers grimaced. "Her poor kids. I wish Fanny and I were living near by. We're too far away to be of any help."

"Nothing you can do," George said with a sigh. "Nothing we can do but watch. Vesty is a stubborn woman and won't take advice, leastways not from us. Just hope that she's trustin' the right people, and don't lose sleep over it. I'm turning in on that note."

"Me too," Powers smiled. "We leave early tomorrow."

Vesta's health deteriorated quickly after the New Year 1859. Sarah nursed her but watched helplessly as the disease took over her daughter's body. On January 10, Albert Toms helped Vesta make a will, which was witnessed by him and William Roche. She appointed Zebulon

Landon and Thomas McMicken as guardians to her children with instructions that her property be equally divided among the children when they reached their majority. She trusted that these men could arrange to pay off her debts and keep the land, as she said, "upon which I have so long resided." She made special mention of a clock, which she said had been given to her by a friend and which she left to her eldest son Alexander with instructions that he never sell it. Her signature was weak and scratchy, as if the effort to write was the last thing she did. Vesta died that evening with her sons about her and Sarah sitting by her bedside. Sarah accepted her death stoically, but in the middle of the night she awoke crying uncontrollably.

A couple of days after the funeral, Albert Toms registered a mortgage on her property at the Registry Office. The mortgage was dated February 10, 1859. For 163 Canadian dollars, Vesta's lands facing Norfolk Street and running along Union Street came under Toms's power to lease or sell them within one year if the principal at 20 percent interest were not paid. The memorial of mortgage was witnessed by William Roche on February 13. There was no signature from Vesta, nor was there need of one by law. The appointed guardians of the property were unaware of the mortgage when the will was read. Actually, Aquila Walsh, the Registrar, had also witnessed the mortgage, and, it was only by chance, a few months later, that he mentioned it to Zebulon Landon in passing. Landon was alarmed. Only the eldest son Alexander was working and he barely made enough for his own subsistence. The rents on the land paid for the livelihood of the other two boys who were still at school. The trustees and members of the family discussed ways to deal with the great debt that had been imposed so surreptitiously on the land and concluded that it could not be paid. There were questions as to whether the dying Vesta was too ill to understand that she was mortgaging her land at the exorbitant interest of 20 percent and whether the official change in currency from pounds to dollars confused her. If the lands had to be mortgaged to raise money, would it not have been more reasonable for the trustees of her will and guardians of her children to arrange for the mortgage? Sarah was made anxious by the news. She feared for her grandchildren and tried to take over Vesta's role as a mother by cooking for them and keeping the house clean. She was depressed after Vesta's death and worried excessively over little things that formerly she would have tossed off as another inconvenience.

The mortgage was not paid; Albert Toms allowed a grace period of some weeks, hence the property and houses were his by law. The sheriff served an eviction notice, and, faced with the Simcoe constabulary, Sarah and Vesta's sons had to vacate. Avery Shaw appeared in Simcoe, and, claiming the second son as his own, assumed guardianship over the youngest two boys. Alexander stayed on with Thomas McMicken as a blacksmith. Vesta's boys came to see Sarah before they left for a village in the north called Collingwood where Shaw had married and settled down. Sarah told them to write to her and tell her how Shaw was treating them. She mistrusted Shaw, resented his wife for taking over Vesta's role as mother and feared for the boys.

Over the years Sarah became close to her next-door neighbour, a white woman from Norfolk County, who married a shoemaker from Ireland. Her name was Elizabeth Lucas. Sarah thought of her as a dependable friend, although she was half Sarah's age. After Sarah's cottage burnt down, the Lucas family moved to the centre of town, but the two of them remained in close contact. Now Sarah went to live with Elizabeth Lucas. She told her daughter Mary that she felt safer living with white people because she suspected her house had been burnt by prejudiced whites, and moreover, living in a white family reinforced her own identity as white. Elizabeth had come to love and respect Sarah over the years as a friend and neighbour. When Sarah asked to move in as a boarder, although she knew that Sarah's mind was troubled, she was flattered that Sarah would turn to her in need. Her round pleasant face and plump body gave Sarah the reassuring impression that her experience of the world did not extend beyond Norfolk County. Her husband, although an Irish Catholic, thought little of Bill Mathews, and she stayed aloof from political opinion.

Meanwhile Tom McMicken and Zeb Landon appealed to the Court of Chancery on the grounds that Vesta had been too ill to understand the terms of the mortgage. It was going to be a slow process. The injustice of it all moved both the guardians to come to talk with Sarah and try to give her hope. There was fairness in the world, they said, and she would see it in the appointment of a good lawyer to argue the case.

Sarah smiled obligingly at these men whom she had known from when they were young. She hid from them her fear that a farmer and a blacksmith had little chance of beating a lawyer and large property owner in the courts. When they left, she went to the offices of the Gore Bank to see Duncan Campbell. She was driven by the conviction that he alone could save her family. Henry Groff, Campbell's faithful clerk, told her that Duncan was away and would not be back for some weeks. Her sad expression prompted him to ask if he could do anything. Yet when she mentioned the mortgage and the loss of the land, Groff became abrupt with her.

"We can do nothing," he said. "Mr. Toms is acting within the law. I'm afraid that you must accept the loss. I have pressing matters to attend to, Mrs. Lewis."

Sarah walked mechanically to the door, which Groff, impatient for her to leave, held open.

Elizabeth Lucas had little time to spend with Sarah; she had to care for her husband and children as well as two other boarders, but she allowed Sarah to help her cook meals. Sarah visited Mary for a talk every morning, but Mary too was busy with her household chores and tending to her small farm. Sarah spent hours knitting for her grandchildren or just staring out the window of her room and watching seasons mature and fade away into the next one. Her thoughts carried her back to her youth on Brown's Island and the people she had known, including her sisters. She tried to avoid thinking of the violence, the humiliation, and the cruelty by concentrating on happy days with her husband and then on the people who had helped her to escape. She thought of her friends in Simcoe who had passed away and of others who moved away and no longer kept in touch with her. Squire Campbell had a large family to care for and was often away on business. She saw him on the street on occasion, and one time he tipped his hat to her and they exchanged a few pleasant words about John Lewis's business achievements. She looked forward to John's letters, which Elizabeth Lucas read to her, but he had not visited her for over five years. Fanny too visited her rarely. Fanny offered to take her to Norwich for two or three weeks, but Sarah did not want to leave Simcoe, where she felt relatively safe.

Sarah celebrated her seventieth birthday in Mary's home. Mary and her daughter, Henry's son John and George Smith entertained her with a meal and cake. They toasted her with home-made wine and young John Lewis played his guitar for her. Smith could not refrain from talking politics. Mary and Sarah listened to his insights and predictions of war in the United States with apprehension. Late in the evening as Smith got ready to escort Sarah to Mrs. Lucas's home, someone knocked urgently at the door. Smith opened it to Henson Johnson and invited the tall, taciturn church elder to come in.

Johnson had a worried look. He took Sarah's hand in greeting but did not smile. He looked about him as if he did not know what to do next.

"I'm coming late, I know," he said, his deep voice betraying a nervousness.

"Sit down, Henson, my good fellow," Smith said gently.

"No, I must go on," Johnson murmured. "I have bad news." He looked uncertainly at Sarah and added, "John Anderson, our friend from Caledonia, has just been arrested for murder."

"What!" Mary cried. "What did he do?"

"It's the old crime he talked about, killing a white man when he escaped. Someone told on him, a friend who quarreled with him over some property. Told the Brantford police and Mathews has him in the Brantford jail," Johnson said quickly.

Sarah's face reflected dismay and shock. Smith moved to her and helped her to sit down. "Does Maria know?" she asked fearfully.

Johnson nodded, the expression on his lean black face acknowledging Sarah's friendship with Maria Parker.

"Mathews again!" Smith cursed. "I heard that the Attorney-General made him Justice of the Peace! We're in deep trouble now."

"Goin' to members of Wilberforce Society," Johnson murmured. "Let them know."

"I'll talk to Tisdale tomorrow morning," Smith said. "He'll get the abolitionists in his group to select a lawyer. This is going to be a huge political battle. Come, Sarah, I'll take you back."

"No need," Johnson said. "I'm goin' her way. She'll be safe with me," he smiled at Sarah.

"Yes," Sarah said, and saying good-bye hurriedly, her dismay still visible on her face, she left with Henson Johnson.

"Poor Maria," Sarah said as they walked along the boardwalk. "I must see her tomorrow."

Johnson grunted. "Poor us," he said. "The mood's turned against us what with the killing last year and Mathews spreading rumours of more murders by blacks."

They walked the rest of the way in silence. As Sarah thanked him, Johnson told her that he had an intuition that Anderson would be freed and that all would be right again. Sarah gave a small giggle, which surprised Johnson, but he said nothing and watched her hurry indoors. He had seen the mind break down under pressure. Sarah's reaction was like a warning. Fearing for Sarah's sanity, he walked to his next destination.

The newspapers took sides and whipped up a controversy. At first, the public paid little attention to Anderson's plight, but within weeks it became a *cause célèbre* in North America on the eve of the Civil War in the United States. It frightened many blacks with its negative implications and made a fearful impression on Sarah. Was an escaped slave to be sent back to face a court in a slave state where he would find no justice? Canadians were adamant that he should not be, but Canadian politicians and courts had to work within the confines of American pressure and the law. Sarah's fear of enslavement and humiliation began to haunt her again. Mary tried to make her see that her fears were irrational, but the implications of the Anderson case for all escaped slaves preyed on many minds, not just in the black population but in the abolitionist societies, which sprang into action.

The new Liberal Party, that had come out of the Reform Party of the 1850s, accused Attorney-General John A. Macdonald of putting all persons who had escaped slavery in danger of being deported to the States on false charges. Feeling the political pressure, Macdonald instructed Mathews to require evidence of criminality sufficient to sustain a charge in Canada. Mathews, furious at the growing opposition, succeeded in further inflaming whites, already tense from riots between the races, by claiming that Anderson urged blacks in Missouri to rise up against white slave owners.

Bill Mathews kept Anderson in irons in the Brantford jail and alerted the sheriff in Missouri where the alleged murder took place that members from the dead man's family had to come to identify Anderson. Mathews, certain that he had a dangerous killer in his hands, would allow no blacks to visit him. He had Anderson's minister forcibly removed when the Reverend tried to visit. When no one came from Missouri after four weeks, Sam Tisdale demanded that Mathews release Anderson under habeas corpus. Mathews, delaying as long as he could, had to accede. Tisdale's group of abolitionists spirited Anderson away to a secret location. Hours later, a representative from the Digges family arrived at Mathews' office, and the infuriated Mathews, unable to find Anderson, complained to the newspapers.

Anderson found refuge in the home of Maria Parker in Simcoe. Very few knew this, but George Smith, in an effort to reassure Sarah, told her. Sarah, sensing that her future was somehow bound up with the fate of this man, asked Maria if she could see him. Maria, protective of her charge, refused gently but firmly. As one of the small group responsible for hiding him, George Smith took pity on Sarah and brought her to meet him when Maria was out shopping. Sarah brought him a large cherry pie. She was surprised by Anderson's mild manner after all the pain he endured.

"Pleased to meet you again, Miss Sarah," he said, extending his hand.

Sarah shook his hand and smiled into Anderson's eyes where she saw a sadness and a kind of quiet bewilderment.

"I brought you something to eat," she said. "People like my baking. I hope you do."

"I'm no different from other people," Anderson smiled. "Thank you, Miss Sarah."

"Sarah's been asking me about you," George Smith said. "Thought you could answer her better than me—sort of put her mind to rest."

"Do my best," Anderson said, waving Sarah to a chair and sitting near her. "What have my problems been doing to you, Miss Sarah?"

"I just wanted to see that you were not a murderer," Sarah said. "You are a kind man wanting freedom like everyone. What is going to happen to you?"

"Mr. Tisdale tells me to hide out long as I kin. If we kin slow down the process, we kin get time to mount a defense. That's all I kin say. The rest is up to the court, I guess, although I hope I don't have to spend time in jail again."

"Our people will keep you safe," Sarah said. "But you can't trust everybody."

"I'm ready for what's to come," Anderson said. "We learnt that, didn't we? You just stay ready, Miss Sarah. Everything will work out okay."

"I trust in the Lord," Sarah said. "But I get frightened and my mind feels heavy. I don't know why, but I needed to see you. I needed to hear you say what you just said." She stood up and took a step towards Anderson.

He stood up and embraced her. They hugged one another for a couple of minutes as tears streamed down Sarah's face. Then George touched Sarah on the shoulder, and she stepped away from Anderson with an expression of relief.

"You do me good," she whispered.

Anderson watched her go out with Smith and a great worry came into his eyes. What remained unspoken but deeply understood was the memory of years of slavery.

Despite the efforts of detectives employed in all parts of the province, the authorities could find no trace of Anderson. The blacks of Simcoe knew where he was hiding, but no word escaped their lips. Police officers from Detroit, Blodget and Gunning, searched through the summer months. They watched the biggest black communities first, such as at Amherstburg, Chatham, and Dresden. Local officers prowled the taverns listening for loose talk and looking for clues. A police officer from Brantford, Richard Yeoward, traveled to the neighboring towns, visiting Life Henry's bar in Simcoe and the old Norfolk Tavern in Port Dover, where he hoped to find whether fishermen had spirited the fugitive to distant ports. It seemed incredible to Bill Mathews waiting at the Brantford Court House that no trace of "that nigger" could be found.

While the plodding, methodical Blodget stayed in Detroit directing the overall search for Anderson, his detective partner Gunning hired a Mohawk Indian named Shave-Tail to help him track down the fugitive. Gunning was a thin man with a sharp nose and Shave-Tail was a lean, wiry man with brooding black eyes. Their appearance in the villages and towns of southwestern Ontario caused a sense of dread in the inhabitants as if they were representatives of a foreign power determined to find guilt in whomsoever they might come across. They got no cooperation. Shave-Tail spoke only with other Indians in the area and walked the streets at nights to look for telltale signs. He hunted through the forests in the area, particularly near Otterville and along the Big Creek, where a great range of white pine was being cut down by loggers in whose camps Anderson could find protection. An Oneida couple admitted that they had seen Anderson on horseback in the company of whites and blacks near Simcoe shortly after he left Brantford, which brought Shave-Tail to an area near Simcoe called "the Indian woods." Gunning refused to believe that Anderson would hide so close to Brantford, particularly when Sam Tisdale, the ardent abolitionist so vociferous in demanding his release from custody, lived there.

A traveling American salesman overheard two white abolitionists in one of Simcoe's bars discussing a decision to transfer Anderson to a hiding place that George Smith was arranging and, on reaching Detroit, reported what he had heard to Blodget for the $1000 reward.

Blodget sent a message to Gunning, who, shame-facedly admitting that he had been wrong, put Shave-Tail on the scent. The Mohawk was outside Smith's residence when Smith left from his back door in the small hours of the morning. He trailed him stealthily through the streets to a small house in the black quarter in the south-west corner of town. Smith knocked on the door, which opened and a Negro stepped out. Shave-Tail recognized Anderson from the description given him: about five feet, six inches, well-built with broad shoulders and intelligent-looking. He watched the men, engrossed in conversation, walk a distance down the street. Moving silently away into the night, Shave-Tail, his black eyes shining with excitement, slipped into the hotel where Gunning was sleeping and went to Gunning's bedside. He stood for a moment listening to the snores and whistles that emitted from the sleeping detective and reflected on the wisdom of reporting on Anderson to this representative of a nation that had tried to destroy his people. He was a practical man, however, and he reminded himself of the money he would earn; moreover, Anderson was sure to be found in any case. He reached out and shook Gunning's shoulder vigorously. Gunning sat up in fright.

"Got him," Shave-Tail said. "Get arrest warrant from Brantford."

Gunning rubbed his eyes as he gained his composure. "Good work, my man. You keep watch here while I get Bill Mathews, okay?"

Shave-Tail nodded and moved to the far end of the room while Gunning lit a gas lamp and began to dress his thin body, its shadow looking fat on the wall behind him.

"Are you sure it's Anderson?" Gunning asked.

"Sure," Shave-Tail replied sharply. He added after a moment. "Think Smith will move him tomorrow night. Must act quick."

Gunning grunted. "Go to the stable and see that my horse is ready. I'll be down in a minute." He pulled a large chamber pot from under the bed and squatted over it as Shave-Tail swiftly left the room.

When Gunning arrived at Mathews' office in the Brantford Court House hours later, he excitedly called for an officer to arrest Anderson. Mathews, cautious at first, then jubilant as Gunning told him the details, rubbed his hands with glee and called on Yeoward and two younger officers to ride to Simcoe. Hurriedly preparing their equipment and arming themselves, they set off immediately. Recent rains had made the roads almost impassable in some parts. They arrived in the late afternoon and made arrangements with the Simcoe magistrate and jailer to be prepared to receive a prisoner at midnight—for that is when they decided to make the arrest. In the meantime, Shave-Tail watched the house in which he had seen John Anderson. Having hunted game all his life, he knew that prey could escape accidentally. He waited all day without eating. About supper time as the sun began to fall into the trees and the shadows lengthened over the dirt streets, he saw a couple of white men enter the small house. Presently Anderson appeared and walked with them for several blocks to a large stone house with a flower garden in front of it. Could it be the home of a rich abolitionist? he wondered. A middle-aged black man opened the door as the men approached the front steps. Shave-Tail instinctively stepped behind a tree before all four men looked around them and up and down the street. He saw them enter the house quickly and close the door.

Shave-Tail stood behind the tree for a quarter-hour. He dared not move as he knew that someone might spot him from a window of the house. Then, after scrutinizing every window facing the street and being certain that no one was on watch any longer, he walked casually to the corner and, turning it, loped in long strides to the Mansion Hotel where he found Gunning meeting with Officer Richard Yeoward in his hotel room. On Yeoward's map of the town, he pointed out the house to which Anderson had been taken.

"That's Reid's house!" Yeoward exclaimed.

"Who's he?" Gunning asked in alarm, afraid that they would meet an obstacle to making the arrest.

"He's a rich black man—prominent in this place. But he can't stop us," Yeoward said reassuringly. Yeoward was a self-composed, outwardly confident man.

"I've got to telegraph Mr. Blodget in Detroit to come here in case we meet with any trouble," Gunning said.

"Don't," Yeoward warned. "A telegram can be seen by several people in its transmission. Wait until after we make the arrest."

Gunning thought for a moment and then said as if angry with himself, "Of course!"

Although Shave-Tail offered to keep watch on Anderson's new hiding place, Yeoward insisted that he remain in the hotel room with him and Gunning. They sent for food and spent the hours before midnight discussing the issues that had been raised over Anderson's impending extradition.

"Your government is no friend of the United States," Gunning said angrily to Yeoward. "It's a straight case of murder and it won't turn him over."

Yeoward shook his head. "The question is, where the trial should be. We don't think he can get a fair trial in Missouri."

Gunning, looking perplexed and annoyed, went over and over the details of witnesses' testimony as if by citing the facts he was presenting the truth.

Shave-Tail laughing said that Gunning was wasting his breath. "White man's law does not want truth," he smiled. "It wants victims."

Both whites fell silent. Yeoward went to collect his two fellow constables sleeping in an adjoining room. Asking Gunning to lay low at the hotel, as he feared the appearance of an American at the arrest scene would incite the opposition, Yeoward led the two officers behind Shave-Tail through the lamp-lit streets to the imposing home of John T. Reid.

All was quiet, except for the sounds of the men's footsteps over the cinders. Signaling that Shave-Tail was to watch the back of the house, Yeoward and one constable knocked at the door. The other constable stayed in the street. A head appeared briefly from a second-story window. Yeoward knocked again and called "Police!"

The front door opened a crack. Yeoward pushed it open with his shoulder and confronted a middle-aged black man in his dressing-gown and slippers.

"We have a warrant for the arrest of John Anderson," Yeoward shouted. "Where is he?"

Reid tried to stare Yeoward down. "This is a respectable home," he said. "What business do you have disturbing my family at this hour?"

Yeoward held the warrant for Anderson's arrest before his face. "You may be liable for harbouring a fugitive," he warned.

A voice sounded from behind them. "It's all right. If I'm wanted, I'll be glad to oblige the officers." Anderson stepped into sight, dressed in his pyjamas. "I'm John Anderson and I'll be ready to go with you in a moment."

Yeoward seized him by the wrist. "We'll give you five minutes to dress," he said sharply. "And I'm not letting you out of my sight." Instructing the other constable to stay at the door, he followed Anderson to his room, a small space just big enough for a bed, and waited while he dressed.

Reid sent his eldest son to tell Sam Tisdale what was happening.

When Anderson was ready, Yeoward put handcuffs on him and led him by the arm out of the house. Reid shouted at them that they were arresting an innocent man. His loud voice resounded through the streets, and people began coming from their houses to surround Anderson and the constables as they walked through the dark to the jail house. By the time they reached the courthouse, a huge crowd of blacks had gathered to shout at the constables for breaking the peace and arresting a good man.

The magistrate was waiting and legitimized the arrest. Anderson said not a word and stood head bowed waiting to be taken to a cell in the jail beside the Court House. Samuel Tisdale burst into the courtroom at that moment but stopped short of interrupting the proceedings. He looked chagrined, and, turning to two other whites who ran up breathlessly behind him, he instructed them to get as many supporters as possible into the streets to demand that Anderson be released.

Sarah was awakened by the noise. She lay in bed listening to the news being shouted by blacks and whites as they walked the streets to rouse support. She heard Elizabeth Lucas and her husband dress hurriedly and run from the house. She felt depressed and anxious. Anderson stood for the right of man to be free. And now he was captured and imprisoned. Her body began to shake. She panicked and sensed her heart racing. She got up and paced her room. She no longer heard the shouting in the streets. A loud roaring in her ears blocked out all other sound. After some moments of calling on all the will she could command, she was able to calm herself. She sat on her bed and feared for her safety. The men in command might turn against her and her children and send them back to slavery, she thought.

Gunning telegraphed Julius Blodget in Detroit announcing Anderson's imprisonment in the Simcoe jail. Blodget caught the ferry to Windsor, the train for Paris, and the stage coach to Simcoe. Blodget had a large blank face and his figure was indistinguishable from the average man, which allowed him to pass through neighborhoods without notice. He walked the streets and tried to get a sense of the inhabitants before he went into the Court House at the hour set for Anderson's hearing.

A mustachioed man from Missouri was testifying that Anderson had been a slave and had escaped. The magistrate, dubious of whatever the Missourian was saying and constantly interrupting to ask for proof, reflected the general skeptical attitude of the people to the evidence against Anderson. Blodget sat beside the thin, hawk-nosed Gunning. There had been a mob of blacks outside the prison the previous night, Gunning said; they threatened to rescue Anderson. Many people could be hurt, he warned. Blodget nodded understandingly and glanced about at the angry faces listening to the proceedings. When the magistrate ordered the Missourian back to his state to secure more evidence, the anger abated only to rise when the magistrate acceded to the request of the Crown attorney that Anderson be transferred to the Brantford jail. As Anderson returned to his cell, the spectators broke into small groups and talked animatedly among themselves. Blodget instructed Gunning to take Anderson to Brantford after supper. Then, hoping to get a few moments of relaxation before the quarrelsome, possibly blood-letting confrontation he would face in the evening, he sauntered over to George Smith's barber shop on Peel Street to observe the notorious Black Pimpernel in person.

There was a sign above the door declaring that Smith cut the hair of gentlemen and ladies and shaved anyone. Blodget walked in and met the quick look of Smith who was cutting the hair of an elderly gentleman. Smith smiled archly at him and pointed to a second chair just being vacated by a customer. Blodget had wanted to be shaved by Smith so that he could engage in conversation with him but being presented with an empty chair he felt obliged to sit in it. The black barber assisting Smith finished collecting from the departing customer and turned to face Blodget. The direct brown gaze, the lean face and upturned nose startled him. The loose-hanging arms, and finally the mellow voice with broad accented vowels made him absolutely sure that this barber was John Brown, a man who had been accused of killing the woman Indian Sue at Cleveland two years ago. He glanced away into the mirror before him and, hiding his surprise, he ran his hand over the stubble on his face.

"Give me a shave," he said in a voice deeper than usual. He had seen John Brown in Detroit where the fellow had worked as a barber before going to Cleveland. He hoped that Brown did not recognize him, and, from Brown's confident manner, it appeared that he had not. Controlling the trembling in his hands, he stretched back in his chair and received the lather that Brown applied to his face. At least, in this condition he could hardly be recognized by his own mother, he thought.

He marvelled at his incredible luck in securing two runaway slaves guilty of murder. The one case would help to substantiate the other, he thought. As Brown shaved him, he watched through half-closed lids via the mirror George Smith chatting with his customer. Smith had a charming manner and was ready with witty repartee that brought laughs from those around him. He was a formidable adversary because he was so intelligent. Blodget waited patiently for Brown to finish shaving and then, standing hurriedly, as if he had an appointment, he paid Brown without looking at him and left the store. He went directly to the Court House where the same magistrate who had heard the Anderson case was still in his office. He procured a warrant for Brown's arrest and accompanied a Simcoe constable back to the barber shop. Brown was in the act of cutting a woman's hair when the constable placed a handcuff on his wrists and arrested him. Brown, gaping in disbelief, tried to speak but his words stuck in his throat. Blodget took the scissors from Brown's hands with a smile and put them on a side table.

"You don't remember me, do you, John? Detective Blodget from the Detroit Police. You remember cutting my hair years ago when you were a slave, don't you?"

Brown glanced embarrassedly at Smith, who was regarding the scene with a stoic seriousness, and said to Blodget, "Seems you look familiar now. Why you arrestin' me?"

"For murder," Blodget said, looking Brown sharply in the eyes.

"Don't be alarmed, Miss. He is innocent of the charge," Smith said to the woman in Brown's chair. "And I shall finish your hair in a moment." He glared at Blodget. "You are upsetting my business with your preposterous charges. Go back to Detroit and leave us alone, for God's sake!"

"You are next, Smith," Blodget replied angrily. "We're on to you."

"You had best get back to the safety of the Court House," Smith warned mockingly and looked round at the crowd beginning to assemble to watch the arrest.

Blodget followed the constable with Brown in tow into the street and, pursued by a group of young black men, hurriedly walked to the prison where Brown was locked in a cell with two white thieves. Although Blodget was proud of himself, he began to notice the animosity building against him in the Simcoe community. He was hooted at in the streets and called a bounty hunter. The stories of blacks being arrested on unproven charges and whisked away over the border without trials in recent years had alarmed people throughout the province. Police turned over runaways for money to reward-hunting Americans. For that reason, many blacks gathered outside the prison to keep a silent vigil. When the news circulated that Anderson was to be transferred to Brantford, Sam Tisdale led a huge crowd of whites and blacks in protest.

Tisdale, his face hot with anger, addressed the protesters from the roof of the Registry Office, which overlooked the park in front of the Court House and prison. Anderson was innocent of murder, he cried, and only guilty of pursuing his dream of freedom. John Brown was absolutely innocent of the charge against him because the crime happened a month after Brown escaped to Simcoe. Tisdale informed the crowd that Blodget had telegraphed for a witness and a detective to come from Cleveland. All those who could testify when Brown came to Simcoe must appear in the courtroom at Brown's extradition hearing. Men and women in the crowd sang out in agreement: "Yes, indeed." "Hear the man."

Tisdale told them that the notorious Bill Mathews sent several mounted constables to assist in the transport of Anderson because the small Simcoe force could not prevent his rescue. Tisdale was messianic in his zeal. He looked like a firebrand of righteousness, his blond hair and blue eyes illumined in the torchlights like some avenging angel. His accusations worried the magistrates and police. The background of many of the citizens—American Loyalist refugees from persecution, house burnings, and mob violence in the States, and others who fled from persecution in Europe, whether from starvation, Highland Clearances, or religious intolerance—made them instinctively sympathize with former slaves. With a large segment of the whites philosophically against them, the authorities moved quickly to get Anderson to Brantford before they faced the wrath of the whites as well.

After Tisdale had finished speaking and there was a lull as the people waited for some form of active effort to charge the prison, Anderson was ushered in ankle and wrist irons into a carriage at the back. A score of mounted officers took up positions on either side of the carriage. The formation moved forward at a command from the lead officer, Richard Yeoward. A boy saw the action and excitedly ran to the front of the prison to shout out that Anderson was being taken away. The crowd surged after the carriage and some young men ran in front of it to stop it. Yeoward ordered the police to take out their swords and hold them ready. The gesture was sufficient to deter any interference. Sam Tisdale and some other white abolitionists ran up shouting to let the carriage pass but to follow it to Brantford. The crowd sensed the wisdom of this and shouts of watching for any devia- tion in the route, any attempt to hijack the prisoner, resounded in the night. The crowd followed the prisoner down Robinson Street to Norfolk. Sarah heard the commotion. Elizabeth Lucas called out to her to see the procession, and, her curiosity overcoming her apprehension, she went outside to watch. The torchlights, the shouting protesters, the determination of the police, and the plight of Anderson, who was locked away in a closed carriage, altogether frightened her. The large police presence reinforced her fears that the government was turning against coloured people. Wanting to flee back in the house but fasci- nated by the spectacle, she followed the carriage until it reached the highroad to Brantford as mounted protesters replaced the crowd on foot and melted away into the darkness.

Elizabeth Lucas stayed close beside her.

"Don't you worry, Sarah," Elizabeth said quietly. "Mr. Anderson's going to get a fair trial, and if the people have any say in the matter, he's never going back to Missouri."

"They're taking him back there now, aren't they?" Sarah asked plaintively.

"No, my dear, just to Brantford."

Sarah could not accept this and she shook her head vigorously. "You can't trust them, Lizabeth. You can't trust people these days.

Things have got to a pretty pickle." She laughed suddenly at that. "Things are in a pickle."

"Come, Sarah. We'll go inside. You need to rest." Elizabeth put her arm on Sarah's back to guide her.

"Oh my! Inside! Can we be safe inside?" she laughed. "They'll get us inside."

"You'll be safe here," Elizabeth said, her round face wistfully sad as she steered Sarah back to the house.

"My grandchildren weren't with those persons, were they, Lisabeth?"

"No. They are all safe at home."

"Home," Sarah giggled. "Once my home and gone. Well, all I can say is, good riddance!" she chuckled to herself.

Elizabeth Lucas humoured her in a mild, calm voice as she thought that Sarah's mind had become unhinged at seeing Anderson's removal.

31

Sarah confused the Anderson case with the litigation over Vesta's land. When she heard that Anderson was kept in irons in a Brantford jail cell, she thought of Alexander, Vesta's eldest son. Mary took some time to convince her that Alexander was free and working as a blacksmith with McMicken. Sarah's confusion was not to be wondered at because the Anderson case had spread confusion throughout the province over the right of extradition under the law. Abolitionist parties in the United States sent representatives to confer with Canadian abolitionists. The British abolitionists, who had become irrelevant in Britain after the slave trade was abolished, seized on the issue to bring themselves back to prominence. Canadian newspapers in opposition to John A. Macdonald's conservatives charged the government with complicity with the slavers of the United States. In reaction, Macdonald toured the province to placate the Orange faction of his party which he had betrayed by agreeing to the establishment of Catholic schools throughout the province in order to effect a union with Lower Canada. Macdonald welcomed the Anderson case in hopes that it would distract people from the issue of religious schools. He spoke in Simcoe in the fall and won over his listeners with his charm and diplomacy. He held a special audience with black leaders and white abolitionists to assure them of his concern in the Anderson case. George Smith was completely convinced that Macdonald would prevent Anderson from being extradited and would thereby keep Canada as a haven for escaped slaves. As far as most blacks were concerned, the liberals were tainted with their reformist past and American republicanism, which, in turn, stood for slavery, regardless of how strongly liberals denied it.

Sarah was in the courtroom when Blodget brought in witnesses to the murder of Indian Sue and listened in dread as a white woman swore that Brown was the killer. Simcoe residents testified that Brown was in Simcoe at the time of the murder and thus outswore the witnesses from Cleveland. The court gave the Cleveland authorities more time to produce further evidence, but, when no more was forthcoming, Brown was declared innocent of the charge. Although the people of Simcoe felt that justice had been done and now looked to three Toronto judges to free Anderson, Sarah was overwhelmed with foreboding. Two judges ruled that extradition could not be denied. Public meetings all over the province damned the judges and insisted on an appeal. Sarah sensed that Anderson was doomed and went to see Maria Parker, who followed the case in the papers.

"Don't look so gloomy, Sarah," Maria said lightly, trying to cheer her up. "John's got too much support now that the British have taken up his cause."

"If he loses," Sarah said, looking distraught, "we all lose."

"Listen!" Maria said impatiently. "I been reading all the papers. John has got powerful friends. Besides, what court is goin' to ignore those huge rallies for him in three countries? And are you goin' tell me that a Canadian court is goin' to go against a ruling by a British court? No, Sarah, stop worrying."

"And the civil war?" Sarah asked her, searching her face as if trying to read the truth there.

"It's goin' to be a long war and it's got nothing to do with us. It's not in Canada, Sarah. For God's sake! stop worrying. You are safe, I'm safe, your children are safe. The only thing concerns me, is John Anderson comin' back to live with me in Simcoe now that he's such a big shot."

Maria, unable to dispel Sarah's sense of doom, escorted her gently to the door, kissed her cheek, and told her to go home and get some rest. Sarah's mental state worsened. As Maria predicted, the Queen's Bench in London, England, intervened with a writ of habeas corpus, and one of the Canadian judges noticed that the warrant against Anderson was defective because Mathews had failed to use the word "murder," and thus the three judges declared that Anderson should not be in custody. To Canadians, Anderson became, as one newspaper wrote, in reference to the Italian liberator who had just routed the Bourbon army, "a black Garibaldi", and his victory in court was celebrated with a sleigh ride about the streets of Toronto in February 1861. The Americans were furious but as they were drifting into Civil War they soon forgot the case in the press of other matters. The British abolitionists invited Anderson to England, where as a hero he spoke at Albert Hall in London to a full house. The blacks in Simcoe celebrated with a big dinner for everyone who had contributed to Anderson's release. Maria Parker and Sam Tisdale were the guests of honour. Although George Smith tried to persuade Sarah to accompany him to the festivities, she told him that it was not true. She believed that John Anderson had been sent back into slavery.

George recognized in Sarah's confused mind a fearful uncertainty that blacks were feeling generally. He still mistrusted the Reformers, who, running in the local elections, tried to persuade blacks to vote for them because of their vociferous support for Anderson; Smith publicly supported Macdonald because it was his steadfastness that finally got Anderson his freedom in a tricky political situation. Despite the flightiness of her manner, Sarah had lucid moments in which she called the Anderson case just "show." What she detected from the whole affair was a growing resentment against the coloured population playing itself out in small ways that were not dramatic enough to attract the attention of newspapers.

In the early months of the Civil War in the States, the Southern Confederate Army seemed to be winning. All the abolitionists in the world could not stop the spread of slavery if the North was defeated. Such thoughts sent Sarah into long periods of silliness in which she uttered gibberish and sang children's songs from her days as a slave in Virginia. Elizabeth Lucas discussed Sarah's declining mental health with Mary Smith. Could it be, they wondered, that the hardships of Sarah's life had worn down her mind? At least she was harmless—just a flighty woman who periodically talked gibberish to herself. Elizabeth agreed with Mary that Sarah would be better off under her care, and when Mary asked Sarah to move in with her, Sarah gave her a look of gratitude. "I wanted to ask," she murmured, "but didn't want to impose."

Sarah's mind quickly replaced the Anderson case with worries over Vesta's children. Although the court guardian, a lawyer from Toronto, who was appointed to their case, seemed an ambitious young man, Sarah feared the worst. The land was sure to be taken from them, all those years that she had spent tending it, cherishing it, all that it had meant as a symbol of her emancipation and the pride of achievement, was to be stolen. Her experience with courts in Virginia told her that the confrontation in the courtroom would be a sham.

Sarah went with Mary to hear the lawyer argue the issue of the validity of the mortgage at the Court of Chancery, which came to Simcoe in the fall Assizes. He was able to throw doubt on the motives behind the mortgage, although it could not be denied that Vesta's estate had received the money from Toms. That was the problem. Even though the administrators of the estate were not aware that the money represented a mortgage, they had used it. The judge reserved judgment and the Court moved on to its next stop on the circuit.

Sarah went for long walks about Simcoe and into the countryside. She felt less alarm when she was with nature. She returned to the Culver farm and sat for hours by the grave of her little girl. She touched the tall poplar that had come to stand for the success of her son John. She knew fewer people now and recognized no one but old friends. Charity and William Rusling left Simcoe early in 1861 when their house burnt to the ground. There was some talk that it might have been arson because he had formed a Temperance Society that was becoming influential politically, but since the distilleries and taverns continued as before, the suggestion was dismissed by most citizens. The Ruslings moved to Norwich near to Fanny and William Powers' home. Sarah distressed acquaintances by her moments of distraction and sudden bouts of silence, and they stopped speaking to her. Maria Parker had given up on her and called her a bitter old woman best left alone. Maria herself was bitter over John Anderson's deserting her for the abolitionist cause, although she looked through the papers closely to catch news of him touring England. When it was reported that he migrated to Liberia, she had to accept that she would never see him again. Sarah's friend Richard Plummer was no solace. He drank too much wine all the time now, which increased his delusion of being a Scotsman so that he spoke with a brogue. Sarah sympathized with him because she knew his Scottish blood claimed him when he was inebriated, but people recognized him only by his skin colour. She heard him cry out "Caledonia!" and quote from Shakespeare's sonnets and sometimes from "Macbeth" when he acted out the dying scene of the Scottish king in front of small crowds who gathered in the street. She recognized in him a failing in herself, but she did not try to communicate with him. She knew that she was no longer capable of conversing coherently. Laughing, giggling, smiling to herself, Sarah seemed to be losing all contact with reality. Only when she was alone on her long walks in the fields and along the Lynn River did she feel happy with herself. The rest of the time she ached with worry, although the subject of her worry became indistinct, appearing only now and then in the form of the lost property or the Civil War.

Sarah walked by the land that had been Vesta's and stared at the cottages on it to see the tenants when they appeared at windows and hung out their laundry in the spring sunshine. Toms rented Vesta's old house to an immigrant family. The burnt-out shell of Sarah's cottage lay untouched. The spring floods coursed down Union Street as they always had. Jerry Curtis, the blacksmith, still ran his business on the back of the property. He would call to her, but she kept to herself and hurried away. She knew that she should recognize people who were friendly to her but could not. When she received clothes from her son

John, she remembered him, and when he sent cheques to Mary for her board and lodging, she felt a momentary protective presence of a child who lived far away.

Sarah repressed many ugly things that had happened to her, but now the memories of beatings and the faces of men who had raped her came to confront her more insistently. She was no longer able to blot out the bad thoughts with memories of her children and her pride in their accomplishments. Her daughter Mary and Elizabeth Lucas were the only people that she felt comfortable with and whom she always recognized. Mary was like a staff that she could lean on; Henry came from Hamilton to see her occasionally and brought his dependable personality to soothe her troubled mind; Fanny did not visit now but her success in raising a respectable family gave Sarah an added sense of accomplishment in certain clear moments when, too, she remembered Israel and Vesta as giving her trouble, but with strong character in the face of adversity; John's good-looking face came sometimes to her mind. When she thought of Duncan Campbell, he figured as the young Scotsman with whom she had lain in the Windsor tavern. When she saw him walking in the street, she no longer wanted to speak to him. Her life was becoming a blur with lucid intervals. She could manage to look after herself, do her own shopping, and cook in Mary's kitchen, although Mary prepared all the meals. But she had no sense of perspective, no consciousness of herself moving in a larger world; everything seemed up close to her as if crowding in upon her. She began to get irritable and quarrel with Mary for no reason. The townspeople regarded her as an eccentric character because she wore good clothes, cut a commanding figure, and exchanged money for fruits and vegetables at the stands in the market in a business-like manner, yet she laughed to herself, recognized no one, and walked through the streets and into the fields for most of the day, like Old Horace used to do.

One hot day in August in a fit of pique, Sarah took her belongings from Mary's house to the home of Mrs. Benedict, a spry young lady who had befriended her, in the next street. She felt that Mary's vigilance over her was becoming oppressive. She told Mary that she felt safer in a household of white people, but she giggled as she spoke and her manner had become so flighty that Mary doubted that she knew what she was doing. Mary blamed George for discussing the crushing victories of the Southern armies in front of her, but George laughed and said that Sarah could no longer understand the war.

Sarah seemed to settle down and agitate less. She did not go out unless it was for a purpose such as to buy something or to see a circus that had come to town or to hear an outdoor band concert on the common. But in the third week in her new lodgings, her grandson Alexander paid her a visit. She recognized him and asked him about the court case with a sudden clarity of mind that surprised him. No decision had been made, he sighed, but what was worse, he had heard from his brothers that they were badly treated by their stepmother. The youngest had been forced to sleep out in the cold as punishment and Avery's own son, the middle boy, came in for canings frequently. Avery's son stayed only because he wanted to help out his younger brother as much as he could. Avery Shaw spent many weeks on the road and meekly submitted to his wife's demands when he was home. Sarah's mind took her back to the abuses she endured as a slave and envisioned her grandsons suffering as she had. Alexander tried to calm her by saying that nothing could be done since they were far away in Collingwood and he had told their court guardian, who said that he would look into it. These words, said as soothingly as Alexander could express them, failed to keep Sarah from plunging into depression. She began to moan with pain and rock in her chair. When he left, Alexander asked Mrs. Benedict to keep a close watch on his grandmother as he feared that she was sinking into a crazy state.

Sarah spent a sleepless night in bed, and, waking early at dawn, she dressed quickly, put all the money she had been gathering over the months into a purse, and laughing softly to herself, went directly to the stage coach station to take the earliest stage to Paris. The driver Hank Power had just retired and the new man did not know her. The roads were hard and dry. The coach made swifter progress than usual through Burford and on to Paris on the Grand River, at which she could catch the train from the West going to the settlements north of Toronto. Sarah had only a hazy idea of where she was headed, but she had her grandsons in her mind, which, she felt, was guidance enough. She did not purchase a ticket at the station but sat in one of the cars and paid the conductor when he passed through the train. She said only one word "Collingwood." When the conductor told her that no train ran to Collingwood, she repeated the name. Shaking his head, he gave her a ticket for Barrie on the shores of Lake Simcoe, the closest stop to Collingwood, and she paid the requisite fare. She seemed to settle down and appear relaxed now that she was underway.

Mrs. Benedict, who had assured the Smiths that she could care for Sarah, became alarmed when Sarah did not appear for her mid-day meal and sent a boy to tell Mary Smith. At first, Mary and George expected Sarah to come in from one of her long walks, but when she could not be found by nightfall, Mary informed the police. Some days later a constable learned from the stagecoach driver that he had dropped off an old lady fitting Sarah's description at Paris. As far as the Simcoe constabulary was concerned, she had gone out of its jurisdiction. She was someone else's problem.

Mary Lewis telegraphed Henry asking if Sarah had come to him in Hamilton and, if not, to help find where she had gone. Henry asked at stagecoach stations, railway stations and went to near-by towns to ask the black communities for news of his mother. There were no leads. Mary also wrote Fanny but their mother had not come to Norwich. Mary, worried to the point of panicking, took the coach for Paris and spent a couple of days in the village searching its streets and asking storekeepers and passers-by if they had seen an old woman with a touch of Negro blood wandering aimlessly. No one had and no official at the rail station remembered selling such a woman a ticket. Sarah had disappeared into a chasm. Sick with concern, Mary returned to Simcoe and wrote a despairing letter to John in New York City. John was the only person that she knew was powerful enough to move people to find their mother.

John Lewis was prospering. The more the animosity between free and slave states increased, the more frantic was the trading between the two. He handled the distribution of raw cotton to manufacturers in New York and to England and shipped finished products to the South in huge amounts. At first, the returns had been greater than he could have imagined. His older partner John Haviland, tiring of the pace, sold his share of the firm to John, which became the John D. Lewis Company. He invested in machinery and warehouses to meet an increase in demand for goods.

He was a creature of the present—a self-made man—who was no more and no less than the physical person that moved through the nefarious business world and high-living night life of a great city with antennae alert for danger. And danger and treachery he had in abundance on all sides and at all times. He was often in court—once on the charge of attempted assassination.

Two men arguing near a police station in the early hours of the morning over the dividing up of money paid them to murder a merchant were overheard and arrested. They confessed that John D. Lewis promised them a large sum to kill a former employee who took his trade secrets to a rival. John's lawyer, A. J. Dittenhoffer, called it a crudely constructed web, of which, he suspected, the intended victim was the principal weaver. John, after two weeks in jail, was released for lack of evidence.

John asked himself sarcastically what would have happened if the fact that he was the son of an escaped slave had been submitted as evidence? He reasoned that his black ancestry meant nothing to him other than the traces of it that he saw in his mother. Why should he allow his enemies to destroy him for that one slim connection to the past, of which he had no knowledge, no empathy, and, when he thought about it, no real sympathy?

The secretive life John led made him a lonely man. He filled the void with the high-spirited life he led in the taverns and at the theatres. His work gave him a reason for living, and, as his business prospered, he became more content within himself. He made some friends among his fellow merchants, but his closest friend was Frank Wilder, who worked as a porter in his firm. Wilder was a heavy-built, athletic young man, who accompanied John on his rounds to the night spots and to meetings with the more unsavoury men with whom he had to deal to have his goods moved. Wilder became his confidant. A man of steadfast loyalty, without ambition for himself, street-smart, he remained at John's beck and call, always ready to lend him assistance, not just because he was paid to do it but because John's security was the reason for his existence. Such devotion surprised and pleased John immensely. His housekeeper provided affectionate care for him, and, over time, he found her indispensable to him. Although he could not trust these people with his secret, he felt safer with them than with anyone because they were in his employ and therefore unable to presume upon his friendship to ask questions. A couple of his closest business associates named their sons after him, and he remained in affable but aloof relations with them for years. No one could penetrate the veneer of the man. His great wealth attracted many people to him yet he kept them all at a distance.

He kept watch also from a distance over the education of his daughter in a convent in a small town about thirty miles north of the city. Occasionally he visited the girl and brought her presents. He always paid a visit near Christmas. He was tempted to bring the girl to live with him when she grew older, but, unable to look after her properly, he left her at the convent.

The loneliness at the core of the man would have been insupportable in the early years without his mother's love. He related his achievements to her with pride and had to visit Simcoe, despite the risk, every few years, to hear her voice and hold her hands. The burning of her house had an impact on him. It was as if someone had threatened his very being. When he learned that she was safe with her good friend, he soon dismissed the danger and was caught up in his business and the politics which affected it. If he had taken a closer interest in the affairs of his family, he might have intervened with his wealth to deflect the tragic events which unfolded in Simcoe

He, however, worked hard during the day to save his dry-goods firm from the threatening recession brought about by the ceasing of trade with the South and enjoyed the company of the girls and young men at night with Frank Wilder, whose sense of humour in a light satirical vein kept him amused. When he received Mary's letter reporting his mother as missing, his life changed. His worry made it impossible for him to enjoy himself in the old way. But whom did he know who had the clout to move the authorities to find Sarah? Theo Hunt no longer came to New York City and no longer lived in Simcoe. He was somewhere in Michigan.

John wrote to Duncan Campbell but waited in vain for a reply. Duncan knew that Sarah was addled in the head and an embarrassment and burden to those who had to care for her. He just did not wish to become involved in Sarah's problems. His interests lay far beyond Simcoe in that great important world of finance. Exasperated at the apparent indifference to his mother's fate, John wrote to Sandy McPherson asking desperately for help. The strain of having to keep his private affairs to himself without a soul to discuss them with or to help him deal with difficulties became great at times. He needed someone to confide in, and McPherson, having been a substitute father for him in the old days, made a good and discreet listening post on the rare occasions he unburdened himself to him. McPherson ran a dry-goods store in Brantford and practiced law on the side. He did not relish scouring the countryside looking for a needle in a haystack, as he expressed it, but, always an admirer of Sarah for her beauty and resourceful personality, he wrote to several people, including Judge Mercer Wilson, now one of the most influential citizens in the province, who made extensive inquiries.

Sarah had got off the train in Barrie and taken a stagecoach to Collingwood village on Nottawasaga Bay off Georgian Bay about thirty miles from Barrie. Its citizens made their living from fishing, building boats and servicing the surrounding farming population. When Sarah wandered the streets and rocky beaches, the climate was warm and welcoming and the trees were turning golden and red. She did not find Avery Shaw's home and she did not see her grandchildren because Shaw did not live in Collingwood but rather some miles out of it along the coast. She became more confused when she could find no one who knew the family. People paid little attention to her, presuming that she was crazy but harmless. December came and the snows fell. It was growing colder. She spent all her money and depended on handouts of food from the local churches. Vagrants were common in the area because black farmers in disputes over title to their lands often lost them despite all the heavy work they had done.

Sarah knew only that Collingwood had been her goal and could not leave it. A few days after Christmas 1861, on the complaints of some citizens, who worried that the old lady would die in the streets, the mayor asked the sheriff to take her to the newly-constructed jail in Barrie. At least, there she would be warm and fed.

The jail or prison was a low-lying stone building built on a rise at the back of the town, which fronted Kempenfeldt Bay. The cells were small—just big enough to accommodate a bed. Sarah, bewildered, went into one of them. It was punishment for vagrancy. No effort was made to discover where she came from. She was regarded as incapable of providing for herself and would be kept until she regained her sanity, or until someone claimed her.

Sarah was a pitiful sight with her ragged clothes, her erratic gestures, her teeth chattering with the cold, her handsome face strained as if caught in some inexpressible anguish, her hair clotted with dirt. Yet at seventy-one, she still had a fine figure and commanding presence. The jailer, Alex Lang, a man in his forties of middle height and with a bored expression, remarked on her unusual looks when she was taken from the wagon and led into the jail. By the nature of his job he had to have a hard heart toward his prisoners, but his heart softened when he saw Sarah who had the characteristics of a lady yet was so worn, distraught, and lost in mind that it seemed she would never recover her senses. A woman who assisted him, Charlotte Poory, took responsibility for making Sarah wash herself and don the coarse prison garb of brown skirt and blouse. When she took Sarah to her narrow cell and locked the iron-grilled gate behind her, she heard a wail of despondency and turned to see Sarah asking the wall for her grandchildren. She seemed to be praying to God to keep her grandchildren safe.

"Poor soul," she said to Lang. "She has suffered over some wrong that was done to them."

"We can't tell, can we," Lang smiled. "She could be imagining the whole thing. But she's a pretty lady. By the brownish colour of her skin I'd say she had Negro blood."

"She has a kind of accent from the Southern States, I think," Mrs. Poory said. "But she looks Anglo-Saxon. She could have come from one of the communities forming along the shore of Lake Huron and been brought to Collingwood by boat. But then, she must have been wandering for months in her demented state."

447

"You think she comes from the Southern States?" Lang asked with a frown. "That's a long way to walk, but crazy persons can do remarkable things."

"Poor old soul." Mrs. Poory shook her head. "Deserted by her children like so many are these days. We'll be kind to her, Alex. Try to humour her."

Alex did not know what Charlotte Poory meant by that last remark. The prison authorities had just passed a regulation cutting down on the food served in prisons. Henceforth prisoners could eat meat only once a week. Did Mrs. Poory mean that he should break the regulations and feed Sarah more meat and vegetables than she was allowed? Or did she mean that he ought to give her more time than was usual away from her narrow little cell? Or did she mean to just talk to her as if she were sane? Whatever she meant, Alex Lang was not in a position to humour anyone. He frowned at Mrs. Poory for suggesting that he soften his attitude to any one of his prisoners, despite his own inclination to make an exception in Sarah's case. He had to keep her confined to her cell because there were male prisoners who could not be trusted when a female was available. As for food, this female prisoner seemed to eat little. When he tried to talk to her, she spoke only of her grandchildren and mumbled the names of Edward or Edwin and Thomas. Perhaps, he thought philosophically, she will mention another name that might lead to discovering her identity. In any case, she was lucky to have been picked up when she was. Another few nights exposed to the freezing cold after Christmas would surely have killed her.

32

Now that warmer weather was coming and the roads would be more passable and travel less difficult, George and Mary hoped that Sarah would come to their door some day as if returning from a long walk. Bill Mathews and the Brantford constabulary, embittered over losing the John Anderson case, were uninterested, and the Simcoe constabulary was too small to devote any man to the case of a missing person. Least concerned were the authorities, whose philosophy required each person to be solely responsible for himself and expect help from the government only when a serious crime was committed. When the snows melted in the spring, a woman's corpse was found in a wooded area beyond some farmers' fields in Simcoe. The local police announced that it was Sarah, but when Mary Lewis saw it, despite its state of decomposition, she knew it was not her mother.

Meanwhile the war between the states brought alarming news. Whole regiments of young men were destroyed by the simple expedient of marching them straight into blistering cannon fire. Some young Americans fled to Canada to escape the draft and were called "butternuts" and "copperheads" by American patriotic newspapers. The hard times, the bleakness of the village of Simcoe, the general feeling of despair, these were the heavy shadows that followed the lives of Canadians. Mary and George Smith struggled to sustain themselves. George, in addition to running his barbershop, became a tailor with Mary as an unpaid employee.

In May of 1862, the Chancery court judge finally ruled on the property of Vesta Lewis; he awarded it to Albert Toms, who now called himself Squire, and celebrated his victory with his wife. He sold the property to Henry Groff, Duncan Campbell's faithful clerk, who had always had his eye on it because it was convenient to the bank where he worked.

Fortunately Sarah knew none of this. She, who so loved the open fields, gradually lost her health confined in a tiny cell where she laughed and muttered to herself. Occasionally she complained that Squire Campbell would not have allowed her to be so closely confined if he knew. Lang discounted her lucid moments as a part of her madness. He was interested in knowing her identity, but such matters were the responsibility of his superiors; he was a jailer doing his duty.

Did he report what he heard to the mayor of Collingwood, who in turn contacted Duncan Campbell? And did Campbell see her disappearance as an opportunity to unburden himself of a part of his past that had been an embarrassment to him for years? Or did the mayor think there was no possible connection between this old lady and one of the country's prominent men?

The hot summer of 1862 was unbearable in that little cell. Sarah caught a fever in mid-August and sickened. Mrs. Poory nursed her, but Sarah grew worse. Her silly laughter and mumblings, incoherent phrases, and the stressful signs of madness gradually ceased and sanity returned. On her last day she was clear in mind. In her soft southern accent she told Mrs. Poory and Alex Lang, who sat by her bed, that she had come to Collingwood to find her grandchildren. Her worries over their mistreatment by their stepmother had motivated her. She spoke again of Squire Campbell and declared that if only he knew where she was that he would restore her to liberty. Jailer Lang may have pitied her then, but his expressionless face betrayed no emotion. There was a break in the weather in the afternoon of August 19 as north-west breezes brought cooler air through the narrow windows of the prison cells, and Sarah, holding Mrs. Poory's hand, passed away.

Lang looked on while Sarah died. She had been so very different from the thieves and other petty criminals that he had in his charge. At the inquest the next day, he testified to her gentleness and her kind disposition that came through her madness to impress him; she was a true and handsome lady, he said.

There was no money for burial. A couple of grave-diggers found a spot in the Wesleyan burial ground on the hill behind the prison and they dug a grave into which Sarah was lowered in a cheap wooden coffin. Mrs. Poory and another woman arranged the body for burial and followed it to the grave. Charlotte Poory said a prayer while the men held their hats. When the small group left, the gravediggers began filling in the grave. Such would have been the end of Sarah's story if John Lewis was not so desperately seeking her.

It was McPherson's letter of inquiry to Judge Mercer Wilson, who asked his contacts in the courthouses throughout the counties, that finally brought word that Sarah was locked up on the order of Mayor McCall of Collingwood. Jubilant, McPherson wrote to the mayor, who confirmed that she had been a prisoner in Barrie but died a month previously. An angry McPherson rode to Simcoe to inform George Smith, who related the distressing news to Mary. At least, Mary consoled herself, Sarah had died in a shelter, but she wondered at life's cruelty, that Sarah's strong mind, which brought her and her children through tribulation, should betray her in the end.

When John Lewis heard from McPherson, he was wracked with guilt. His dear mother, who had cared so much for him, could not depend on him in her direst need. Instead, his continuous court cases, suits over undelivered material, delinquent payments, and real estate contracts had meant more to him than her welfare. But how was he to know? he reasoned with himself. He could not have located her faster than those who were living there, could he? Yet the self-accusation which he could not avoid, that he had not looked for her lest he be connected with her Negro past by strangers in authority and risk revealing his origins, stayed to torment him. After a week, he composed himself to write to McPherson to see that a tombstone was erected over her grave with the words: "Sacred to the memory of Sarah Lewis, native of the U.S.A., who departed this life August 19, 1862, aged 72 years." Jailer Lang had the tombstone erected and asked for $23 costs. John sent McPherson the equivalent of $18, making a mistake in the exchange rate and obliging McPherson to explain to Lang that he would send the rest later. Whether John was too busy to make up the difference or just did not care about small sums, the jailer waited for ten years before he received the full amount. It came about in a strange way.

In 1872, sitting in his prison office late one summer evening, Alex Lang, hearing the office bell, opened his door to a gentleman wearing a dark suit and a linen coat, who requested a private interview with the jailer. Lang welcomed him into his office. The man had a slight olive complexion, very dark hair and fascinating dark eyes burning with energy. His visitor asked about the circumstances of Sarah Lewis's imprisonment and death. Surprised that someone with such fine clothes and gentlemanly deportment should ask after Sarah, Lang then remembered the description of John Lewis given him by the jailer in Simcoe with whom he had discussed Sarah's death. When his visitor told him that he wanted the interview kept secret, he knew this was Sarah's son. The visitor, who did not offer his name, listened attentively with a look of great sadness as Lang related her last days to him and asked to see her grave. Since it was already dark, and he was leaving on the seven o'clock morning train, they arranged to meet at six in the morning.

Lang was up and waiting when he saw John Lewis walking up the road. He accompanied him to the graveyard and watched as the man fell into a sombre state, his expression infinitely sad as if the fellow had lost his usual control and was at the mercy of emotions that welled up to bring tears to his eyes. After several minutes of silence, the man seemed to regain his composure and, turning to Lang, asked about Sarah's grandchildren. Lang, who thought that they lived in Collingwood, told him of Sarah's concern for them. John pressed him to look into their needs. John's concern for Vesta's children came from his desire to honour his mother. If Sarah had been so moved by their plight as to go half-insane with worry, then he would make sure her effort would not be in vain. When Lang complained about receiving less than the cost of the tombstone, John gave him ten dollars and asked him to send all information and receipts for his expenses to McPherson in Brantford.

John stopped in Brantford to see Sandy McPherson on his way back to New York City to tell him what he had arranged with Lang. He instructed him, once more, to keep his identity secret. McPherson told him that surely there was no reason for him to fear the past, but John was adamant that he tell no one that he was acting as his lawyer. He wanted to break all ties with this land of his youth, he said bitterly, implying that his mother's unhappy end had to do with the disinterest of her community in her plight. McPherson guessed that he visited his mother's grave so long after her death because he was busy maintaining his firm during the tumultuous years of the Civil War and commercial competition thereafter. At age fifty, John exuded confidence, wealth, and a sharpness of mind. He went to see Leonard Sovereign, Duncan's one-time rival as the richest man in Simcoe. Sovereign told McPherson later that John talked about his mother as if she had been an angel living on earth for an allotted time. When Leonard asked if he were going to see Duncan, John shook his head angrily. He seemed to think that Duncan had betrayed his mother's trust. The hurt in his eyes at the mention of Duncan's name was apparent. Sovereign surmised that John wanted Duncan to know that he had avoided him, as if slighting him to make him aware of what he thought of him. McPherson thought otherwise, that John wanted to avoid an awkward situation; moreover, with his mother dead, the relationship between Duncan and himself lacked meaning.

When Alex Lang located Vesta's sons, now adults, working as labourers, John, through McPherson, sent them money to buy farmsteads. Two years later, John became a subject of interest to lawyers and law courts in New York City.

His lawyer, A.J. Dittenhoffer, a heavy-set man with deep-set eyes that could bore through witnesses, lost a litigation case to John Lewis, and since he had served John's interests for years, he resented what he considered John's shabby treatment of him. John, paranoid about lawyers, wrote his will by himself, leaving many thousands to his porter friend Francis Wilder, and some few thousands to his housekeeper, his executor and his godsons. The following month, on a hot day in August 1874, John was hurrying through Central Park in New York when another carriage veered in front of his. To avoid a collision, John swerved his horse, causing it to crash his carriage into a tree against which John smashed his head and died instantly. Since he was one of the richest men in New York City, perhaps in the country, through his many real estate deals, his heirs were easily persuaded by Dittenhoffer to challenge the will when they learned that some mysterious nineteen-year old girl by the name of Lizzie Barton Taylor, who lived in a convent, was to inherit the bulk of his estate.

Lizzie would receive the income from the estate at the age of twenty-one until she married, when her income would stop. At her death it would be given to her children. If she never married, the interest from the invested estate after her death would be used for the upkeep of her and John's graves, which were to be beside one another in Greenwood Cemetery. Dittenhoffer could understand John's reluctance to have his wealth fall into the hands of Lizzie's husband, who might well be unscrupulous, but his directions were so amateurish that

Dittenhoffer knew that he could disprove the will in probate, and, in the process, make a good deal of money for himself. Having once overheard John say that he came from Toronto, he put an advertisement in the Toronto *Globe* asking if there were relatives with an interest in the Lewis estate. Judge Wilson in Simcoe saw the item and got in touch with Dittenhoffer, who employed a law firm in Simcoe to begin looking for direct relatives. Sarah Lewis should have received his wealth, but she being proven dead, the real inheritors had to be Sarah's legitimate children, Henry Lewis Jr. and Mary Smith. The news that they might be incredibly rich stunned brother and sister, who, nevertheless, tempered their joy with the caution of people who had more downs than ups in life.

The news brought Mary out of the despair that afflicted her in the years after George Smith disappeared. Since his underground railway activities ceased after the Civil War and left him with a boring life of cutting hair and watching helplessly as more and more opportunities for advancement for young blacks were curtailed, George decided to make a fact-gathering trip through the northern states to report to the blacks in Canada on the advisability of returning. Whether he was recognized by one of his old enemies and secretly killed, whether he decided to make a new life for himself without informing Mary, or whether he died suddenly, perhaps accidentally, and the authorities, as in Sarah's case, made no attempt to find his relatives, one could only hazard a guess. Mary, so accustomed to seeing him come back from one dangerous mission after another, held onto hope for the first couple of years, but then she succumbed to her worst fears. George's exploits as the Black Pimpernel were forgotten as the older black leaders died and the younger generation of blacks in the towns of Ontario drifted back to the States to make better lives for themselves, among whom was Henry's son John.

Henry's wife Ellen, who left him for good and took up with that high-living band of swindlers to whom she had been long attracted, heard with delight from the lawyers that Henry could be fabulously rich. To avoid her importunate questions, Henry telegraphed to Mary that he was coming to Simcoe to buy a farm and settle down. Mary welcomed her brother. Not only would Henry relieve her loneliness, but she and Henry could plan their strategy with their lawyers together.

Henry visited Hollidays Cove in the summer of 1876, forty years after he left. He wanted testimonials from his former neighbours verifying that he and Mary were the only legitimate children of Sarah. James W. Brown, Jacob A. Brown and James "Miller" Campbell willingly obliged him when he came to their residences. They broke out the good wine and treated their former slave as an honored guest as they reminisced about the past. The men were about Henry's age; they had been playmates as children. The gruesome aspects of slavery and the inhumanity of Miller Campbell's Uncle James were forgotten or not mentioned. They all remembered Sarah, her beauty and her dignity. They were amazed by Henry's prospects of great wealth, and a little envious. His prospects gave Henry, whose personality had become assertive over the intervening years, great respect in their eyes.

When Henry left Campbell's home, he walked where the slave cabins had been, since they were destroyed after the Civil War along with other vestiges of slavery, and stood on the hill overlooking Brown's Island in the Ohio River. The menace had gone from the landscape. Sarah's fears on looking up to these hills were just a memory that came back to him then. But memories were menaces in themselves, and, despite holding the affidavits in his hand that in a way testified to his courage in returning here and to a change in race relations, he felt unwelcome. As he walked through the noise and confusion of an industrialized town and saw the wrenching alterations in the landscape that large plants, blast furnaces and huge machinery were making, he waited impatiently for the train to carry him back to his farm in Simcoe and Mary.

Since Sarah's daughter Fanny Powers had been dead for a couple of years, Fanny's daughter filed a brief claiming that her mother was a legitimate daughter of Sarah and Henry Lewis Sr. and "intermarried" with Powers. Her claim was denied on the testimony of Henry, who remembered that his father wanted to harm the little white baby. Newspapers in New York announced in headlines that two mulattos as next of kin could inherit John Lewis's estate, thus bringing down with a crash John's carefully crafted image of a financial wizard of Spanish origin. Dittenhoffer had his revenge.

Dittenhoffer considered it ironic that John Lewis's great loves were his mother and his daughter, neither of whom he could see often because the former had been a slave and the latter illegitimate. He arranged for a lawyer in the town of Haverstraw, north of New York City, to interview Lizzie Barton Taylor in her convent there. She was to be twenty-one in October, when she could make her own decisions. The lawyer reported that the Catholic order was eager to get control of her inheritance; but since she would receive just the interest from the estate, the lawyer thought that she and the nuns would be more amenable to negotiate a settlement when she reached her majority. In the following year, the New York Supreme Court put aside John's will and ordered that Lizzie receive the interest on the estate until she married or died, whence the income would be paid to Henry Lewis and Mary Smith. Dittenhoffer wrote the lawyers in Simcoe that they had the basis to force a compromise. Since the property was heavily encumbered with mortgages, taxes and assessments, and the remaining surplus was small, a compromise had to be arranged after years of wrangling in order for Henry and Mary to gain anything at all.

An aged Sandy McPherson went to Simcoe to attend the funeral of Duncan Campbell, who died just short of his ninetieth birthday. In the last forty years of his life, Duncan looked after his land interests and gave kindly advice to his debtors. Quite a little crowd turned out to bid him good-bye. Most of his contemporaries were dead, except for his old rival Leonard Sovereign who greeted McPherson at the funeral. Others such as Judge Wilson had followed Dr. Duncombe to California and warmer points south. McPherson, finding an opportunity to talk with Duncan's eldest son, asked him if he had come across two ambrotypes of John D. Lewis, which Duncan mentioned in an affidavit that he had received from him. McPherson was curious to see them as reminders of the past. He received a rather curt "no" and surmised that the subject of John Lewis would not be entertained by the Campbell family.

Henry Lewis and Mary Smith were among the farmers forced by the long depression to sell their lands and migrate to the States, joining the black community who went in search of work. McPherson missed the gaiety, the good fellowship and the natural comedy that he associated with his black friends in Simcoe, particularly George Smith, whose gentleness with children and animals he admired as an unexpected trait in one who dealt with violence and intrigue. William Plummer, Richard Plummer's son, who, after his father died, was the town's best orator and a prize graduate of the Simcoe grammar school, still kept a home in Simcoe, but that was because he worked as a sleeping car porter for the Canadian Railways. One day McPherson sought him out to ask about the Black Pimpernel. Plummer said old George Smith remained "disappeared", never to be heard of again, and he added laughing, "just like about everyone else." McPherson thought of George Smith as symbolic of his time; it just disappeared.

Undeterred from his sentimental quest for some token of those days, he drove his carriage to the southern part of the Gore where Joseph Culver's farm used to be. There, still standing, was the poplar that Sarah had planted at John's birth. A survivor, it stood with a few newer poplars as a windbreak in a farmer's field while much of the great forest in the vicinity had been leveled years before. He looked for the grave of John's twin sister but that had been run over by the plough. The poplar, though, had strength and resilience; it reminded him of Sarah. As he looked up at the bare branches, hinting of buds and the coming spring, Sarah was laughing as she whirled to an Irish reel that, in those early days, captured his heart and raised his spirit.

Note: The events and characters in this novel are taken from life. Sarah's grave, despite John Lewis's care to have her remembered with a fitting tombstone, disappeared when the Wesleyan burial ground in Barrie gave way to development.

Many thanks to the several friends who read the ms and gave me their advice, and a special thanks to Michelle Rustan and Enid Bloom who copy edited it.

I am indebted to Mary Zweirzchowski of the Mary Weir Public Library in Weirton, W.Va. (formerly Hollidays Cove) for her encouragement, for the articles she sent me and, with her husband Dave, for taking me to the scenes that Sarah would have known. My thanks as well to June Welch of Weirton who gave me information on the Campbell family.

Of the several libraries in Ontario who kindly helped me in research, I wish to thank, in particular, the volunteers at the archives of the Eva Brook Donly Museum in Simcoe, Ontario.

PRINCIPAL CHARACTERS IN THE NOVEL

Molly Kinney--Col. Richard Brown--Honor Brown   Hugh Brown
      Nell--Grady   Richard Brown Jr   George Brown
      Fanny--Dick Dawson   Rachel--Beseleel Wells
      Sal (Sarah)--Henry Lewis
        Henry Lewis Jr--Ellen Mince   Rev. Doddridge
        Molly (Mary)--George (Black Pimpernel) Smith   Philip Doddridge
      Sal--George Brown   Alex Caldwell
        Fanny (m. Bill Powers)
      Sal--James Campbell--Margaret MacDonald
        Israel   (John and Candor)
      Sal--Samuel
        Vesta
      Sal--Duncan Campbell
        John Lewis

REBELLION

Loyalists	Rebels
Duncan Campbell, Capt.Norfolk Militia	Dr. Charles Duncombe
Mercer Wilson, Capt Norfolk Dragoons	Eliakim Malcolm
Allan MacNab, Col., Loyalist forces	Bill Powers
William Kerr, Col., Indian forces	Col. Alfred, St. Thomas
	Bill Mathews, later mayor

Black community, Simcoe	Sarah's white friends
Richard Plummer, orator, tailor	Lucinda Landon
George M. Smith, barber	Mr and Mrs George Kent
Jerry Curtis, blacksmith	Sandy McPherson
Henson Johnson, blacksmith	Joseph and Phoebe Culver
Maria Parker	Charity and Bill Rusling
Isaac Dorsey, farmer	Elizabeth Lucas
John Anderson	